VIRA
MODERN (
660

Shena Mackay was born in Edinburgh in 1944. Her writing career began when she won a prize for a poem written when she was fourteen. Two novels, *Dust Falls on Eugene Schlumburger* and *Toddler on the Run* were published before she was twenty. *Redhill Rococo* won the 1987 Fawcett Prize, *Dunedin* won a 1994 Scottish Arts Council Book Award, *The Orchard on Fire* was shortlisted for the 1996 Booker Prize, and in 2003 *Heligoland* was shortlisted for both the Orange Prize and Whitbread Novel Award. She is a Fellow of the Royal Society of Literature and lives in Southampton.

By *Shena Mackay*

Dust Falls on Eugene Schlumburger/Toddler on the Run
Music Upstairs
Old Crow
An Advent Calendar
Babies in Rhinestones and Other Stories
A Bowl of Cherries
Redhill Rococo
Dreams of Dead Women's Handbags
Dunedin
Such Devoted Sisters: An Anthology of Stories (*editor*)
The Laughing Academy
Collected Short Stories
The Orchard on Fire
Friendship: An Anthology (*editor*)
The Artist's Widow
The World's Smallest Unicorn and Other Stories
Heligoland
The Atmospheric Railway
Dancing on the Outskirts

DUNEDIN

Shena Mackay

virago

VIRAGO

First published in Great Britain in 1992 by William Heinemann Ltd
This paperback edition published in 2016 by Virago Press

1 3 5 7 9 10 8 6 4 2

A CIP catalogue record for this book
is available from the British Library.

ISBN 978-0-349-00719-9

Typeset in Goudy by M Rules
Printed and bound in Great Britain by
Clays Ltd, St Ives plc

Papers used by Virago are from well-managed forests
and other responsible sources.

MIX
Paper from
responsible sources
FSC® C104740

Virago Press
An imprint of
Little, Brown Book Group
Carmelite House
50 Victoria Embankment
London EC4Y 0DZ

An Hachette UK Company
www.hachette.co.uk

www.virago.co.uk

for C.H.

ACKNOWLEDGEMENTS

I am very grateful to the Francis Head Fund, administered by the Society of Authors, to the Royal Literary Fund, to Deborah Rogers and to Richard Bates of Discript and Rachel Cusk.

CONTENTS

PART ONE

New Zealand 1909

I

The rain stopped as the *Inverness* rode into Otago harbour on the high tide under an escort of albatrosses. A rainbow flashed out over the bay, ribbons of coloured light intensifying into a broad curve from the island to the waves of the Pacific. A gauzier rainbow fluttered below its arc, the spectrum in reverse. Dazzled into silence, the passengers on the wet deck clung to one another, many of them in tears, the long voyage over and the New World glittering at the end of the beams which streamed from the fingers of God as a sign that all would be well.

Men who had uncovered their heads, women in hats and bonnets and wide tartan shawls or 'screens', and children looked to Jack Mackenzie hoping for some blessing or affirmation of the miraculous or thanks for deliverance, and would have fallen to their knees or joined their voices in praise on the diamond-hung ship, but the minister's binoculars were raking the bright green hills sloping upwards to darker growth against the slate-blue sky. Already, in his imagination, he was far away, halfway to the snowy peak of Mount Cook with a knapsack full of antipodean alpines, and a Mount Cook lily within his grasp.

The women who had sailed to join pioneering husbands and fiancés, the disgraced sons sent to redeem themselves in sheep farming, the opportunists and ne'er-do-wells, the children taller and thinner after weeks at sea, stood in awe until the shouts of crew and gulls returned them, from the awareness of themselves as at once individuals of destiny and specks on the ocean, to practicalities.

Here and there white buildings sparkled in the emerald grass and the boundaries of farms stood out as the sky blazed into sapphire. On the quayside black umbrellas folded like the wings of cormorants and the sound of bagpipes with a melancholy undertone, a hint of lament even in welcome, came over the water. At that, some of the passengers were quite undone; they had set sail to the strains of 'Will Ye No Come Back Again', leaving loved ones diminishing in an ever-widening wake.

Jack Mackenzie was the first passenger ashore: he had determined from the moment the ship left Glasgow that he should be, no matter who he had to elbow out of his way. The elders of St Enoch's church unwound themselves in a small black knot from the tumult and came forward to greet him, puzzled to find him alone and, his distinguishing stock and collar apart, dressed in tweeds more suitable for the grouse moor than for the pulpit. Jack Mackenzie pumped papery calloused hands, and clapped frail black backs heartily, a big glossy auburn fellow like a fox in a parliament of fowls. Eventually they found, among the people streaming off the ship, hugging, kissing and bewildered, Mrs Mackenzie, obviously with child, looking greenish in the regatta atmosphere, and holding tightly to the hand of a small redheaded girl in a grubby sailor dress, and boy in a kilt. With them was a young servant girl struggling with the hand baggage. As Jack Mackenzie introduced his family, shaking and straightening the children for inspection and berating the servant for her tardiness in getting them ashore, one of the elders was shocked to see the tip of the maid's tongue, pink and pointed as a licked strawberry ice-cream cone, thrust out at the minister's back. What kind of menagerie was this they had been sent, to replace the Craigies so tragically taken from them?

The party was conducted through the crowd towards the wagonette which was to take them to their new home, Louisa Mackenzie and the children engulfed by a group of ladies of the congregation. Their luggage would be delivered by the shipping company's carrier. The maid screamed, bringing them to a halt. She had seen a cannibal, black as the Earl O'Hell's waistcoat, lounging against a pile of crates, eating a pie. The children stared at the first black person they encountered in their new country, gripping their mother's hands.

'Come along, Lilian. You're attracting attention. What on earth's the matter with you?' demanded Jack.

'Yon p-pie,' she gibbered.

'It's a perfectly ordinary mutton pie,' said the chief among the elders testily. 'One of Galbraith's from the look of it.'

'You'll find, Mr Mackenzie, that most of the natives are a living testament to the wonderful effects of Christian teaching and the brave struggles of the early missionaries, some of whom were witness to quite dreadful scenes of carnage and debauchery. Of course, there has been a certain amount of interbreeding among the less desirable elements, as you can see. The unfortunate products of miscegenation ... ' He pointed the ferrule of his umbrella at a pair of barefoot children with coppery skins and red lights in their knotted hair.

'Well, they look bonnie enough. Our guid Scots blood has done them no harm, evidently,' was Jack Mackenzie's unsatisfactory reply. He poked his own son between the shoulders with an admonition to watch where he was going, the big tumfy. The Maori, having finished his pie, took a handkerchief from his trouser pocket and wiped his lips. He gave a brief nod to the wide-eyed Pakeha children being dragged away, the land undulating under their wobbly legs, beneath the fading rainbows. Then on the edge of the throng and tumult were other dark faces, blue-black hair like magpies' wings, women in gaudy clothes, with bluish patterned chins, selling fish from flax baskets.

'Well, Mr Mackenzie, there'll be all kinds of things ye'll be wanting to know. St Enoch's is no a . . . '

'Indeed yes, Mr Cameron,' Jack interrupted. 'I'm particularly interested in the flightless birds of the region – although entomology's really my field. The island's geographical isolation and consequently unique flora and fauna make it fascinating to a student of the natural sciences, which in my humble way I am.'

'Quite so,' said Mr Cameron, agitating his furled black wings.

'I feel we know you already, Mrs Mackenzie,' one of the ladies, who introduced herself as Miss Kettle, was telling Louisa. 'We've read all about your little family in the *Outlook* – that's our church newspaper.'

'Fancy,' said Louisa faintly.

'I'm sure little Alexander and Kitty will be happy in Dunedin. We've some fine schools here, and there are plenty of nice children for them to make friends with. There's a reliable

6

girl up at the manse, Madge, who was with the poor Craigies; she'll be able to take your own girl in hand.'

Mistress and maid felt some criticism was intended. Lilian had the look of one who, as an orphan from the foundling hospital, was accustomed to being taken, however unsuccessfully, in hand and who was resigned to riding with the baggage in the cart while the family crowded into the wagonette. It was pulled by a cross-eyed skewbald that the driver, Robert, introduced to the children as Solomon. Lily was jolted along in some trepidation at meeting the reliable Madge.

Madge stood on the verandah of the white house beyond the hedge of macrocarpa sweetbriar and honeysuckle, shielding her eyes with her hand. Behind her tall dark figure the windows of the manse blazed golden. She took command at once, ordering a surprised but obedient Jack to take his wife upstairs to rest, directing Robert with the bags and taking the children by the hands, pulling them towards the subdued silk print of her best frock.

'So you are Kitty and Alexander. Do you get Sandy?' she asked the little boy, who nodded.

'Yes, he's Sandy to the family,' said Lilian pointedly.

Madge looked at Lilian standing uncertainly on the threshold, her knuckles white on the handle of her cheap suitcase, feeling usurped, unsure if she were to be nursery maid, kitchen maid or disregarded entirely. Madge let go of the children's hands.

'You'll be wanting a cup of tea,' she said. Madge had filled vases with roses and prepared a meal. It transpired that she had decided against engaging a cook and a girl was employed to do the rough work. As Lilian carried a tray up the stairs of her new home, she thought that Madge, who ruled the roost, with her bright eyes and clever parrot's face, was well-disposed towards her.

That night Madge was woken by a scream. Lilian was lying in the moonlight, her eyes wide with terror.

'Lilian, what is it?'

'I had a dream . . .'

Madge patted the bedclothes beside her.

'You'd better come in with me for a while,' she said.

Three days after the Mackenzies' arrival Louisa gave birth to a baby girl. They called her Jessie, after Louisa's mother. Jack had wanted Flora but Louisa looked so frail and tearful lying there that he gave in. The child was baptised Jessie Flora Mackenzie.

Some weeks later Sandy, home from school where the proprietors were the Misses Dunce and Dumbrell, stalwarts of his father's congregation with a taste for the tawse, interrupted his father in his study. He hovered, fiddling with a piece of scrimshaw, a delicate ivory schooner, until the tip of a mast snapped between finger and thumb. Hiding the ship behind a Bible on the desk, Sandy spoke.

'Father?'

'What is it, Sandy?'

The boy's timid voice irritated him. It was not often that Sandy addressed a question to his father. Jack carefully drew out a flower from the green glass collecting jar and laid it on a sheet of paper to dry. His thoughts were of an illustrious predecessor, the Reverend W. Colenso, whose extensive travels in the wilds of North Island and anthropological studies excited his envy.

Jack had been reading Colenso's essay on New Zealanders, written for the Dunedin Exhibition of 1865, that morning and had put it away with a grudging respect for the man's erudition and frustration at his own limitations, both scientific and those imposed by his calling and his family.

'Well, Sandy?'

'What's the difference between flotsam and jetsam?'

'Flotsam is found floating on the sea, and jetsam is jettisoned overboard and cast up on the shore. It is perfectly easy to distinguish between them. F and J.'

'Yes, Father,' said Sandy, but asked, 'Might not flotsam become jetsam then?'

'Don't be impertinent. If you've nothing better to do than waste my time . . .' The minister concluded his explanation. His vague idea of sending Sandy to Knox College at a later date was dissolving; the residential theological college, in its magnificent building overlooking the city from the heights of Opoho, was never to embrace young Sandy Mackenzie, although later in life, jetsam washed up on the coast of South-east England, Sandy would say that he had been educated in the School of Hard Knocks and had graduated from the University of Life. When the occasion warranted it, he laid claim to Knox College as his alma mater.

Perhaps, his father wondered briefly, the boy's talents would lie in business or even the law, where his gift for prevarication and general slyness might be put to profitable use. He watched his son back out of the room to seek, no doubt, the company of the maids, and sighed. He noticed at once that his pretty little ship had been damaged; perhaps one of the maids, the foolish Lilian, dusting his desk, disobeying orders? There would have to be an inquisition. His thoughts turned to Myrtille, the dark-skinned laundress who washed and ironed the household linen.

Once, riding far from home, he had come upon a *marae* and had glimpsed women dancing in soft, slow, swinging rhythms. Although he had searched, he had never found the place again, and would have thought he had dreamed it had not the patterns of the carved posts and painted lintels of the *whare runanga*, the tribal meeting house, impressed themselves on his memory almost as clearly as the magnificent massive women. In his imagination Myrtille swayed among them in the undulating line of the *poi* dance, in the golden age.

He saw her as Rousseau's Noble Savage, or Eve naked before the Fall, in a garden where he and she might wander far from the strictures of Presbyterian Dunedin. The words of Diderot, in his *Supplément au Voyage de Bougainville*, came to him, with their warning to the Tahitians that one day the Christians would come 'with crucifix in one hand and the dagger in the other to cut your throats or to force you to accept their customs and opinions; one day under their rule you will be almost as unhappy as they are'. He put the picture away from himself, but not before regarding for a moment or two, with moistened eyes and lips, dark girls with blossoms in their hair in a languorous dance on the shore of what Bougainville had named Nouveau Cythère after the island where Aphrodite rose from the sea. Myrtille was among them, bending and swaying under the Southern Cross and all the stars of the whispering South Seas. His sympathies would have been entirely with the two sailors Webb and Gibson who had fallen in love with Tahitian girls and deserted from the *Endeavour*, but that the pair of fools had been caught and brought back in ignominy and flogged. A plan was hatching in his mind to inveigle Myrtille into accompanying him on a botanical or entomological trip, meeting at a secret rendezvous far from the haunts of man, into mountains or bush so primitive as to be out of the sight of God too. Perhaps an expedition to the ruins of an ancient Maori settlement, a remote and desolate hill fort, a *pa* half buried under forest or shifting sands, where fragments of bone and stone ornaments and weapons might give the jaunt a geological slant.

While he was engrossed in lascivious speculation his wife was walking beside the Waters of Leith, weeping for their namesake in Edinburgh. Her husband might be happy with his church or groping about in old middens for the broken bones of moas but she was not. The thought of the vast ocean all around them filled her with desolation. She was necessarily busy most of the time and she was lonely almost always, even when the children were with her. The island was beautiful and she despised herself for being unhappy and weak in what Jack had pointed out more than once was an earthly paradise. Often when she encountered Madge and Lil together she had the feeling that she was interrupting something and crept away, an interloper in her own house. She hesitated at the kitchen door. The maids' friendship reminded her of the companionship of her sisters, and their kindness to her made her more wretched than ever.

During the voyage she had lain in her cabin, feeling ill and fearing for her unborn baby, while Kitty and Sandy scampered terrifyingly about the decks, and Jack pontificated, bringing her tales of porpoises, whales and dolphins dancing and cavorting over the waves and albatrosses gliding on vast motionless wings. She had been fearful that Jack would let the children slip into the sea while she lay sick and unknowing, unable to move, or to swim come to that. She had secretly shared Lilian's fears that on landing they would be seized by people with tattooed faces and eaten; thus she was also forced to wish that the horrible journey would go on for ever. Jack had told her that there were few Maori – and those scattered and unwarlike – where they were going, and had attempted to divert her with tales of the massacre at Murdering Beach and the destruction of the wooden city of Otago. She had recoiled.

Murdering Beach, dark and bloodstained, haunted her dreams. Jack told the story with some enthusiasm, reading from a contemporary account he had found in one of the books on New Zealand that he was studying as they sailed. In 1811 a sailor named Tucker had stolen a preserved head from some Maori near Riverton. Six years on, a whaler called the *Sophia* anchored at the Otago Heads and a boat with seven men landed on Whareakeake, Murdering Beach, to buy some potatoes from the natives there. Tucker was recognised as the thief of the dried head and the sailors were attacked. Four of them made it back to the ship, where they found a hundred and fifty Maori on board, trying to take the crew prisoners. The crew set about them with huge sealing knives, slaying sixteen; many more Maori jumped overboard and drowned in the fast current. The chief, Corockar, was captured. All night a watch was kept on the canoes drawn up on the beach and early the next morning the natives approached the *Sophia* calling for their chief whom they feared was dead. Corockar was paraded on the deck with his hands bound. He called to his rejoicing subjects to bring a large canoe-load of potatoes, presumably to pay for his release. A canoe was paddled by two men towards the brig, then one of the sailors shouted, 'The canoe is full of men!' A large number of men were concealed under mats in the bottom of the boat. The ship fired a volley into their midst. The Maori, armed with spears and clubs, jumped overboard and tried to pull the canoe over to the brig. There were nearly forty of them, to the whalers' fourteen. Several were shot and run through with boarding pikes trying to board the *Sophia*.

Corockar jumped overboard and was shot in the neck. Two of his men swam to him, and most gallantly, according to the eyewitness account, took him to the shore, but he died. The next morning, Christmas Eve, a great number of Maori assembled on the beach, lamenting and crying for their chief. The sailors determined to destroy the Maori canoes lest they attempt to take the brig again.

One boat was landed, and the Maori ran away. The crew sawed up all forty-two canoes and took them for firewood. The Maori rushed the boats but failed to wound anyone. On 26 December, a fine summer day, the whalers decided to destroy the Maori city. They set fire to it and in four hours the city of Otago, perhaps the finest in all New Zealand, was a heap of ashes.

'Not a very happy Christmas,' said Louisa. She had seen pictures of canoes, intricately carved, and elaborately ornamented houses. In her head she heard the whisper and then the crackle of flames consuming wood.

'The stolen head was offered for sale in Sydney some time later,' Jack told her. 'It was the first to come on the market. I don't know how much it fetched.'

'But who could possibly want such a thing? What became of Tucker, the man who stole it?'

13

'Killed by the natives in the first attack.'

'I expect they ate him,' said Sandy, who with Kitty had come in and listened silently to the story.

'Cooked and preserved in his own fat,' agreed their father. 'I wonder what they're cooking up for us in the galley tonight. Louisa, you really ought to make an effort to join us, instead of lying there like a dying duck in a thunderstorm. Come on, a turn around the deck would do you the world of good, bring the roses back to your cheeks.'

At that unusual softening of his tone, pale red bloomed and faded in her face as she replied: 'Yes, I think I shall try to get up now, I really think I'm beginning to feel a little better.'

It was said partly in obedience to his wishes but mostly to get them out of the cabin, which smelt of the sickroom, before she was engulfed by the wave of nausea which had risen at the image of pieces of roasted sailor in jellified fat. It brought to mind an old story, and the thought of St Nicholas raising from the dead, and miraculously reassembling the chopped bodies of three boys which a rascally innkeeper had mixed with pork in a pickling tub was too much for her. Had a pig scrambled out too, shaking the brine from its snout with squeals of rejoicing? She thought not, as she wiped her face, and considered the livestock in the ship's hold.

Nevertheless, she managed to sit with the family at dinner, Kitty at Jack's right hand, Sandy in disgrace for some misde-meanour, probably awaiting a postprandial whipping. She could take only a spoonful or two of soup. Jack, as the only clergyman on board, had been appointed to ask a blessing on the food at mealtimes. He had also presided the previous day over the burial at sea of a crewman, sewn into a canvas shroud, who had died of natural causes. 'We therefore commit his body to the deep, to be turned into corruption, looking for the resurrection of the body, (when the sea shall give up her dead) ... '

In Kitty's dreams shoals of rotting canvas sacks and fish skeletons bobbed in the ship's wake. The dead sailor who had snarled at her once, in response to a childish question, loomed over her bunk, dripping and half eaten by fish. Her father, roused by her screams, comforted her.

Had he been a religious man, the minister would have been awestruck by the wonders of God's creation which he observed from the deck; as a sensualist who had entered the Church at his father's behest and who nourished an amateur passion for the natural sciences, he performed his duties with more enthu-siasm for marine life than for worship.

'I take my text this morning from the Book of Job, Chapter XLI, verse 1. "Canst thou draw out Leviathan with an hook?"' He had read with a heavy heart of the seas round the Australian and New Zealand coast running red with the blood of whales and seals from May to October as the whaling fleets pursued them to their breeding and mating grounds until they were hunted almost to extinction, of the Sodom and Gomorrah that man had made of the beautiful Bay of Islands, the site of the notorious whaling station. Darwin had called the white popu-lation there 'the very refuse of society' and had been pleased to leave behind the debauched riffraff who plundered the seas and reduced their living creatures to blubber. The stench of boiling oil hung over the passengers and crew grouped on the deck as Jack accused: 'And you ladies in the congregation might pause to think, as you lace your corsets in your vanity, of the cost of that whalebone, of the protracted agony of a noble beast, of mothers heavy with young, of calves and fathers of families slain indiscriminately, of that cache of oil in the head of the sperm whale, shed for you, which in the sight of God is as precious as the ointment in the jar of alabaster with which a sinful woman anointed the feet of Jesus Christ . . . '

There were murmurings, uneasy shiftings and blushes, as if Darwin and whalebone corsets in a sermon constituted profanity. Those familiar with the word sperm were outraged; Louisa felt her dress billow like a bulky sail at the references to mothers heavy with child, and stared scarlet-faced at the sea. And yet, his vulgarity had been redeemed, even blessed by divine approval, when at the words, 'Oh ye whales, and all that move in the waters, bless ye the Lord: praise him and magnify him for ever', a school of porpoises had risen, leaping and curvetting over the green waves, joining in with the congregation.

To return to Myrtille, as the thoughts of Jack Mackenzie did with such frequency, she might have been described as a piece of the jetsam he so despised. Her position in the community was anomalous, her ancestry mysterious. One of her grandfathers had been among the first convicts shipped to Botany Bay, after he had spent a year or so in the rotting hulks at Woolwich. He had escaped from the penal colony and made his way to New Zealand, landing at the disgraceful Bay of Islands where he was very much at home. When gold had been discovered in Coromandel he had joined the rush for riches but had failed to make his fortune and thence had travelled to the diggings at Gabriel's Gully in Otago. Myrtille's mother, the product of his dalliance with a girl of the Ngai-Tahu tribe, had been left in a little basket of woven flax on the doorstep of a missionary family who, while not treating the child as one of their own, had fed and clothed her and given her the rudiments of an education. At the age of eighteen she had married a Frenchman who had signed on as cook on the *Musselburgh*, one of the early freezer-equipped ships, setting out with a cargo of mutton from Port Chalmers. The *Musselburgh* went down in a freak storm with the loss of all hands and five thousand frozen sheep. Myrtille's mother, now a widow, found work at the woollen mill at Mosgiel to support herself and her child; but her spirit was broken. When Myrtille was thirteen, an epidemic of measles swept through the population, taking with it some fifty people, most of them Maori who had little resistance to the white man's disease. It seemed that Myrtille's mother had called upon her aboriginal ancestry to release her from this life, for she gave herself up to the illness, turned her face to the wall and died. Thereafter Myrtille was taken in by an old laundress, who taught her her trade and left her the ramshackle *whare*, her coppers for boiling clothes, primus stove, pieces of crockery and knick-knacks when she died.

On summer evenings Myrtille could be seen sitting outside her open door on a bleached seagrass chair with a book lying on her lap. When it grew too dark to read she stared at the stars. Sometimes she disappeared for days: Jack Mackenzie had encountered her one night miles from home walking where glow-worms glittered at the edge of the bush. He had reined in his horse and invited her to mount behind him. She had declined, and he had ridden on, troubled, with his killing bottle and leather specimen cases. Another time, he had passed her on the steps of the Carnegie library, where she had responded with a regal nod when he had raised his hat in surprise as much as politeness. She wore her beauty carelessly, as if its loss would mean nothing to her. On the occasions when she sat with Madge and Lil in the kitchen she joined in the conversation and jokes but was always apart, even when they plaited her blue-black hair or piled it up with combs and decked her with their finery. There was a darkness in all the stories Myrtille told, of tribal wars and mothers who killed all their children, deaths by drowning, betrayal and murder by the settlers. There was also a sense of loss for old customs, traditions and ceremonies that had never been hers but were like beautiful fragments of a dream that glitter for a moment after a sleeper wakes, and fade like glow-worms.

Myrtille and Louisa Mackenzie might have been friends had it been possible for them to know one another socially, but Myrtille did not belong to the Ladies' Guild or the sewing circle and was never invited to tea by anybody, although she had an infuriating air that suggested she would decline to come if asked. Once, Louisa looked up from her sewing and unthinkingly waved it in greeting to Myrtille on her way to the Mackenzie wash-house, and turned away in confusion at the thought that Myrtille might sway over to the ladies in their circle of rattan chairs under the cabbage tree with a basket of crumpled nightwear and underclothing and spirit her away for a stronger brew from her blackened billy. Thereafter she was careful to observe the proprieties, secretly envious of Myrtille's independence, and intimidated by her scornful mien.

Miss Kettle, who employed a washerwoman who knew her place, angered by her arrogance, imagined Myrtille's shack to be littered with *pipi* shells and the greasy bones of mutton birds. She desired to see Myrtille seated on the stool of shame in the kirk, draped in the white sheet of penitence, head bowed in confession of unspecified sins. That would humble her, the Hottentot! But she was thwarted by Myrtille's refusal to enter the church.

Louisa for her part wondered what force propelled Miss Kettle from her narrow bed each morning, her days spread out around her like the repeated pattern of a dingy patchwork quilt. When entertained by Miss Kettle, she could not dismiss the impression of drinking tea and eating scones in a coffin. Outside, a *tui* called, its mimicking notes competing with the cuckoo-clock to mark the tortured passing of the minutes, at the same time mocking with its freedom of sunshine and blossoms and rain. Miss Kettle's little wooden pet bird in its dark brown house made her sad, while the heavy fircones which weighted the mechanism held time looped in their chains. The scent of lavender was underlaid with darker tones of meat: the rabbits which charmed the Mackenzie children and plagued the farmers and gardeners were the staple of Miss Kettle's diet, small joints bled on the ashet, the big oval plate that had belonged to her mother. She wore their skins in a tippet round her shoulders.

St Enoch's was not one of the fashionable Presbyterian churches of Otago and Southland. It was small in comparison with First Church, whose very name suffused the new minister of St Enoch's with a bitter sense of having been cheated, and Knox Church in George Street, and even with St Andrew's and North Dunedin. There were Sundays when his eyes raked his congregation – the pews of rusty black dresses and soberly bedizened bonnets in Sabbath hues, the great soft lads in kilts lolling against their mothers, men with the Saturday night drink throbbing in red threads on their cheeks and noses, and those nearer to God in the gallery, the hantle of good families in their reserved seats – and thought it, overall, the flotsam and jetsam of Dunedin. Then his eyes rested on his own uncomfortable brood, and he bombarded them with burning coals. They had passed already through the ordeal of Family Prayers, when family and servants knelt together after Lil had cleared away the breakfast debris, and the week's sins were laid, black and scarlet, on the white cloth at Father's place at the head of the table. Kitty and Sandy were never to hear the words 'Though your sins be as scarlet, they shall be as white as snow' without seeing that white starched cloth and swallowing on the sick, boiled-egg taste of fear. It rose in the throat of the child whose turn it was to read from the enormous family Bible with its slippery pages, and also in the mouth of the sibling who anticipated the other's halt and stumbling version of the Scriptures, and inevitable disgrace.

There were not many of the congregation who could nuzzle up to their shepherd like favoured sheep after the service; most slunk away on goatish legs with cloven hooves splitting their tight polished boots and telltale horns peeking from hat brims and bonnets. This morning the little flock was disconcerted by the smile which played across the minister's red mouth as he mounted the steps to the pulpit, tapping the beat of a metrical psalm with his fingers on his Bible as he was ushered and shut in to his wooden hexagonal by an elder. Somebody was going to get it. Every Sunday Sandy nourished a vain hope that his father would not be able to escape but be imprisoned there like an angry genie in a bottle. However hard he tried to remember it, he would have forgotten the text by the time his father demanded it of him at the luncheon table. In vain would Kitty kick his ankle; he would not dare to lift his eyes to her silently mouthing face. Lamb would congeal on his plate, rosemary needles warped in wrinkling gravy; mint sauce would wobble gelatinously; pudding would pass him by.

Once he had written the text on the cuff of his shirt, and its discovery had brought terrible consequences. Lil had comforted him later, as he buried his sobbing head in her warm speckled throat that rose from the unbuttoned neck of her white blouse. He had felt sheltered under the wing of a white speckledy-feathered hen; but when he had put out a finger to trace the curve, just visible, of a pair of warm freckled eggs, the hen squawked and battered him with a brutal wing, leaving him doubly condemned and lonely. She had been sharp with him for a long time afterwards. 'Like father, like son,' she had clucked; 'What's born in the blood is bred in the bone', Madge had added, with glittering yellow eye. Their words had been shaming, menacing and incomprehensible, but the boy treasured these sayings in his heart. He puzzled over them now, as he watched his father in the pulpit. He screwed his eyes guiltily shut to blot out the wicked image of his father's fingers clutching Lil's breast, and clenched his eyeballs until a drift of kaleidoscopic stained-glass dots silted over the figures of the minister and the maid. The minister's voice tailed off, and Sandy looked up to see him absentmindedly forming his fingers into a gun, aiming and firing. Miss Kettle fell, in the general gasp, like a wounded swamp hen, in a flurry of brown bombazine.

People hurried to prop her up, holding their breath against the mothbally exhalations from her open mouth, the vapours of her Sabbath fast. The minister, recalled abruptly from his prospected hunting trip, waited impatiently for the restoration of order and declared testily: 'I take my text this morning from the Acts of the Apostles, Chapter ten, verse thirteen.'

'Why did he shoot Miss Kettle?' Sandy whispered to Kitty in the cold vestry which smelled of mildewed hymn books, as their father disrobed.

'Miss Kettle fainted!' said their mother, but she had seen him fire the gun, as everybody must have done. Her anxiety was not allayed by the giggles and squawks which escaped from Madge and Lil's irreverent mouths on the way home.

Miss Kettle perceived that her eschewal of breakfast had been a sin of pride, and that retribution, in the form of the public humiliation of fainting in church, had been swift and just. Her jowls mumbled penitently in anticipation of a small chop with mustard, followed by tapioca garnished by a ruby or peridot of jam. Nevertheless, she could not masticate away the image of the minister pointing an imaginary gun at her. After the service she shook off the enquiries about her health as a fowl shakes off the dirt of a dustbath, and hobbled home alone, much troubled.

'He must be a good man,' she reasoned, unpinning the grouse-claw brooch from the lapel of her good coat, and setting it in pride of place among the hatpins in the pincushion. 'A Godly man. He must have entered the ministry for the love of God, for it was certainly not for the love of his fellow man.'

She smoothed her thin hair, and noticed that the silk of the pincushion was not, as she had always thought of it, the bright purple silk of thirty years ago, and that the grouse claw was a little bald under its dull cairngorm. 'I suppose they will see me out,' she thought, with a pang of pity for her shabby old friends.

'I'm a silly, vain old woman.' As the pearls and pigeon's egg ruby of her pudding slipped down, she choked at the sudden thought of God's finger on the trigger. For what was Jack Mackenzie but an instrument of God?

2

The tin was painted with brown and purple mountains, fir trees
and a tumbling cataract and, in letters of gold, were the lines:

> O Caledonia! stern and wild,
> Meet nurse for a poetic child!
> Land of brown heath and shaggy wood,
> Land of the mountain and the flood,
> Land of my sires!

It contained shortbread, shipped from Edinburgh to the antipodean manse above Dunedin Bay, and was to be taken on the
seaside picnic. Kitty had been told to pack it. She and Sandy,
already seated, looked towards the sea, while the baby's view
was the flicker of sunshine through leaves and wicker and the
white fringes of the canopy under which she lay. The cradle was
swung aboard; Solomon's grey-and-white spotted hindquarters
twitched into glossy motion, gravel sprayed from the wheels, and
a calico blind rolled down at an attic window. The little wooden
acorn at the end of its cord rattled against the sill, and was still.

'Where's the shortbread?' Sandy cried. 'We've forgotten the

shortbread!' He turned to accuse his sister. 'Mother told you to get it from the kitchen!'

He didn't care for it himself but he had been promised the tin and was willing to martyr himself on the thick dry sugary fingers and scalloped petticoat tails.

'It isn't fair! Why should he have it?' Kitty pleaded yet again.

'I need it. I need it to keep important things in.'

'I need it too. I need it more than . . . '

'Neither of you shall have the tin.' Their father silenced them with characteristic diplomacy. 'Your mother and I shall eat the shortbread in our own good time, and then I shall use the tin myself. "O Caledonia! stern and wild." Who can tell me who wrote that?' he enquired genially of their sulky faces. 'Come on, come on!'

Sitting opposite them, he flicked the ankles of his unpoetic children with the tip of his ebony stick.

'Robert Burns?' Their mother attempted to deflect the storm. She had been too busy unwrapping the rest of the parcel, cutting the string free of red blobs of sealing wax to pay much attention to the tin, abstractedly agreeing that Sandy might have it.

Jack Mackenzie smote his forehead with his knuckles, dislodging his hat, which sailed onto a bush. Sandy, forgetting that mishaps which occurred to Father were not funny, laughed.

'Sir Walter Scott! It was Sir Walter Scott, Father!' Kitty tugged at her father's sleeve, but he seized the reins from Robert, who was driving them, slewing Solomon's head painfully. They skidded to a stop. Sandy was pitched out by the scruff of his neck onto the stones, landing on his hands and knees.

'Hat.'

Sandy handed it to him with a bloodied palm.

'Drive on, Robert.'

Kitty watched the graze of her brother's blood dry on Father's forehead. She turned her head and saw Sandy, in his round linen hat, grow smaller as they trotted away. She saw him lift his fishing net and hurl it after them. Now, she knew, he would cry. Then, as she remembered Sandy's whispered tearful threat, made one unhappy night, to kill Father, she pictured the Maori greenstone axe, decorated with feathers and dog's hair that hung in the hall, with two small hands circling its shaft, splitting Father's head and cleaving the bone with the terrible sound of the butcher hacking a pig's foreleg, or the soldiers breaking the thieves' legs on their crosses. She looked at Mother, but she had her head bent over the cradle. Baby Jessie responded to her mother's tickling finger with a gurgle of happiness. Then Father was chuckling too, as if the day had not been spoiled, and Mother then, and Kitty smiled back at Father, the four of them complete, bowling along to the picnic. Her face ached with the burden of being Father's favourite.

'I've half a mind to turn back for Sandy . . . ' remarked Jack, at ease among the cushions in the sparkling morning, pleasantly full of eggs and bacon, with the prospect of an appetite for luncheon sharpened by the sea breeze.

'Strange,' he mused, 'Ironic . . . '

'What is, dear?' Louisa prompted as the wheels sped along, not turning back for Sandy. He could not have told her how he had been reflecting that an expedition led by the explorer after whom bougainvillaea had been named had probably brought venereal disease to the innocent Pacific. There were instances of it, he knew, in his own congregation.

'I was thinking about plants.' He laid trails of tropical blossoms in her lap, rather than the corrosive flowers of gonorrhoea.

'Yes, plants are strange,' she was ready to agree. 'And ironic, I suppose.'

Jack was at his nicest when being botanical. She swayed, her hand on the cradle, sick at heart for Sandy, blind to the tiny pinkish flowers of carmichaelia that sprigged the verge.

'*Mackenzia*' or '*Mackensia*'? What a feather in his cap that would be. To find a new species and have it named after him. *Mackenzia officinalis*, should his discovery add to his repute by bringing medicinal benefit to mankind. Jack wished with all his heart that he could have sailed with Cook on his first Pacific voyage, in the company of the botanists Banks and Solander; he wished that he had been Banks. *Terra australis incognita* – the romance of that name! Banks, the wealthy and gifted amateur, youngest president of the Royal Society, designer of a ship with a gallery deck for artists and musicians – too top-heavy, alas, to sail – an eater of vultures, and cockatoo pie. He wouldn't mind a slice of that himself. Raised polished crust, with a crest of golden or rosy feathers.

'*Banksia*. Not a particularly distinguished plant, would you say?' He considered enviously a specimen with seed pods so hard that only the heat of a bushfire would split them.

'No, indeed,' said Louisa. She could think of few less distinguished. 'And not a particularly pretty name. It seems rather conceited to name a plant after oneself, I think.'

'You do, do you?'

'Fuchsia is nice,' said Kitty, 'and dahlia.' Then she squirmed at her mother's narrowing eyes, feeling silly, as she often did when alone with Father and Mother, as if she had forgotten to

27

put on her clothes; a crab without a shell. Of course Jessie was there, but she was too young to count.

'I think . . .' Mother began to say.

Jack's mind had hopped to penguins; 'Jumping Jacks', Cook's sailors had called the formal little fellows who bowed to them from the waters of Dusky Bay. A penguin waddled, vestigial wing raised to silence the applause, onto the platform at the Royal Society, to deliver the lecture which would make his name.

'No, you don't, I'm afraid,' he said mildly, and added, 'Robert Burns'. His thoughts lighted on an evergreen shrub with white, sweet-scented flowers and dark lustrous berries. Myrtille. His surplices and stocks returned from her hands with a faint, fresh sweetness in their starched folds, he slept in cotton and linen smoothed by her irons. The maids, Madge and Lilian, called her Myrtle, but he dissolved Myrtille, a scented purple pastille, on his tongue. 'I will plant in the wilderness the cedar, the shittah tree, and the myrtle, and the oil tree . . .' Isaiah.

Kitty shivered at the thought of salt water assaulting her scratches and stings. Perhaps, without Sandy there, she would be able not to paddle, and would have to stay on the sand with the baby. Sandy's disgrace had been all her fault. If she had brought the shortbread . . . but she had left it deliberately on the kitchen table. If she could not have the tin, she did not want the shortbread to be eaten. She scratched an itchy leg guiltily and watched a speck of blood ooze through the thin white stocking.

Tormented by sandflies, from the shadow of the bleached parasol Louisa watched children lift glittering ribbons of seaweed and wave them in banners above their heads as they ran down to the sea. She saw Kitty skip back from its edge. Jack, at a distance, was sauntering along the shoreline, from time to time stooping to pick up something, his trousers rolled to the knee, his hat on the back of his head, crammed tightly down. Jessie slept in the shade. Louisa rolled down her stockings. She felt the sun on her ankles. She unpinned the cameo at the high neck of her blouse, whose prim ridges, set by Myrtille's goffering iron, were going limp in the heat. A little breeze played in a delicious triangle beneath her throat. The sand felt cloying beneath the soles of her stockings and, with a glance at Jack's receding back, she slipped them off. How white were her toes, the nails like pale shells; a prism played along one shin and then the other, a tantalising little rainbow. She pulled her skirt as high as she dared, and lay back and closed her eyes, but she could not rest. At a discreet distance along the beach Robert was eating something out of a paper bag; she could see him, squinting through the sun, trailing sand into a pyramid with the fingers of his free hand. His white shirt was open to the waist, over his brown skin; his heavy boots stood clumsily side by side. New freckles stippled her legs and her arms below the pushed-up sleeves of her blouse. She sat up, irritable, and took out, once again, from her pocket the letter that had come in the parcel from home. Tears dripped onto the cheap paper, blurring the laboriously written words.

'Louisa! Make yourself decent, woman!'

Jack's great shadow was over her; his face bubbled with perspiration.

'You're crying! What's wrong? Is it because I sent Sandy home? I'll make it up to him.'

29

She shook her head, her hair tumbling from its pins in reddish profusion.

'I had planned to punish him, but I won't if you don't want me to.'

'Of course I don't want you to – he did nothing. It's not that . . .'

How could she tell him that she was crying because a canary had died in Edinburgh? As if sensing at least the provenance of her grief, he dropped to the sand beside her. 'Dinnae greet, lassie. Tell me what's wrong, and I'll put it right for you.'

Boldened by his softening, she picked up his big hand.

'I want to go home.'

He scrambled to his feet, brushing sand from his knees.

'Is that all? I'll tell Robert to get ready at once.'

'I don't mean home,' she wailed. 'I mean Home!'

'It's the heat. You've had too much sun.'

Jessie woke and started to cry. Louisa clasped the baby to her. She wanted to howl with her. 'I want to go home. I want my mother and my father and my sisters and their bairns and my wee brother.'

Jack was throwing the picnic things into the basket. Kitty came towards them slowly, shivering and shaking herself like a dog. Her father, splashing her playfully at the water's edge, had suddenly grabbed her ankle and she had fallen, her shrieks turning to gulping terror as the salt engulfed her nose and mouth. The blue ribbons on her sailor collar had run, leaking indigo onto the white. She saw that there would be no cluttering bite – the piece you were given when you came out of the sea with your teeth chattering.

'Myrtle will deal with it,' said her mother, stabbing the neck of her blouse with her brooch. Her nose looked red and beaky, as if she had been crying. She seemed not to care about the stained frock.

'Myrtille will deal with it,' said her father.

He called to Robert to get Solomon hitched up. He wondered if Robert had been watching the minister's wife lying there, her skirt round her knees, her hair all tumbled, her blouse disordered, like a wee hoor. He chafed at the long ride home.

'Early to bed for you, lassie, I think,' he said, looking at Louisa.

'I'm not a bit tired,' Kitty protested.

Louisa saw herself running down the beach, tearing off her heavy skirt, swimming strongly out into the ocean with Kitty on her back, pushing Jessie's basket in front of her through the waves, swimming home. She reached back her hand and towed Sandy along beside them.

There was a bit of grit embedded in Sandy's hand; he could see it under a jagged flap of skin. A hot salt surge of disappointment flooded his chest as the others trotted towards the sea. His fishing net lay stupidly where he had thrown it. He picked it up and made a half-hearted lunge at a butterfly. Father had a killing bottle in his study, which no one but he was allowed to touch, as if they would want to. He imagined the bottle enormous, a giant hand plunging Father into the poison, his little legs kicking from the neck. Father skewered with a pin to a black velvet pad.

'I didn't mean it,' he said to God. 'I wasn't really committing murder in my heart.'

Father was threatening to get him a proper fishing rod; Sandy hoped that he had forgotten, since he had seen Robert reel in that fish with a hook through its eye, a lump of silvery bloody jelly, and the fish battering itself on the stone until the eye was ripped out. Kitty had screamed and run away, which was all right for girls to do, but boys had to like things like that. Robert had made him carry the catch into the kitchen, five fish pierced through the lower lip by one big hook, and then the sticky skeletons piled on the plates for Madge to clear away.

'I thought you were going for a picnic?'

It was Myrtille, with a two-handled basket of washing on her shoulder.

'I decided not to go on the picnic.'

'But your Papa has gone, and the others?'

'Yes.'

Sandy swiped at the grass with his fishing net. Myrtille half put out a hand, as if to ruffle his sandy hair.

'I think you did want to go with them. Would you like to come with me, I'm going to have some lemonade.'

Sandy shook his head violently. 'I've got to go home. Thank you.'

'Well, I am going to sit in the sun with a cool glass of lemonade while the water boils.'

'Myrtle . . .'

'Myrtle, Myrtle . . .' she mocked.

She walked away on her bare feet.

'Myrtille has a foot in both camps,' he had heard his father say, 'but she belongs to neither of them. I fear that she does not even pay lip service to the tenets of the Church.'

'Myrtle!' Sandy wanted to shout after her. 'Is it true that

you've got the head of your great-grandfather on a shelf in your cottage?'

He could see it, tattooed, rolling its eyes and lolling its tongue at the lemonade, paying blue lip service.

'It's *tapu*. That means sacred or magic. It's a sign of respect, to keep the head,' Madge had said one day in the kitchen. 'The relatives come to honour it every year, apparently, although I've not seen them in the time I've been here. They don't cut the heads off any more, of course.'

'Well, I think it's unChristian!' Lil said. 'The thought of it . . . ugh!'

The children could feel the hairs standing up on their arms. They agreed with Lil. Then she giggled. 'Would you keep my head on a shelf, Madge, as a sign of respect?'

'Respect is something that has to be earned, Lilian Morrison, and the state of your cap and apron earns you none, that I can see.'

Lil rolled her eyes and stuck out her tongue like a tiki. She was so bold. If the children had done it they would have got a slap from Madge. Lil did get a slap but she just giggled the more, and they could see that Madge wasn't really cross.

'Wouldn't the heads smell,' asked Kitty, 'as they decomposed?'

'They're preserved, you goose. Now, out of my kitchen. Lilian and I have work to do, if some people haven't.'

Lil giggled. Lil was a giggler. It drove Father mad. Sandy tested the rottenness of 'decomposed' on his tongue. Kitty was always bringing out words like that; it was as if she had a secret store of marbles, bigger, brighter, and shinier than his.

Imagine Father's head, on the mantelpiece, with his stock and bands and his pipe. Sandy ran towards the house. He stopped

33

to untie Hamish, the rough yellow dog, from the iron peg sunk into the ground outside his kennel, and saw two eggs lying under the hedge. He carried them, still faintly warm, into the kitchen. There was nobody there, only a heap of peapods in the colander and a pot of shelled peas beside it. Sandy put the eggs down carefully and took a handful of peas. There on the table was his tin, the cause of all the trouble, sent from his maternal grandmother to fatten them up for the cannibals who populated this Presbyterian city. The parcels from Edinburgh, with their string blobbed in red sealing wax, always made Mother sad.

'Mother, why are you melancholy?' Kitty had asked once, when there had been a comb of heather honey.

'As if there aren't bees in Dunedin ...' was all Mother had replied.

'Is there no balm in Gilead?' Father had asked.

Melancholy. It had a grey-mauve tinge, like faded lavender; a cloudy marble. The house felt melancholy. He decided to creep up to the maids' room and surprise them. Then he had a wonderful idea. He tiptoed upstairs and found his box of charcoal.

'I'm sure I heard somebody, Madge.'

'There couldn't be anybody. Myrtle's gone. The dog didn't bark. They won't be back for hours.'

She punctuated each reassurance with a kiss.

The attic door burst open. A tattooed face thrust in, yelling, a half-naked savage with feathers in its hair, brandishing a greenstone axe at the tumbled bed; the maids in their white petticoats screaming.

Then Lil was upon him, shaking him, shouting, 'How dare you burst in here? How dare you?'

34

The greenstone axe clattered to the floor and the Maori warrior crumpled under the falling kiwi-feather cloak as the whole miserable day engulfed him. Then Madge had him in her arms soothing, 'there, there, he's only a wee boy,' imprinting him for ever with rough cotton lace, feathers and moist warm skin.

When the family returned, Sandy was found in the kitchen, with streaks of charcoal and dried tears still on his face, being fed shortbread by the maids, decorous in their black dresses and white aprons.

'What on earth does he think he's at?' Jack demanded. 'What's going on here? Explain yourself! Have you forgotten you're in disgrace? Well, have you? And how dare you untie that dog?'

Sandy, choking on shortbread, could not explain himself.

'Och, don't be so hard on the lad. He missed the picnic, after all,' said Madge boldly. 'He's just a wee boy.'

'I am not hard on the boy. Allow me to know what's best for my own son. Everything I do is for his own good, so that he will grow up strong and honest and manly, into a son I can be proud of. Get yourself cleaned up, Sandy, and get off to bed. You'll not be wanting any supper after that shortbread.'

When her husband was safely shut in his study Louisa crept upstairs with a bowl of bread and milk sprinkled with sugar.

'Why does Father hate me?' Sandy whispered.

'Of course he doesn't! He loves you, and always remember, Sandy, that Mother loves her precious boy more than anything in the world.'

If Jack, engrossed in a tray of insects, some with heads no bigger than the heads of the pins that impaled them to their meticulously written labels, had heard her words he might have recognised that his harshness to Sandy was rooted in jealousy. He felt quite differently towards Kitty, so affectionate and bright; she, he had decided, was destined for university. She should have every opportunity to make the best of herself. She was to fulfil his hopes; Sandy on the other hand would never become the honest fellow his father could be proud of. He retained his pleasure in dressing up and disguises, and even if the maids had been fooled only for a minute by his impersonation of a murderous Maori, he had quite convinced himself as he sneaked up on them and sprang his attack. In time he would progress from amateur dramatics, with his pleasing light tenor voice, straw hat and cane, to professional deceit, and his late father's clothes would provide the costumes for some of his most successful performances. Dressed in them, he had more in common with Jack Mackenzie than his father would have cared to admit.

3

'"God wants the boys,
The merry, merry boys,
The noisy boys, the laughing boys,
The thoughtless boys.
God wants the boys, with all their joys,
That He as gold may make them pure,
And teach them trials to endure;
His heroes brave He'll have them be,
Fighting for truth and purity.
God wants the boys!"'

'Sandy Mackenzie, I'm warning you! Any more disruption of my
Sunday School and I'll be having a word with your father. Girls,
now!' Miss Kettle pointed her baton and the girls' voices took
up their verse. Sandy Mackenzie was stuffing his handkerchief
in his mouth, convulsed by his imitation of her.

'"God wants the girls,
The happy, happy-hearted girls,
The loving girls, the best of girls,

The worst of girls.
God wants to make the girls His pearls,
And so reflect His holy face,
And bring to mind His wondrous grace;
That beautiful the world may be,
Filled with their love and purity.
God wants the girls!"

'Together now.'

The noble boys and gentle girls, with Miss Kettle's elderly soprano wavering above them, joined together in the last verse, 'God wants us all', and closed heartily on 'God save us all!' Miss Kettle was weighing up the humiliation of having Sandy Mackenzie gibbering like a monkey, pulling faces, inciting other boys to misbehave and generally undermining her authority, against the distasteful task of confronting his father. Perhaps a quiet word to Mrs Mackenzie might be better. She felt sorry for that gentle girl, for it was evident that the minister was a domestic tyrant. It was apparent, too, that he favoured Kitty over her brother; perhaps if he were not so hard on the boy, young Sandy would not feel compelled to play the goat when he was not under his father's eye. Miss Kettle had come to dread Sunday afternoons; she suppressed a sigh as she turned up the day's picture on the big hanging book of coloured illustrations of Bible stories; 'Jesus Stills the Storm'. If only that tragic accident at Rotorua had not befallen the Craigies. Miss Kettle scolded herself for bemoaning her own subtle loss of status under Mr Mackenzie's rule, almost blaming the Craigies for her unhappiness, when they had suffered such a terrible fate. Almost the most horrible aspect of it all was Jack Mackenzie's ill-concealed amusement, that glittering moustache failing to disguise the quirk of his lips, when the Craigies were mentioned, and overhearing the Mackenzie children's voices, sharp and clear from the garden: 'What shall we play?'

'I know, let's play the Craigies at Rotorua.'

There followed two loud splashes from the pond.

The fatal furlough had progressed as follows. Angus Craigie, a martyr to gout, had determined to try the efficacy of the thermal pools at Rotorua, and, having a holiday due to him, had booked himself and his wife Jamesina into Brent's Bathgate House, Rotorua, Auckland. The Craigies had set out in fine fettle, taking with them clothes to suit the variations of temperature they might encounter, fishing rods, and their photographic equipment, for they were keen amateur photographers, proposing to provide the congregation of St Enoch's with instructive entertainment on their return. They had sailed on the steam launch to the volcanic island of Mokoia, in the middle of the Rotorua lake, where the Maori chief Tutanekei had dwelt and where Hinemoa, famous in legend, had swum the three miles across the lake to see him. They had seen the steamy columns of Whakarewarewa rise against dark hills, smelled hot sulphur and iron, seen the setting sun turn forests to crimson fire, scrunched through the Manuka scrub. They had captured snow-capped mountains and mud volcanoes, geysers and boiling pools in sepia, mementoes which were eventually to make melancholy viewing for the shocked congregation of St Enoch's. The Craigies were determined to make the half-day trip to Tikitere, eleven miles from Rotorua, and set off in good spirits with a group of fellow tourists, Mr Craigie feeling regenerated by the thermal baths which he had taken.

The inferno at Tikitere did not disappoint, with its billowing steam, boiling pools and mud geysers; it had been called rightly 'Hell's Gates'. There the hydrothermal action is so powerful that the earth vibrates as if indeed suggesting horrendous sub-terranean activities, although the springs are famed for their remarkable healing properties. Some slip of the earth's molten crust that day, some particularly strong tremor and rise in tem-perature, or fury from below perhaps, shaking the ground and boiling the water – nobody could say which it had been – made Mrs Craigie stumble and fall. Her husband, in steadying them both, plunged with her. Whatever the cause of the disaster, the Craigies were dealt with as cruelly and efficiently as a pair of lobsters in the hands of a chef.

The horror of their end, the shoes slipping on the earth's wet lip, the hissing cauldron, haunted Miss Kettle. At least it was quick, she comforted herself; at least they went together, strong in their faith. The shock and choking mud would have killed them instantaneously, unlike crustaceans who, if not stunned before being plunged into boiling water, can take some time to die, battling with boiled claws up the sides of the pan.

Another matter, graver than Sandy's misbehaviour, was also troubling Miss Kettle, breaking her sleep and causing indiges-tion which the white powder she stirred into a glass could not soothe away.

Louisa was checking the fresh laundry, referring to a small black book with a rectangular window in its cover, on which was written LINEN. Many years later, Kitty would come across this book in a drawer lined with a brittle paper of bleached and breaking roses exuding a distillation of summers locked in wood, and would weep at the schoolgirlish hand in which the sheets, pillowcases, tablecloths (rectangular and round), traycloths (embroidered and drawn-thread-worked), napkins, dishtowels, glass cloths, and towels were listed so importantly and painstakingly in ink which had rusted to the colour of old thin blood.

This morning Kitty flung into the room in grass-stained muslin.

'Father says he's going shooting! You've got to stop him.'

'One of Aunt Ina's table napkins is missing . . .'

'You're not listening! Did you hear what I said? He's going to shoot *kakas*, parrots! He's polishing his gun! You mustn't let him go! And *kakapos*! They can't even fly.'

'I'll thank you not to use that tone of voice with me, Miss. Your father's business is his own concern.'

'But, Mother, you can't . . . Remember what Father said about killing the whales when we were on the ship?'

'That will do. Hand me that towel, please.'

It was true; Jack had no compunction about killing when the gun, net or poison was in his own hand.

Louisa noted the green streaks on the white dress and could not exert herself to say anything. She started to hum; flocks of parrots might well explode in shuttlecocks of brilliant bloody green feathers if that would take her husband away from Dunedin for a day or two. He could make the feathers into a headdress, cloak and skirt for all she cared, and perform a grotesque, stamping war dance and protrude his tongue, and fall backwards with a feathered spear impaling his chest. 'May God forgive me, I didn't mean it,' Louisa muttered as she realised that she had just committed murder in her heart. In her contrition she thought of home, and tasted raspberries in her mouth, the

41

little red and yellow Scottish raspberries which grew where the rabbits came out of their sandy caves on summer evenings. She heard the soft call of the wood pigeons who cried, 'Take *two* cows, David. Take *two* cows, David.' That was what her grandfather had told her their throaty calls were saying, but he could not explain why they advised it incessantly, or who David was. Here in Dunedin the moreporks, owls cried out for 'More pork, More pork.' When they called in the daytime it meant that rain was on its way. And there was the *tui* or parson bird, with its bands of white feathers at its neck, just like her husband's stock; the garden flickered with melodious little ministers.

'Après moi le Delage.'

Jack had materialised.

'I beg your pardon, dear?'

He caught her eye staring at his chest, where the spear had entered. His finger scrubbed impatiently at the spotless cloth, the jagged bloody wound, as he said: 'Oh, please don't. I was merely attempting a very feeble pun. But, as I may have remarked before, I don't make jokes for *your* amusement.'

'I am sorry, Jack. Please tell me, and I'll promise to laugh.'

He looked at her face for a sign of irony or subversion, but her tongue flickering nervously out like a lizard's to moisten her lips for laughter and her strained skin stippled with freckles, as if she had caught the sun through a motoring veil, betrayed a serious and irritating desire to placate.

'Miss Kettle has called to see you, sir,' said Madge round the door.

'Excellent, excellent. Show the good beldam into my study, would you, Madge,' he said savagely.

'I have, sir.'

'My misdirected attempt at humour,' he said over his shoulder to Louisa as he left the room, 'was inspired by the fact that Ross, McBride and I will be travelling in a hired Sunbeam. The others will follow in the Delage.'

He stumped off to his study, where Miss Kettle would be slithering about on the brown leather chair, having acquainted herself with the letters on his desk, or the books on his shelves. Those were all theological volumes and botanical works. Certain other books were under lock and key, and the key lived on his watch chain. Grizelda Kettle, who was now examining a glass case of butterflies pinned to black velvet, claimed a connection with Charles Kettle, the surveyor who had laid out the plans for the 1,400 acres of Dunedin and who had landed there in 1846, and so she had ordained herself a power in the congregation. What could she want now, the minister mused. Perhaps some falling-out with Mrs Potts, an elder's wife, some slanderous remark at the Ladies' Guild about her ancestry, which would provide the long-awaited opportunity to remark 'A case of the Potts calling the Kettle black'. Too much to hope for; not even Mrs Potts could have whispered an accusation of the taint of Maori blood at the pale Grizelda Kettle, not seated but standing, sour as a vinegar bottle on the carpet.

'My dear Miss Kettle, what a pleasure ... but you would appear to be working up a fine head of steam ... what seems to be the trouble?'

He aimed an imaginary gun at the ceiling and Miss Kettle was astounded, faint as at blasphemy, to see the fleshy lips, which uttered the most sacred words of bread and wine, form a pink popping sound: pow, pow, pow. It was true, then, that he had aimed his gun at her from the pulpit.

'I feel it my painful duty ... there has been some talk ...'

'Talk? Talk? There will always be tittle-tattle, Miss Kettle, for those with nothing better to do than to listen to it. What talk? Out with it, woman!'

Jack watched her throat redden like a turkey's wattles at this affront, until she was all suffused with angry crimson, forcing herself to stand her ground.

'People are saying that you neglect your duties, that they cannot come to you for comfort or guidance. That your heart is not in your ministry.'

'What nonsense is this? Which people? Who is saying that? Who has sent you here, or have you come on your own initiative, propelled perhaps by some feminine pettiness, some imagined slight?'

As Jack was at once blustering with relief and reeling in horror from the thought that the desiccated old biddy might possibly cherish romantic notions of him, Miss Kettle herself recoiled from the frivolous flaunting petticoat and crumbling petticoat tails of shortbread which his words conjured up. She trembled in blotchy frustrated outrage before his self-satisfied body, his male complacency as unassailable as that kauri wood great desk, should she bruise her toes kicking its thick glossy legs. She was aware of all its horrid little drawers and winking handles, the bland-faced shagreen, the knives and sharp pens and squills and quills.

'Won't you sit down, Miss Kettle?' he said, insultingly late in the day, indicating with the casual sweep of his hand that it was of no importance which chair she chose and that he would rather she was gone.

'If the matter is of importance, Miss Kettle, you must

speak now, for I plan a short vacation from the ardours of office.'

Then Miss Kettle might have realised that she had been wounded by a random bullet and was not his selected prey, but she stood, pale now, struggling to say what she had come to say, aware that she had failed already.

'I really cannot be expected to exercise any authority in my Sunday School class, when the minister's own son ...'

'Ah, it's about young Sandy you've come, is it? Well, well, I might have guessed ...'

He was rubbing his hands as if with soft soap.

'Boys will be boys, eh, Miss Kettle? We should not forget that we were young once ourselves!'

The thought of the two of them, the minister in knicker-bockers and herself in her school pinafore, conspiring in some playground naughtiness defeated Miss Kettle. She bowed her head, words unsaid, rumours undenied, and with a muttered 'Good day' departed, leaving him still washing his hands, master of his smug paraphernalia, in his perverse benevolence towards his son. Louisa came flying out of the kitchen, barging blindly into her, igniting the acid fire of indigestion in her bony chest.

Halfway home, Miss Kettle was overtaken by Michael Flannery, the odd-job man, in his ramshackle cart pulled by his shambling mare Nellie, the pair of them drunk as lords. Michael offered her a lift, as if she would be seen dead in that conveyance, sitting on a pile of old sacks with a scythe and a pair of tin kettles, a broken chamber pot and empty bottles rolling around in the back. 'Jack of all trades, master of none,' sniffed Miss Kettle to herself, and thought of the minister. And of that tarbrushed washerwoman. Everybody had seen the way he looked at her.

In the kitchen Madge, seeing her mistress's eyes bulging yet again with tears, almost snatched a linen napkin from her fumbling fingers. She folded it in half, and in half again, then turned up an inch all round the square she had made, and pleated the whole into folds. Then she turned back the three central pleats, and a fleur-de-lis bloomed in her hand. Louisa clapped her hands like a child. Hers were always triangles.

'Oh, pretty! Let me try.'

Madge, who knew all the subtle etiquette of linen, regarded her effort, with pursed lips.

'Not bad, for a first attempt. I'd a friend once could make wee gold chairs from the wire round champagne corks.'

'Could she? How clever. I should like to have seen that.'

'Aye, she was gey artistic-like. I'll show you how to make a bird and the cockscomb and the mitre and the slipper when I've the time,' Madge promised, although privately she judged them to be beyond the mistress's capabilities.

Left alone in the kitchen, Louisa rejected again the ridiculous notion that she was jealous of Madge. She had the children, and Madge was but a servant. Who could do everything better than she could. Who had no house, no husband or child. Who slept in an attic. In a single bed. Who was often singing, although not as sweetly as Lilian, and laughing. Who didn't hear the terrible miles of the sea between here and home beating in her ears night and day. Who had a friend to share secrets with. Who wasn't frightened all the time, swamped by grey salty waves of anxiety. Who, she suspected, laughed at her master behind his back.

She wanted to go up to the maids' room and sit on a bed and kick off her shoes in the simplicity of their lives. The family, the congregation, this house; it was as if she wore a heavy iron corset, dragging her down. She wandered into the pantry and began counting, distractedly, the jars of jams, jellies, preserves, pickles and bottled fruit. She peered into the meat safe, a cabinet of perforated zinc, and a picture came into her mind, of the man in the iron mask, and then of herself, head locked into the meat safe, her long hair growing and growing, so that she could not see or speak, until it strangled her, and tendrils of red hair wound in and out of the perforations. When Lil came to collect the clean linen she found the table afloat with white water lilies, which proved to be two dozen, less one, perfect fleurs-de-lis; she gathered them up and placed them on top of the pile of folded sheets.

Lil could not forbear to comment, 'I detect the hand of Madge in this.'

'Lilian, are you ever . . . homesick?'

'I count myself fortunate in having everything I could wish for here, madam.'

'You're very kind,' Louisa heard herself say. Probably the wrong thing to say. Yes, probably the wrong thing to say.

She ran out of the room; the wrong thing, always, always. Bumped into Miss Kettle; she was like a demented clock chiming silently, running up the stairs wringing hands, ringing wrong wrong wrong.

'Words fail me.' Jack, entering the bedroom, snatching up a bowl of pot-pourri, crunching dried rose petals in his fingers, trickling crimson, scented dust into the white latticed dish. No, that's what's happened to me, words fail me, Louisa did not say.

'Say something. Explain yourself. Rushing out like that, knocking Miss Kettle flying. What will people think? As it is there have been complaints that you are failing in your duties as the minister's wife.'

That night Louisa woke to the cry of an owl.

'Myrtille.'

Jack, tasting bittersweet, bruised purple fruit, stumbled forward and fell into scratchy twigs and harsh little leaves.

'Jack! Wake up! You're dreaming!'

Louisa was shaking him, standing beside the bed in her white nightdress, her hair in a scrawny pigtail.

'What? What's the matter now, can't a man get some sleep?'

'You were calling out – I thought you were having a bad dream.'

He had one hand under the bedclothes; the other shot out and grabbed her wrist.

'I was. Come in here with me and kiss me better.'

She resisted; he could feel the tension in her arm.

'Come on, you're shivering.'

'Why were you calling out "Myrtille"?'

'Was I? Well, I'll tell you. I was having an awful dream about the laundry. Come away in, and I'll tell you all about it.'

'Oh Jack! I've just got Jessie off to sleep. I'm so tired. Please . . .'

A sudden jerk pulled her sprawling on top of him, as a wail came from the nursery. Louisa felt foolish, undignified. He had his mouth on hers, his arm across her neck, squeezing until she had to open her mouth. She saw herself as if from above, spreadeagled, nightie in ungainly billows round her legs. She

48

bit him. A mouthful of bristly cheek. He roared; the baby was screaming. Then he pulled her down again saying, 'That's better. At last you show some spirit.'

Desperation that somebody, one of the children, should come and see her gave her the strength to twist away, run from the room to the nursery and pick up the wet, frantic baby, holding her fiery face against Jessie's hot head. Little bodies that she could clasp, kisses from innocent mouths, that was all she wanted.

Jessie was not hungry, she had just been fed, so Louisa started to unpin the damp napkin. To her consternation, Jack's feet were thudding up the stairs in fury to the maids' room.

'Mother! What's going on?'

Sandy and Kitty stood, in their little white nightclothes.

'Nothing. Come on, back to bed with all of you!' She put the soothed baby down in the cradle and crept back to her own bed.

Jack threw open the door so violently that it crashed against the wall. 'What do you mean by letting the baby ... '

Madge and Lil shrieked and pulled the bedclothes to their necks, lying there side by side with terrified eyes. The empty bed screamed at him.

Jack closed the door. As in a dream, he followed the baby's cries, startled by Kitty appearing like a white moth in the moonlight. Louisa flickered into the shadows.

'Away back to your bed now.'

'Jessie's crying again.'

'Father's going to her. Off you go now, before you catch cold.'

The unearthly hour, the moonlight throwing rectilinear shadows through the banister rail, Father's voice, bemused and tender, made Kitty feel that something strange was happening that night. The house was altered, like a house in a dream, their house and yet not their house. There came a scraping sound from the maids' room, like something dragged across the floor.

Jack sat heavily in the rocking chair, shoogling the damp baby on his knee. 'Shoo shaggy, o'er the glen, Mammy's pet and Daddy's hen.'

The baby, in the unaccustomed haven of her father's arms, gazed up at him.

'Well, Jessie, what are we to make of that?' he asked softly.

Jessie stared at him as if wisdom from a time before the cradle lay in those unblinking eyes, as if she were assessing his features for the first time and saying, 'So this is the father I have been allotted'. Then, as if satisfied, she fell asleep. Jack sat for a long time cradling the weight of his daughter, fondling a tiny foot through the long nightgown, in a confusion of protective love and uncomfortable desire at the memory of the maids in each other's arms.

When the door closed behind Mr Mackenzie, Madge leaped up and pulled the chair across the room, wedging it under the door handle.

'That's the last time anyone comes bursting in here. I'm fitting a snib to this door the morn. First Sandy, and now him. Is there no peace in this house?'

Lil lay stricken, paralysed, her great wide eyes staring at horror and disgrace. She was like ice when Madge climbed back in beside her, took a frozen hand and chafed it gently. She wrenched her hand away, pulled her nightgown on and flung herself the short distance to her own bed, dragging the covers over her head.

'No use shutting the stable door when the horse has bolted,' came Madge's muffled voice, calm through the blackness. Lil's head emerged.

'Oh Madge, are you no feart?'

'Why should I be? You had a bad dream and I took you into my bed to comfort you. What's to be feart in that?'

'Well, I am. I'm – terrified – that they'll send me away from you!'

'I'll never let them do that. What did I tell you? It's you and me, together for ever. He may pay our wages but we are not his slaves. His does not own us body and soul. We are not Russian serfs and we're not black slaves on the plantation, we're free and able-bodied Scotswomen in a Christian household.'

At that Lilian visualised denunciation in the kirk, and wept.

'But it's wrong, loving each other the way we do. It's wrong. I keep seeing his terrible face, staring at us. Like God and Adam and Eve.'

Madge came over to Lilian's bed. 'Is it wrong? Does it feel wrong when I take you in my arms?'

'No.'

'Does it feel wrong when I kiss you? Like this? And this?'

'No. No. I don't know.'

Madge lay awake long after Lil had fallen asleep. It was true that Lilian had had a bad dream, and that she had taken her into her bed to comfort her, but that had been on her first night in a strange land, when Madge had been the mother, the sister Lilian had never known. She remembered clearly her first sight of Lil, standing out, for her, among the clutter of Mackenzies, clutching her cheap suitcase as if it was all she had in the world, which it was, her fair hair slipping untidily from a bashed felt hat, her big frightened eyes, the colour of wild hyacinths, her fine ankles above the clumsy shoes, with a crooked darn just above the delicate bone. She saw her putting her things in the closet, ashamed because they were so few; the way she stroked down the skirt of her Sunday frock with a sigh told Madge that she was a girl who would like to have pretty clothes and dancing shoes. She should have them, Madge decided, although there was little prospect of jigging in Dunedin. Orphaned herself, and a few years older, Madge had flourished in the blast, while Lilian seemed a frail plant to be uprooted and blown about by the wind. Nothing Lil had done in her life had been her own decision; dreamily, often incompetently, she had always done what she had been told to do, whether it was learning her tables or being let off school to help with the lifting of the tatties; leaving school, slaving in the kitchen of a big house at Fochabers or being promoted to maid and passed on from there to an old minister in Elgin and thence to a family in Edinburgh. When the family had moved to England, a position had been found for Lilian with the Mackenzies. It had been taken for granted that she should accompany them to New Zealand; Mrs Mackenzie needed help with the children; there was another on the way, and the mistress as sick as a dog every morning; and the Mackenzies were all the family she had.

Lilian had a singing voice that reminded Madge of rowan-berry jelly when you held the jar up to the light. The first time Madge had heard it, above the raspberry canes, where Lilian had thought herself alone as she picked the fruit, everything was still around her. Madge had felt the brush of wet leaves against her face, had felt the cold red berries in her hand, had seen with such longing a clear burn tumbling through bright stones. She could have bent down and scooped a handful of pure icy water and tasted her childhood running through her fingers; and then Lilian had come across the grass, carrying a bowl of berries, her lips and apron stained, going as red as a raspberry at seeing Madge and knowing she had heard her singing.

Lilian could have them all in tears, even the minister, when Mrs Mackenzie played the piano and she sang the old Scottish songs and the songs of Burns from Mrs Mackenzie's beautiful embossed blue and gold volume illustrated with 'numerous engravings'. 'This selection from the Poetical Works of Robert Burns includes such of his popular Poems as may with propriety be given in a volume intended for the Drawing-room; and nearly all the Songs which are usually published.' Then, as they all wandered together among the green braes, the flowery banks o' bonnie Doon, pulling the gowans fine, how the minister's fine tenor soared on: 'And I will come again, my love, Though it were ten thousand mile': Madge had to dash away the tears as Lilian sang 'Bonnie Wee Thing', and Louisa thought of her babies. Louisa could never bear to join in on 'Fare thee weel, thou first and fairest! Fair thee weel, thou best and dearest!', for Kitty had been the first, and she knew her voice would break at the thought of severing from any one of her bairns; her voice, soft, heartfelt and unreliable, warbled and wantoned through the flowering thorn, and Madge dreamed of the wee shop she and Lil would have one day; sweeties in glass jars, bright green soor plooms and striped clove balls, Highland toffee and home-made tablet, cut into squares and sold in paper pokes.

Sometimes Robert, leading Solomon from the stable, for the

53

minister had given him permission to use the horse, heard them singing. He had had hopes of Madge, a fine-looking woman, tall and slender with a cloud of dark hair, and, parrot-like in profile, with a mouth that looked too soft to house that sharp tongue. He had assessed Lil too, pretty as a picture; but those two were as thick as thieves, and now he had his Donalda, the young woman he intended to marry.

'Oh Myrtille at thy window be, it is the wish'd, the trysted hour!' Jack was thinking. It was the wished but not the trysted hour. His wife was a winsome wee thing, never more so than in the light of the candles on the dappled walnut wood of the piano, but he could wish he were the lad born in Kyle, with his Jean, his Mary, his Tibbie, his Phyllis, his bonnie Lesley and all of them, and his Myrtille, whom Robert might visit with impunity; 'We are just friends, Mr Mackenzie, nothing more', and whose name Robert, like the maids, pronounced to rhyme with spurtle, the stick they used to stir the porridge. He should never have entered the Church to please his parents; he should have stuck to his guns.

The morning after Jack had burst in on the maids dawned dreich; they were heavy-eyed, Lil with weeping and Madge with lack of sleep. A bird came down the chimney of the master and mistress's bedroom, dragging soot all over the white counter-pane as Madge tried to catch it and Mrs Mackenzie fluttered in a corner until the wild thing was released through the window. Lil took it as an omen, sure that such an occurrence spelled bad luck, despite Madge challenging her for any proof that there was such a superstition. She was on edge too, expecting, like Lil, a summons to the study. The rain kept dinging down all morning, and Myrtille, coming into the kitchen for a crack, could not amuse them, even with a story of a Maori woman who, years ago, had killed her babies in turn and suckled puppies at her breast in their place, until the wife of a missionary pointed out the error of her ways.

'Och away' was all Madge said, and Lil looked as if she had been crying already, so a few more tears were hardly flattering to the storyteller. Robert came in, dripping, and put on the table, with the other purchases, a small brown paper package containing the bolt Madge had asked him to get.

'Will I put this on for you?'

'I'm perfectly capable of doing so myself, Robert, thank you.'

Still the command from the study did not come.

By the evening Lil was a trembling wreck, crying over broken china and spilled milk. When they went to bed Madge drew the bolt and pronounced, 'It's clear that he has no intention of saying anything, and why should he indeed? Except to apologise for disturbing two innocent ladies in their boudoir, and that's too much to hope for.'

4

Jack Mackenzie had turned away Miss Kettle, who would have been willing to adore him chastely and work her fingers to the bone, not difficult in her case, in embroidering kneelers and pincushions and needlebooks for sales of work, and knitting and sewing little garments for heathen babies. It was she who had fashioned the blue silk collection bags with appliquéd fleurs-de-lis, which had been relegated to the Sunday School when Jack Mackenzie had expressed a preference for a brass plate, and she who had tried to instruct Kitty in crewel work: 'All needles are cruel,' said Kitty, whose sewing was specked with blood and tears. Many small snubs followed the occasions when Mr Mackenzie, his mind on the expedition which had horrified his daughter, had seemed to shoot Miss Kettle from the pulpit in front of the whole congregation, and again in his study, when she had steeled herself to do her unpleasant duty. Jack had returned from the trip with the soft body of a deer roped to the roof of the car, and a small pig, and feathery passengers lolling all over the back seat. Mr Bell, of Bell's Royal Garage in Manor Place, had not been pleased with the state of the Sunbeam, and Jack's children had shrunk from the booty. Disgruntled with them, he had made Sandy carry armfuls of dead birds to the buggy and drive with him to the taxidermist in Caversham. The shop window was of horrible fascination, for it contained the tableau of a school where a hunch-shouldered kiwi in a mortar board, holding a book in one foot and a tawse in the other, presided over a class of small birds and rats seated at miniature desks, and in the corner stood a Maori dog in a dunce's cap. Jack Mackenzie, who had been the Dux of his own school, as he reminded Sandy often, was very taken with the display. While Jack negotiated with Mr and Mrs Forsyth, the sprightly and cruel old surgeon and seamstress who seemed to have injected their elixirs into their own veins, Sandy prowled round the shop, brought up short by the kittens' tea party where the fluffy guests in their party dresses and sailor suits were waited on by a tabby maid wearing a black dress, lacy cap and apron.

Jack had been in good spirits as they bowled home, singing 'Annie Laurie' and giving Solomon sharp little flicks of the whip, raising his hat and bowing to people he knew. Sandy was in some distress, hiding it with a sickly smile; while fiddling around unnoticed, he had knocked a seahorse to the floor and in stepping back had trodden on it, crushing its tail. The smashed thing was burning a hole in his pocket. Had he not been so afraid of his father, had he not been called a liar and a fool so often, he might have confessed, got it over with and offered to pay for it with the sixpence in his pocket. As it was, he added the seahorse to his hoard of undiscovered crimes and concomitant dread, and remembered that he had no right to the sixpence either. A quarter of a mile from home, they saw Myrtille trudging along with a basket of washing balanced on her shoulder. Sandy was astonished when his father reined in the horse and jumped down, lifted his hat and handed Myrtille into the buggy. He then stopped at their gate and told Sandy to get down while he drove Myrtille the short distance to her home.

Sandy's worry about the seahorse was compounded by an uncomfortable feeling which he could not define. He hid the seahorse in his room wrapped in a handkerchief at the back of a drawer, deciding that it must be restored to the sea next time they went to Ocean Beach, rather than interred in his secret burial place in the garden, the repository of the results of several previous accidents and regretted petty thefts. He had nightmares of his father discovering his hoard. As he closed the drawer he thought about the burial at sea, from the *Inverness*, and the waters closing like green glass above him as the sailor spiralled down and down to the bottom of the sea. Davy Jones's locker.

Meanwhile, Jack helped Myrtille down and took her basket of washing himself. She tried to take it but he insisted on carrying it in. He set it down on the clean, swept floor and looked around. There was a seagrass chair with legs riddled by borers, a shelf of books, a seagrass table on which stood a kerosene lamp and a stone jar of fuchsias, a primus stove and an upturned packing-case holding a few utensils. He could see a narrow bed with a patchwork cover in an alcove. Beyond this room, half sunken under a grassy roof, was the laundry where Myrtille boiled his stocks and surplices, and a few yards away, concealed in a green bower, the dunny. Jack paced the room.

'What in the name of ...' His voice rose; it came out as 'Niname ...'

A head grinned at him from a triangular shelf set in the angle of two walls.

'Don't touch it!'

He stared. The hair was startlingly white against the leathery skin whorled and stippled with tattoos; the blue-scrolled chin, plucked with tweezers formed by two mussel shells, was beardless. It was perfect. The prize exhibit, the *pièce de résistance* of his collection.

'Where did you get it?'

'It is my great-grandfather.'

Myrtille lied. She repeated the story she had concocted for the maids: her great-grandfather had been a tribal leader, as renowned as the great Te Kooti Rikirangi, who had been betrayed and treacherously murdered by a rival tribe, his body eaten and his head preserved as a spoil of war. His followers, bent on vengeance, had counter-attacked and after the ensuing massacre had retrieved the head and passed it down through the family ever since. Now she, Myrtille, was the custodian of the honoured relic, and she in turn would bequeath it to her own son, should she have one. From time to time members of her scattered family gathered here to pay their respects to their illustrious ancestor.

Jack did not believe a word of it.

'What year would that have been, when the massacre took place?'

'Don't go any closer. It is *tapu*, forbidden; he is still powerful.'

'What was his name?'

'Tara-whai.'

'I see.'

Indeed he saw. In plucking out of the air the name of one of the most renowned chiefs, of legendary bravery, she confirmed not only that she was lying but that his knowledge of history was greater than hers. Concealing a smile, he turned from the head as if he had lost interest, and studied the books on her shelf.

'There's one book I'm looking for. That I don't see here.'

'And what might that be?'

'The Word of God.'

'Fancy.' Myrtille mocked the good ladies of Dunedin.

'No doubt you keep it at your bedside, for instruction and consolation at your morning and evening prayers?'

Myrtille spread her arms across the alcove, a dark angel in a workaday dress barring the way.

'Do you say your prayers, lassie?'

'Not to your God.'

He turned on his heel, with a glance at the sacred head on the shelf, and said: 'I see where my duty lies. I shall expect you in my study at four o'clock this afternoon.'

'I have decided to start a wee Bible class,' he told Louisa at luncheon, taking his napkin from its silver ring and unfurling it with a starchy crack on the soupy air before bowing his head to ask a blessing on the meal.

'Amen. I'm sure that will be a good idea, Jack.'

'Yes, I think it will fill a need. I recruited my first pupil this morning. Myrtille.'

'Myrtle?'

Her own napkin ring rolled off the table and onto the floor. Jack stopped it with his foot and retrieved it, examining it for dents, and handed it to her, as perfect as a halo.

'Thank you.'

60

'Yes. Myrtille. She is a lost sheep who I am determined to bring into the fold – the first of many, I hope. I'm looking to her to set an example and bring other lost souls, women, children, men too, I hope. This is just the beginning. That young woman is no fool, Louisa; she has books on her shelf: Scott, Barrie, Dickens ... but I could not help but remark her disgraceful want of anything but novels. She possesses neither Bible nor prayerbook.'

He relished a mouthful of melt soup, concocted by Madge from mutton and sago, carrot and onion, and expelled a clove delicately into the bowl of his spoon as Louisa wondered how he knew which books Myrtille had on her shelf. She contemplated the fern in the green lustre bowl on a lace cloth that was white against the dark polished wood.

'I am sure it is only her lack of education which has held her back,' Jack continued, 'and the lack of any spiritual guidance. By the time I've finished with that young washerwoman, she'll hold her own with any of the elders of the kirk. Loath as I am to criticise my predecessor, *de mortuis nil nisi bonum*, but Craigie was badly at fault there; more a fisher of salmon and trout than of men, I fear.'

He was pleased with his judgement, until he considered that it might have been applied more to himself than to Craigie. Lilian cleared away the soup plates and brought in the meat and vegetables. Jack was proud of his vegetable garden; with Robert's help it was flourishing. The Craigies' fruit trees were heavy croppers, and big peaches, rosy and golden as sunsets, as pigs' haunches, bloomed under glass in the conservatory at the back of the house. It was a wonderful year for peaches; after all the bottling and pickling, the eating of fruit warm from the tree, the puddings and pies, they had thrown the bruised bits to the pigs. There was an espaliered peach tree too, spread out against the fence, which fruited as never before.

While Jack and Louisa ate, Jessie slept under a tree; Kitty and Sandy were at school, having finished the dinners which their mother had packed herself, playing in the sunshine until the big hand-bell summoned them in to afternoon classes. Louisa and Jack lapsed into silence.

'Wait till I tell you, the minister's starting a Bible class, and guess who's to be the first pupil?' Lilian challenged Madge when she came back to the kitchen from checking the baby.

'No' us, I hope?'

'It's Myrtille, that's who!'

'Och away.'

'I'm telling you. I heard him say.'

'I wouldnae like to be in her shoes, then. Not that she wears any, mind.'

'Will she tell him that Robert goes sneakin' across the grass to her at night, I wonder?'

They heard Robert removing his tacketty boots at the door. Lilian was stacking dishes, Madge running a knife around the fluted edge of the prune mould when he came in.

'Something smells good.'

'Sit down then, Robert, till I give you your meal. Tell me,' she asked innocently as Lil carried the pudding through. 'How's Miss Cruikshank, your fiancée, keeping?'

'Donalda's very well, thank you, Madge.'

Louisa plunged the spoon into the mottled glossy castle and served her husband a quivering rampart, herself a small slice. She was fair sick of the food here; stewed sheep's trotters, stewed sheep's tongues, melt soup, kidney soup, mock-turtle soup made from beef and half a calf's head, gravy soup, mutton, mutton and rabbit. She found herself less and less able to stomach it. Jack thought about Myrtille.

The high-necked blouse which Myrtille wore to Bible class that day was more distracting than her usual *déshabillé*: the fine pleats, the mother-of-pearl buttons marching with the self-righteousness of the Band of Hope; the brown wrist against a starched and buttoned cuff. She had dredged up a pair of shoes which sat demurely side by side like docile pupils. Scents of the sea, soap and woodsmoke mingled in her hair. She was attentive and quick to learn, but as she bent her head over the little red catechism, Jack had an uneasy feeling that she was laughing at him.

Louisa, passing the window, saw her dark head lift and her full lips frame some doctrinal question, and was glad. She wished that Miss Kettle could witness her husband at his pastoral work, gathering in that lost sheep, for she had been stung on several occasions lately by hints that Jack, with his botanical expeditions and hunting trips, was failing in his duty. She had woken that morning to the sun gilding her bed and a breeze fluttering the curtains into organdie bridal veils. The tiredness she had felt since Jessie's birth left her like a ghostly garment dissolving in the radiance of day, vanishing like the shadows of a pair of fantails. She felt strong and, brought to her senses by a sharp slap of happiness, renounced her misery. The tuis were calling in the garden; she surprised her husband with a kiss, the first bestowed not taken. Her children were healthy, Lilian was singing in the kitchen; the morning was as sweet as a comb of heather honey. She saw that it was she who must direct, must take up the threads like skeins of wool, playing them out through her fingers, gathering them in. The grey tenement with its shared bed in the press, the close where she played ball or skipped with her sisters, the communal washing lines on the flat roofs, the canary's empty cage, were set aside, no less dear, but fading beside this house with a verandah, of which she was the mistress.

She leaned over the paddock fence to watch Solomon, unconcerned, cropping grass, the patches on his skin wrinkling as he flicked flies with his mane. She could have flung herself over his back and galloped for miles and miles astride his glossy hide, all of a piece with him through flowering, spiny bush, across mountains and plains to the Clutha river roaring and tumbling through its golden hills, if her day had not been hanging in front of her like a sampler of tiny cross-stitches spelling out her tasks.

PART TWO

London 1989

5

Olive Mackenzie had dismissed the National Gallery, the Royal Academy, the Hayward and the Tate as places of refuge from Sunday afternoon, had dismissed anywhere she might run into anyone she knew, however remote the possibility, and so she had ended up in the Horniman Museum, faced by a tragic lobster in a glass tank, whose plight, surely worse than hers, did nothing to cheer her. Made from astonishing bright blue suede, shading into green and purple on its massive claws, almost filling its prison, it seemed to be signalling desperately with its delicate and sophisticated antennae. 'Why pick on me?' she almost said aloud, and hurried past. Then she stood staring into the mossy stones and clouded glass of an empty tank. 'Crustaceans have no rights,' she thought, shivering in her thin shell, remembering a crab she had seen in a Chinese shop in Gerrard Street, picking its way on its stilettos over the backs of its folded fellows, walking towards the window, skidding on ice.

She thought at first that it was the back of Terry's head that she saw in the café. Her tea had slopped into the saucer as she walked towards the table; but her heart stopped several times a day at the sighting of some false Terry Turner, and this one turned out to be some loony who smiled as she set down her cup with distaste among the dirty crockery.

'Would you like a biscuit?'

An antipodean loony holding out a cracked biscuit in cellophane.

'Of all the pick-ups,' she thought, 'this is the crumbiest.'

She turned up her cigarette lighter until it was like a flame-thrower, almost shrivelling the cellophane, scorching his smile. She smoked very little but a cigarette could be a useful repellent.

Since Terry had left her she had exuded some essence which attracted every loony in south-east London; they homed in on her like insects on garbage, flapping the wings of soiled coats, thrusting trembling proboscises as if to engorge their scaly bodies on her. A ranting Rasta had made her the target of his ravings at the bus stop yesterday; a girl had threatened to shove her teeth down her throat on the stairs; the conductor had implied that her Travelcard was a forgery. At the age of forty-four she was transported by violence back to the time when she was fourteen and it seemed that she could not walk a hundred yards without some man exposing himself to her.

The youth at the table was mildly turning the pages of a book of Russian short stories. The pale green dusk of Yalta; white nights in St Petersburg ... she wished she were young and reading Dostoevsky, holding her book up to the window to catch the last light on the page, or lying in the long grass on the edge of the hockey field, the white sleeves of her blouse rolled to the elbow in the languorous dinner hour of her last term at school, with a green and golden future beyond the book's edge. The young man at the table was wearing a shirt with the dingy whiteness of the launderette, carelessly buttoned fake 501s on his long skinny legs; his ankles were bare above lichened trainers which took up too much floorspace. She should have brought her brother with her for protection, but she knew that he would have refused. He would be sitting at home in his grey cardigan of shame, in a surfeit of newsprint, a rat on a rubbish dump, nosing out gobbets of disgrace, sinking long yellow teeth into the soft exposed flesh of sexual secrets. His teeth had not really grown rodent-like, it was just that they, like the rest of his body, had become discredited. She was sorry for seeing him as a rat. He rose early on Sundays, slinking to a distant paper shop for his weekly fix, now that they could not enter Cosy Corner, Prop. S. & J. Patel, Newsagents. Olive's papers landed with a thud on the end of her bed and she woke to William hovering with a breakfast tray. Last Sunday, her birthday, there had been a nosegay of garden flowers in Mother's Stuart crystal vase, cut like a thistle, between her coffee cup and plate of toast, and suicidal greenfly had adhered to the newsprint, determined to be squashed. The books section had been missing, so she knew at once that it contained a review by Terry. She had retrieved it later from the bin, preferring to destroy it herself. Friends had come for a late lunch, carrying wine and flowers. She had memories of singing, 'It's my party, and I'll cry if I want to . . .', and she had. As William kept the glasses filled, and the empty bottles piled up, people admitted between sips that they couldn't drink the way they used to because it took so much longer to recover, and wondered what damage they had done; a little circle of old friends wreathed in smoke in the garden, released for the weekend from the world of post-feminist power-lunching on Perrier. If anybody was a rat it was Terry, not William who had hung his cardigan on a bush and tried to look happy. William Jack Mackenzie, named for his father and grandfather. Now Olive Schwarz, *née* Mackenzie, named for nobody, left half her tea and rose from the cafeteria table, stumbling over the foot of the young man sitting there, hoping she had hurt him.

'Sorry,' he said. 'My feet are much too big.'

Olive bit back a line from a Fats Waller song and returned to the museum. In fact it was not the feet which were too big, but the trainers, which looked as if they had been purloined from someone's dustbin.

A Chinese water dragon, sprawling along a branch, trailed a green beaded leg, wrinkled at the knee. Little children were bumping against her legs, pushing to see the axolotls and the slumbering geckos.

'Dreaming of Mexico.' The mad Colonial again. Olive moved away angrily.

The place was cluttered with complacent families. A father squatted to explain something to a child.

'You ethnographical imbecile!' Olive wanted to scream. 'What is the point of pontificating about dinosaurs? This is what we come to, look! This is all we are.' A troupe of skeletons grinned from a glass case. She thought of the water dragon; green stockings wrinkling and laddering, moccasins losing their beads. Among the painted deities, the masks, beads, shells and feathers, the ancient brilliant parakeets, she came upon a human skull, halved horizontally to make a begging bowl. It was shaped like half a walnut shell, or tortoise's carapace, its interior polished to ivory, indented with feathery traces of the brain. Whose head was it? Who had halved and buffed it to a shine? What coinage had clinked into this bony gourd?

The New Zealander, ambulant among the exhibits, kept Olive in the corner of his eye. South-east London Sunday afternoons in cemeteries and small museums: how he loved them. He had been happy in bitter parks anticipating spring, and now that he had a home, these excursions had become a luxury. Transported by the book he was reading, he believed himself to be Russian, a student in a Moscow museum. The warm thin smell of tea had lured him into the cafeteria, where he had loped up to the samovar and exchanged his last kopecks for a thick white china cup and a packet of biscuits which had Nice printed on them, and they were. The yellow fruit cake embedded with bright red cherries looked good too. He dunked a biscuit in his tea, remembering a sheet of polythene which he had seen on his way there, dancing on the grass outside a block of flats, glittering and crackling in the sun as it took the wind and billowed and folded itself into shining geometrical shapes, as if it were delivering an invisible giant bouquet to somebody on one of the balconies. He opened his book, a library book borrowed without a ticket, which he intended to return and was trying to find his place when the woman sat down at his table. She might have been Russian, with her black bobbed hair and dark mournful eyes and heavy red lips. He almost wished her 'Dos vedanya' but offered her a biscuit. In reply, she had almost burned his hand off with her lighter, and placed a cigarette in her unhappy mouth. Then he had been sure that there was a Great Russian Soul beating under that faded tomato-coloured sweatshirt. She wore Mexican silver earrings, and a ring with a black stone. He tried once more in the aquarium, but she strode away. When she headed for the exit, he followed, but he wanted to visit the little menagerie in the park where he was on terms with the wallabies, so he let her disappear.

'South-east London really is the pits,' Olive thought, wrenching the steering wheel. 'I don't think I can stand living here much longer.' She drove past buildings faded like old music-hall queens, raddled, with dust in the folds of their skirts and broken fans, past people hitting their children while waiting for buses that would never come. Rain hit the windscreen, and at once it, and the road, were full of what they used to call dancing dollies; silver spirals pirouetting on glass and tarmac. Through the arc of the wipers she saw the New Zealander, half under a tree. There was a rumble of thunder, and a spark of lightning. She aquaplaned to a stop and looked back. He seemed to be smiling, his dripping face turned upwards to the leaves, as if he would uncoil a long tongue like a giraffe's and eat them. She reached over and opened the passenger door: 'I must be mad,' she thought . . . '"the naked torso of a woman found in a dustbin in Forest Hill, south-east London, has been named as that of forty-four-year-old Olive Schwarz. The dark-haired divorcee was identified by her brother William Mackenzie, forty-six, of the same address. This is the second time that tragedy has struck Mr Mackenzie in less than a year. Last May while leading a school party . . . " If that idiot stands under that tree for much longer he'll be smiling on the other side of his face . . . frazzled to a crisp by lightning, as he deserves.'

She stuck her head into the storm and yelled. He whirled like a corkscrew on one leg and then galloped towards the car, a huge flightless bird, an emu or rhea or moa that had burst its glass cage, a kiwi. Then he was in the passenger seat, dripping.

'Where to?'

'Where are you going?'

'That's not the point. Tell me where you want to go, and I'll drop you off. I hope you realise that I don't make a habit of offering lifts to young men . . .'

" . . . Police combing the area with tracker dogs for missing items of clothing and jewellery unearthed a silver and onyx ring. 'That was Olive's lucky ring,' her brother William Mackenzie wept as he identified it . . ."

'Well, where do you want to go, or don't you want a lift?'

'Crystal Palace,' he said, just as she was about to undo her safety belt, to flee, abandoning the car with him in it.

'Is that where you live?'

'No, but I've always wanted to go there. I live in Waverley Road. Do you know it?'

'I do,' she said grimly. 'I'll take you to Crystal Palace.'

After she had dropped him off, she reflected that offering a lift to a young man had landed her in her present desolate state. Terry Turner AKA Turncoat. Opportunist, liar and deceiver. Anomalous product of a mobile home immobilised, its axle embedded in concrete.

'It was very claustrophobic, a confined space. It was horrible. I remember as a boy I had to lie there in my bunk night after night and watch my parents making . . .'

'Oh, Terry . . .' Olive had seized his hand and kissed it.

'Ovaltine.'

The storm that had sluiced Forest Hill had been local. William, contrary to his sister's expectation, was not at home, but in Ruskin Park some miles away, where the virtuous were mowing and manicuring the world's surface, good husbandmen, while he sat, vaguely hearing their humming and clipping, on this bench under the dripping pink candles of a chestnut tree, attracting arboreal detritus like a municipal statue, a stone man oblivious to a quick squirt of white on his brow. He picked a petal from his knee, rolling it into an oily ball between finger and thumb. Petal. Patel. Late P. Two Japanese boys were playing frisbee. A little girl on a bicycle, head down, glasses, pink track-suit, sped past him on the path, riding out some fantasy. Behind him, under a hawthorn flicked with tiny buds, a stream made a put at being elemental in spite of the wreath of toilet paper on the bush. The Japanese boys moved obliquely away, the disc spinning between them. Where was the little girl? What were her parents thinking of, letting her out in a park alone? Didn't they read the Sunday papers?

Two men were serving life sentences for the murder of Pragna Patel. One was the Panamanian who had pushed her onto the line in the Metro. The other was William Mackenzie, the headmaster who had taken a party of fifteen-year-olds on a trip to Paris. Pragna's parents had not wanted her to go.

'You ask them, Sir. *Please*! They'll listen to you.'

They had listened to Sir, standing side by side behind the counter in the newsagent's. A little brother was cutting out paper dolls, busily pretending not to show off. A guard in a gingham overall was posted on the door, admitting blazered schoolchildren two by two. The afternoon must be the worst time for the Patels, William was thinking now, when the pupils of Pragna's school came in to buy and steal sweets and crisps and drinks at the time that she used to come home.

74

William had learned that when people say 'You mustn't blame yourself', they think you are to blame in some way. He did blame himself, even though the inquest had cleared him of any negligence. He blamed himself almost every moment of the day and night, waking screaming in a sodden, strangling tangle of sheets. The horror of the child's going. The nightmare of the police, the telephone calls to London, the journey home. Some of the other children on the trip were still receiving counselling as far as he knew, their lives marked for ever.

Technically, he was not to blame. He had been standing further away from Pragna than were his two colleagues, explaining a map to one of the boys. The group had been well-behaved and adequately supervised. Along the platform came Ramon Gonzales, sometime pimp and pickpocket, every trembling finger scarred by the razor blades which the gangs used in training their apprentices to dip into handbags and pockets with the utmost delicacy. There was a babel of voices in his head and he was sick to his stomach. He saw the crowd of kids gabbling about him in a foreign language, jeering at him, mocking, pointing at his stained trousers and split shoes, the voices growing louder and shriller and more threatening, the ribald laughter bursting his eardrums, until beyond endurance, he grabbed one of them and threw her.

None of the English party had noticed him, until it was too late, and horror went into slow motion. Of William's two fellow teachers, one had left the profession entirely, and the other had left London and was teaching in Bradford. After all the legal business, the devastating memorial service in the school hall conducted by the children, William had seen neither of them again. The school had planted a tree in Pragna's memory. Within a week it had been vandalised, the broken sapling making a metaphor which even the dullest English student could take.

'Sir?'

'Snyder!'

His former Head Boy stood there in front of the bench, his hands on a baby buggy, a woman at his side.

'Liam, I should say ... excuse me, a touch of hay fever ...' He wiped his eyes. He did not remember Snyder's mother from any parents' evenings or social occasions.

'Allow me to introduce my wife. Rosetta, this is Mr Mackenzie, my old headmaster.'

'Pleased to meet you.' Mrs Snyder glared at him.

'My daughter, Chantal.'

William rose and held out his hand to Rosetta Snyder, who took it briefly in hers, heavy with rings. A tangle of auburn hair fell onto the shoulders of her tight white linen-look suit jacket which, like her short skirt, was concertinad with creases everywhere it touched. Her skin had a coppery tone; a gold cross swung in her deep cleavage. She might have been any age between twenty-eight and forty. Snyder would have been nineteen.

'I must congratulate you, Liam. And this is Chantal? She's beautiful.'

At this Rosetta smiled, revealing a wide gap between strong white teeth. As she bent over the child, black underwear was outlined against her white skirt.

'What are you doing with yourself these days?' asked Snyder.

'Oh, this and that ... you know ...'

'Life goes on,' said Snyder. 'I'm in the property business

myself. Estate agent. Give us a bell if you're thinking of placing your property on the market, I'll see you right.'

'Thank you, Liam. I will.'

He watched them walk away, the wheels of the buggy rolling, Rosetta rolling in her white stilettos, Snyder slim as a knife in his chinos and what William assumed were a designer polo shirt and trainers: a family.

He honked into his handkerchief. Snyder had known that he was crying and had been kind to him.

He put Snyder's flashy card in his wallet. Snyder, paterfamilias.

The two Japanese boys were coming along the path towards him. One of them was wearing shorts and a white T-shirt and carrying a tennis racquet. They passed William, laughing, and he saw that the legs of the boy who held the racquet were the tiniest, most endearingly bit bowed under the exiguous shorts, gilded by the afternoon sun to the golden curves of a pair of compasses; the limbs of a very young Buddhist deity. William was propelled off his bench by the interpretation that might be placed on his thoughts. Was it not possible, he argued, to delight in something simply because it was youthful and beautiful and ephemeral? His teaching years whirled in a kaleidoscope of arms and legs in vests and shorts and coloured team bands. Had there never been a desire for forbidden secret softness? Never, he exonerated himself: pedagogue, not paedophile, never pederast. He stood on the path, shaking the images from him, brushing a petal from respectable trousers. Yet, he had at once picked one boy as his favourite, censored the other's hair, which needed cutting, as sternly as any horticultural judge, as too raggedy a blue-black chrysanthemum weighing down too slight a stalk. He had too much time on his hands, too much time to search a bankrupt soul, and dredge up dross.

Although the Case of the Norwood Builder was not one of Sherlock Holmes' more spectacular adventures, William liked to think that it conferred a certain sinister distinction on his part of London. Less leafy, more urban now than then, and than when Camille Pissarro painted Norwood, Dulwich and Crystal Palace, the suburb is still full of blossom in the spring. Buses lumber in heavy traffic up the hill where carriage lamps once glittered in black rain and snow blurred the pale green streetlamps. Pissarro's brother lived on the site of West Norwood Woolworths, on the opposite side of the road from the cemetery where the dead stare disconcertingly from coloured photographs or lie in the splendour of decay in great flaunting mausoleums which prove the mortality of marble and mortar and the supremacy of grass, briar and bush. Beyond Knight's Hill are secretive parks and half-hidden walks through what were once the gardens and woods of large houses; somewhere, lost, is Beulah Spa, a fashionable watering-place whose brilliance gushed briefly, and trickled away.

Not far from the peninsula where St Luke's church stands, in a quiet road of double-fronted houses, number ten is distinguished by the peacock tiles of the curved path which leads through the unkempt garden to the front door. Bright blue and green stylised feathers give it a Moorish aspect as it sparkles in the sun and glows richly after rain. They had decided William to buy the house twenty years earlier. The price he had paid as a young teacher with a small inheritance from his father had seemed horrendous then, the house a folly and a financial millstone, but he had fallen in love with it. Had he baulked at the provenance of his father's money? He had not. Now the house was worth at least twenty times what it had cost him, and with the mortgage paid off, William might have been a contented man, had not his life ended almost a year ago.

Unmarried, childless, his career terminated in public odium, he had lived alone until his sister Olive had moved in, not without qualms. Was there not a whiff of failure about a brother and sister living together? Distant filmic echoes of a boy being bribed to escort his ugly duckling sister to the Senior Prom? In fact, they were a tall and striking pair, Olive dark and vivid and William with thick straight grey hair, dark eyebrows and a melancholy look. Lately he had infuriated Olive by affecting the demeanour of an old man; she had kidnapped and murdered a shuffling pair of checked slippers but had been unable to get her hands on the grey cardigan which gave his shoulders a premature stoop.

When William had bought the house it was without the slightest doubt that it would be filled one day with the sound of running feet and children's laughter, that a blue aluminium climbing frame would rise from the yellow leaves on the lawn, where the previous owner had hung an old tyre from the tree as a swing. 'It's a family house,' the estate agent had repeated. 'It needs a family.' William had agreed. There had been parties there with cousins' children and the children of colleagues, but eventually the rope rotted and the tyre fell and disappeared under grass and weeds.

Occasional sardonic barks of laughter from Olive, usually at his expense or that of Charlene her assistant, or some customer in her shop, disturbed the gloom of the house as the spiders, moths and woodlice, with whom he had led a peaceful co-existence, scurried for their lives at her approach. Olive had found a nest of earwigs in the damp wood of the cutlery drawer in the sink unit. William had expressed amazement but in truth he had known they were there and had not cared. Brochures began to arrive from people called Poggenpohl, Schreiber, and Smallbone of Devizes, and the house was cleared of its indigenous population. One insomniac night William had watched a procession of ants heading for the back door with suitcases; then he had realised that they were carrying grains of spilled sugar. All that remained, except for casual intruders, were the specimens that their grandfather, the Reverend Jack Mackenzie, had brought back from New Zealand and which lay in glass-fronted drawers in small brass-bound chests and which nobody dared touch in case they crumbled. King of the exhibits, mounted on a brass plate, was a tuatara lizard, ancient and powerful with the socket of a third, vestigial, eye set in its faded, silver-blue head.

6

Some hours after Olive had dropped him off in Crystal Palace Parade, the boy from New Zealand left the park to a few drenched sports fanatics and the life-size models of prehistoric beasts which lurked in the grass and lakes and foliage, and set off for home. It had been a good day. His name was Jay Pascal and he was nineteen years old, dark-eyed, with loose black, blue-tipped curls recently barbered by a friend's Swiss Army knife. Jay felt he was getting the hang of London now, as he made his circuitous way to Waverley Road, in no hurry.

Jay had crossed the Pacific innocently optimistic that he would find the house. The vastness, noise and dirt of London had appalled him. After several weeks of wandering, lacking an *A to Z*, lacking everything but the clothes he stood up in and a plastic carrier bag containing a book and his blunt and grubby shaving and washing kit since his passport and money had been stolen, he had surmised that he was getting close. He knew the name of the road he was looking for but the directions given by such passers-by as deigned to stop vanished even as he expressed his polite thanks and he realised that he had been watching a bird or speculating on the meaning of a slogan on a T-shirt and not listening at all. One night as he searched the grey serpentine streets with ghostly gardens he heard birds singing in the trees. 'Nightingales', he thought and stood enchanted, looking up into the pollarded clumps of leafy twigs which concealed diurnal birds charmed from sleep by the streetlamps. He stretched out behind a hedge in someone's garden and slept until the whine and glassy rattle of an early milk-float woke him.

He came to a café where men were already eating breakfast, smoking, reading newspapers before beginning or ending their working day. He was sick with a hunger that pounded in his head behind his gritty eyes. He went in and walked up to the counter, intending to offer to wash dishes in return for breakfast. Before he could speak, in the silence that had fallen, the proprietor, perceiving him to be a loony, slammed down a yesterday's sandwich in front of him and told him to bugger off out of there. Jay ate the sandwich gratefully in the street but he had been shamed in front of the men in the café. It had been companionable inside, in the smell of tea and cigarettes and frying food. He took note of the name: Double Egg Café. He would come back one day, clean and shaven with money in his pocket, and order a double-egg breakfast with all the trimmings. The works. Had he been permitted to join them, he could have asked the men if they had heard the nightingales, if it had been a magical phenomenon or if nightingales were common in these parts.

As he walked on, he attempted to restore his self-esteem by imagining the scene which should have taken place in the kitchen: 'Well mate, I can see you've had experience in the catering trade, them plates haven't sparkled like that since the day they left the factory, and you're a dab hand with the old tea towel too. Don't suppose I could interest you in a permanent position by any chance? There's a nice little room at the back, decent wage, all the scoff you can eat – come on, lad, whaddya say?' If he had a friend, a mate, someone to talk things over with, share; sometimes his tongue felt like the clapper of an old bell, rusting in his mouth, so that if he opened it nothing would come out but a few rusty flakes. He could see why so many people talked to themselves in the street.

Waverley Road. Jay's heart leaped at the name. He turned into the road, suppressing the thought that when he arrived he wouldn't have the faintest idea what to do or say. All his unfocused hopes lay in that house. When he found it, he had to grab the gatepost, dizzy with shock. *Dunedin* was derelict.

The name was just discernible on the gate. *Dunedin.* Jay traced the letters embossed in blackened brass, with their echoes of Dunroamin and lost Edens. Broken glass glittered on the verandah that hung like a torn hem from the brickwork; wooden boards blinded the basement and ground-floor windows but those upstairs reflected jagged shards of spring sky, and one was barred with bent iron rods. An attic window wore a draggled half-petticoat of lace. A white lilac spread across the dark-green, nailed-up front door; a buddleia sapling waved from one of the chimneys. The hinge had fallen off the gate but a rusty padlock and ropes of long grass and bindweed held the gate fast. There was a side gate, marked 'Tradesmen's Entrance, No Hawkers, No Circulars', but Jay was not going to enter that way. He put one hand on a rotted post and vaulted over the front gate, landing in the garden of *Dunedin*.

He looked back. On the opposite side of the road, across the traffic, a woman in a yellow sari, pursued by an army of purple irises, did not pause from ladling water with a saucepan from a red plastic bucket over the seedlings she had been planting out when he noticed her a few minutes ago. This was not a street to foster neighbourly vigilance. Some front doors stood open on passages that led to rented rooms and stairs with the allure of broken combs, or teeth in a decaying mouth; a few front gardens had flowering rockeries and beds, others bloomed with dead cars in drifts of blossom, and the wreckage of furniture and television sets and fridges. There were bluebells everywhere.

It was easy to enter by a basement window. He landed on glass, in a cellar, in darkness and mould, and groped his way past metallic and wooden obstacles to the square of diffuse light at the far end of the room. He came to the foot of a narrow flight of stairs. The smell of mildew and ammonia grew stronger as he edged his way up the broken treads. In the kitchen he looked through a chink in the boarded window onto the back garden, at the skeleton of a greenhouse floating on a lake of broken glass, resting his hand on a cast-iron stove, and withdrawing it in alarm. The stove was warm. It could have been the sun, he told himself, but everything else in that dank interior was cold. He stood, hearing a blackbird's singing, staring into the scullery, and beyond it, into a room without a door, at a naked lavatory bowl gushing a fountain of dry cement.

Jay forced himself to go on, past rooms strewn with mattresses and heaps of rags and black plastic sacks, past ribs of lath poking through the plaster, through bad smells and freckles of light and pools of sunshine like melted butter dripping through the hardboard at the windows; he saw dim coloured pastilles

84

of light falling from the glass in the front door as he climbed the main staircase, under a ceiling swagged with cobwebs. A human snore came from somewhere below him.

He stood on the threshold of an attic room, the one with the lace at the window, a servants' room with a dado of faded fruit. An iron bedstead was propped against one wall, and a mottled mirror, a servants' looking-glass, against another. The floorboards were surprisingly sound, although the ceiling sagged and a stain on the floor indicated a leaking roof. What might have been a dead bird lay on a heap of soot and brickdust in the grate of the green-tiled fireplace. A picture lay face downward on the narrow mantelpiece. Nobody had thought it worth scavenging. He turned it over; it was a photograph, cheaply framed, the glass intact, speckled with age and mildew. Two young women in long dark dresses and white caps and aprons sat on the railing of a wooden verandah: they were not looking into the camera, they were smiling at one another. Across the bottom left-hand corner was written in spindly copperplate: 'Madge and Lil. *Dunedin* 1910.' Jay sat on the floor, studying their faces.

'What the hell do you think you're doing?'

He jumped up, clutching the picture.

In a whirl of furious bluish hair and whipping garments, a woman launched herself across the room at him, knocking the photograph from his hands and pinning him to the wall with a knee.

'This is a private house. You've no right to come sneaking in here.'

'You're hurting me.'

'You're not from the council, are you?' At the sudden

85

suspicion her knee ground bonily, agonisingly, in his stomach. Tears came to his eyes. He thrust her away from him.

'I'm not from the council, I swear. I've come to live here.'

Her eyes rolled like cloudy blue marbles veined with red filaments.

'You can't stop me. I've got as much right as you to be here.'

She laughed a harsh gust of combustible breath into his face, revealing brown striated teeth and shockingly pale gums.

Jay glanced at the picture on the floor. 'You – you're not a ghost, are you?'

No, the memory of her solid knee ached.

'I've come all the way from New Zealand ...' Jay's voice broke; it made him sound so lonely.

'For this? And I thought I was the one who was supposed to be mad ... what's up, feeling a bit homesick, are we?'

Homesick. An empty beach. A narrow bed in a row of narrow beds, far-off children's voices. The woman waited in a long shimmering cone of sunlight, sparkling like the blue fairy in *Pinocchio* through his tears.

'Och, I suppose you can stay. There's room for another – plenty of room ...'

'Who else lives here?'

Jay looked round the attic room, intending to make it his own.

'Just people. *Dunedin* is where the ruined people live.'

'I could bring up one of those old mattresses from downstairs.'

He saw that the bedstead leaning against the wall had no body, just a head and tail. He could prop his mattress between them, making it a real bed. Put up a few pictures; Madge and Lil would do for a start, to make it homey.

'They're taken,' the woman was saying. 'You'll have to get your own from a skip. I'm Kirsty.'

'Jay.'

They shook hands.

'Do you know the film *Pinocchio*?' he asked.

Kirsty's attention had wandered. She was addressing a wood-louse which had rolled into a ball in her hand.

'What are you doing inside on a beautiful day like this, you silly wee slater? You should be out in the sunshine.'

Jay followed her downstairs, through the house and into the garden.

'I'm sorry I pushed you,' he said. 'I hope I didn't hurt you. You took me by surprise.'

'You? Hurt me? Huh!'

Then he felt foolish as she stared him up and down, as if a right hook to the jaw, which was missing a tooth or two, or an eye like a stormy sunset was the currency in which she was used to deal, clenching her fists as if his white smile inspired murderous impulses.

'I don't suppose I could have a drink of water, could I?'

'There's a tap over there.'

'Beauty.'

She watched him gulping the rusty water from his hands, in his shirt laced with cobwebs, his hair powdered by plaster and brickdust. He picked up a mossy tennis ball, half severed by time and weather; two earwigs fell out and an empty, yellow-banded snail shell. He was fiddling with the jagged edges of the green tennis ball, trying to fit the hemispheres together.

Kirsty laughed suddenly, jerking her arm upwards.

'Nothing but blue skies from now on.'

87

She strode towards the house, leaving him alone in the garden, throwing and catching the ball which had lost all its bounce.

By the time he had encountered Olive, his room had been fixed up nicely. He had a bed, and Madge and Lil and a pretty piece of wrapping paper he had found were on the wall; his book and a jamjar of flowers stood on the mantelpiece. He had cleaned out the fireplace; the lump lying there had proved to be a bird when he had gently blown the soot from it, a swift lying with folded wings, peaceful as a dead nun. Jay had buried it beside a hidden Solomon's seal, under the arching stem hung with holy white, green-tinged bells. The thing which made his room really his was the key he had found in the rubbish in the grate; he could lock his door, and was safe, unless a drunken shoulder should come splintering through.

The once-handsome manse belonging to St Andrew's church, since a warehouse for second-hand office furniture, had become a skipper where vagrants dossed down. Once the scene of decorous and dutiful tea parties, it had opened its doors, figuratively speaking, to the itinerant homeless of south-east London. Undeterred by the 'No Hawkers' sign on the gate, they effected entry, as Jay had, through the cellars while the house awaited demolition. Pigeons flew in and out of broken upstairs windows and a family of foxes lived in the garden. Best of all in Kirsty, who could be very unpredictable, Jay had found a sort of friend.

Another resident, Denny, spent his days on the steps of Brixton tube station with a scrawny Lurcher named Gnasher, and a can of beer in his hand; in the evenings he could be found, alongside the woman who played the comb-and-paper and sold drawings in felt-tipped pen stuck with glitter and sweet wrappers framed in gold and silver sticky tape, trying to flog tins of dog food to late travellers. The dog food was the gift of a regular who loathed Denny but worried about the dog condemned to live on the dirty and crowded steps. She had offered to take Gnasher, who was either mild by nature or suffering from chronic depression, for a run in Brockwell Park but Denny had refused to part with him. He was, after all, his meal ticket and kept him in booze. Often Denny and Gnasher dined together in the littered kitchen of *Dunedin* on Pedigree Chum, food of Supreme Champions at Crufts, with Gnasher keeping a wary ear cocked for rats and foxes. Jay had sat with Denny on the steps of the tube among the hustlers who begged for change, humble, aggressive or mad, while the old black man with scarlet knots in his hair had called out 'Flowers for your lady love, flowers for your lady love,' offering leftovers from the daytime stall to late travellers. Jay thought of the women he had met in London; there was the girl who had let him share her sleeping bag one wet night; Kirsty; and that Russian-looking woman in the Horniman who had given him a lift. He would have liked to present the Russian with a bouquet better than a bunch of shrivelled tulips.

Jay avoided the other residents and visitors to *Dunedin* as much as he could; he was afraid of them, with their burning brazier and bottles and fights. When he could, he brought a bottle of cider home to negotiate a safe passage, but punches had been thrown at him and an empty bottle, and once an iron bar had flown through the air as he ran up the sagging staircase.

Now that the vast old asylums with their high walls and

intricacies of railings and bars, fire escapes, glassed-in walkways in the sky and labyrinthine corridors were being demolished, smashed to red-brick rubble in their parkland and gardens, their residents were discharged into what they had been taught to call the community. Some people were placed as families in supervised units where their neighbours were not as welcoming as they had been led to believe; others scuttled away like insects under a lifted stone, singly or to form colonies in church porches, doorways, squares and parks, on waste ground and under the arches of flyovers.

Those who were not transplanted enlisted in the scattered, disaffected army of the deranged which terrified, disgusted and molested citizens in the street, on buses and in the underground. The hearts of the populace hardened against them; there were still some who would give money to a mendicant with a dog, to an importunate mother with children barring their way in the tube, or to a lad in a sleeping bag in the Strand, but as the number of beggars grew daily and the country slid into recession, they grew fewer. The dispossessed lurked around cash machines and lay in wait, they leered through restaurant windows, they forced bona fide drinkers outside pubs off the pavements with their blue breath and curses; they had lost eyes and teeth in fights and limbs from gangrene, wild stinking matted verminous creatures displaying human potential which inspired hatred and fear. There were those who had decided that something must be done about them. Private enterprise was engaged to trawl the streets in the dead hours before dawn, after the soup-runs mobilised by volunteers who still cared, and before the refuse carts lumbered into motion. Rumours of disappearances circulated in crypts and on park benches and in derelict houses but nobody walked into a police station to register a vagrant as a missing person.

Sometimes Denny brought people home. Jay, in his attic, heard their voices, laughing, cursing, arguing far below him, the sounds of a guitar and singing. With his door locked, he slept snug as a bug in the rug he had unrolled on his floor, one of the trophies he had discovered in the wonderful world of skips.

7

Wednesday was Olive's free day. She would leave her little shop in the hands of Charlene her assistant, rise late, and lunch with one of her friends. As most of the local shops were closed on Wednesday afternoons there were few customers and Charlene, she knew, welcomed the opportunity to entertain her own, unemployed friends. Stock-taking would reveal missing items of jewellery. The once elegant door of the shop had become a patchwork of leaflets advertising Dance Workshops, Black Women's Writing Circles, Iridology, Aromatherapy, Self-Defence and Self-Awareness classes, Palmistry, Goat's Milk Cheese, Reflexology and an occasional maverick card offering Relaxing Massage. The shop was called 'Ideas' and often a customer would approach the small semicircular dais where Olive was enthroned behind a curved glass case and enquire, 'Have you any ideas?' or 'Got any good ideas?' Boiling oil, Olive would think, on a bad day, or suicide, or I've an idea that I might change the name of the shop, jingling the flight of wind-chime parrots as she gestured towards the abalone shell and turquoise set in Mexican silver, the fake art-deco and silver art-nouveau fairies and dragon-flies, the Japanese dolls and lumps of quartz and crystal, as she laughed and chatted on the telephone. Then customers felt as if they were at a cocktail party to which they had not been invited. The more timorous purchased a postcard or a tube of tuberose or jasmine joss sticks before they hurried out. Charlene would sigh, and bring her a cup of soothing, if unfortunately diuretic, camomile tea.

This particular Wednesday Ashley, the friend with whom Olive had planned to have lunch, had rung to say that she had a long meeting and could not make it. Olive suspected at once that her friend could not face another confrontation with her broken heart across a restaurant table. William suggested that she join him in the mad Italian café in Streatham to whose tepid pasta he had become addicted, but she declined.

Covent Garden was full of pregnant women, dehiscent fruits in dungarees and billowing dresses, bellying her off the pavement. She had a beer, which brought sad thoughts, and bought a dress in Monsoon. As she wrote the cheque she realised that the dress would look far better on Charlene. Olive Schwarz, a bitter fruit with a hard stone at its heart. If she had stayed married to Schwarz she might have had a daughter to go shopping with, like that woman she had just seen screaming at an elephantine girl in the doorway of Laura Ashley, both of them in tears. In her imagination, she held the bright dress against Charlene, tropical on her dark skin.

Danny and Olive Schwarz, married in Hastings, repented at Leicester. They had met in a shop which specialised in art deco, one Saturday afternoon. Danny had been teaching at Sussex University then, and not long after their wedding had been offered a job in the north. Three years as a faculty wife had persuaded Olive that she was losing her own faculties, although they had lived in a charming house, to which she returned often in her dreams. His affair with one of his students had been her trigger, or excuse, for leaving him, scrupulously taking only the things which belonged to her. Most of Danny's possessions had been placed in a hired skip which had been collected and driven away by the time he had returned from the conference in Tel Aviv which had given Olive her chance. She had thought afterwards that it had been generous on her part to go to such trouble to appear the jealous and heartbroken wife, when in reality she cared not a fig about his infidelity. She had left him the bill for the skip.

As she sat on a seat in Covent Garden thinking about this, and how odd it was that she had once been married to a man who she thought of rarely, and regretting a silver art-deco lamp in the form of a kneeling nymph clasping the moon like a luminous netball someone had thrown her, she became aware of a figure facing her.

A deranged woman with bluish hair was demanding scissors to cut the thread cruelly embedded in a pigeon's foot. Bemused, Olive produced a pair from the little emergency sewing kit she kept in her bag. The operation was completed as satisfactorily as was possible without further injury. While Olive fluttered squeamishly to one side, the woman pocketed the tiny silver antique scissors and said, 'He'll be all right now. That'll cost you a pound.'

'I beg your pardon?'

'It's a pound for one foot. Two pounds for two.'

'How much is it a metre?' asked Olive, but the joke was lost.

Realising that she was becoming street theatre, as in a dream she found herself opening her purse and paying up.

'What about the scissors?' she called after the woman.

'There's no charge for the scissors.'

Olive took refuge in the Transport Museum where she consoled herself by buying a dark-green poster showing a lighted excursion bus travelling home from Reigate to Stockwell in the blue dusk, past a full moon shadowed by a black cypress tree – 'The Homeward Way In The Cool Of Day'. She and Danny had driven to Reigate one day, and called in at the library to ask about local places of interest. The library manager had looked baffled, and then directed them to a small natural history museum. It was open only one weekend in the year, they found, but it was set in a pretty garden, as they saw through the locked gate. They had driven on to Brockham for lunch, and walked along the banks of the river Mole until they had come to a secluded wood full of bluebells and wild garlic. They had returned home in the cool of day, pungent with crushed garlic, with a big illicit bunch of bluebells strewn on the back seat.

She remembered the young New Zealander in the Horniman Museum, and at once she knew that he was living in *Dunedin*. She was surprised that she had not realised it as soon as he had mentioned Waverley Road. She knew that the house had been taken over by squatters, but she could not bear to think about it. It was not her responsibility, but oh, if she could have got her hands on *Dunedin* before it was too late. Herself and William, the last rotting fruit on their branch of the family tree.

How she despised them both. Eyebrows were raised imperceptibly when she said that she lived with her brother; it was thought at once that there must be something unnatural in their relationship. Nowadays it was just not done. When the lease had run out on her flat she had moved in, paying him a reasonable rent which he found very useful. 'It's expedient,' she would feel forced to explain, 'just until I find another flat. William rattling around like a pea in a pod in that great house ... it seems the sensible thing to do ...'

There were those among her friends who suspected her of altruism, who thought that William would have killed himself if she had not moved in to prevent him. People had noticed that she made no pretence any longer of looking for a flat. The interior of the house was taking on the sepia tones of an old photograph, as if the pair of them had been consigned to the past. The improvements Olive had promised seemed to have been shelved.

She had been walking aimlessly for some time and now found herself in Soho. She bought some cheese and, tempted to eat it on the spot, went into Valerie's for a glass of lemon tea and a cake. It was full of strangers; she sat jammed between two of them, wishing that her tea was not so hot. A fat Italian baby reached over and grabbed her beads. She almost gave them to him, but the fist was uncurled and removed by an apologetic mother. Olive sucked bitter lemon juice through her teeth.

She mistimed her homeward journey and was faced with the choice of lingering, perhaps meeting someone for a drink, or travelling in the rush hour. She decided to brave the crowds. Early tourists contributed to the crush; tiredness and heat turned intolerance to hatred on sweating faces, and Olive remembered that old advertisement for Amplex that used to unnerve travellers in the tube. It was not until Vauxhall that she managed to get a seat. And then she saw him.

Her body contracted in a dragging pain. Her insides turned to water. Her mouth hung open, her breath coming in harsh gusts as she drank in greedily the sight of him. She had never felt such desire before, for any human being, animal or object, jewel or work of art. She was shocked by her own passion. His face was wise, although his fretful movements in his mother's arms were those of a child of six months or so. He would never be older than he was today; he seemed in touch with the infinite, his eyes heavy with the secrets of the universe; he could only grow younger as he progressed into baby speech and his stumbling first steps. His little back arched stiffly in a white knitted suit banded with lemon across the chest and at the cuffs and ankles, terminating in grubby feet that trod restlessly his mother's knee. She was struggling to control a folded pushchair that kept rolling away and a shopping bag, but Olive was not interested in her or her difficulties; she was admiring a tiny gold ring in the lobe of the baby's ear, a small black apricot, neat and flat like her own.

'Aren't your ears set close to your head?' the hairdresser had said last week, pushing one, flushed pink from her ministrations, gently forward with the tip of her comb.

Olive had burst into tears.

'That's the nicest thing anybody has said to me for ages,' she explained. It was also the first time anybody had touched her for some time.

'Have you tried oil of evening primrose?' the girl had asked. 'My mum finds it very helpful.'

Until now, she had disapproved of jewellery on children, but she had to admit that it looked perfect on him, as on an Egyptian cat.

As they approached Stockwell, the mother made no move to rise. That meant they were going to the end of the line.

At Brixton, the mother stood, balancing the baby on her hip, wrestling with the pushchair and her shopping.

'I'll hold him while you sort yourself out,' said Olive.

He was in her arms. The doors opened. She was out on the platform. She heard a scream behind her as she was swallowed in the surge of people shoving towards the escalator. The heat and bad temper of the time of day were in her favour. Nobody reacted to the mother's scream; everybody was too concerned with fighting up the escalator and getting to the bus stops. The baby, who had been shocked into silence, opened his mouth to yell as they reached the street, but his voice was drowned by the traffic and a preacher shouting at people to repent, and the vendors of Hard Left tracts.

Olive, who had often cursed it, now blessed the fact that nobody bothered to queue for buses any more. She saw one coming and shoved through the crowd, thrusting herself and the baby onto the platform and up the stairs. She sat down beside a youth with a personal stereo. He had his eyes shut, and would not be able to identify her. The bus was one of the few which had a conductor, but he took her fare impassively without giving her a second glance. 'Tsk tsk tsk' went the hissing headphones; the bus stuttered through heavy traffic and slow lights, and the baby, heavy on her lap and too wise, or too bewildered, to cry, was quietly sick on her skirt.

A woman across the aisle gave Olive a sympathetic smile. 'Kids, who'd 'ave 'em?'

Olive grimaced as she mopped with a tissue, but she didn't really mind. Well, you don't when they're your own, do you?

'Nearly home,' Olive soothed as they approached the front gate. As far as she knew the only neighbour to have marked their passing was an African Grey parrot suspended by one foot from an inner window frame.

'See the birdie? Pretty Polly.'

How nice the house looked from the outside, she thought, as they walked up the peacock-blue tiles between roses coming into bloom.

William was sitting at the kitchen table when she came in, in her creased and stained skirt, with a baby straddling her hip. He looked round to see if there was someone behind her, and saw that she was alone with the baby.

'What a day!' exclaimed Olive, sinking down on a chair and kicking off her shoes. 'I popped into the shop and there was Charlene in a terrible state. Her cousin's husband had just dumped the baby on her – he was distraught, his wife's run off, he had to go to work – he works nights – Charlene had to go to see her mother in hospital, and anyway she's totally incapable of looking after a baby, so I said I'd take him. What else could I do?'

'I'm not sure I've taken all that in,' said William.

'I've brought you some nice cheese.'

She dumped a paper bag on the table.

'Cambozola?' Those little blue bits of delicate decay in the creamy white.

'No. That cheese has become such a cliché. Someone I know saw her cleaning lady buying it in the Co-op. Something else.'

'What's his name? What does he eat, and where is he going to sleep?'

'Theodore.'

Theodore. Gift of God.

William felt suddenly uneasy. He looked round for a bag of

99

baby's provisions. The baby, who had been regarding William steadily, started to squirm and thrash in Olive's arms.

'The thing is, his stupid father dumped him without even a bottle. No nappies, no nothing. One of us will have to nip out and get some things.'

'Well, don't look at me. I shouldn't have the faintest idea what to buy.'

It was much better that she should go. William might talk.

'I'll go. Doolally's will be open. I shan't be long.'

She gathered up her purse and a bag.

'Aren't you taking him with you?'

'Don't be silly. He's tired. Try him with a banana, if you like. Peeled and mashed.'

'Peeled and mashed,' mocked William, over the baby's head; as the front door banged. He fetched an old tartan travelling rug and sat the baby on it propped up with a cushion. The baby screamed.

'Now, Theo, just be patient. These things have to be done properly.'

He sterilised a saucer and a spoon with boiling water from the kettle, and dried them with the tea towel that was lying on the draining board. Theo grabbed at the spoon. William had not known that one medium-sized banana contained such a volume of pulp. Wiping the child's face, and his own, William did not fall in love with Theodore as Olive had; rather, the solemnity of his gaze, the trust with which he surrendered himself to this clumsy stranger, inspired the feeling of intense, spurious happiness about to shatter into a salt spray of tears that he experienced sometimes on top of a bus.

Since the tragedy on the Paris Metro, the red-and-blue signs of underground stations betokened entrances to hell: he spent a lot of time riding about on buses. From the top deck it was possible to see into the jumbled storerooms above shops where a profusion of faded boxes and discarded artifacts gathered dust, to look over gardens at roses and refuse sacks, to glimpse people's lives in domestic interiors made poignant by distance; still lifes in high kitchens made momentary statements of universality, as he cruised past in his spaceship observing this alien civilisation. A wedding party spilling from a terraced house onto a narrow pavement, children dressed like nylon carnations running in and out, a man wearing a carnation in silver paper standing by the dustbins eating a plate of canapés in the traffic fumes, or a pregnant woman carrying a bowl of fruit salad wrapped in clingfilm between the flourishing roses of a garden path, or the white, ivy-wreathed façade of a ruined synagogue behind which shimmered a graveyard of wrecked cars, or Hume's Botanical Institute which he meant to visit but never had – sights like these held for him mysteriousness shot through with longing. Occasionally he travelled with a bottle in his pocket, and then such human activities, or the baby green conkers left when the chestnut blossom had fallen, were made more unbearable by the knowledge that he would remember nothing of what had moved him so. Fragments of schoolgirl conversations seemed charged with arcane profundity:

'If the car's there, it means he's gone to Croydon; if it isn't, he hasn't, know what I mean?'

'I was really gutted, know what I mean?'

Now he never did know what they meant, any of the garrulous exotics, who might have been his pupils; he could interpret neither their language nor their lives, their vehement, violent, rambling anecdotes, all cutting across each other, none listening to any voice but his or her own. Graffiti burned into his brain; an aerosoled message on the wall of an off-licence haunted him: 'Say Hey Lady Marcia You Know I am the One that Called you.'

Now he held a cup of milk to Theo's mouth, wondering if he was weaned and worrying that he might be allergic to cow's milk.

Olive entered Dooley's – known to herself and William as the Doolally shop – on the final bars of Elgar's cello concerto, from which only yesterday she would have fled, and the tail end of a political discussion between Mr and Mrs Dooley. Since Terry's defection she had been unable to listen to anything noble or sad, but today she could face the music.

'Well, we've lived for so long in what we now all have to refer to as Thatcher's Britain that I can't even remember what it was like before. Isn't that right?' Mrs Dooley demanded of Olive, who she had never seen before. Olive, unlike William who was a regular here since he had shunned the nearer shops where he was known, had refused hitherto to patronise the shop.

'Absolutely,' Olive agreed.

She was humming as she took her wire basket, blithely and wilfully unaware of the enormity of what she had done, in crossing to William's side of the chasm that divided him from most of the human race, in joining the company of those wrecked vicars and schoolteachers and Brown Owls, *ses semblables, ses frères* of the Sunday press. She recognised the tune that she was humming as an advertising jingle as she selected an enormous packet of disposable nappies and was surprised to find that she had been, unaware of it, as absorbent as the elasticated diapers which she chose. Elgar had been replaced by a tape of Dusty Springfield's Greatest Hits. The Dooleys' young son Keiron carried in a tray of cacti from the pavement; they, like the kumquats turning blue, the albino aubergines, the long-handled dusters like rainbow candyfloss, the inflatable women's legs in red high heels and the helium-filled parrots, all the stock in fact, had the look of impulse buys from some doolally Cash and Carry. Olive paused at a pyramid of tinned salt fish and ackee; would they be ambrosia to a gift of God? She put a tin of Ambrosia creamed rice in her basket anyway but decided that otherwise Theodore should have fresh fruit and vegetables, puréed if necessary in the blender. She picked up too a little pair of Taiwanese dungarees – hardly Oshkosh or Benetton but they would do for now, and a red, green and yellow striped T-shirt. Mrs Dooley admired them as she put them into the bag, and then poured four pounds of Jersey potatoes on top of them. Olive was looking forward to cooking for the first time for weeks.

'It's not that I object on principle to your being a dyke,' Mr Dooley was telling his daughter at the back of the shop, 'if that's what you've set your heart on. It's the thought of all that money we wasted on the guitar lessons that breaks my heart.'

'Dad, you're missing the point somewhat, as usual ... '

'Love! Your generation doesn't know the meaning of the word! There's more to life than compact discs.'

In the street Olive realised that she had not thought about Terry Turner for almost two hours. For a year she had been at ease in her body, walking at ease in the world, enjoying in their irregular liaison a feeling of domesticity she had never known in her marriage. Then he had put her out one morning for the dustmen to take away.

Later, lying in bed, William heard Olive moving about in her room, the floor creaking, the child's half-cry in his sleep. The radio was buzzing away beside his bed, bringing a phone-in that he did not want to listen to but lacked the energy to switch off. He did not wish to hear Florence of Peckham's solution to the problem of English soccer hooligans abroad, or Margaret of Stratford's views on Hong Kong; he did not need to be reminded of refugees living in cages while he lay insomniac and smoking in his comfortable, if fuggy, bed in a house which could shelter several families. The news summary interrupted the programme. A coach carrying British schoolchildren had crashed in France. He saw blood and broken glass, the distraught headmaster ... then he became aware of a woman's voice. It was tearful, young, and black ... 'I just want to say – whoever's got him, please give him back. I just want my baby back.' She broke off in an incoherent, heart-wrenching gurgle. Then a man's voice said, 'You know who you are. Somebody's holding him, we know. Just tell somebody where he is. Nobody's going to hurt you or nothing. We just want Jermaine back safe and well.' William looked down at his arms; the hairs had risen vertically. His scalp crawled and the underarms of his pyjama jacket were wet with prickly sweat. His legs itched. He shivered violently. He took a drink and his teeth rattled on the rim of the glass.

'Oh God, what am I going to do?'

He paced the room beating his arms against his chest, slumped onto the edge of the bed tugging at his hair with both hands, and sprang up to pace again.

'What am I going to *do*?'

He pulled back the edge of the curtain fearfully. The street was still and empty with white ghosts of roses blanching in the lamplight.

William, barefoot, his pyjama jacket, striped and buttoned to the neck and tucked into his trousers, giving him the look of an old tousled little boy, stood outside his sister's door in the colourless light of a no-man's-land of time between night and day speckled gold by the song of an insomniac thrush. It was the second time that he had approached her room. He had always been a bit afraid of Olive and tonight he felt physical fear again, of a frenzied white figure who in daemonic mother love might lunge with a dagger in the darkness. At the same time his ears strained for sirens, the running feet of a posse of vengeful rescuers, a brick, a petrol bomb crashing through the window. At last, demented with terror and lack of sleep, he turned her doorknob, entered her room and stood with the roaring of his own blood drowning the sound of their breathing. Then he slid one foot in front of the other towards the sleeping child and placed his hand over his mouth. For a second, he might have been a murderer. Then he lifted the baby in an armful of bedding.

Ten minutes later, he drove past a traffic island in a pool of coarse diamonds, a shattered bus shelter, all spidery glass. The empty road was full of malice. Invisible, evil faces stared from the drivers' seats of parked cars; Theo, or Jermaine as he now knew him to be, whimpered on the back seat, wedged in with blankets. William's hands were wet on the wheel; he dared not drive too fast lest the child roll to the floor. A lorry overtook him at speed and its articulated tail swung crazily, almost hooking a line of cars from the kerb. The driver made an obscene gesture in the mirror, which William was afraid to return. A police car shrieked past. His heart was a choking lump of pulsating meat, his hands clamped rigid as he waited for it to swerve in front of him, forcing him to pull in. Only when its tail lights disappeared and it did not make a screeching U-turn and come doubling back did he taste blood in his mouth where he had clamped his teeth on his tongue.

He was caught by the lights on Denmark Hill. He sat in the deserted road waiting for them to change. A homegoing taxi drew up on the other side of the road. They waited, the throbbing of the taxi's motor drilling through his head. A car drew up behind William. The lights stayed red. He cursed the unblinking red eye. With that bastard sitting on his tail, he might as well have had a BABY ON BOARD sticker on his rear window. Just as Jermaine started to howl, the car pulled out and overtook him, and the taxi driver with a shrug that said 'bugger this' shot across the broken lights. A blue light was bearing down the hill. Forcing himself to keep to the speed limit, William drove on to Camberwell Green where he lost the police car at the roundabout. He drove back up Denmark Hill.

Here and there a lighted window indicated human wakefulness in the Maudsley Hospital. The main gates were locked. Instead of steering across the road into King's College Hospital, as he had intended, William drove into the Maudsley outpatients' emergency entrance and, leaving the engine running, took the baby, startled, damp and heavy, from the car, and placed him on a dun strip of grass.

Once out of the hospital, speed was paramount. It was not until he had left the phone box in the side street and was back at the wheel that the enormity of what he had done hit him. He shook violently, his knees actually clashed; he had to hold them down, grasping his thighs in both hands. The police, he knew, could trace a callbox almost instantly. He got the engine started and the car kangarooed noisily forward. A hundred yards or so down a quiet road, he had to pull over. Flecked with vomit, he drove home through back streets of houses where innocent early risers were beginning to start their simple day, tasting the sour and terrible knowledge that he had left the baby defenceless on the cigarette-strewn, drizzled grass where dogs and drunks had peed, in the grounds of a mental hospital, prey to rats, or marauding patients or a pack of hungry, abandoned dogs. He should have left Jermaine at King's.

He had done this in defence of his sister, or had he? He had done it for Jermaine, then. For his weeping young mother and his father, hardly more than children themselves from the sound of their voices. For Olive and the little family he had put himself at risk to lay a baby on a plastic carrier where slugs and snails would drag their slimy trails across his face. He had done it for himself, to expiate some of his own sin. A thought slammed into his brain: what if Jermaine had started to crawl, towards bushes, over broken glass, towards the railings, towards the road, across the car park, where an exhausted doctor stumbled into a car, reversed, heard a soft thump and, thinking he or she had struck a bag of rubbish, drove on. He could not bear it. No more. Surely a baby could not die of exposure on a mild, if drizzly, morning. Surely he was already in encircling arms; please God let them be the warm official arms of a nurse or a night porter. The pale sky was split by sirens zigzagging like lightning through the birdsong as he drove.

He lay on his bed, exhaling smells of sickness and fear through his clammy muzzle, one hand on his battering heart, the other throttling the neck of a whisky bottle, as the birds built up, twig by interlaced twig, a thicket of song, which was shattered by a long wail of loss and disbelief from Olive's room.

William switched on the radio in the kitchen for the dreaded, longed-for news summary ... 'safe and well' ... Thank God. Then the voice of the mother, still tearful ... 'Whoever took him's a sick lady ...'

The father, interrupting, 'She's not a lady, she's a monster.'

'Yeah, well, we don't bear her any grudges but I would say she needs help so no other parents have to go through what we went through. Perhaps she's a mother who lost her own baby ...'

Olive knocked the radio to the floor, where it played on unperturbed.

'Sanctimonious cow – couldn't she think of anything original to say? Mouthing clichés and platitudes. Thief! And you're no better, you murderer. You've killed your own sister. You dumped my baby in a loony bin!'

William left the kitchen without speaking.

A photofit picture of the baby-snatcher appeared in that evening's *Standard*. It might have been anybody, but it would just take Mrs Doolally to put two and two together. Olive studied the picture as if it had been of somebody quite unknown to her. Apparently the woman had been smartly dressed and well-spoken, had been spotted on a bus, was in her mid to late thirties. Considerably younger than Olive.

She thought of hiding in her room for ever but the idea of

the stillness, the silence, William's presence in the house, his breathing, the bulk of his body, his being, were intolerable, like rough wool on burned skin.

Later, she realised that she had never seen anybody, even Terry after a bender, shaking from head to foot as William was, a ravelled grey thing fumbling a set of car keys onto his keyring.

'I've locked your car. You are not to use it. Just pray that nobody got the number.'

He forced the keys between the hard metal rings with their cheap red plastic tag and slid them round until they hung next to his front-door key.

'I've locked the spare keys in the boot.'

Olive felt the impotent humiliation she had choked on when a teacher had confiscated her penknife at school. She could have plunged the blunt blade into the teacher's heart. She stared at William's grey cardigan, blurred in twisted cables of shame.

'Don't ever speak to me like that. As if I were one of your delinquent pupils. You're not a headmaster now, in case you've forgotten.'

The words which should never have been spoken breached the carefully constructed wall of pity and respect and a bitter tidal wave of silence engulfed the kitchen. A bluebottle banged its head on the window pane, zizzing angrily and desperately at the glass. Which one of them would dare to let it out, the murderer or the baby-snatcher? The air buzzed with antagonism; they would stand and watch a fly beat itself to death. When it became unbearable, William braved the waters and forced up the window on its risky sash cord, flinging the iridescent crumbs of two blue corpses after the live one into the air. He knew that Olive was thinking 'Pity he couldn't be bothered to save the life of a child, but the tender-hearted wimp seeks to expiate his guilt in small acts of mercy, such as rescuing a bluebottle, in the hope that a lifetime of atonement will secure redemption. As if he didn't know there is none.' Olive thought, 'He is thinking, "At least I did not *wilfully* deprive parents of their child."' Sanctimonious shit. I want Theo. I just want him.'

She felt the little arms round her neck; the weight, the softness, was pierced by a pang of baby powder.

Through ears clogged with tears, she heard soft objects being stuffed into a black plastic sack, and the clash of the dustbin lid. Disposable nappies thrown away unused, incriminating tiny T-shirt, dungarees made in Taiwan, all muddled up with coffee grounds and banana skins and the detritus of two single adults, awaited dustbin day, or doomsday.

'I only wanted to have him for a little while,' she wept. 'I would have given him back.' And at the same time a voice insisted, 'He would have been happy with me. He loved me. Oh, Theo! I miss you so much. I want my baby back.'

8

Deprived of her car, Olive had to travel by bus to the shop. Wave after wave of black and blue-blazered, huge, terrifying schoolchildren swept over the bus stop, chewing, smoking, scuffling, swearing, spitting on the pavement, crushing, shoving aside intimidated adults and small children as they swarmed onto the bus, leaving casualties in their wake, convent and comprehensive bound. Had she not burned with hate for William, Olive might have pitied those who had to teach them; as it was, she exacted small and inadequate revenge in surreptitious kicks and elbowings, while her heart grew murderous. Theo would grow into one of these louts, whom even their mothers surely could not love, mouthing obscene patois at those appalling girls. She thought of her own schooldays, when walking down the road three abreast, not wearing a hat, or eating in the street, were forbidden lest they impede or offend The General Public, and carried the penalty of a Detention. How civilised that seemed now. Her eye lit on a small boy with his mother; that was Theo a few years on. What energy, what charm, what grace boys have at that age, before they turn mean, into those great restless, loose-jointed, loud-mouthed boys vibrating with anger.

*

The flock of abalone parakeets whirred upwards in panic in the draught from Olive's entrance and would have flown to safe perches had they not been tethered by their strings. Charlene took in Olive's lacklustre hair and red-rimmed eyes. There was no shock of recognition of photofit or identikit.

'You shouldn't've come in.'

'Evidently.'

A half-unpacked crate spilled paper streamers over the floor; a hungover harlequin doll slumped on the counter, a perfect painted tear trembling on his cheek for his sins of the night before; the greetings cards were ruffled in their racks. A joss stick smouldered among the burned-out candles. Obviously, Charlene had had some friends in and had arrived too late in the morning to tidy up before Olive's entrance.

She had interrupted a conversation between Charlene and a youth with hair shaved into a pillbox on the side of his head, who was rotating the postcards impatiently, as if waiting for her to leave. She went into the back room to hang up her jacket. It hung like a ghost in mid-air as she was frozen by these words:

'. . . bottled him, innit.'

'What do you mean, bottled him?'

'Broke a bottle on his head, hit him in the face with it, vodkar in it and all. His mouth's out 'ere, innit.'

Olive saw a huge swollen lip, turned inside out, pink running red, screaming, burning raw spirit mingling with blood.

'No, I don't feel sorry for him at all,' the youth was disagreeing. 'Listen, if someone was to throw a brick at your niece's head, right, whatsaname, Grace, right, how many men in your family would go after him? There's your brothers, your dad, Mark, Curtis, Paul, Marvin, for a start, at least ten men . . .'

Words she had blocked out, Charlene's mother's overheard comment as she left the shop after her first, and last, visit came back to her: 'Me spirit don't take to her.'

That was the justice they meted out to those who injured them. Olive saw herself in Casualty, her lip brutally and punitively stitched with a darning needle, a crewel needle, to form a hideous scar. Bottled. Branded. Scarfed against the taunts and curses of strangers. She came back into the shop, her face half-concealed by a gauzy strip of Indian silk, carrying a tray with two mugs of coffee. Charlene's friend had gone.

'Got toothache?'

'A touch of neuralgia. I've made coffee, and then let's get this place tidied up.'

Olive flinched as a woman bumped her way backwards through the door with a pushchair; she was beginning to feel sympathy with William's furtive life.

'He's asleep and I didn't dare leave him outside,' the mother said with a certain self-righteousness, as a wheel caught a wicker basket of dried flowers and overturned it. 'These baby-snatch cases always have a copy-cat effect, don't they?'

'You can't be too careful these days,' Charlene agreed, scooping up splintery flower heads, glancing at the door as if a deranged woman, a molester in a mac, the Erl-King, would all stride in at any moment to snatch the sleeping child. 'I think women who steal babies must be sick in the head,' she added, as if presenting a revolutionary psychological breakthrough.

'Much safer to bring him in.' Olive attempted to unite them in a trio of concerned sisterhood, and pulling her scarf tighter across her face, forced herself to lean over the infant. A person would have to be hard up to want that one. She inhaled the sweet smell of talcum powder: the odour of Theodore. She put her hand to her lip. She felt, through her back, the customer mouthing 'What's up with her?' and Charlene's whispered 'Faceache'.

'Faceache's going to the bank,' she informed Charlene.

'That's what I like about you, Mrs Schwarz, you can laugh at yourself. That's a rare gift, you know.'

Olive stomped out with the previous day's takings. Her eye was caught by a new notice among the jumble of cards on the door:

> *GOOD GRIEF* BEREAVEMENT COUNSELLING.
> GROUP AND INDIVIDUAL SESSIONS.

'Is this for real?'

'I think it's a very good idea,' Charlene said. 'Mourning Therapy. Many people don't give themselves permission to grieve properly.'

'Oh, shut up,' Olive said inside her throbbing head.

She passed a telephone, hesitated, retraced her steps, and found that it took cards only. She went into a newsagent's and bought a phonecard for £2. She dialled Terry's number. On the third ring a blast of tenor sax hit an ear already aching with the weight of a savage and bizarre brass and bloodstone earring. 'Hi, thanks for calling. Please leave a message and I'll get back to you.' The insolence. The pretentiousness. Olive crashed down the receiver. 'That's two more quid you owe me, bastard.' She pictured him in bed with some girl, while the answering machine went up in flames, combusted by her hatred. The fire engulfed the bed. Two naked figures beat desperately on the window, and fell back, blackened, into the swirling smoke. A fire engine, swooping and sawing through the traffic, shrieking at the bumbling cars in its way, passed her. 'Too late,' said Olive. 'Good Grief.'

Her bank was a disagreeable place, smelling of cigarettes, anxiety and incompetence, with little dangling broken chains which had once held pens stolen long ago. The queue moved laboriously up the narrow confine until Olive counted that the bell which signalled a vacant position would ring three times before it was her turn. Third bell. At school, first bell was a warning, second bell a command, and third bell meant the goody-goodies were at their desks with opened books, the teacher tapping impatiently on hers. Grass-stained girls were ordered to roll down their sleeves; ghosts of gravy and mashed potato, unfocused longing, indolence were in the air, birdsong, girls' cries and the clop of tennis balls. Out in the street, traffic glared on melting tarmac in heavy fumes; Olive remembered the heat haze over asphalt on a tennis court and a girl named Chloris Sparks hitting the ball into the shrubbery, so that they could spend the lesson pretending to search for it. She had once placed a fallen rhododendron petal, a pink, a purple, a white, on each of Olive's fingers. Chloris Sparks had notched a record number of detentions on the illicit belt which dragged in her grey skirt; other girls competed to write her lines. 'Chloris Sparks, Chloris Sparks, I'm tired of saying your name,' the headmistress had sighed. Olive had never tired of it. It was Chloris Sparks who had discovered the way into the air-raid shelter, where the cognoscenti had smoked packets of five Weights and Woodbines. Chloris had disappeared one day. At length a malleable teacher had been persuaded to disclose that she had gone to live in Brighton. For several weeks there had been talk of an expedition to find her, but it had never been mounted.

'In a moment,' thought Olive, forcing her way through lumbering shoppers, 'I am going to start thinking that my schooldays were the happiest days of my life; a lost Eden of white aertex and bottle-green knickers ... I really must make an effort to keep my shoulders back.' She shrank from slumped bare backs in sundresses, upper arms like batter dropping from a spoon, cleavages criss-crossed by time. She pictured Chloris Sparks, faded and tinted in raffish splendour, queening it in a peeling stucco pub, or doing voice-overs for local radio, or conjuring outlandish fortunes from a crystal ball in a Byzantine booth in a seafront arcade. Everybody on the pavement seemed so defeated, and yet how did they carry on from year to year, putting one foot in front of the other without, she suspected of most of them, any spiritual spur or consolation? Whatever this thing called the human spirit was, she felt she did not have it; and felt a lack in herself like a fleeting, inexplicable vision of possible bliss, a house glimpsed from a train, a gate opening on a distant field, a fragment of memory, blue as speedwell, sharp as sapphire, lost for ever. She saw a notice in a hairdresser's window: *Reduced Rates For OAPs On Wednesdays.*

Charlene was in the back when she returned, unpacking huge cardboard boxes which when emptied had to be demolished, the dangerous staples wrenched out, and stamped flat and carried outside to await the dustmen's pleasure. The air was pungent with motes from a smashed jar of peppercorns and explosive with Charlene's sneezes. 'What a self-indulgent sneeze that girl has,' Olive thought, at a particularly volcanic burst. 'A Tissue! A Tissue!' Charlene's sneezes seemed to shout, demanding some audience reaction; sympathy, applause, or the suggestion that Olive change places with her. Olive sighed heavily as she inscribed a card in bold italic. Once she had not asked of her staff anything which she was not prepared to do herself; 'There was nothing in the job description about cleaning floors or bashing boxes,' Charlene had complained recently. Olive had given her a basket of chipped soaps. 'We must all pull together,' she had murmured vaguely. Now she Blu-Tacked her notice to the shop door, and dusted a bare patch on a shelf. An old woman, killing time, was poking about in a pile of Peruvian knitted children's caps.

'Has the bath stuff come?' Olive called to Charlene.

'What stuff?'

Charlene appeared, glad of any distraction.

'Aloe vera.'

The old woman turned round, as if about to respond to a greeting.

Olive's blank look met the lined face under the cap of scarlet, viridian, acid yellow and magenta stripes which the old woman had perched on her head. The ear flaps dangled. Charlene sniggered, setting the parrot mobile tinkling as if sharing a joke; the old woman beamed, a bit puzzled.

She backed out, still wearing the child's cap.

'Bye bye, Vera,' Charlene snorted.

The kid over-reacted to everything. She was watching the old woman read the notice which she had just stuck on the door, shaking her head. 'She hasn't paid for that hat. Go after her, Charlene, there's a good girl.'

'Poor old thing. Let her keep it, brighten up her life a bit,' said

Charlene comfortably. 'Besides, all the colours will run when it rains. You should've seen my little niece in hers, all the colours of the rainbow. You had to laugh but . . .'

Olive froze. 'Have you finished unpacking that order? I'm still waiting for the aloe vera, and the jojoba.'

'My sister was going to sue you for child abuse. As it was, I had to pay to have Grace's coat cleaned but that beetroot colour never came out.'

Olive strode through to the back. 'Magenta.'

She was answered by a sneeze from Charlene, on her hands and knees among spilled peppercorns.

A shaven-headed girl in shorts came in and spent a long time selecting an earring.

'Don't you find that awkward, when you've got a cold?' Olive asked her, referring to the stud in her nose.

The girl put the earring on the counter and left the shop.

The mention of little Grace had stabbed Olive, leaving a panicky ache in her chest. She wondered if she was sick in the head, as Charlene had suggested, and dismissed the idea. Snatching, no, rescuing, Theo had been a mad impulse, an impulse, but she had been quite rational. Of course he would have had a better life with her. He had loved her. His little hands. His ears. His pristine feet. She hated William, her hands were round his scrawny throat, bashing and bashing his vile head against the wall.

A woman's face burst round the door.

'I just want to tell you I think your notice is ageist and disgraceful! I shall never patronise this shop again!'

She ripped off the card and flung it to the floor.

'What was all that about?'

Charlene picked up the crumpled card. '"No Reductions For Pensioners On Thursdays".'

She stared at Olive, constellations of unspoken thoughts whirling round her head.

'I'm sick of hypocrisy, of establishments paying cynical lip service to the lie that this is a country which cares about old people. When everybody knows the old fools would be better off dead, and the sooner the better for all concerned. Hairdressers, health shops, dry cleaners! It makes me sick.'

'I think old people are brave,' said Charlene.

'God preserve me from the self-righteous!'

At the thought of the bus journey home, the waiting, the shoving, the standing jammed up against other members of the hated human race, and William at the end of it, Olive burst into tears.

'No, seriously, I think old people have got a lot of courage. My grandfather ...'

'No, seriously, Charlene, I don't wish to hear again how your grandfather came over on the *Windrush* in nineteen-whatever with only the zoot suit he stood up in and a cardboard suitcase ...'

She expected, half hoped, that Charlene would lose her temper, hit her, storm out, but the girl said gently, 'Look, Mrs Schwarz, I'm not speaking to you as your employee now, but as a friend. I think you really need help.'

'Oh, lock up, lock up, Charlene. Let's call it a day.'

'You go on home. I'll see to everything here. And I do really think you ought to see your doctor.'

'Stop being so bloody nice, I can't bear it.'

She scrubbed at her eyes with a tissue, and heard herself spit out the words, 'You think. You think. You'll see to everything. Don't you ever have a moment's self-doubt? Your niece, your grandfather. Is it your deliberate intention to undermine me, to point up the fact that I have no role to play in this ridiculous world? If it is you're doing a great job.'

'Here's your handbag.'

At the door, Olive turned and, with a tremendous effort, managed to say, 'I forgot. I bought you a dress. I'll bring it tomorrow. How do you like those soaps?'

'Well, I'm not really into lavender. I gave them to my grandmo—' She bit it back, and swallowed it on a laugh.

Olive managed a watery smile.

She could not face going home, but what was the alternative? Seeking out that mad boy Jay? Ringing Terry's number and putting the phone down when he answered? Ringing one of her friends? She stood at the bus stop among the Kwik-Save shopping bags and wept. See your doctor, that's a laugh. She remembered her latest visit to the surgery, before she had lived with William, where she had outlined the general malaise which disabled her. Dr Rosen looked at her and gave his diagnosis: '*Mittelschmerz*.' On the way home from the surgery she had bought a jar of Epicure crinkle-cut beetroot. She ate it from the jar with a fork, standing over the kitchen sink, watching carmine splashes turn blue in the sediment of cream cleanser on the white surface; one of the legion of women who eat joylessly, furtively and guiltily because they have nobody to cook for, standing up at stove or sink as though they are not worthy of a plate. And as she ate she had reflected on her interview with the doctor.

'Is it terminal?' she had asked.

'In most cases, no . . .'

A flick of beetroot juice had flown from the tines of her fork onto her white shirt. She had taken off the shirt and soaked it in a mild bleach solution until all that remained of the stain was a tiny violet bruise. She thought of that now, and imagined Charlene's niece, all the colours of the rainbow in her stained coat. A small boy bounced a football against her leg. His mother hit him. He howled. The day was like a tired and dirty child, with ice cream on its breath and dried in a scum around its fractious mouth, who should have been washed and put to bed. But there were hours more to be staggered through.

The weeping fig in the sitting room had grown into a tree which cast shadows over the ceiling and walls; its cascades of leaves bent its trunk almost to the floor and its branches were supported by strings suspended from the top of the yellowed window frame. Behind its green gloom the window panes, inaccessible, were cloudy, furred on the outside with the grey accretions of traffic in the street and dried rain. Flourishing, dark and glossy, it threatened the ceiling. The inhabitants of this little jungle moved about the room, not knowing where to place their bodies, touching a leaf, roughly folding a newspaper, too distraught to straighten the pages properly so that it had to be opened and slapped and flapped, its clumsiness irritating to the folder and its papery rasp grating on the ears of the listener. A cushion would not sit properly on its chair and got thumped and replumped as all the furniture slouched and seemed to shift uneasy feet. A mould of silence grew between the faded medallions of the wallpaper as a spider running along the branch of the weeping fig showed itself the only creature present with a sense of purpose.

The painting on the wall, of a stout man in a clerical collar, holding a top hat, stick and gloves, seemed to draw the light into itself until the eyes stared out with a brilliant glitter and the hairs of the moustache bristled like the pelt of a predatory animal.

'Go to the ant, thou sluggard,' William thought, watching the spider, avoiding his grandfather's eyes. In the portrait hanging opposite, his grandmother's dress was bleached to the colour of washed-out ladies' smocks at the end of spring. There was no cat or dog to nudge the knees of the grandchildren of the manse as they sat, or to importune for affection, food, or fresh air. There was a parrot but it was made of coloured glass and hung in an oval lead frame on a chain, above the words 'Fine Feathers Make Fine Birds'. One green segment of a wing was missing, where Olive had kicked an infant shoe through it in a rage.

William shattered the silence.

'Do you recall me mentioning a boy called Snyder? Liam Snyder?'

'Wasn't he a bit of a pain?' Olive's voice was as faded as her grandmother's dress.

'Oh, I don't know – no more than the others.'

'What about him? Is he in trouble?'

Olive saw a boy lying on asphalt with a knife stuck into the pullover between the lapels of his blazer.

'No. I ran into him the other day. He's an estate agent. He's married.'

'Then he is in trouble.'

'What do you mean?'

Was this a new bitterness about the married state?

'Don't you notice anything that goes on around you? The collapse of the property market? You spend your life travelling around on buses, I should have thought you might have noticed the thousands of For Sale signs tacked to unsold houses, or the closed-down estate agents with their floors covered with unopened mail ... apart from reading those endless newspapers of yours that clutter up the place. I don't know what to do with them. One feels so guilty just throwing them in the bin. Although that's where they belong ... '

'You could recycle them into logs. Or get a kitten and use them to line its litter tray ... '

'How I wish they'd never invented that stupid hole in the bloody ozone layer. Life's becoming one long guilt trip. They might at least have waited until I was dead.'

'Snyder's got a little girl, Chantal.'

'Then let her cope with saving the bloody planet.'

It struck Olive at that point that it was the first time William had referred to one of his pupils since the accident, and she had spoiled it. She tried to think of something to retrieve the situation.

'Wasn't he, though, a bit of a pain in the ass?'

'No,' he said. 'In the heart, now. They all are.'

He stood up. 'I debated whether to tell you but I suppose you ought to know. There was a new photofit picture in tonight's *Standard* – didn't resemble anybody as far as I could see – anyhow,

"Must we to bed indeed? Well then,
Let us arise and go like men,
And face with an undaunted tread,
The long black passage up to bed."'

Olive stared into the parchment folds of a fan in the grate. A metaphor for dying, or simply a bedtime rhyme for children? Stevenson; she could look it up, but wouldn't. She took two glasses through to the kitchen and dumped them in the sink. One cracked. She held it up to the light, seeing the irredeemable fissure in its old fragile shell through tears: the curse of a happy childhood. Well, there had been moments of happiness, brittle as glass. She found the paper; a deranged-looking old bat with staring eyes; nothing to do with her.

A mile or two away, Jay Pascal was also thinking about going to bed. He had had a disappointing day; somebody had told him of a place at King's Cross where they hired casual labour for kitchen work. He had slept rough the night before to make sure that he was one of the first in the queue, and at five o'clock he had been one of a swelling group of unemployed, students and derros hoping for a day's wage. Jay had been jostled and pushed aside when the blokes arrived to choose. He had not been picked. He had earned a couple of quid helping tourists with their cases before uniformed station staff had come running at him with silver luggage trolleys. He had escaped with bruised shins. He would have been ashamed, and bored, to sit all day with a plastic cup and a notice saying 'Homeless and Hungry. Please Help', but nobody wanted his help. Anyway, he consoled himself, he wasn't homeless. But nobody wanted him.

Night had been falling by the time he got back to Brixton station, using an old one-day Travelcard he had found; it wasn't honest, but what could he do? He had to eat, and so far his plan to grow vegetables in the garden of *Dunedin* had been thwarted by a lack of seeds; his offer to work at the garden centre near

Herne Hill in return for money or plants had been rejected. He had come up the escalator and passed Denny sprawled drunkenly on the steps that led to the street, with a can of lager in one hand and a notice hanging round his neck: 'Legless and Lazy. Please Help'. Gnasher had been watchful beside him. Jay had contemplated taking the dog home, but his lead, attached to the spiked collar, had been wound tightly round Denny's senseless hand. Denny's upturned Afghan cap had been empty.

Jay had crept into the house. All had been quiet. As he had tiptoed past the half-open door of Kirsty's room, he had been arrested by the sight of her kneeling in the moonlight. She had been pulling what looked like a large painted tin from under the floorboards. She had prised off the lid and lifted something out. At his indrawn horrified gasp she had whirled round, holding by the hair an ancient, wizened and tattooed shrunken head. As Jay ran for his room, she had laid the head gently back in its bed of tarnished excelsior and closed the lid.

Jay had locked his door and dragged his bed against it: she should not have held the murdered souvenir by what was left of its hair, for that was the most sacred part of the head, imbued with, and probably still emanating, *tapu*. Taboo, forbidden, especially to the likes of Kirsty, and in a strange land.

9

When Olive entertained her women friends William usually went out, or lurked in his room, for fear of overhearing something ribald or gynaecological. Tonight, having come downstairs for a book, he passed the kitchen, where they all sat round the table in an aubergine smoky haze, and heard the voice of Lizzie, who, in their slight acquaintance, he had rather liked, saying ' ... And what about William, then? How does he get his rocks off?' He didn't know what she meant, but he guessed, and fled before he could hear Olive's answer. She was bearing her bereavement well, he thought acidly.

'Is that you, William? Come and join us for a drink,' someone called, and a burst of laughter gusted up the stairs after him. Thenceforth Lizzie was damned in his book.

He hated them all then, as he sat in his chintz armchair twisting his unopened book in his hands, seeing them as a coven of witches, lips glossy with food, flushed with wine, ashtrays among the dishes, indulging in what one of them would have referred to as an inter-course cigarette. Perhaps he should join them and introduce the topic of baby-snatching? 'Anybody watch *Crimestoppers* the other night?' Voices mingled with the

roses on his carpet and buzzed round his feet. Then the music started vibrating the floor, as unidentifiable and insistent as that which escapes insolently from personal stereos on the bus. He found himself straining his ears as he read to pick it up. He thought he detected Peggy Lee singing 'Is that all there is?' He suspected dancing. He sneaked into the bathroom and got ready for bed, where he lay trying to read himself to sleep as usual, lonely and outnumbered. Catch Olive behaving like that with her girlfriends when Dad was alive; the Dansette's plug would have been ripped out of the socket and the records smashed, and serve her right. Wishful thinking of course; Olive had always been Daddy's pet. It seemed hours before the telephone began to ping and the minicabs began to pull up and the louche lot were disgorged into the street at last.

William had burned at Lizzie's words and the thought that they were laughing at him, or perhaps pitying. It was true that he had not felt the feeblest spark of desire since the accident. He wondered if Olive was serving up such details as she had of his affair with Anne and its demise; if so, they would make slim pickings, as Olive, for all her inebriated insight, knew almost nothing of Anne. And understood less. Anne, a big cream-coloured full-blown rose, had been, still was for all he knew, the school secretary; his mainstay and right hand. The sound of women's laughter almost tempted him for a moment to signal her in the darkening evening, to see if she remembered their old code.

It would not have taken a master cryptologist to break it; it was as simple as a=I, a=z or a=b. His one ring on the telephone ('Was that the phone?' 'I didn't hear it', or 'Must be a fault on the line, it often does that') signalled 'Ring me as soon as you're alone.' Her 'Bill, there's a problem with tomorrow's timetable' meant 'I can't get out to meet you as planned'; while his 'I'm so sorry to intrude on your evening. Something's cropped up – could I just have a quick word with Anne?' translated as 'I miss your wife so desperately that I am unscrupulous in disturbing you and risking embarrassment to her, and the contingent disarray of emotions, casting a blight on her night'.

Afterwards, William had discovered that all their colleagues had known and that he and Anne had moved among them with his headmaster's gown and her school secretary's understated elegance devalued by hypocrisy and illicit sex. The tragedy which had demanded of him his resignation marked the end of an eight-year love affair. His pain was subsumed in the horror of a pupil's death. Anne's grief was compounded by fear that somebody would shop them to the gutter press, but no one had betrayed them. She was a spoiled Catholic, married with two children who were not quite at ease with the awkwardly avuncular Bill. William – he was Bill to no one now that Anne was gone – had rebuffed her in his unhappiness and shame. She had wanted to comfort him despite her dread of scandal. Now he wondered if she had felt some relief that she had been disburdened of the unpleasant task of ending it herself and hoped that she had found peace of mind with the removal of guilt and subterfuge when her family had formed a neat moral square again.

His own guilt at what had been stolen from a man he liked and respected was much more acute now than it had been when blurred with passion and jealousy and resentment. Alone, he saw himself as a thief who had siphoned off emotions which should have fuelled the marriage. The shared jokes, the songs, the music, the parks where they had walked, the revelation of her deepest feelings to him, had all been robbed from her husband, Matthew. Then there were the flowers which Anne would say she had bought on the way home from school, scenting Matthew's house, the presents which had to be hidden or assimilated into the family picture; the currency of deceit. Then there were the children.

William learned through the local press that his school, which had served the community well for a hundred years, was under the threat of conversion into a city technical college. Staff morale, as high as could be expected in the political circumstances until the tragedy, was low now with teachers uncertain of their futures. He imagined, despite the assurances of the scheme's advocates, the local authority and private enterprise in cahoots, the pupils sitting in rows at word processors, keying in the basics of self-interest and greed. In his own time there he had been forced to watch art, music and drama dwindle through lack of staff and resources; now, he suspected, they would fade from the curriculum altogether. Language would be taught without literature, for the purpose of concluding deals in Europe, and sport, much restricted already, would be confined to egocentrically competitive games of squash. He read the reports and followed the court cases and appeals with a dull depression which was too damp to flare into anger. It was not his battle now.

He had driven slowly, in Olive's car, past Anne's house a few months ago. It was a Tudoresque semi, with a stained-glass galleon on the front door, in a little frayed snippet of ribbon development with a dreary parade of shops which made drivers on the dual carriageway remark: 'Imagine living *there*.' They couldn't. The place had no heart, no centre; it seemed too bleak a location to foster any community spirit, yet its inhabitants were always among the first to frame their windows with fairy lights before Christmas, which cheered or depressed travellers on their way, and implied a feeling that this was home. It was to Anne. A winter flowering prunus stood in a circle of earth with shivering pink blossoms on its leafless branches like the blobs of wax on bunches of twigs that William remembered from vases of his youth. The two black cats, Mack and Mabel, sat either side of the Christmas tree with its electric stars, looking out into the electric blue dusk. A girl detached herself from the light of a streetlamp and walked towards William's idling car. He got back into the stream of traffic, leaving her bare-legged in her stonewashed denim miniskirt and white high-heeled shoes on the freezing pavement, and contemplated a conviction for kerb-crawling outside his former mistress's house. The girl looked about fourteen.

Naturally neither he nor Olive mentioned Lizzie's crass and invasive question in the morning – although Olive did have the grace to blush when he came into the kitchen or it might have been the exertion of loading bottles into a box, for the bottle bank, which reddened her face.

'I hope we didn't keep you awake?'

He opened the window, letting in a rush of rainy air. The draining board was heaped with dishes and cutlery.

'There's quite a lot left. You could have it for lunch, and there's fruit and cheese.'

'I'll be out for lunch.'

'Oh God, we might as well be married. Or in the nursery. I'm going to work.'

'I don't need or want to be placated with your leftovers. Shall I give you a hand with that box of bottles? It looks rather heavy.'

'I can manage. I'm out this evening.'

She staggered out in a jiggle of green glass. The front door slammed and shivered in its frame. William waited. He heard the box crash down satisfyingly outside the locked garage door, as she remembered that she was without a car, and angry heels on the peacock tiles of the path.

He found the Peggy Lee record and put it on. 'Is that all there is?'

He had a spoon in a dish on the top of the stove when the front door bell rang. Ashley stood there, pale, blond, in a short black skirt.

'I think I must have left my diary here last night. Would you mind if I had a look? It's got everything in it – I'm absolutely lost without it.'

William held open the door and she stepped inside.

'I've rung the minicab people and they haven't got it. It's just got to be here or I may as well kill myself now. Work, contacts, my entire life!'

Ashley worked in Hatton Garden, for a company which manufactured scientific instruments – optical, medical and nautical – and exported them all over the world. She had started in the workshop, learning to grind lenses, bevelling prismatic edges, and had worked her way up to an executive position. She had recently celebrated twenty years with the firm and, enthusing slightly bemusedly over the engraved glass punchbowl and glasses with which she had been presented, wondered where the time had gone.

William followed her into the kitchen, where she pulled up

cushions, dragged open cupboards, investigated the draining board, and flung open the stiff doors under the sink which hid the pedal bin. William restrained her, feeling the bone under washed silk on her thin arm.

'There's no way it could be in there.'

She was persuaded not to tip the garbage from last night's meal onto the floor.

William was mildly excited by the thought that the diary had spent the night in the house, and annoyed that he had not read it in the furtive dawn light.

The fat Filofax was located in the sitting room. Ashley whirled on sheer thin ankles, clasping her entire life between black covers to her heart.

'I don't suppose you've got time for a coffee?'

'Well – I'm so late anyway . . . you haven't got any Nurofen, have you?'

'There's something called Remorse in the bathroom cabinet.'

'It's called Resolve.'

Later that afternoon William idled outside the newsagent's, reading the cards in the window: 'Ebony Massage; Unisex Massage; Wedding Dress Worn Twice Only As New; New Young Massage; Let Me Massage Your Cares Away in Comfort; New Unisex Massage, Pleasant Surroundings; Transsexual Massage – He-She Male . . .'

Lost in a reverie, wondering if he would qualify for the Ebony Massage, and if not, whether he would have a case under the Race Relations Act, fantasising someone's front room in the flats opposite, soft toys bundled behind the sofa covered with a thin brown-and-orange plaid rug, *Neighbours* on the telly, with the sound almost turned down, a baby screaming and rattling the bars of its cot in the bedroom, the grey light strained through dingy ruched blinds.

'They all seem to be for massage.'

He was startled by a woman's voice at his side.

'Yes, it's a good place to live if you've got a bad back,' said William.

'I was looking for someone to pave a patio, and do a bit of general gardening . . .'

'Gardeners do seem a bit thin on the ground,' he agreed.

The woman looked ordinary enough, middle-aged and a trifle *déshabillé* perhaps but not worryingly so.

A pleasant prospect of rolled shirtsleeves, sand and water, sloshy cement and the fragrance of drenched plants warmed him like sun on his back. A deal was struck, addresses and telephone numbers were exchanged, and William was engaged to report for duty at Mrs Handisyde's Tulse Hill house in two days' time. They shook hands on it, William's grip a little crushing as he winced from the blow to his ankle struck by a Dunn's River Nurishment can tossed from the window of a passing bus. He rubbed his sharp bone and set off for Doolally's, wondering how to seal the shiny new tools which he must purchase against the corrosion of Olive's scorn. Somewhere in the house, he knew, was a Reader's Digest book titled *Your Gardening Questions Answered* which, he felt confident, contained a section on paving patios. He had ordered it, with a free gift of secateurs, in a vain bid to win a Grand Prize Draw. He was passed by Rosetta Snyder, grim-faced, pushing a screaming Chantal in the buggy. He had a horrible fear that she was going to place a card in the newsagent's window: after all, had not the bottom fallen out of the property market, he reflected as he watched her strained stonewashed jeans disappear through the narrow shop doorway?

Doolally was serving a woman with vegetables, routinely and spiritlessly extracting the maximum innuendo from the leeks she was shovelling into her bag, when he realised that she was one of the nuns from Our Lady of the Rosary up the road, in mufti.

'There you go, Sister; lovely pair – beautiful couple of melons for dessert. On the house.'

He dropped the fruit in her bag in penance.

'Bless you, Tom,' she thanked him. His name was Bob, but she had been playing the washboard in a skiffle group when her Vocation came, and never entered his shop but the plaintive strains of 'Hang Down Your Head, Tom Dooley' twanged on piano wire through her memory, inspiring the misnomer and an unaccountable warmth towards the old reprobate in the ravelled Crystal Palace bobble hat.

'Just cut the bruised bits out. Sweet as a nut, they are, Sister!' he called after her.

'Right you are, Tom.'

'Wonderful sense of humour, some of them nuns. Very broadminded, you'd be surprised.'

He treated William to a wink.

'What can I do you for, sir?'

William fancied there was a sneer in that last syllable, a reference to his disgrace.

'I don't suppose you've got any parsley, have you? I couldn't see any out the front.'

He felt himself pushed against two tall weeping figs in pots as the shop filled up. A baby buggy nipped at his heels; he was aware of something sticky on his trouser leg at toddler level and a scuffling behind him as Doolally fished a bunch of dead coriander triumphantly from a bucket.

'Your lucky day, sir. This is your continental parsley. Couple of hours in the fridge and it'll be right as – Oi, mind me bananas!'

A youth, hand on a pile of fruit boxes, vaulted over the display in a flash of turquoise and pink, and held a knife across Doolally's throat, while another, purple and yellow, shoving people aside, grabbed at the open till. Child screaming, mother screaming, cursing, wrestling with buggy. Doolally gibbering, eyes rolling, rolls of grey stubble bulging over knife blade. William seized a weeping fig in either hand and swung one heavily on the shoulder of the boy with the knife, and the other, in a shower of earth, stones and dead leaves from the pots, on the head of the one at the till. The boy fell and scrambled up, executing a breakdance flip over the tottering display, headbutting an old man out of the way, followed by his companion who clutched his shoulder with his good hand. A woman had run to the wall phone at the back of the shop and dialled 999 as William with his trees charged after the youths, thrusting a weeping fig across the ankles of the first and bringing him down on the pavement as the other collided with them in a tangle of feet, bodies and leaves. They grappled on the pavement; William felt the slither of bright nylon in his hands, smelled sharp sweat, as a hail of potatoes flew from the shop door, with Doolally's shout: 'Not the bleedin' Jersey Royals! Use the Desirees!' One struck William painfully on the back of the neck. The boys had twisted free and were fighting to mount a bicycle, one on the saddle, the other on the crossbar. A cauliflower lobbed by Kim Doolally smacked William on the ear, as he wrestled with the handlebars, and was shaken off. He grabbed a tree from the pavement and spoked the back wheel, as the vengeful see-sawing of a siren swooped through the traffic and two white cars screeched up and six policemen flung themselves out. The boys were spreadeagled on the pavement and handcuffed, lying like garish burst balloons in their deflated shell suits.

After an exchange of formalities and addresses and instructions, when the squad cars had driven away, Kim Doolally put a mug of sweet tea into William's hand and laughed. He looked down; the mug bore a red heart and the words GIVE BLOOD, and he saw that he had been stabbed in the wrist. As soon as he noticed that, it began to hurt, but not so much as his ear, which was throbbing violently and swollen to twice its size.

'Reckon you've got what they call a cauliflower ear, mate!' Kim was convulsed by her own wit.

'Never mind cauliflower ears,' grumbled Doolally. 'Them weeping figs is sixteen quid apiece. Cost you twenty down the market. I wouldn't mind, only the wife's only just gone down the bank not half an hour ago. There's only fifteen in the bleedin' till!'

His words recalled Kim to her ideology.

'Capitalist swine!' she said. 'And you're no better, just a tool of the oppressors in the Class War.'

She took a Swiss Army knife from her pocket and jabbed it accusingly at William, before slitting open a pitta bread and inserting a slice of processed cheese from the packet she had speared from the fridge.

'That sarnie looks a trifle dry, my dear. Could I not tempt you to a spot of mustard?' Doolally enquired in silky tones. 'Or piccalilli perchance?'

'Why, thank you, Daddy, dear.'

Kim reached for a yellow jar.

'Don't you dare!' Doolally roared, baring his teeth, like a sweet old grandmother turned wolf.

William put down his mug. 'Thank you for the tea. I'd better be going. You haven't got a packet of plasters, have you?'

'Kim! Packet of Elastoplast for the gentleman. Fifty-two p., *if* you please, sir.'

Doolally came after him into the street flapping a plastic carrier, scooped up the bruised cauliflower and several potatoes from the pavement, and dropped in the remains of Kim's packet of cheese slices.

'There you go. Nice colly cheese for supper, bit of mash, lovely grub. Might as well have these while you're at it. Twenty nicker down the market. Don't tell the missus.' He winked.

'No, really, I . . .'

Doolally backed into the shop which was filling up again as William struggled with the broken trees which Doolally had thrust under each of his arms. As he set them down and tried to apply a plaster to his bleeding wrist he heard, 'Fat chance of me being a bloated capitalist with you eating all the profits. And I noticed you wasn't backwards in coming forward with that colly to chuck it at them poor deprived lads that you're so sorry for now. Could've took that geezer's head off with your rotten aim. No wonder they chucked you off of the netball team.'

'I was aiming at him, not them.'

William found that the plasters were a special Doolally

brand, which did not stick. He did not know if he believed Kim or not. He left the weeping figs at the end of the bus queue, where they looked no more dispirited than anyone else, and took his agonising ear and his vegetables home, where his own weeping fig spread variegated gloom.

'Well, what were they like?' Olive, who had come home while he had been at the police station making his statement, asked, on being told of his adventure.

'Young. One black, one white.'

He could see that she shared Kim Doolally's opinion of his valour.

'Well, I do think the police might at least have driven you to Casualty and then to the station themselves, after your display of public spirit. Did you see the lads there?'

William shook his head and winced.

Half-closed blackened eyes, split lips, ruptured spleens and kidneys, youths on remand hanging themselves in their cells loomed in the evening air of the kitchen. A blackbird sang on the laburnum outside the window, black on yellow, hurting them.

'I had forgotten that you are on the other side of the law now,' said William.

'Like you.'

A broken bicycle, a broken doll, a torn and scribbled book lay between them.

The front door bell rang.

'There's someone at the door.'

'So?'

'So answer it.'

The bell sounded again.

'Well, go on, then!'

'You get it, if you're so keen. I don't want to see anybody.'

Brrr brrr brrr brrrr!

William sighed, and backed down, as he always had.

At first he thought it was one of the youths come to get him; then he saw that it was a young woman dressed in a similar shiny shell suit.

'Mr Mackenzie? I'm Jenella Abdela from the *Streatham Guardian*. I believe you was involved in thwarting an attempted robbery at Dooley's Fruit and Vegetable Emporium this afternoon. They say you was very heroic, and congratulations on that, Mr Mackenzie. I won't keep you a minute. If you could just tell me in your own words what occurred. Mind if I bring my bike in, you can't trust anybody these days, can you?'

'Hello, Mrs Mackenzie, you must be very proud of your husband,' said the reporter, preceding William into the kitchen.

Olive exhaled deeply and dropped the knife she had seized on realising that it was not the police, come for her.

'This is Ms Abdela from the *Streatham Guardian*. She's left her bike in the hall,' said William desperately signalling Olive to rescue him.

'Good thinking,' said Olive. 'You can't be too careful nowadays, can you?'

'If you're *making* tea, Mrs Mackenzie, I'm gasping. Anythink herbal would be all right.'

'Rosehip and Hibiscus? I find that makes a pleasant alternative to ordinary tea at any time,' Olive said, reading from the packet, 'Limeblossom? Apple and Cinnamon? Wild Raspberry? Golden Slumbers?'

'Not Golden Slumbers, thanks, I'm driving! That is, I've got the bike.'

Olive put biscuits on a plate. 'Do you take sugar?' She decided she could not be bothered to suggest that they adjourn to another room, and said, 'Actually, I'm not Mrs Mackenzie', wondering what she'd make of that. Headlines formed in Olive's head as the reporter fished the bag from her tea, and looked speculatively at William, frowning a little: 'Grey Cardigan In Washday Sex Romps With Pantyhose. Have-A-Go Hero's Love Nest Of Shame With Baby-Snatch Sister. Shamed Head Is Have-A-Go Hero. Mr Patel of Cosy Corner, Grand Parade, commented, "All credit to Mr Mackenzie, but I only wish he had shown the same have-a-go heroism when my young daughter who was in his care was attacked by a drug-crazed homicidal maniac in the Paris Metro. That said, I congratulate him on being nominated for a Community Service Award."'

William was looking distressed.

'Really, Ms Abdela, it was a very minor incident, of no news value whatsoever. I'd really rather you didn't print anything. There must be more important things going on . . .'

'Like the fire at Woolworths, you mean, or the baby-snatch case? I've just come from there as a matter of fact, interviewing the parents. Thank God they got him back, little Jermaine.'

After too long a pause, it was William who agreed, 'Thank God.'

'Poor little thing,' said Olive. 'Have they found the person who took him?'

Sourfaced old bat, Jenella thought, obviously couldn't care less, not a spark of human feeling in her.

'Not yet. But they will. They always do. Anyway, Mr

Mackenzie, what you did wasn't nothing. If everybody showed your initiative, the streets would be safer for all of us to walk on. What did you say your occupation was again?'

'I – I'm retired.'

She made a squiggle in her notebook which Olive and William assumed meant unemployed. Or even pensioner, Olive thought, in that awful cardy. Unless she does know already who he is.

'I'm sure I know you,' Jenella Abdela suddenly said to Olive as she negotiated her bicycle through the front door. 'Your face looks really familiar.'

Olive saw the hideous photofit enlarged to poster size.

'No. It can't – I mean, it could, I own a shop, you might have seen me there. *Ideas . . .*'

'Of course! That's where I got these earrings. Unbelievable! I love your shop, I'm always browsing round it!'

She shook the great silver manacles in her ears delightedly.

'Of course,' said Olive, 'I've been trying to place you.'

Later that evening William saw Jermaine again. He was on the television screen, on *Newsroom South-East*, in the arms of his mother Nicola. Looking over the top of his head, she was saying, 'I don't bear her any grudge. Maybe she's a mother who lost her own baby, or who can't have children. I feel sorry for her, she must be a sick lady. I think she needs help.'

Jermaine's father, Junior Kincaid, was holding by its arms a huge blue teddy bear, making it somersault through the air. He said: 'She's not a sick lady, she's a monster. I don't think she needs help, I think she needs to be locked up for a long time so no other parents have to go through what we went through.'

William heard the phone ping. Olive was ringing somebody.

10

At home in Temperance Terrace, Terry Turner's telephone rang. He had an intuition that it was Olive, something in its tone, and did not pick it up. Temperance Terrace is in a quiet, almost rural road behind Norwood High Street, a row of brick cottages built in 1891 by a forgotten philanthropist who lies in Norwood Cemetery with a holly tree like a deranged dryad dancing on his broken tomb. Two or three of the houses, including Terry's, retain their terracotta beading and the egg-and-dart mouldings above their front doors. Several have been pebbledashed and furnished with blank aluminium-framed windows and frosted-glass sliding outer doors which open onto the street, where silver-haired men in beige windcheaters and trousers walk to and from the shops several times a day. Their narrow gardens are bright pictures of begonias, alyssum, lobelias and salvias. Some front borders feature a row of unusually tall love-lies-bleeding, with leaves like elephants' ears and flowers which trail over the low walls and bleed and bleed in long soft dark red fountains on the pavement. Terry's had a pale montana which grew up to the windowsill of his flat.

Terry had come to London several years earlier from the Sub

Rosa caravan park in Redhill, where his parents still lived in a mobile home, via the University of Southampton, where he had gained a 2-2 in English. Terry Turner was something of a pioneer in having a telephone. Until he came along nobody in his family had possessed one, or driven a car, booked theatre tickets or a restaurant, eaten, drunk or done any of the things that Terry had learned to take for granted. He had shared a room in Brixton at first, in the days when he looked as though he had forgotten to remove the coat hanger from the jacket of his Oxfam suit. His first novel *Wraith Rovers*, a tale of a ghostly football team, set in a deserted village, and written at the time of the miners' strike, had attracted some attention. He followed that with a collection of stories, *The Meat Rack*, whose title story told of the short, summarily ended career of a rent boy at Piccadilly Circus. Then he was offered some reviewing. He had also written screenplays for television and a script for a film which had never been made. Slightly less gaunt now, his adam's apple not quite so painfully prominent, he had moved into the upper half of number two Temperance Terrace one winter morning, cleared out the backlog of mail-order catalogues addressed to his predecessor Mrs Joyce Jauncey, and taken possession of the floral umbrella she had left behind.

After the friend who had helped him move had driven the hired van away and Terry had arranged his possessions, he had looked out of the window and seen that it was snowing. As a meteorological phenomenon this was in no way remarkable, especially on a December morning, but what gave this scattering of white flakes its strangeness was the absence of anybody to whom he could remark, 'It's snowing!' The first fall of the year was entitled to an exclamation mark, in tribute to its pristine state, before it became a commonplace grey nuisance. There should be a flurry of activity; sheep brought down from the hills, logs stacked in sheds, horses shod in winter shoes, chains wrapped round wheels, tennis racquets strapped to feet as makeshift snowshoes, the runners of sledges oiled, all in a cold crackle of excitement; whereas he was standing at the window of a suburban street watching his neighbours, she in her green coat and he in his beige jacket zipped against the wind and an acrylic Russian hat, making their morning trip with their shopping bags, sharing the weather.

He had recently got rid of his car, a game little Citroen, mostly rust, which had doubtless been recycled into a baked bean tin as there was so little metal left on its chassis. Its demise heralded the ending of an affair. Terry had realised the deadly implications of possessing wheels when involved with a single mother with children and pets. Never again. Life had been interrupted by tedious and time-consuming trips to hospital casualty departments and visits to the vet. After he had pocketed the ten pounds the car had raised he had been assaulted by an incoherent phonecall from his girlfriend, from which he gathered that she had travelled back from the vet's in a minicab with a dead dog on her lap while the driver's radio blared out 'Don't worry, be happy', despite her tearful pleas for it to be turned off. Then she had spent hours digging a grave with a trowel until her hands were blistered and bleeding, while her sobbing daughter held a torch.

'At least he wasn't playing Old Shep,' Terry had remarked.

He hadn't heard from her again. Not long afterwards, he had met Olive Schwarz at a book launch. He had thought at once that she must be some distinguished writer, visiting from abroad perhaps, with her olive skin, simple expensive haircut, loose tunic and trousers of silky burnt orange and cinnamon, and heavy jewellery of jumbled silver, glass and amber. He had felt tricked when she revealed that she was merely an old friend of the author, and he had been edging towards a more interesting circle of people when it had struck him that he was in with a chance.

'I thought *The Meat Rack* was wonderful,' she said. 'Devastating. That poor boy ...'

Terry, to whom rent boys, now that he had written about them, were of as much interest as a box that had held a take-away pizza, assumed a concerned look and attempted to divert her with a Marlboro Light from a crumpled soft pack: 'Or are you one of those bores who's given up?'

She was, but took one and, encouraged, continued, 'It makes one's blood run cold to realise just what can go on in children's homes, and the terrible risks those runaways face in London, not to mention ...'

'I like to think *Meat Rack*'s done its bit to make people more aware ...' Terry interrupted before she could mention anything more. He tapped her glass: 'What are you drinking? White?'

'Oh, just mineral water, thank you. I'm driving.'

'Oh, are you? Where to?'

'South. Near Herne Hill.'

Later, Olive would think that if she had said Hampstead, or Barnet or anywhere north of the river their acquaintance would have ended then. As it was she drove Terry home, and stayed the night. They had been shy with each other, a bit clumsy and apologetic. Olive pretended not to notice the small cigarette burn on her shoulder.

'What's this?' he said, kissing it when he discovered it. 'Birthmark?'

'Ouch, don't. Actually, you burned me with your cigarette. It doesn't matter.'

He got out of bed and came back with the bottle of wine they had opened earlier. He took a drink, and passing it from his mouth to hers, choked and sprayed it all over her. That seemed to break the ice.

A year later it had happened. The only wonder was that it had taken so long to happen. Terry and Olive had been sitting side by side watching television and eating corn chips with a taco dip when he had become aware of a cracking in his ears. The sound of crunched crisps was the sound of falling out of love. Terry willed himself not to hear it but the fragmented bluish shards filled his head like the noise of an army of locusts chomping through a brittle harvest. Terry knew the pattern; now that he had become aware of her eating, nothing would escape his notice: her laugh would grate, her endearments annoy, her voice on the telephone irritate him into cruelty which would baffle and devastate. He must bulldoze the foundations of the future they had planned before the walls grew any higher.

He decided that the kindest way would be to tell her that he was engaged on work of such intricacy and intensity that it was necessary for him to renounce the world for a while, to become a sort of hermit, hermetically sealed from the distractions of life. Her reaction was not what he had hoped. He was affronted by the value she placed on his work, she who had hitherto accorded it an importance and worth that even he had occasionally thought a little exaggerated. Now she was claiming equal status with literature and pressing for parity with it. Having failed in that bid, she began bargaining.

'Even hermits must eat,' she wheedled. Terry pictured himself lowering a basket from his window and pulling it up filled with goodies daintily arranged by Olive.

'I'll come round in the evenings to cook, then you'll still have all day to yourself,' she said.

'That wouldn't work. It would be just the same as now except that we'd be trapped here every night.'

'Trapped?'

'I didn't mean trapped exactly – just that I need to be entirely alone for a while.'

'All work and no play makes Terry a dull boy.'

'You understand nothing, do you?' Terry shouted. 'My work is my play. I thought you realised that. This is my life we're talking about here.'

'And mine.'

His silence denounced her presumption in equating the life of a retailer of knick-knacks with that of an artist. He took a cigarette from the pack on the table and a song came to him. He sang it under his breath. 'I saw the Marlboro lights, They only told me we were parting – those same old Marlboro lights that once brought you to me . . . '

'Well, I'm glad you're so cheerful at the prospect of not seeing me. Sitting there humming!'

Olive swept the bowls of chips and taco sauce to the floor and slammed out of the flat leaving the tulips she had brought quivering in their vase.

Terry felt a rush of adrenalin at her exit. He stepped over the mess to his typewriter and reeled in a sheet of paper, convinced by his own performance. Ten minutes later he switched on the radio, drifted over to the window and leaned out over the clematis sprawling on the sill. 'You won't be seeing rainbows any more,' Roy Orbison sang. Behind him the paper on his typewriter read: 'A4 Bond the quick brown fox Marlboro Marlborough Olive Oyl oleaginous oleander' – a not untypical day's work. Terry went to the kitchen and returned with a plastic spray to squirt water on the dusty leaves and rather drab mauve flowers of the montana, which had been planted by his predecessor in the strip of garden. The couple downstairs never watered it or cut it back but still the plant flourished.

'Keeping her memory green.' A neighbour's voice startled him.

'I never knew her.'

As he closed the window he thought that, in a way, he did know Mrs Joyce Jauncey rather well. He had built up a picture of her from the junk mail and shrink-wrapped catalogues addressed to her which formed the bulk of the mail that came through the letterbox of number two. The downstairs people extracted their own post and left Terry's and Mrs J's on the mat. Sometimes, as he read the catalogues, it seemed as if Mrs J was there at the kitchen table opposite him easing her feet out of her Light 'n' Lovely beige slingbacks and snuggling them into her ever-popular softee slippers, blue or beige floral with foam-lined upper and a braid trim, before shuffling over to administer a dose of Baby Bio to the relic of her final Christmas in Temperance Terrace; the last faded pink bracts had fallen and two green leaves flapped from the scarred bony stalk of an abandoned poinsettia, like the wings of a parrot which has plucked out all its feathers in a pet shop. Terry felt that if he were to turn and look at the wall behind his chair the Egon Schiele print would have dissolved and restructured itself into the hanging display cabinet which housed her collection of ceramic thimbles and miniature historic houses, each hand-painted and hand-crafted. He had come upon the leaflet describing this set, one of a limited edition of 5,000, crafted for the connoisseur, on the floor of the built-in cupboard with amazing expandable hanging rail and clear plastic shoe-caddy containing one odour-eater. The last of the series, J. R. R. Tolkien's house, absolutely free, had arrived after Mrs Joyce Jauncey's departure and the tiny work of art stood appreciating in value on top of Terry's bathroom cistern. Terry was often on the point of putting the poinsettia out of its misery, but vague hopes of fresh leaves and the intention of presenting it to his mother at Christmas prevailed.

He went into the kitchen where a bouquet of asparagus brought by Olive lay on the draining board, still in its white paper.

'It was all over Brewer Street, I couldn't resist,' she had said, conjuring up a street of green stalls heaped exclusively with pale green stalks and rows of asparagus growing through the cobbles among the squashed fruit and sloughed skins. He had seen some himself in Brixton market beside a card on a metal spike, which read, 'Grass £1.50', and had rejected it as too expensive. As he cut the string from Olive's bundle he heard a woman's voice remark, 'Corst, they used to call it sparrow grass in the olden days.'

Shaken, he decided against sharing an aphrodisiac delicacy with the ghost of Joyce Jauncey and opted for a Menu Master boil-in-the-bag vegetable curry, with added extra garlic as a precaution against the supernatural.

After Olive's departure he kept his answerphone switched on night and day. He did not return the calls, pleading, angry, once drunk with restaurant noises in the background, which she left on his machine. Then, after a few days, the calls stopped and, emboldened, he gave a dinner party for four, a squash in his small room. Although it cost him dear in Marks and Spencer and he was astounded by the time and energy expended on a fairly simple meal, Olive did not fly in like a vengeful harpy to wreck it, nor did Mrs J put in an appearance, even when somebody knocked J. R. R. Tolkien's house into the loo. Terry, despite the failure to materialise of a plot for his novel, knew he had made the right decision about his life.

The tulips were flinging themselves into ever more extravagant attitudes, snaking out of the tall glass vase, performing wild colours as if inventing bizarre and hectic hues might seduce time into extending their stay or deceive it into allowing them to scatter their seeds. At last they could hold on no longer and the petals fell to the table, denuding vulnerable pale green heads circled by sooty stamens. Terry felt that it would be sacrilegious to crumple the fallen petals into the bin on top of the orange-smeared, cigarette-end-filled dishes of a take-away. He scooped them up and carried them, glossy and slightly greasy, to the window and flung them out. Olive, standing below, her hand hovering towards the door bell, received a flock of petals in her upturned face and dashed at them with her hands, thinking herself under attack from red and yellow birds.

'Olive! What are you doing here? Why aren't you in the shop?'

His face showed not a flicker of surprised pleasure.

'It's Wednesday. I just . . .'

'I'm working. I can't be disturbed. I told you.'

'I know. I just thought . . . look, I'm sorry about that stuff on the carpet, I hope it didn't stain . . . '

'Olive, you're not being fair. I told you I had to be a hermit. It's not out of choice. I've just got to bury myself in my work, for as long as it takes.'

'I won't stay. Just let me come up for a minute. *Please*, Terry. I do understand, I promise . . . I *know* how important your work is.'

Terry started to pull down the window. Two neighbours in matching polo shirts were approaching. Olive put a basket on the step and turned away and began to walk.

'Olive!'

Terry was leaning out. 'I'll call you. We'll do lunch.'

As the neighbours passed the woman with tears running down her face one turned to the other and said, 'I'll call you, Bill. We'll *do* lunch. The yuppies have landed.'

Terry would have heard that with mixed feelings: he was an avid reader of style magazines who, when it suited him, would stand at literary parties with a can of beer in his hand glowering working-class scorn from beneath his dark lock of hair. He was the only child of a school caretaker and a hospital cleaner who wrapped him, literally, in cotton wool, for he was a premature and sickly infant who eventually thrived on his coddling. His parents were elderly, so much so that when Terry graduated they were put on the spot, having to choose between that ceremony and the Darby and Joan outing. To his enormous relief they opted for the coach trip to Polesden Lacey. They would have been unaware of the graduation had not the blabbermouth mother of one of Terry's former schoolfriends let it slip in Safeway's. The old couple had stood bemused with their basket at the checkout behind her exotic trolley while she contemplated offering them a lift to Southampton, and decided it was unthinkable. Then a fragment of old film, of girls' dresses like white peonies and black silken tasselled mortarboards flickered in his mother's memory; the ghost of Gordon Macrae materialised in Eastmancolor at the side of Shirley Jones at their daughter's graduation in *Carousel*, to the strains of 'You'll Never Walk Alone'. Mrs Turner felt tears prickle her eyes as if she had missed out on something, while her husband packed the tinned Irish stew, lard, and pink-and-white biscuits into the shopping bag. Terry had sent them a photograph of himself in cap and gown which took pride of place on top of the television, next to the glass lighthouse filled with layers of different-coloured sand he had brought back from a school trip to the Isle of Wight. One wall was a collage of postcards, views of abroad, and school photographs.

Returning from his visits to Sub Rosa, Terry felt sick with anxiety for the future. What would happen when one of them popped his or her clogs and the other was unable to cope? He had visions of the crimplene twilight of a geriatric day room where ancient babies lolled and writhed and fretted in high chairs with trays attached and no coloured beads or toys to play with, while children's television blasted away in a corner. He had seen such a place on his visit to an uncle who had served a five-year sentence there. The kindest thing he could hope for was some calor-gas disaster which would despatch them both instantaneously, or a leakage which would lull them into a sleep from which they would not waken. Poignantly enough, there was a pair of painted clogs, he remembered, hung by the front door, which he had brought back from Amsterdam with a small salami-like bottle of Genever gin which had never been opened. He had no idea of what a mobile home, if undemolished by gas, would fetch on the market.

Terry was not dissatisfied with the progress of his career; of course he wanted more fame and more money, but these would come. After the publication of his first novel, literary societies and organisers of small festivals had begun to invite him to read, and kept him waiting in provincial hotel lounges among stipples of egg and shreds of cress on the nightmarish orange-and-brown swirls of carpets which did nothing to quell his nausea. He had drunk warm water from aluminium beakers in school dining halls with embittered English masters, smiling modestly at the other teachers' declarations that they had read nothing that he had written; he had almost apologised for having had the temerity to pick up a pen at all. It was as if his efforts, scrawled over with red ink, had been scraped into the waste bucket with the scornful plastic spatula of the dinner lady, who mistook him for a particularly gormless new boy. He had sat in front of semicircles of chairs, against a background of the books of Booker winners and contenders, in branch libraries which had forgotten to put up the poster advertising his appearance. There he had read to those mutinous members of the library staff who had been captured before the door had been locked, and one or two defaulters who had arrived just before closing time in the vain hope of sneaking their books undetected back on the shelves. He had consoled himself with the story of the eminent biographer who had once delivered a two-hour lecture to an entirely empty hall. Once he had attempted a feeble joke in response to a question from the audience: 'I have been searching in vain for many years for the magic formula. I would be fascinated to know how a young chap like yourself went about getting his stuff in print.'

'I slept with my publisher.'

In a corner of Surrey he would always be known as a homosexualist.

He had played these theatres of the absurd for a nominal fee, or none, and as often as not his hosts had forgotten to reimburse his travelling expenses and he had been too proud or too shy to remind them. The shoulders of his jacket hung ever more hollowly. More than once he had had to hitch home; he had been stopped by the police and had spent several hours in the cells before a call to Myles, his agent, persuaded them that he was not in possession of stolen books in Norwood High Street at 3.45 a.m.

To those who could cope with someone much thinner than themselves, his air of poetic poverty increased his attraction; his clothes, though second-hand, were stylish and picked out with care from charity shops. He learned how to say no to those invitations which would have diminished him emotionally and financially, and with his slightly increased affluence his face lost a little of its poignancy. It had still been hollow when he first met Olive, and his clean, lank black hair had flopped over his brow and had to be pushed back constantly with an impatient or weary hand. There was no doubt that he was photogenic.

A few days after Olive's visit Terry found himself on an Intercity train heading westwards to his first stint of teaching creative writing, co-tutor with the formidable novelist Una Ogilvie, once a notorious beauty, whose books he had never read. Terry's chief reason, the fee apart, for accepting the invitation to replace the scheduled writer on the course, Declan O'Donohue, a dissolutely glamorous figure, was that Olive would have no idea where he was and so would not be able to get at him with telephone calls which blighted his day. He had told nobody apart from his agent where he was going. He had left no special message on his answerphone, partly so as not to alert potential burglars, and also in the hope that Olive would assume that he had gone abroad for some time. Now he was debating the wisdom of his acceptance as Una Ogilvie's head swayed onto his shoulder in the taxi which had met him and Una at the station. Una had travelled First Class. It came to him that Ogilvie was Olive with a G.I. He would have been even more alarmed had he overheard the conversation which had taken place that morning between the two resident organisers of Amberley Hall: 'It's not Terry Turner I'm worried about, although he's a disappointment of course, but I believe he's quite professional. Una Ogilvie scares the life out of me. You know she's just been barred from the Poetry Society . . .'

Through the rear window of the taxi, which was in fact a tenderly cherished aquamarine 1969 Corsair, Terry saw a little group of people with holdalls and rucksacks staring after them. A large woman ran a few steps, waving her arms, then faltered into defeat.

'I sussed them out at once, on the train, as our students,' Una observed. 'We'll be seeing enough of them during the week, without having to conduct workshops in the bloody taxi . . .'

She poured a Bloody Mary into the cup of her thermos flask, holding it between practised knees.

'Workshops?' bleated Terry.

'Oh yes.'

She was grinding black pepper from a large wooden pepper-mill onto her drink. Terry had a vision of himself in a carpenter's apron, standing among curls of planed wood.

'What exactly *are* workshops?' he asked through a mouthful of nails. She handed him the drink and proceeded to pour one for herself.

'Oh, you know . . .' she said vaguely . 'Chin chin.'

'Cheers.'

Terry recalled the shame of being the only boy in his class to fail woodwork: what crucifixion had he set up for himself, he wondered, drinking deeply of the cup. A fine drift of pepper made him sneeze a red spray onto his white knee. Una scrubbed at it with a purple tissue, adding a mauve smear. His fear, suppressed on the train, that he might be expected to sleep with her, resurfaced.

With her floppy black hat wreathed with poppies, the sooty stamens of her eyelashes, the crushed red silk of her wideskirted dress, she reminded him of the Poppy Fairy in a church hall pantomime. The glamour of the production, his first love flitting across the stage to declaim 'My gift is the gift of joy. Fairy friends, fairy friends, here am I, scattering joy to you,' came back to him. In place of a wand with a silver-paper star and the giant dried poppy seedhead, from which the fairy had scattered joy, Una had a black parasol with silk tassels, a little ravelled, and her peppermill. Beneath the hat she was white and delicately veined blue, fragile as an egg or a baby bird.

'Look!'

She gripped his knee with a surprisingly robust claw and pointed through the window at two figures standing knee-deep in daisies on the opposite side of the narrow lane. As she spoke, one of them was dropping a disconsolate thumb in the exhaust of a passing tractor.

'Isn't that Hope McCrow and Sean Desmond? Who were teaching the course before ours? God, they look a mess. What can have happened to them?'

'Workshops,' said Terry. Had those ragamuffins been their predecessors, two scarecrows who had uprooted themselves from the field, or just a pair of locals attempting flight?

'"A foolish thought to say a sorry sight."'

Una gripped his knee again.

'Terry, we're in this together, right? Us against them. We must stick together, OK? A united front, what say you? The two of us. And you of course,' she added graciously to the driver, who had turned to stare, almost putting them in the ditch. 'I can see you're One of Us. To the three of us!'

She raised her cup in a toast. Terry responded with a plastic clink.

'Have a drink.' She poured a refill, peppered it and passed it to the driver, who took a hand off the wheel to receive it.

'The Three Musketeers!' he said, winking at Terry, who leaned forward to touch his cup with his as the car lurched onwards; then Una responded with the thermos, and they bowled along towards Amberley with the spirit of goodwill overlying the sickness of fear.

'I trust you are well supplied, Terry dear.'

'Well, no, actually. I didn't think . . .'

He realised now why her suitcase, which of course he had carried, had been so heavy. He had assumed that it contained books and had panicked at the thought of the Ed McBain in his own bag.

'I know a little place where you can stock up,' the driver volunteered. 'Many of the tutors find it very handy. The panic usually gets to them hereabouts.'

'Excellent,' said Una. 'Take us thither, Porthos.'

'Which one am I?' Terry asked. Needless to say, she had bagged Aramis, or was it d'Artagnan. Surely that made four?

The driver pulled over into the hedge to allow a bus, which had been gaining on them steadily, to overtake. Several faces slewed round to gaze at them.

'Those will be your students, I reckon,' said Porthos with what Terry, in so far as he was capable of analysis, decided was malignant satisfaction. 'Nemmind, we'll overtake them later on.'

'Good,' said Terry firmly. 'I think it's important that we be there to greet them, don't you, Una?'

'Oh God,' she replied, 'I can't remember the title of a single bloody book I've ever read. Quick, tell me some writers! Tell me the titles of my books!'

Porthos broke the embarrassing silence.

'Pheasant! There, in the hedge. Did you see him? What a beauty. Pity I missed him; nemmind, the wife's got a couple in the freezer. You'll see a lot of wildlife in these parts. Henry James. How about him?'

'Good man. Phew, thank you, excellent. You don't happen to remember any titles, do you, or the plots of any of his books, I suppose? Or any of mine by any chance?'

She dredged a notebook and pen from her enormous black leather sack.

'Nobody's going to test us on Henry James,' Terry said with more conviction than he felt, aware of a yawning chasm where his knowledge of Henry James, indeed of all English and foreign literature, should have been.

'You never know. Who else is there?'

'Prowst,' said Porthos. 'He rates quite high in my own personal canon.'

'Don't know him. Should I? What did he write?' Una's pen was poised.

'*À la recherche du temps perdu.*'

'Oh, that Prowst. Well, nobody can reasonably expect us to have more than a passing acquaintance with *his* plots.'

'Either of you interested in history?' asked Porthos. 'I only ask because . . . '

His hand hovered towards the glove compartment as Terry made the mistake of nodding into the driver's mirror.

' . . . I happen to be working on a historical verse-drama set in the reign of the Merry Monarch. You might be interested in having a look at it.'

A heavy bundle of typescript, held together with a rubber band, landed painfully in Terry's lap. Through tear-filled eyes, he noted that it was typed on both sides of the paper. He tried to slide it onto Una's knee, but she wasn't having any.

'In conception, it's a kind of mixed-media offering, if you like,' Porthos was explaining as they fought silently behind him in a grim game of pass the parcel. He pulled into the courtyard of a small pub with a sign depicting a hare about to be torn apart by a pack of hounds.

'You'll find there's quite a bit of madrigal dotted about, and the comic relief is provided by a troupe of licentious Morris Men who form a sort of *leitmotif* . . . '

If there was one moment when Terry regretted bitterly his

decision to break with Olive, it was when he half-fell from the car, clutching that manuscript, onto the cobbles and chickweed of the forecourt of the Hare and Hounds set among inescapable fields, and watched Una pour the last drops of Bloody Mary down her throat, in preparation for having her flask refilled.

'All For One and One For All!'

She barged through the door into a startled saloon.

'Amberley Hall, I presume?' asked the landlord, of the taxi driver.

'Amberley Hall, Ted. You have surmised rightly, good mine host.'

'We are two very ill, travel-worn people,' Una explained as she tottered into the great dining room of Amberley Hall on Terry's arm. 'So you must all be very kind to us.'

A sense of mutiny recently quelled emanated from the faces down either side of the refectory table. Someone started a derisory slow handclap.

'A troublemaker,' hissed Una. 'We'll have to keep an eye on him! There's always one rotten apple,' she added loud enough for all to hear. Spoons of sandy crumble were suspended between bowls and mouths. Two plates of ratatouille congealed at a smaller table which had been set across the head of the long one. The company was halfway through its pudding. Sweeping the assembly with a radiant, unfocused smile, Una poured custard from a gravy boat over her stew, and added a generous dollop to Terry's.

'Well, this is very nice,' she said brightly, shooting out a hand which closed like a Venus Flytrap on the bottle of wine that a tactful hand was in the process of removing. Terry saw that it was the frosty mitt of Sandy, one half of the residential staff.

'Who's the Merry Monarch?' he asked Una.

'Bluff King Hal,' she replied. 'Or was it Good Queen Bess?'

Terry realised that, although Una was drunker than he was, she was in the more fortunate position of having been first choice as a tutor, whereas he was a feeble substitute for the man in whom these people had invested not only good money but their literary aspirations. He thought that he heard a female voice remark that designer stubble was *passé*, and ran a hand over his chin, feeling it grow bluer under his fingers. He was a man who needed to shave twice daily, but there had been time for nothing but dumping in their horribly adjacent rooms in the converted pigsty their bags, Porthos's typescript, and a sheaf of poems from Ted the landlord of the Hare and Hounds. He had grabbed a last terrified slurp before their tightlipped hosts, Tom and Sandy, escorted them to the dining room, explaining on the way that the course was under par, as two students had asked for their money back on hearing of the defection of Declan O'Donohue.

'I was a bit puzzled by some of the symbolism in your latest book, Una,' the man on her left was saying, chummily, seeking to establish himself as an ally by refilling her glass.

'I'm aware that you students take turns with the catering,' she replied, 'and I should be extremely grateful if you would be so kind as to spread the word among your fellow cooks that in my personal canon the lentil and the chickpea have no place.'

'Oh. Absolutely. Er ... you remember the passage, page twenty-seven, if my memory serves me right, where Hugo and Atalanta, and I hope you won't mind me saying this, I'm not sure that their relationship entirely works in the context of the novel, where they present the peacocks to Gillvray, and it's obviously meant as some sort of votive, ceremonial . . .'

'Or celery, for any other purpose than stirring Worcester sauce into a glass of vodka and tomato juice. Fennel, yes, indeed, but celery, raw, braised, or otherwise, is a definite no-no. Or anything which has been within a furlong of a sesame seed. I am horribly allergic to sesame and suffer the most dramatic reaction to it.'

Terry became aware of a voice, like a mouse at his elbow, squeaking something about 'primary sources'. A question mark hung at the tail end of her words. Terry looked deep into the sauce boat for salvation.

'Well . . .'

At that moment his plate was removed by Tom, his moist mouth clamped in disapproval in the thicket of his beard, and replaced with a bowl of cold crumble.

'I'm afraid there doesn't appear to be any custard left,' he said pointedly. Terry, grinning weakly, noticed the unpleasant way Tom's hair was disposed under his chin and down his neck. He turned to his questioner on primary sources, in an attempt to be seen conducting a serious literary conversation, but her courage had scampered away. He was never to hear her utter again.

'Jolly decent of you, Terry, to step in at such short notice,' a man leaned across her to say, 'especially to fill in for Dec O'Donohue. A hard act to follow, as they say in showbiz. I'm looking forward to your reading tonight, whatever anyone else might say . . .' Terry's ratatouille lurched up his throat, and he had to gag himself with his handkerchief.

'I must say,' the speaker lowered his voice and jerked his head towards Una, 'the old girl seems in good form. Mungo, by the way. A pedagogue, for my sins, which fact will not be too evident, I trust, in the novels I've brought along for you to pull to pieces. I'll drop them into your room later, so you can have a go at them before we meet tomorrow.'

Terry grasped weakly the hand which the pedagogue was extending dangerously close to the mouselike girl's nose.

'Mungo,' he said. 'Good to meet you.'

After dinner the company adjourned to the large barn where Una and Terry were to give their reading. Una was a heavy weight on Terry's arm. He was carrying her books, seven of them, as well as his own, as her free hand was burdened with a bottle of *Arc De Triomphe Rouge* and a corkscrew.

'I did explain about the kitty, for the wine, didn't I?' Sandy asked again.

'Good idea,' said Una. 'Perhaps we can do a bit better than this tomorrow ... a trifle less *ordinaire* ... '

Terry paused dramatically at the barn door, causing a small pile-up.

'I know!' he cried, 'Why don't we put on the show right here in this barn?' and fell flat on his back, pulling Una down with him. Through the engulfing darkness he heard Mungo chuckle; he expected writers to behave badly, and he was getting his money's worth.

Terry woke, very seasick and fully dressed, to the knowledge that he had somehow behaved appallingly. A sailor was standing by his bunk with a mug of coffee.

'Drink this,' the sailor said, revealing himself as Una in

a matelot T-shirt and sparkling white trousers. Her hair was caught back in a jaunty ribbon.

'Come on, drink it. You'll feel better. I've brought the list of the students you're seeing individually today. I've seen my first five, and the bugger of it is, Terry, some of them are bloody good.'

'What's the time?'

'Gone ten. Come on, drink up.'

She looked unbelievably trim and shipshape, pulling back his curtain which somebody must have drawn at some stage, with an agonising rasp, like a giant Elastoplast being ripped from his skin.

'Go and dance your hornpipe somewhere else, Una, go away, please, and stop looking so bloody professional . . .'

'But that's what we are, Terry,' she said, as if the previous day had been a dream. 'Professionals. We've got a job of work to do, and we owe it to everybody, the students, Tom and Sandy, and not least ourselves, to do that job to the best of our ability.'

Shamed, Terry took a gulp of the black coffee. Too late he realised what he might have known, that Una had added a hair of the dog.

As the week progressed, or passed in blocks of knowing and unknowing with Tom and Sandy's faces ever more distant, coldly disapproving lamps flickering at the edge of his darkness, his insides began to feel as though they had been scoured with Ajax and Brillo pads so that only regular lubrication with alcohol assuaged the pain, soothed the nausea and removed the impression of a cart-horse's iron shoe from the back of his head. Terry now conceived of Una as a praying mantis preserved in formaldehyde. More than once he had woken fully dressed on her bed with the brittle insect in his arms, and when he staggered into the kitchen messy with other people's breakfasts he thought that the students fell silent. By Thursday only Mungo turned up for his informal seminar in the pub. That was the evening that the guest reader was expected. This shy person in an ethnic dress with little brass bells on drawstrings at neck and waist was quite overwhelmed at the welcome she received and was at once convinced that she had been invited by mistake. Before supper she had been accosted and taken aside by six different people who poured out their grievances to her. Three of them had begged for a lift home with her in the morning.

'Terry, Sandy and I need to have a talk with you.'

'Not now, Tom. I've got a stack of manuscripts waiting for me and I must do a bit of reading before supper.'

Terry broke away and ran in a shambling gait through knee-deep wet grass to his quarters, startling white-faced bullocks into stampede. His desperate intention, apart from escape, was to sort out the avalanche of paper, including Porthos's mixed-media offering which had slid from his desk and lay on the floor, hopelessly muddled and sullied with muddy footprints. He was in tears when the supper gong sounded. Each new leaf he turned over seemed ringed by a wine glass or unnumbered or upside down. Vowing to stay up all that night to make sense of it, he went to take a quick shower before supper. He woke naked and bemused standing in a flood with cold water trickling onto his head.

Una's tribute to professionalism was a diaphanous white dress over layers of white petticoat, a white velvet snood and long, yellowed-white shoes on her narrow feet. She wore one elbow-length buttoned kid glove, and carried the other, taking her place at the refectory table.

> "'And like a dying lady, lean and pale,
>   Who totters forth, wrapp'd in a gauzy veil,
>   Out of her chamber, led by the insane
>   And feeble wanderings of her fading brain ...'"

Mungo said softly.

'What was that?' Una turned on him.

'I was remarking on the moon. Shelley.'

'Oh. Well, hail to *thee*, blithe spirit!'

Una lifted her glass to him.

'How very refreshing to encounter somebody literate in this philistine age in this God-forsaken spot. I can see you and I are going to be friends. Tell me all about yourself. Where are we, by the way?'

Mungo, who had spent with her hours of intimate revelation of his disappointments, marital difficulties, and hopes, had bent his head with hers in close analysis of his text, and two of whose novels, bedizened with spilled face-powder, lay on her dressing table awaiting her verdict, fell to silent contemplation of a moth which had dissolved in a wine glass into grey powder and disembodied wings floating on a ruby circle.

Terry was pretending to eat, forcing fragments of food into the tide of wine which threatened to burst through his head. He saw that a woman whom he had passed earlier at the payphone was crying and being comforted by the man on her left.

'What's up with her?' he asked his neighbour, whom he

thought he recognised as Jan, who taught children with special needs.

'She misses her kids. It's the first time she's been away from them. Beth invested a lot in this course, and I don't just mean money.'

Terry felt under attack.

'Blame Declan O'Donohue, blame it on the bossa nova, blame all your charms that melt in my arms but don't blame me.'

'I'm glad it's such a big joke to you, Terry. You can just take the money and run, leaving a lot of broken dreams behind you. This was Beth's first chance to do anything for herself, she's got four kids and ...'

'Oh well,' said Terry. 'You know what Cyril Connolly said about the pram in the hall.'

'That's a problem you'll never have to face, I'm sure. You're far too selfish.'

Their plates were removed by somebody on kitchen duty.

'And that's another thing, folk here have bent over backwards to create nice meals; they take it seriously as part of a sharing experience – what this week's supposed to be all about, and you don't bother to hide your contempt for their efforts.'

'I'm not well. I'm ill. Very ill, but I'm doing my best not to let people down regardless of how I feel.'

Jan snorted. 'You've got a bad case of alcoholic poisoning. Just look at yourself!'

She held up a spoon as a looking-glass. Terry pushed it away. He clenched his fists to prevent them seizing her do-gooder's grey helmet of hair and grinding her face into the peach cobbler which had been placed in front of her.

'It's Una's fault. I came here in good faith.'

'"The woman whom thou gavest to be with me, she gave me of the tree, and I did eat,"' Jan mocked. 'No, I'm sorry, Terry, that won't wash.'

Terry disengaged a pastry circle from his pudding, staring into his plate as if the fibrous peaches were the fruit of the knowledge of good and evil. A buzz of conversation and the clatter of cutlery went on down the long table.

'I thought the purpose of a kitty was that everybody put the same amount in and took the same amount out, as it were,' someone was saying. At any moment knives and forks would whizz like apache arrows round his head. A peach like a poached egg or a raw scallop swam into his spoon.

'For goodness' sake, eat it. It might do you good.'

Down the table the guest reader, in training for the evening's bout, sipped mineral water, wreathed in cheerful talk and laughter.

'The great British public clasps the mediocre to its middle-brow heart,' thought Terry. The underside of his pastry was putting out soggy fronds like a culture grown in a laboratory jar.

'Your enmity and spite will get you nowhere.'

He stared at Jan, unfocused, not realising he had spoken his thoughts. There was nothing welcoming or motherly about that large grey sweatshirted bosom.

'If you want to drink yourself to death, that's your problem. If you want to play the tormented genius, fine. Only, do it in your own time and don't think you have the right to destroy others in the process. Frankly, Terry, you're not that good a writer.'

Terry sat on with an empty space on either side of him while the table was cleared, her words clanging in his head.

He was woken violently by a snore and realised he was in the sitting room. Hostile eyes were glittering at him, and a woman was reading them a story. He sat upright in his sagging chair and concentrated on the pink-and-blue paisley patterns of her dress.

He came to again and looked round wildly, draining someone's glass. A horse had kicked him in the head again. He was at some party but he had no recollection of getting there. People were having a silly conversation about someone's Aunt Etty, who apparently always wore boots and carried an umbrella.

'She likes booze and she likes a snooze,' said a girl, 'but she never gets drunk and she never snores.'

'Yes,' replied Jan. 'She does get squiffy or even pissed, if you'll pardon the expression, on Schweppes or Schnapps, but she won't touch whisky or gin.'

'Jan's got it! Brilliant!'

Terry certainly hadn't got it. Who was this person? Was it all directed at him?

'She buys it at Woolworths or the Co-op. She refuses to go to Sainsbury's or Tesco, in fact she boycotts them,' added Mungo.

'Terry ought to get it, even if Una doesn't. So should Bill but not Sue or Miranda or Beth.'

The log fire had collapsed in embers and a charred cigarette packet. It was obviously late.

'I hate to be a party pooper,' Terry said, 'but I'd better be going. Great evening, thanks, but I've got to work in the morning. Can I ring for a minicab? No, it's OK, I'll take a chance with a black cab. I could do with some fresh air.'

Nobody moved as he lurched out, upsetting a small table with a lamp.

169

As he made it up the extraordinarily long and potholed drive it came to him that he didn't know who of that blur of faces was his host or hostess. He would send flowers tomorrow when he remembered. Yes, that would be a nice thing to do, he decided, as he swayed between the high hedgerows, trying to flag down a black cab in the empty blackness of a country lane.

Terry awoke in Dulwich. Some good Samaritan must have picked him up, and had set him down on the edge of the South Circular. There was straw in his hair. The sky had the clarity of vodka. By instinct rather than by thought he started walking down the road. Foxes and rats had raided the dustbins in the night and torn open black sacks of rubbish, so that the residents of this respectable street would emerge, groomed for work or school, to find their secrets scattered over the path and front garden or the contents of someone's bathroom waste-bin strewn across the pavement in the unforgiving early light.

The walk home seemed to go on for hours; traffic was building up into congestion. The righteous passed him slowly in clouds of diesel fumes but he could not face the throbbing of a bus or any human contact. Safely inside Temperance Terrace, he took a swig of vodka and crawled into bed. Before he fell into a coma he whimpered for his mum, but he had sent her on a Saga coach tour of James Heriott's Yorkshire.

A day or so later when he opened one sticky eye it was to catch the green eye of the answerphone flashing peremptorily. He ignored it. When he felt well enough to place one foot in front of the other, feeling strangely light-bodied with a head swollen into the sort of stone ball that decorates imposing gateways, he negotiated the kitchen. There was an inch of Aqua Libra in a bottle in the fridge, which he used to swallow four aspirin. After a painful shower he shaved himself with the tenderness of a compassionate nurse barbering a terminal patient. It was not until he had gathered up his mail from the hall and settled on the sofa with the Sunday papers that he discovered, with disbelief and horror that electrified his hair, and cast the paper from him with a curse, that something appalling had been taking place while he had been sprawling in an alcoholic nightmare. Thousands of Chinese students had been crushed by tanks and shot in Tiananmen Square, Beijing.

An ice-cream van came down the road chiming plangently on to the hot Sunday air that felt as heavy as asphalt and was almost as blue-grey. Terry felt strong enough to face a little food. Unfortunately, the obvious solution was the Chinese take-away. Terry felt he should make some gesture, but what could he say: 'Awfully sorry about Beijing, old boy'? Large fish bumped clumsily up and down a tank which was much too small. As he carried his food home, the trees inky against an aquamarine sky, the single star and thin gold wire of the new moon provoked a desire to see Olive again; to retrace the steps he took in the early days, nervously under an uncertain spring sky, and let memory, like the sudden rough scent brushed from a wet flowering currant bush, catch his throat in sharp recall of the feelings he had had then.

In imagination Terry sees himself making the journey into what was once a foreign land, a cold paper cone of flowers spattered with star-shaped drops in his hand. The rain has strewn with green confetti the pavement that blooms in the dusk like a patch of bluebells glimpsed through trees. The passionate fruits glowing in stained glass on closed front doors, fan-shaped wall lamps bathing a room in voluptuous apricot, a man in a kitchen performing some domestic task like a priest at an altar, tempt him to stop to gaze, and at the same time heighten his expectancy and quicken his steps. He passes under the cherry tree heavy with rain and lavish blossom and lifts the weighty wooden gate and walks the wet, petalled path to the front door. The bell sends an electric thrill through his finger to his heart. Olive stands there and the paper moon swinging in the hall throws a magical light on carpet, paintings, doors leading to rooms not yet entered. In the kitchen, a ragged bunch of parsley stands in a glass on the draining board, the corkscrew like a little wooden Provençal woman in wooden cap and skirt waits beside a bottle of yellow wine and green grapes. Yellow and green peppers and aubergines are piled on a plate. All these things are for him; they have been planned and chosen, the vineyards and pastures and orchards of Sainsbury's have been plundered for him. The flowers he has brought are placed in a heavy glass carafe with a green tinge. The evening can begin.

Of course that was Olive's old place that he had imagined. Life had not been so sweet once she had moved in with brother William. Nevertheless, he would like to see her soon. He wanted her now, to soothe away the horrors of Amberley Hall.

caddish cravat, bowler, brown trilby or sandy hat sporting a small feather, and sandy moustache which stroked the rim of a glass of pink gin. 'The perfect pink gin,' he instructed his children, 'is the colour of the *Financial Times*.' William had absorbed that information at an age when he could just about decipher the hyphenated syllables of the text of *Chicks' Own*, *Rainbow* and *Playbox* comics; he had never found it useful. The Pink'un, the racing paper or the *FT*, protruded from Father's frayed pocket, matching the pink rims of his eyes as well as his gin.

Sandy Mackenzie had not lived to enjoy for very long the fruits of his final successful business venture. William had inherited a wardrobe of ties, three blazers with crested pockets, a fistful of bad debts, and half the proceeds from the insurance policies which were paid on his mother's death, which followed less than a year later. From time to time William observed, in a bar or on a bus, a man who might have been his father a few steps further down the road, when the money had been frittered away and the mortgage defaulted: a shifty chap keeping up appearances, eking out the cigarette held between shaky, nicotined finger and thumb, with oiled gingery strands combed across a freckled scalp, or an ill-fitting toupee, cut too square. these occasions he was glad that Dad had got out while the going was good.

remembering Dad, William had to smile when a blind man glasses passed the window at a brisk pace, tapping white stick, carrying a tin. It was the guide dog which his suspicions, a Rottweiler in harness. Among his things William had found two dog collars, one tartan disc engraved 'Jock', the other made of celluloid

174

11

The street where William and Olive lived was planted at intervals with rowan trees. One grew from a square of grass in the pavement outside their house, a Chinese Hupeh rowan whose silver leaves turned lacquer-red in the autumn, with berries that ripened from pale green to porcelain white. William was standing at the window, his finger on the trigger of a transparent g... of emerald window cleaner, cloth in his other hand, thin... about his father, whose birthday it would have been, w... to sing 'O rowan tree' to his wife's piano accomp... Perhaps the council had planned to protect the res... witchcraft, William thought, or had chosen trees... on urban pollution; either way, the birds were... about the ornamental fruit and left the chir... until all the reds and oranges on the nei... gone.

His father Sandy had been a *flân...* tebank, a master of double bluff; n... have been assumed, would have... part, in shifty gingery suede s... well-brushed but shabby in...

and secured with a gilt paper fastener in place of a stud. Jack Mackenzie's collar studs and cufflinks had been scattered long since, like Mother's bits of jewellery and hatpins, among pawnshops all over London. Oor Jock, the wee soul, had been a curly-coated Airedale cross, with an undershot jaw which the family thought endearing, and strangers intimidating. He was a beer drinker who had his own pint mug at one hostelry – in his role as Major Anstruther, Dad's instinct led him to fumed oak, horsebrasses from Hong Kong, leaded lights and coloured lanterns, where men in blazers could stretch their legs towards the electric coals and call to mine host for 'similar, if you please, sir, and one for your good self'. The Major's dog was a favourite until he was barred for extracting pork chipolatas from the plates of traditional English Fayre prepared by the landlord's lady wife with her own fair hands. Not long afterwards, one regular confided in another that he was rather worried at the Major's absence, as he had invested a tidy sum in a scheme which the Major had assured him was copper-bottomed, and then, one by one and shamefacedly, the saloon bar crowd confessed to like involvement. Rage and incredulity were the order of the day; the traditional English Fayre congealed and sales of gin rose shakily, but the Major and Jock were long gone.

It was clever of Dad, William thought, to rise no higher than the traditionally bogus rank of major, for he had been one briefly during the war, and, that established, it gave credence to whatever followed. William had loved his father but not his calling, and his teenage rebellion took the form of working hard at school and entering the teaching profession. Olive early expressed extreme childish conformity, demanding pixie hoods, bonnets with rabbit's ears, ladybird plait grips, a miniature coronation coach, a hula hoop, peeptoe shoes, a lemon duster coat, and flinging herself about declaring that unless her wishes were granted she could never go to school again; would run away, kill herself and then they'd be sorry. Their mother would be in tears, Father stormed out of the house and William trembled, all fingers and thumbs with his Meccano or Stanley Gibbons Approvals. After a while the Approvals stopped coming and his stamp collection faltered to a halt while Olive's cheese label album flourished, augmented by matchless examples brought by Dad from Soho delicatessens and pretty triangular foreign stamps which she had appropriated, telling her rivals at school that they were cheese labels. Somehow most of the things she desired so vociferously were provided: she got the Cinderella watch in a transparent plastic slipper, while William hoped in vain for the Hopalong Cassidy version which rested on a saddle. The sight of a child in a frenzy of grief threatening suicide would have chilled the blood of harder-hearted parents than hers; and she *had* run away once, to be found eating toasted crumpets and watching *Heidi* on a friend's television, having effected entry by the scullery window knowing that the family was at its chalet on Camber Sands. Broken-hearted best friends languished in playgrounds all over the South East, left to repair their social lives after Olive's exclusive love, bewildered by her overnight disappearance; there were women, middle-aged now, who, memory triggered by a dry martini, a plastic tray of black calamatas in a deli fridge, or the whirl of two black glossy plaits around some vivacious child's head in the street, wondered briefly whatever had become of Olive Mackenzie. Then they had been little girls distinguished by their ability to draw crinoline ladies in profile, their mutations of ballet steps, or their skill at doing 'acrobats'. Vainly, Jean, Olive's mother, had pointed out that the correct word was 'acrobatics'. She was always getting things embarrassingly wrong. Jean's moral code was immutable: never say anything nasty about anybody's mother. Never run past anybody lame. Never call anybody ugly. Never laugh at anybody's clothes (a tricky one this for William and Olive – Dad: 'Come on, son, cheer up. I'll bet there's not many lads can boast that their mother knitted their Davy Crockett hats!'). Don't say 'Dan Dan the dirty old man'. ('Why not?' 'It isn't nice.') Don't link arms with a friend and chant 'Siamese twins, joined together, Siamese twins joined together' – you never know, you might pass somebody who was a Siamese twin and had lost his or her other half in an operation. Don't say Eeny Meeny Miny Mo, Catch a Nigger by his toe. Never eat a hot cross bun except on Good Friday or an Easter egg before Easter Sunday. And so on and so forth, lest the feelings of even a handkerchief or the last biscuit on a plate be hurt.

How, then, had this woman of such sensibility reconciled herself to her husband's trade? Olive and William had argued endlessly, one sometimes concluding that she was completely innocent as to the sources of his income and the other protesting that she could not possibly *not* have known and was in cahoots and collusion, a wicked hypocrite in a Presbyterian mask. What had she got out of it, then? Two children, a succession of rented rooms of varying squalor, a series of menial jobs, no social standing, no chance to make friends or make a home to which she might invite them with domestic pride, no time to plan and tend a garden and watch it grow; none of the simple pleasures of respectability a headmaster's daughter might have expected. And most painful of all was the estrangement from her family. She had enjoyed a short, heady idyll in the passenger seat of a Morris Minor when Sandy had been in the motor trade selling used cars in Warren Street, and she did have a fur coat, hardly an object of envy or censure among her neighbours, a nicotine-coloured wartime simulated model with shoulder pads, embellished with a barometer of their fortunes, a brooch of gold or silver, or glass and tin. Jean had been thin with dark fly-away hair that defied kirby-grips and turned to thistledown in her later years, whitened perhaps by years of deceit; a Scottish thistle blown into stony urban foreign ground, fearful of being cast with the tares into the everlasting bonfire. Diffident and indecisive outside the home, on her rare visits to the hairdresser she would nod at the woman sitting next to her and whisper, 'Och, I'll have whatever she's having', looking anywhere but into her own sherry-coloured eyes in the mirror facing her. She would emerge with some bizarre and expensive results. 'Mother lived at a tangent to life,' William said. 'Her perception and her morality were her own.'

'Well,' she would say, standing on a rotting wooden draining board slimy with the previous tenants' slivers of pink and green soap, fixing a sere gingham curtain on a string across yet another kitchen window, 'it has possibilities.' Snapping on a perished pair of heavy-duty rubber gloves she would declare, 'It'll be a little palace in next to no time.' And it was. Dining from exotic dented tins by the light of candles stuck to saucers on packing cases, the children were seduced, until the morning broke, into excitement at the wonderful new life in store for them all. Cosy winter afternoons of cocoa and *Children's Hour* on the wireless glowed in their memories, although the flames might be the swift flashy pyre of a table or a bookcase. 'There's nothing your mother can't do with a couple of orange boxes and a traycloth or two.'

In the days when he still cared, before his heart had been scorched, in the days of billy-cans and damp dough roasted on sticks, when he organised camping holidays for his pupils in the summer, William would enthuse on the subject of fire, the magical comfort of mankind in the darkness from time imme- morial. He remembered throwing walnut shells and orange peel and dried-out holly into the open fire on Twelfth Night and watching them burn with green and blue flames, of staring into caverns in the coal, and drying his hair until his scalp roasted, and what Olive called 'glorifying' her hair, kneeling and holding long wet strands to the blaze like an iridescent screen. Those pleasures, and the reassurance of watching your mother baking, and the freedom of fields and woods and run- ning streams were denied to most of his pupils. Lead fumes, tapwater teeming with wildlife, and burgers and microwaved chips did not compensate them for the denial of their human need to be in touch with the elements.

'Just as well,' Olive had said once. 'They'd all be little pyro- maniacs and arsonists given half the chance. Some of them are anyway.'

She thought William touched, through his trouserleg, the brand she had given him with the tongs at the age of ten, when, not realising that they were red hot, she had grasped his leg playfully. He had never quite believed her denial, that she had not known the tongs had been resting against the grate.

'We did set the mantelpiece on fire,' William pointed out.

'That was you. I was ill in bed if you remember. Anyway, it proves my point.'

'Malingering,' said William.

Nowadays the topic of fire was taboo.

When Olive had started to tell him, recently, that Crystal Palace Woolworths had burned down, she faltered.

'Isn't that the Da Souzas' new kitten on the wall?' William had changed the subject, pointing through the window towards the neighbours' garden.

'The wee soul ...' Olive unthinkingly brought it back to Mother.

'Oh, the wee soul!' Mother would cry, pausing to delay some bull-headed tom from his lustful or murderous purpose, or peeking into a pram. 'Poignant' was her accolade. 'How poignant,' she would murmur, looking at a bunch of evocative felt flowers at a Bring-and-Buy in a cold Presbyterian church hall redolent of her childhood; misty-eyed, she would pin the purple-and-yellow pansies drooping from green felt stalks to her coat. Needlebooks with clumsily pinked pages and embroidered violets, French knots, golliwogs with snipped topknots made from little skeins of wool, anything in faded raffia, a cut-steel evening purse, all qualified; poignancy was like charm, indefinable. A lavender bag might exude it, or a dolly's dress with heartbreakingly tiny smocking; while a pincushion, be it ever so lumpy and cobbled by small fingers, failed in its wiles. Being broken or ephemeral did not necessarily guarantee acceptance, nor gaudiness, as evidenced by red-and-yellow cherries on a hat or black rayon splashed with poppies, exclude. An elephant at the zoo could be as poignant as a mother-of-pearl button or a baby's tooth. After her mother's death, Olive had discovered the tooth fairy's hoard in a little pochette she had made at school. The tiniest teeth had fallen apart; hollow at the centre, they were like the halves of miniature tinned pears.

'Pochette?' her mother had queried, on Mothering Sunday.

'It's made of linen crash,' Olive explained.

'Fancy,' said Mother.

'I could've made a handkerchief sachet, only I thought a pochette would be more poignant, and you've only got one handkerchief.'

It was some years after the demise of Jock, the beer drinker in the tartan collar, that Mother was forced to call in the vet to his successor, a saintly cat whose ninth life was ebbing agonisingly away. The vet held the syringe up to the light before plunging blackness over sunny windowsills and baked earth under hot wallflowers, feathery grass that brushed off on a plumy tail, secret milky moonlight and stars, and wind that provoked skittering side-stepping dances, taunting autumn leaves, and knees punctured by contentedly clenched claws. She looked up through the tears that were still falling onto the cat.

'I wonder if you'd mind very much taking a look at my husband while you're here.'

'Really, Mrs Mackenzie, that's hardly my province.' The vet bridled, alarmed at the prospect of administering the *coup de grâce* with a needle to a conman's flabby flank.

'No, I understand that. It's just that he seems a bit – dead.' She led him upstairs.

'Oh dear, it never rains but it pours, does it?' she said, backing against the tiles when the vet pronounced her husband dead indeed. In his opinion it was heart, not drowning, despite the glass of whisky on the bath's curly rim.

'He was without sin, you know.'

The vet swallowed. That was not what he had heard of the not very late Sandy Mackenzie, but if that was how the new widow chose to cope with her grief . . .

'He never caught a bird or a mouse, not so much as a daddy-long-legs.'

The vet followed her down the stairs.

'Mrs Mackenzie, would you like me to telephone anybody? The family? Doctor? Ambulance?'

He looked helplessly round the narrow hall where it was forever autumn, with a flurry of maple leaves on the walls and the polished acorn at the end of the banister.

'He was a candidate for casting the first stone if anybody was, only he wouldn't have of course, the wee soul. He was like my husband in that respect – late husband, I suppose I ought to say . . . Oh dear, there must be arrangements I should be making. I'll have to borrow a spade, Oh God, and the ground so hard . . .'

'That was the best place they ever had,' Olive and William agreed. 'A little palace.'

There was even a tone-deaf piano. They had both left home by the time their father died. It was they, summoned by the first telephone their parents had possessed, who had performed the melancholy task of borrowing the spade and applying it to the frozen earth, and organising the undertakers. Mother was coping with her grief in her own way.

Apart from such members of the family who chose to attend, Sandy Mackenzie's funeral attracted sundry denizens of Fitzrovia, ambassadors from afternoon drinking clubs, the Gargoyle and the Caves de France; a sprinkling of Majors in camel coats taking furtive nips against the cold, three or four ladies with the stiff-legged gait of elderly pub dogs on indomitable painful feet forced into high-heeled shoes; a pug in a shopping basket on wheels, and the Norman Embers Trad Quintet, old pals of Dad, shivering in the sleet in their striped waistcoats, holding their bowler hats low out of respect.

'Exactly the sort of gimcrack affair one had feared,' hissed Hamish, the bereaved brother-in-law, Kitty's husband. They had come down from Edinburgh for the occasion. At their first meeting she had noticed his resemblance to Hamish the yellow dog they had left behind in New Zealand, and perhaps that was what had attracted her to him.

'Just be thankful we're in Peckham not New Orleans,' she said out of the side of her mouth, 'or we'd be sashaying through the streets behind them.'

'Saloon-bar savants hoping for a free drink. Just look at them all – a motley crew indeed.'

He nudged her towards a Major who stood to attention with a row of medals on his chest and a black armband on one sleeve. The other sleeve hung empty in the bitter wind.

'As for those pensioned-off Ladies of the Night! If a man's funeral is a mark of, or metaphor for, his life – would you say that chap, the one-armed one, looks suspiciously bulgy down the left side?'

'Will you shut up! You never got the point of Sandy!'

Olive was holding the hand of some smoothie old enough to be her grandfather, who seemed to think her name was Olivia, and William had brought along a girl in a college scarf on a first date which was not a success.

'I'm sorry, I always cry at funerals,' she had apologised, dabbing her nose with her scarf.

Sandy had managed to be late, provoking subdued mirth among the mourners and a little admiration.

'Trust old Sandy. Always told him he'd be late for his own funeral!'

'You will be too. Think about it,' Jessie snapped, taking the arm of her long-time companion Phyllis. There was a distinct feeling of the drawing up of opposing ranks. Norman Embers risked a line of 'There Was I Waiting at the Church' as the hearse, which had caught up with the mourners, lurched into view.

'Even the minister looks a trifle dubious,' Hamish whispered, not quietly enough, as they repaired afterwards towards the funeral baked meats. 'Type you'd expect to read about in the *News of the World*.'

The Reverend Mr Morpurgo shivered as though a ghost or a goose or an angel had walked over his grave.

'Now, Mr Morpurgo,' said Mother, rescuing him by linking hers in his black trembling arm. 'You must tell me all about the Fifty-Nine Articles. I've never *quite* understood . . . '

At the wake, for such it became quickly with the room thick with smoke that curled the edges of the sandwiches, Mother was heard to say: 'The vet offered to take him away in a plastic bag but I wouldn't hear of it. He deserved better after all these years.'

'Give us The Saints, lads,' someone cried and a little discreet and restricted jiving took place in the hall.

'I wouldn't be in our brother's shoes when he meets Father again,' Jessie told Kitty. 'I mean, God must have told him by now it was Sandy who spiked the communion wine.'

'Well, Father had only himself to blame if Sandy went wrong.

He was never fair to the boy. Remember the day of the picnic, for example – no, of course you don't, you were only a baby – but you must remember how Sandy could never do right in his eyes.'

'It wouldn't surprise me to learn that Father's own copybook was not entirely unblotted.'

'Quite so. Hello, William, how are you doing?'

'OK, thanks. Is there any food left in the front room?'

'Masses. Have you ever seen a bun dance on a table?'

William smiled weakly. 'That was what grandfather always used to say.'

'I know.'

It could not be denied that William, smouldering in a suit of his father's, and Olive, in her customary black, were the handsomest of a good-looking bunch of cousins, sophisticated despite their south London accents.

'Those two will make their mark,' Jessie prophesied, family pride lubricated with whisky embracing the whole flock gathered to mourn the missing black sheep.

Gradually, the young people were siphoned off to Olive's old bedroom with a couple of bottles and their paper plates, decked with holly and robins, leaving Olive's escort uneasily juxtaposed between the cheese straws and a Major who, insultingly, took him for a contemporary.

'Word to the wise, old boy, courtesy of our cousins across the herring pond: "Never bullshit a bullshitter."'

He tapped the side of a boozer's conk, with a watery wink. When Olive came down to show her friend the miniature coronation coach she had rediscovered in a box under her bed, he was nowhere to be found.

The little white horses, now pied with silvery lead where the paint had flaked, trotted in harness towards the ersatz dazzle of the gilded past. Scottish songs and alcohol and easy tears, a breaking feeling in her chest; a Major mopped her up in the bathroom while snow blurred the snowflakes in the frosted glass window. She sought out William, alone in his room, with a book. He read aloud:

> "'Fall, winter, fall, for he,
> Prompt hand and headpiece clever,
> Has woven a winter robe
> And made of earth and sea
> His overcoat for ever
> And wears the turning globe.'"

But Olive knew it wasn't like that for Daddy at all; he was urban and flashy, shabby and fake, and his overcoat was dingy camel-hair, his fingers yellowed to the second joint; but he was too natty and spruce to relish being stuck in the earth, especially when there was a party going on. This was the time he loved, *l'heure bleue*, the cocktail hour, the gloaming, twilight time, where the blue of the day met the gold of the night, when the deep purple fell; a time to shoot cuffs studded with stars, spike a tie with moonstone pin, brush hair with twin silver-backed brushes until it gleamed like the pelt of a fox quivering for the kill or trotting on gingery, black-tipped hind legs with a slender vixen, her Twink home-perm bobbing above a glittery blouse, on his arm.

Nocturnal glamour had fizzled out on raw mornings when blue-and-purple fingers held a sheet of newspaper across a fireplace trying to coax a shovelful of wet coke into flame, when every pocket of every garment had been searched a dozen times, yielding only fluff and shreds of tobacco, when upturned cushions revealed dead matches, crumbs and broken pencils, and the duns were at the door.

There had been a piano in a flat they had rented in Dover, which port perhaps Sandy had thought handy for the Channel should the need arise. Jean had given piano lessons for a while. Olive had hated those strange children clumping through their home with their music satchels, taking their mother's attention while she and William were relegated to the kitchen or bedrooms. Jean lost several pupils as a result of Olive's fearsome glare when she opened the front door to them and conducted them through with the tip of a Maori spear in their backs. Dad played too; popular songs, jazz, songs from the shows. One of Olive's sharpest disappointments had been when Sandy, leaving the house, had said: 'I'm going to buy "Stardust",' and she had awaited his return with a bag of magic golden dust which would grant wishes and make every dream come true, in an excited fantasy of power, spells and flying round the classroom above her awestruck schoolmates. He came home at last with a sheaf of sheet music. Typical, she thought now, of his promises; moonshine, fairy gold that turned to ashes.

There was a tune that Olive always associated with her family; the one that the Trad Quintet, augmented by barrel-house piano, churned out in the front room of the little palace: 'Oh we ain't got a barrel of money/Maybe we're ragged and funny/But we're rolling along/Singing a song/Side by side . . .'; which, when she had heard it first as a small child, had imprinted a picture in her mind of Dad, jacket and trousers

187

billowing in the wind, hat clamped to the back of his head, pushing an empty wheelbarrow with Mum in a floral frock and William and herself all bowling along towards the vanishing point of an empty road.

12

Yes, she was Olive Drab this morning, the dullest colour on the shade card once picked out by the youthful William with glee.

Olive woke to a feeling of general malaise: her head was heavy, her eyes felt puffy and sunken, her legs like the trunks of fallen trees. She knew at once that this was to be one of her Tuesdays. It was only since she had lived with William that she had been free to wallow in them completely. On previous Tuesdays she had run the risk of a caller, landlord, postman, meter man or locked-out neighbour disturbing her smoky *déshabillé*; or the cat which she had then, with unerring feline timing, would catch a bird, send her out for food or need suddenly and dramatically to be taken to the vet.

The idea of her Tuesdays had floated into her mind long ago, she knew not whence, triggered perhaps by something she had read or heard and forgotten, or by someone in a novel holding soirees so glittering that they had become known, and envied by the excluded, as Madame—'s Tuesdays. Tuesday seemed the perfect day; everybody felt Mondayish, which made that day too commonplace; 'One of my Wednesdays' had a wimpishly alliterative whine to it; whereas Tuesday was the day on which one realised that that Monday morning feeling was not confined to Mondays but oozed out of its allotted square on the calendar and spread in a damp grey stain.

From the days when a best friend at one of her schools betrayed her regularly by being absent with conjunctivitis, which Olive never succeeded in catching, she had become aware of the advantages enjoyed by people who had established some temporarily disabling recurring ailment such as that, or later, migraine or cystitis, which could be called upon to absolve them from unpleasant business or social duties. It was a bit late in the day to feign malaria, although she thought she might contract it if she went abroad again; asthma was tricky, and seemed in poor taste as she had a friend whose son suffered frightening attacks; cystitis was rather embarrassing; migraine it would have to be. There was the danger of busybodies warning her off red wine, chocolate and cheese but, as her chosen malady must require lying in a darkened room, these could be consumed in curtained secrecy if necessary.

Once, the mornings when she had found it impossible to face the day had been mastered by her mother advancing on the bed with a thermometer: 'If you're well enough to walk, you're well enough to go to school' had been one of her mottoes, which had inspired fantasies in Olive of scenes of flame and gunfire, from which she emerged heroically crippled. The gangsters of south-east London, however, showed no interest in Sydenham High School for Girls except when they waited outside the gates in flashy cars for their daughters and girlfriends. Olive was fated to rescue from fire only spiders and woodlice scuttling from sticks, and snails on lumps of coalite. In earlier years her mother had been defeated only by chickenpox, measles and mumps; quarantine was imposed rigidly in those days, and the schoolbooks of children with notifiable illnesses were burned. To Olive's mortification, her suspected scarlet fever had been diagnosed as nettle rash before her disgraceful sum book could be tossed into the boiler by Mr Cloke, the mournful-faced, navy-overalled caretaker. Scarlet fever, with its frisson of fatality, and books condemned to a fiery furnace, carried the greatest kudos, run a close second by scarlatina, and rivalled only by double pneumonia. Hours of standing in a wet vest and open pyjama jacket in the freezing night air of a stealthily pushed-up bedroom window had failed to attract the disease to Olive's treacherously healthy chest. By the time of the polio epidemic, she could see that almost anything was preferable to an iron lung, that unimaginable instrument of torture whose name struck fear into the collective heart of schoolchildren, and she had discovered other ways of avoiding school, and recognised that her stay in any one of them would be brief.

Half dozing, half dreaming, thinking about Mr Cloke and heaps of coke and this and that, and pink lesser convolvulus tumbling over tall wooden back gates of gardens in the alleyway on the way to school, in a state of recall so intense that tiny bits of grit glittered as brightly as they had thirty-five years ago; broken bottle glass, beer-brown, flashing golden iridescent rays, short, long, dazzle; green glass, white calcified dogshit, big white bells of bindweed weighing down wire netting in the deserted midday dinner time . . .

'Olive, it's twenty to nine!'

William stood at her bedside with a cup of tea.

'I'm having one of my Tuesdays.'

'Although it's Thursday.'

William was the only person who knew about Olive's Tuesdays.

'No need to look so disapproving. How can I predict the days when I'm going to wake up feeling like a log of wood? As far as I'm concerned it's Tuesday. *Would* you be an angel and ring Charlene and tell her I've got one of my migraines? I'll mend your cardigan, if you do.'

'I don't want it mended.'

The grumpy angel left the room, the grey batwings of his cardigan drooping, the cuffs falling in cobwebs over his hands.

An ideal Tuesday, of course, would not be staffed by William in that ragged cardigan: she heard the brisk clip of hooves, the whirl of wheels stopping, footsteps running up the steps, the ring of the bell: 'Madame is not at 'ome to anybody, Monsieur. She is 'aving one of 'er Tuesdays.'

'*Je suis désolé*, Clothilde. Please give her these orchids ... *Je reviens ...*'

Or: 'Now you children just go along quietly to the schoolroom. Her Ladyship's having one of Her Tuesdays, the puir wee soul. Lying there like an angel, she is, wi' the blinds pulled doon and a handkerchief soaked in that cologne his Lordship had sent over special from Paris, on her forehead, bless her, and I don't want her disturbed.'

'Let them come in for a moment, Nanny,' a voice called weakly.

'Verra weel, Madam, five minutes and not a second longer,' Nanny was saying as the door burst open and a rosy little girl in a white dress and a little boy in a sailor suit dashed in and flung themselves onto the white quilted bed, and into the outstretched arms from which the broderie anglaise fell back so prettily. She caught Nanny's eye as she re-tied a sash and pushed back a recalcitrant curl – how she had cried and Rollo, his Lordship, had teased her the first time those curls had been cut – and discerned a twinkle.

'Cook's making one of her special syllabubs, Madam, and a posset. I'll bring them up mysel', said Nanny gruffly. 'Naebody but me shall nurse my lamb, that I've cared for since – auld lang syne!' her look implied.

'Dear Nanny. Dear Cook . . . '

'Mummy, you smell so beautiful! Shall I brush your hair?'

'Thank you, darling. You know how it soothes me . . . but very gently.'

Falling so sleazily short of the mark, Olive sighed and groped for a mirror from her handbag lying beside the bed. Her face was as she had feared, and scarred with a crease from the pillow. No wonder William had been so unfriendly; she looked like a coconut with her hair sticking up like that, the one nobody aimed for at the fairground, a booby prize. She pulled a comb through the tangled coconut matting on her head. Surely she needn't put on mascara for him, not after all these years, when he still hadn't learned to carry a cup of tea upstairs without slopping it? For her own esteem? She couldn't be bothered. She sighed at the thought of the pair of them and reached for her tea. As cold as ice and as strong as death.

She heard William leave the house and snuggled down in the luxury of being alone. When the door bell rang she cursed and pulled the duvet over her head, but whoever it was would not give up. Probably that fool William had forgotten his key. She thought she heard a faint cry of 'It's me, let me in,' and swung furiously out of bed. She opened the front door and slammed it at once. Behind the shivering glass wavered Terry and a cellophane sheaf of flowers, with the wet blue tiles breaking in wavelets round his shoes. The door bell drilled and drilled her as she dragged clothes from hangers and spilled makeup and wrenched on tights and thrust feet into uncooperative shoes. How dared he! How dared he! She must have looked at least a hundred years old.

'Well?'

He was still standing in the porch when she opened the door again. A floral umbrella simpered beside him, like a new fiancée flaunting herself at the discarded ex-wife. She noted with surprised distaste that his hair had been scraped back into a small ponytail secured with black elastic.

'Well, I wanted to see you, and, well, I see you've still got the blue bathrobe. I remember when we bought it, do you? I always liked you in it.'

'How dare you! And how dare you arrive here unannounced when I'm not dressed, and if you say I never used to mind, I'll kill you with that ridiculous umbrella! And how dare you turn up with a bunch of ready-mixed blooms? I can't think of anything more insulting!'

'What's wrong with them?'

Terry looked into the bright faces of the flowers, remembering many past offences against her idiosyncratic code.

'I bet there's a frond of dreary conifer stuck in there. Yes, of course there is.'

Olive dragged out a dark green branch. Terry retreated from its lash, protecting his head and spilling red, blue, yellow and white insults onto the streaming tiles. He saw that he should have hand-picked a flock of white penitents, vestals from an exotic order, perfumed with the heavy incense of remorse, drooping heads too heavy for their frail necks. Fuck. Even the cellophane cone had a scalloped lacy edge. He stepped forward to retrieve Mrs Joyce Jauncey's umbrella, his disastrous flowers replicated in nylon.

'Smiffy always does things wrong,' he said ruefully.

'What?'

'A character in the *Beano*, you must remember. Like me, he always did things wrong. I've always identified with him.'

'I read the *Children's Newspaper*,' Olive lied. 'And the *Young Elizabethan*.' These worthy publications had indeed been delivered to her house once by mistake but she had not read them and, as usual, had had to beg for reads of friends' proper comics. A blurred image of the Bash Street Kids formed in her mind. How typically, distastefully, sentimental of Terry to identify with a small comic strip character at a moment of adult crisis.

'I can't stand people who are in love with the icons of their childhood. I suppose you watch videos of *The Woodentops* and *Bill and Ben the Flowerpot Men*? How decadent!'

'You know me better than that. Anyway, I've heard you wax lyrical about fag cards and halfpenny chews. You probably watch videos of *Muffin the Mule* . . . '

'Excuse me mentioning it, but something very disagreeable seems to have occurred to your hair.'

The rain was coursing down his face; his shirt was a piece of sodden blotting paper under his soaking jacket. He pressed a button on the umbrella and it whooshed up like a floral rocket.

'Wait!'

Terry had started to walk down the path. He turned, with water spurting from his shoes.

'You can't just show up here and then go. Before I've told you how much I hate you. What you've done. You drowned worm, you slug, you, you BABY-SNATCHER!'

She had run out to him and was shaking him by the wet lapels while the umbrella threatened both their faces.

Terry sidestepped a drowned worm, simultaneously realising that she had taken her imagery from nature and remembering the first tender time, after they had become lovers, that she had pulled together the open lapels of his coat against the sleet in a Soho street as they parted after lunch; and how, with that gesture, his heart had stopped, and when it had resumed beating he was in love with her.

'Olive, I love you,' he said now, as he had not said then.

In the kitchen, wrapped in William's dressing gown, grey and claret squares with a twisted silken cord of claret, drinking William's whisky while his rat's tail dried and his clothes steamed domestically on the radiator, he asked, 'I get the worm and the slug, but why did you call me a baby-snatcher?'

'Oh, it just slipped out in the heat of the moment. I suppose that recent case was on my mind, or something – seemed a useful piece of invective.'

'But you are pleased to see me?' Terry, relieved that Olive had not spotted him with a girl he had seen once or twice, and had not in fact meant 'cradle-snatcher', looked humbly for reassurance.

'Oh, Terry, how can you ask? I've missed you so much.'

'I've missed you too. I've had the most horrible time.'

'Why on earth didn't you ring me?'

Terry had been going to tell her about the terrible time he had had at Amberley, but decided it was better forgotten.

'I didn't know if you'd want me to.'

'How could you have doubted that?' She took a whisky-flavoured kiss from his lips.

'And the book? Dare I ask?'

'Not really. I'm having a few problems. I think it may be my typewriter – I'm thinking about getting an Amstrad.'

William came in, saw Turner sitting there in his dressing gown, drinking his whisky, and said: 'Well, well, well, just like old times.'

13

When Jay had first arrived in London, some spring evenings had affected him with a mild delirium; the hardness of stone and the softness of blossom, the first stars in greenish skies, twigs blurred with green, moist lamps in a daffodil or amethyst haze, curled hyacinths in stone urns and their scent, the shattered petals of yellow crocuses stripped by birds, the slates on the roofs and the pavements like the shot silk of strutting, cooing, mating pigeons all conspired to constrict his heart. What could he do with all that undirected love, when a wispy bunch of straws in a beak brought tears to his eyes? One morning he had passed a school and heard children singing, 'Spring is coming, spring is coming, birdies build your nests.'

He fell in love with people in the tube: a black nurse for her thin legs and feet in lace-up shoes and the whites of her eyes, white as china; a freckled girl in khaki shorts; the olive-skinned arms of a sleeping boy in a grey sleeveless sweatshirt; an elderly woman in a paisley silk shirtwaister. People moved away from him, disconcerted by his gaze. He was lucky not to get beaten up. He had been set upon once outside Brixton tube by a pair of winos but the woman with them had intervened and he had escaped across the road to Marks and Spencer's, where he had hovered so long at the till of a woman with a kind smile for her customers that she had asked him sharply what he was staring at.

'I was admiring your blouse – it's very – trim. Crisp. Smart yet practical.'

A security guard had escorted him to the door.

'How do you go about getting a job here?' Jay was asking – the uniform, a bit military, commanded respect – when he found himself in the street, with a fracas still blazing on the other side, over the traffic. He slunk into the market where he filled a small bag with spoiled fruit and vegetables retrieved from under the feet of shoppers.

Now, in the early summer, he was unsettled, disturbed by the great green swaying pink-and-white pinnacled castles of the chestnut trees in the park. He watched a glossy Rottweiler with a plastic muzzle like a small inverted launderette basket strapped over its jaws attempt to retrieve a stick; he saw a pigeon struggle with the heel of a loaf. Each peck threw the heavy bread over its shoulder; the bird turned and stabbed at it again, in an ever-widening circle.

'Don't mind, do you, mate?'

Jay broke off a lump of bread, chewed it, and broke and scattered the rest.

'Excuse me, can you spare some change, please?'

He accosted two girls on the path. One rolled her eyes and strode on, the other reluctantly unzipped the money pouch hanging from her waist, fumbled and pulled out a pound coin, hesitated as if wanting to change it for something smaller, lost her nerve and thrust it at him, running to catch up with her friend. Jay could see they were arguing. The scornful girl had a point; Jay had read in the *Sun* of people who supplemented their dole or even their daytime jobs with begging, who had their own flats. There were also apparently those who were run by bosses, like pimps, who drove expensive cars and had holidays abroad. He wanted to explain that he was not in that category and there were many more like him but had the sense not to indulge in what would be perceived as persecution by a loony.

As Jay drifted, he thought about the Russian who had given him a lift and was lost in a fantasy of meeting her again, being driven to her house and luxuriating in a bath with golden taps while a cloud of bubbles soothed away the grime and smell of mildew that clung to him; on bad days he felt like a split garbage sack attracting a cloud of flies. The cold tap of *Dunedin* and furtive ablutions in the Gents never left him feeling really clean. After his bath, he and the woman would become friends. He felt both guilty and bereaved by the loss of his book of Russian stories; Kirsty had flung it into the flames one night and he had woken the next day with a head swollen by cider to find nothing remained of it in the smouldering ashes. Anyway, he couldn't remember now which library he had borrowed it from, and the stories were fragmented impressions of white nights and vodka and playing cards. He could sort it out with the woman's help. He had hung about the Horniman on several occasions but she had never been there.

By early afternoon Jay had fetched up near St Bartholomew's Hospital. As he approached it, he was startled by a barrage of bloody aprons ahead. A major disaster. A multiple crash or pile-up, a horrific accident. He ran forward instinctively to help, offer his blood, anything. Doctors were milling about in confusion. Then he saw that they carried placards. He slowed down. There was a van, a television crew, cameras and an interviewer with a microphone. Jay remembered reading in someone's paper that the ambulance men were on strike, so presumably the victims were being brought to the hospital by volunteers. He increased his pace, with a silent prayer for the dead and injured.

SMITHFIELD PORTERS AGAINST HOSPITAL CUTS he read on a banner, and in splashy red letters on a wide gauze bandage SMITHFIELD SUPPORTS BARTS, and two men held placards commanding motorists to toot in solidarity. Those skilled dissectors, the bloodstained conscience of London, were staging a demonstration in solidarity with the surgeons who practised on live meat.

Jay, realising it was a demo, was abruptly embarrassed into pretending to be a jogger. He flapped past with the sole of one shoe gasping like a hooked fish, an ironic cheer spurring him on. Thank God he hadn't offered his blood. The name Smithfield meant nothing to him, and he was as ignorant of the protestors' chauvinism, their marches against immigration some years earlier, as he was of their trade, but he surmised that they were a convention of butchers from their bloody white clothes. Tins and buckets rattled, passing motorists and taxi drivers tooted their approval united in angry and sentimental condemnation of the slaughter by default of the innocents, closed wards and empty beds. Jay might have been seen jogging incongruously across thousands of television screens in the South-East that evening, had his performance not been edited out of the footage.

*

'Dino, I'm hungry.' It was a bellow of despair. The old man stood at the entrance to the espresso bar on the edge of Leicester Square.

'Dino, I'm hungry!'

He stood stinking, causing customers to move towards the back of the narrow, steamy room that smelled of cigarettes and hot food, roaring like a weak bull stuck with banderillas. Behind the counter which held the espresso machine, the battery of tiny white cups and saucers, the slices of pizza, the crusty rolls like mouths gobbling meat and cheese and bright salad, the Italian brothers winked at the customers and laughed. One of them shouted at the old man over the hissing of the machine. The smell of the fresh coffee was exquisite.

'Dino, I'm hungry.'

His voice stuck Jay like a picador's lance, and he went to the counter and pointed to a long roll spilling spirals of tomato and sausage speckled with white fat. It was handed to him on a white plate, shawled in a paper napkin. Jay took it to the doorway and gave it to the old man, who snatched it and tore at it with his teeth, spitting sausage and shiny crust, and shuffled off.

'You waste your money,' the Italian said. 'He'll be back in half an hour with the same story.'

Jay shrugged and returned to his coffee, in a cup so small, and only half-full, that he could not believe it cost ninety p. He saw, in the mirror that lined one wall, a woman watching him with tears brimming in her eyes.

'You *are* good,' she said. 'I wanted to do that, but I was too embarrassed. May I buy you another coffee?'

'Thank you very much.'

'I'm sorry,' she told him, wiping her eye when she returned

from the counter. 'I'm the world's biggest sentimentalist. Any gratuitous act of kindness makes me cry, I don't know why.'

'Lizzie, I'm sorry to keep you waiting. We'd better run,' came a voice behind him.

The woman put down her cup and followed a fleshy man in an expensive suit into the street.

'Was that loony chatting you up?' he heard. 'Begging, I suppose. Really, London becomes more disgusting every day.'

Jay finished his coffee, and Lizzie's. As he followed them out into the stormy light and a sudden burst of starlings over Leicester Square, there came the bellow of an unsatisfied, wounded bull: 'Dino, I'm hungry!'

Jay was hungry. The air was full of the vapours from cones of meat, slowly oozing as they turned on spikes, and as thin slices were shaved by the hairy-armed men sweating in sleeveless vests, the juices of kebabs mingled with the sweet smell of popcorn. He caught sight of the couple from the espresso bar disappearing into a cinema, not knowing that they were part of the audience for a preview where drinks and sandwiches would be served. He wished that he had the price of a ticket. To that man in the affluent jacket, he was a piece of the litter that made this city disgusting. The woman, Lizzie, had said that he was good. He felt as if he were nothing, empty, nobody, as light and dirty and full of air as a paper cup rolling in the gutter. If he were a loony, like that man said, he could go and stand in the doorway of the espresso bar and shout 'Dino, I'm hungry!'; but he was not, and so he set about thinking how he should get back to *Dunedin*.

It was late when he finally arrived. Denny and Gnasher were not home. The lumps of two bodies lay in a downstairs room, dead to the world. One day somebody would not wake and the foxes would dine on him.

Kirsty was awake, with a bottle of cider, and disposed to talk. 'There were five of us, Mary, Elspeth, Nancy, Nessie and me. We were known as the McDonald Girls. You should have seen us when we walked out together. Everybody knew us. Nancy's dead now; Mary's a doctor in Glasgow; Elspeth might have had a singing career if she hadn't married a doctor from Ballantrae; Nessie's a teacher, a headmistress now for all I know, and there's me. We were the tallest girls in the town and all the boys were a wee bit afraid of us, we were that magnificent, with our red-gold hair, the five of us. Ah well.'

'Why did Nancy die?'

'She died of an excess of happiness. It was the night that Duncan Hunter proposed. She ran into the house with her face all flushed and her eyes like diamonds, flashing and sparkling, and the snow melting in her hair, and she was dancing round the room and her dress caught fire. It went with a whoosh up the chimney, like a letter to Father Christmas. It was green shot silk and it melted on her. She melted like a candle. We rolled her in the rug, but she died.'

Kirsty danced perilously between the candles, making a wind with her skirts and shawl that guttered the flames, throwing shadows of witches and ghosts of young girls over the ceiling and walls.

'"Duncan Grey cam here to woo," she sang,' "Ha, ha, the wooing o't." Let that story be a warning to you, my lad. Never wear green. Next to myself, she was the bonniest of us all.'

'What happened to Duncan Hunter? Did he die of a broken heart?'

'He was killed in the war. When Nancy died our splendour fell from us, and we became Those Poor McDonald girls. We carried the smell of burning in our hair.'

She sank into the stained pillow, her legs straight out in front of her and her skirt making a runnel of tweed between the skinny limbs. Her fingers writhed in and out of one another and as she rocked back and forth, Jay saw a laughing girl with eyes flashing coloured lights onto her green dress, twirling round, laughing until a blow from her sister caught her off balance, saw her mouth distorted into a scream as her dress whooshed up the chimney, the snow sizzling in her red-gold hair, three silent sisters, arms lifted in horror, stilled like candelabra, until they started to scream and wrench the rug from the floor under Kirsty's slipping feet, as if she was trying to keep her balance on ice. His impulse was to run from Kirsty and the flames and melting candles, but she passed him the bottle and he took it. When she slept he would run away from this house for ever. In the moonlight one of the candles danced in a draught.

'It's your turn now,' Kirsty said, grabbing the bottle, 'I've told you a story, now you must tell me one.'

'What happened then, after Nancy died?'

'Nothing bloody happened. What do you think happened? There was a funeral. End of story.'

Jay pictured a raw grave gaping in the snow among heather and dark conifers laced and bowed down under the white weight of the snow, and the sisters' red-gold hair sprayed out over the black shoulders of their coats and their eyelids and noses pinkly swollen with crying in faces pinched by the freezing air. Their father's fingers grasped Kirsty's sleeve with frozen iron. He and she stood a small distance apart from the others under a black umbrella.

Jay did not dare to imagine the long, long grey years, the windowless wards and corridors that stretched from that funeral to the derelict present; the smell of disinfectant was in his nose and the taste of metal in his mouth.

To protect himself, he said, 'This is a true story. It's about a man I knew in New Zealand. He . . .'

'Yourself! It's got to be about yourself!' she interrupted.

'OK. Once upon a time, there was a boy in Dunedin, who was me. One day I happened to be sitting in the park reading the newspaper and I read that when people eat frogs' legs, the legs – sorry, this will upset you, I'd better not go on . . .'

'Go on! The gorier and more unpleasant the better.'

She had found a place on her own leg which promised to be both.

'They tear off the legs when the frogs are still alive. Well, when I read this, I was very upset. People just laughed when I tried to tell them about it, although my letter to the newspaper got a response from some Animal Activists, but they wanted to bomb the restaurants and I didn't agree with that. How would it help the frogs to have people with their legs blown off? Not much. So I decided to do something practical to rehabilitate those frogs who had already lost their limbs. I designed a tiny battery-powered wheelchair, about three inches by three, and I gathered up all the frogs from the backyards and dustbins of the restaurants and taught them how to operate this prototype. Then I took out a loan on a business enterprise scheme and rented a unit on a small industrial estate. With the help of the young lad who I had taken on to help me, I was soon turning out a dozen chairs a day. It was his idea that we should make the chairs amphibious, and we also manufactured rubber rings and armbands for those frogs who couldn't manage the chairs.'

A grey groan issued from Kirsty's lap, where her head had dropped.

'We called ourselves the Lilypad Corporation. That was our logo, a frog on a lilypad. Of course, there was a lot of nursing care involved too, and counselling. The great day dawned. It was a damp evening. The streets were slick with rain and the restaurant windows steamed. Inside was laughter, warmth, champagne, dinner jackets and glittering dresses and jewellery, the ringing of delicate glass and heavy silver, and linen napery. Suddenly a waiter screamed and dropped a massive dish with a retractable lid. Hot meat gushed out and then a woman screamed and then another, and people were climbing onto their chairs, shrieking. Through the great revolving restaurant doors came, slowly, slowly, over the liveried flunkey who had fainted, hundreds of frogs in tiny wheelchairs, and each frog grasped a banner which read *'J'accuse!'*

Another snorish groan suggested that Kirsty had fallen into a state of stupefaction.

'The demo was an unqualified success. It made all the media, massive coverage. Soon after we staged the first ever Antipodean Amphibian Disabled Olympics. Some of the contestants were cane toads from Australia. Have you heard of cane toads? They're not natives of Australia; they were imported to control pests but now many people regard them as pests themselves, a plague of toads. Somebody even made a film about them. *Cane Toads*, it was called. They became a bit of a cult; children kept them as pets and dressed them in dolls' clothes and pushed them around in dolls' prams. Now they are stuffed and sold as souvenirs. Some people tried to eat them but word got out that they were poisonous, and the people cried, "Lo, a plague has come upon us, yea, cane toads which do threaten that of our native wildlife which we have not consumed already, and our household pets and even our very children, and do squirt venom from their thighs when we do eat their legs!'"

Jay's shouting did not rouse the sleeping woman. As he crept from the room he realised that voices raised in quarrel, brawl and song had probably lulled her to sleep beside many a brazier, the background music to her troubled dreams. She twitched and flung out an arm.

He thought about that dreadful dream he had had, when Kirsty had knelt in the moonlight holding a shrunken head by the hair. He was pretty sure it must have been a dream, or else a trick of the light. With Kirsty asleep it seemed mad to flee into the night. He crept up to his room.

14

It had been a slow morning; slow enough to set Olive's worries about the future of the shop buzzing like a hive of disturbed bees. She had arrived to find the picture framer's opposite locked and cleared of all its stock.

'They might have said something,' she complained to Charlene. 'Going off like thieves in the night.'

'I knew they were closing down. Rob told me last week, but I didn't realise it would be so sudden.'

'Oh.'

Typical.

'Well they might have had the courtesy to say goodbye. It doesn't do much for the neighbourhood or business to have boarded-up shops all over the place.'

'Somebody said it's going to be a take-away. Caribbean and English food.'

'How come you always know everything that's going on? Nobody tells me anything. Is there something about me?'

'Course not. It's probably just that I'm nosy.'

'Possibly.' Olive was prepared to accept that. 'God, it's like a morgue in here today. Quite honestly, Charlene, I think you might as well go home if you like. I can't quite envisage a rush this afternoon.'

'Well, if you're sure . . .'

'Yes, run along. There's no point in two of us being stuck in here on such a lovely day. Well, hot, anyway. Frankly this weather's getting me down. If only we could have some rain.'

She saw it all through the window – Charlene turning to wave, a white youth pushing a bicycle along the pavement barging into her, Charlene's remonstrance, and the youth punching her hard in the mouth. Charlene fell heavily on her knees. The youth snarled some obscenity and walked on. Olive rushed out screaming at him and picked Charlene up. Passers-by stared. Nobody attempted to restrain her attacker.

'It was my own fault,' Charlene sobbed in the shop. 'I shouldn't've said anything.'

Olive dabbed at her with a wet cloth. Blood poured from Charlene's nose and mouth and her lips were beginning to swell.

'I don't think your nose is broken, and your teeth seem OK, but I think we'd better get you down to Casualty just in case.'

She rang for a minicab, her voice shaky with anger and unshed tears. She played the scene over in her mind as they waited but this time she grabbed Charlene's attacker and threw him to the ground, kicking him and pinning him to the pavement until the police dragged him away. *Which makes me no better than him, the bastard.*

'She been beating you up?' the cab driver asked in jocular fashion.

Neither of the women answered and after he had warned them not to get any blood on his upholstery, they drove without speaking, while his controller's voice crackled through the radio, agonisingly slowly, caught at every red light.

Casualty was unlike anything Olive had experienced. She sat, squeezing Charlene's hand from time to time, the one which was not clasping the bloody handkerchief to her cheek – thinking that she was in some Third World country rather than in a famous teaching hospital on her own doorstep. Whole mad families had taken up residence on the balding black vinyl benches and, making themselves at home, they squabbled, scuffled, ate, cried, slept and stared at the wall-mounted television whose sound was drowned by the noises of the room. Emissaries took orders from the wounded and their entourage and returned from McDonald's with burgers, shakes, cokes and chips. Doctors and nurses would peer into mouths and try to distinguish chocolate and ketchup from blood, and Olive was soon disabused of the notion that blood would inspire camaraderie among the wounded or excite any sympathy. A girl with an abcessed finger accused Charlene of trying to jump the queue and, threatened by her, her boyfriend and the friend who accompanied her, they moved onto a hard chair at the end of the bench. Olive would have stood but Charlene insisted that they share the chair. Awkwardly, Olive tried to read her paper but the words swarmed like midges on a summer evening in incomprehensible clouds and she could not shut out the conversations that fizzed around her.

'She had twins, didn't she?'

'Yeah, a little girl and a lizard.'

Such was her febrile state that she assumed that they were discussing some patient in this hospital, rather than a film they had seen. She had failed to register the notice that informed patients that they must expect to wait at least four hours, and after forty-five minutes she assumed that Charlene had been forgotten or her name mislaid. She picked her way past an ancient couple, one in a wheelchair and the other bloodless and bent from pushing it, and accosted a young doctor who looked as if he should lie down at once on a trolley and sleep for at least a week. He swallowed a multiple yawn and assured her that their turn would come. She returned to find Charlene standing and their seat occupied by a woman with a monkey. Olive recoiled, as a gasp escaped her lips. It was not a monkey that the woman fed from a bottle but a baby, tinier than seemed possible, wizened, and jaundiced to the colour and texture of old ivory.

Ducking her head, her horrified loud exhalation beating in her ears, she retreated to the corridor where people adjourned for a smoke. It was packed, and the lavatory proved no refuge either. Olive took one look and backed out into a nurse armed with an aerosol of air freshener.

What had they done with the lizard twin, she wondered. Had it been placed in an incubator with vital tubes attached to its green beaded body? Or cast by terrified, transparent-gloved fingers, kicking, forked tongue lashing in a silent scream from drawn-back lips, into the hospital incinerator? Or carried home with its sibling in a cobwebbed shawl, in a minicab with over-flowing ashtrays, by its bemused parents? 'I'll take Baby. You carry Lizzie.' Such things happened, she knew from her surrep-titious perusal of William's *Sunday Sport*. Would the mother stand accused by her husband of irrefutable adultery with a reptile, and bear the marks of his revenge, like that woman

standing by the ashtray, trying to inhale solace from a cigarette through bloodied and swollen lips? Whatever happened,
there would be the christening to get through. Olive pushed
through the swing doors, plastic and yellowed with nicotine to
the shade of the sick baby's skin, and found herself in a courtyard among a group of men drinking from cans, ambulance
drivers and visitors from the open wards and outpatients of the
Maudsley across the road.

'Have a drink, missis.'

A can of Carlsberg Special was circling nearer and nearer
her. Olive took to her heels and ran towards Denmark Hill.
She leaped onto a sixty-eight bus just as the doors were closing
and was borne towards Camberwell Green, leaving Charlene
and Casualty behind.

All the time that she had been taking charge of Charlene,
getting her to the hospital, Olive had managed not to acknowledge to herself that it was opposite the place where William had
dumped Theo. Now she began to shake out of synch with the
vibrations of the bus. That baby taking tiny sips at life, like a
grimacing ivory figurine, would not go away. If wishing could
turn it pink . . . Olive turned to glare at a child howling as if her
heart had broken, while her mother read a magazine. She suppressed the impulse to scream at the child to shut up. Either one
cares about children, or one doesn't, she told herself. Either we
are members one of another or we aren't. The child was beating
her fists in incoherent grief on her mother's implacable knee,
her body a convulsive arch of tears. The other passengers kept
their own counsel. The more she travelled around, the more
Olive wondered why people had children, when patently they
neither liked nor respected them. She decided that she might

as well go to Safeways while she was here, and got up, catching the reading mother a sharp blow on the side of her head with her elbow as she passed.

'Sorry.'

It was at the checkout, when a small boy sitting in a trolley waved a plastic dinosaur under her nose, that the lizard baby flashed into her mind, turning the key to the cell where her worst memory crouched, hideous, shameful, but still alive after all the years.

The room had been full of girls and young women. Olive had shivered under a cellular blanket a nurse had given her, like the kind they put on babies' cots, but red. The same nurse had switched on a radio and 'Black is black, I want my baby back' had blared out, while there had still been time to run away. In the morning the girls had exchanged cigarettes, although they had been warned that smoking so soon afterwards would lead to severe headache, but they seemed not to care. Some of them had complained about the breakfast they were given, like girls at boarding school, before they were discharged into a world changed for ever.

The long table, the white vulnerable eggs in thick white eggcups, the breakfast of the damned in swirls of boiled-egg vapours, disinfectant and cigarette smoke – it occurred to her that she might have passed in the street, served in the shop, any of those women with whom she had spent the night that disfigured her soul, and mistaken her for an ordinary person going about her life. Time had built layer upon layer around the corrupt pearl in her heart.

Olive felt that no satisfactory explanation could be offered when, driven back by her conscience, she encountered

Charlene, cleaned up but with split lips still swelling, at the bus stop.

'Why do I always have to pick the slowest checkout?'

She grimaced at the heavy carrier bag she held in each hand, seeing that there was no way Charlene wouldn't notice them. Charlene did not respond. A miraculous black taxi was bearing down on them, and by another miracle, had its light on. Olive flagged it down.

'I'm taking you home.'

Then Charlene had to mumble her address to the driver because Olive could not remember where she lived.

'Sure you'll be all right?'

Charlene nodded. Olive watched her walk up the steps to the front door of the terraced house, past a bright slice of garden that put hers to shame, as the taxi pulled away. Charlene and all her friends were so stylish, in their clothes and their hair, never scruffy; she felt helpless anger at the casual violence which had smirched that glamour, and snapped at the driver when he asked her the best way to go.

'You're the one with the Knowledge.'

She kept him waiting while she dropped off her shopping, and returned, several pounds poorer, to the shop, where no frustrated customers were beating on the door. Once inside, she attacked a pile of invoices with venom.

As she worked, stabbing her calculator, cursing VAT, the prospect of the evening with Terry began to seem ineffably tedious; ending up in his bed, getting up to ring for a cab when sleep seemed the natural thing, sitting in the back of a car driven by somebody who despised her; or worse, rising at dawn to travel home past milkfloats and paperboys, to shower and change for work feeling hungover and sleazy. She didn't like Terry's bathroom, his manky shower, the dead poinsettia, the dirty grouting and the ceramic cottage in the loo. 'I'm too old for this,' she thought. An evening with one of her friends seemed a pleasanter prospect, and her thoughts turned to her aunt Jessie and Jessie's friend Phyllis; knowing almost nothing of their life, she saw it bathed in a stately golden light.

Nevertheless, that evening she sat opposite Terry in a Herne Hill wine bar.

'What's the matter, Olive? Bad day at Black Rock?'

'Not particularly. Yes, actually. Some lout punched Charlene in the face, and we spent hours in Casualty.'

'God! Is she OK? You should have told me.'

'I forgot. Yes, she's fine.'

'But why did he hit her? Was it a mugging?'

'She forgot to be streetwise and objected to him bashing into her with a bike. She said it was her own fault.'

'Christ. But the shock – it's quite traumatic to be punched in the face even if no lasting damage was done. What about emotional scars?'

'I don't know, Terry, can't we just drop it? I did everything I could, took her to hospital in a taxi, held her hand for hours in that hell-hole, took her home in a taxi, told her to take a couple of days off. I'm shattered.'

Terry signalled for another bottle of Montana.

'The mark-up on this wine's ridiculous,' said Olive.

Terry filled her glass.

'Get that down ye, lass,' he said in imitation of his friend Mothersole, whom Olive detested. Then he tried another conversational gambit.

216

'Bloody awful, isn't it?' He showed her the picture of a sinking tanker and spreading oilslick on the front page of the *Standard*. 'Seems hardly a week goes by without some ecological disaster,' he went on. 'Hundreds of miles of the Med coast under threat.'

'I can't afford to go on holiday anyway,' replied Olive.

Back at Temperance Terrace he tried to humour her again. 'I'm going to Cheltenham in the autumn. Want to come? I thought we could drive up, perhaps spend a few days driving around. There are some nice little hotels and restaurants, I believe.'

'Why? My father won some money there once I seem to remember – saved our bacon, for a while anyway. I didn't know you were interested in racing.'

'For the festival. I've been invited.'

'What on earth for? Why you? You haven't a note of music in you. In fact you've got a tin ear.'

Terry switched off the tape of Vivaldi's Four Seasons.

'The festival of literature.'

'Oh. I suppose I ought to congratulate you. No, thanks, anyway. I can't stand those chichi little places in the provinces where everybody speaks in hushed tones and has to go into raptures about the home-made fudge.'

Terry, at a loss for words, put his arm round her and pulled her face to his. After a minute or two he sat back on the sofa.

'God, you're about as exciting as a hot-water bottle that's gone cold. What's the matter, have I got bad breath?'

'No, just winey, as usual. I suppose I'm the same. I'm just not in the mood. Sorry, Terry, I think I'd better go.'

She picked up her bag and stood up.

'What do you want, then? I thought you were pleased we were back together.'

He was hurt and angry.

'I don't know. I just know I want more than this. Some stability in my old age.'

'You should've stayed with your husband, then, shouldn't you? Poor bugger, I bet you led him a right old dance.'

Terry watched her from his window, saw her stop, and walk on. 'Another one bites the dust,' he thought, of the evening. He was wearily confident that she would ring later, but it was possible that she might find the line engaged. He switched on the television, put his feet up and reached for his little black book. 'There are plenty more fish in the sea,' he said, as he was confronted by an oily guillemot on the screen, its bright terrified eyes seeming to be the only bits left alive in that tarred and feathered body.

Part of Olive wanted to run back as soon as she was halfway up the road, embrace him, say she was sorry; after all he was all she had. William and empty rooms leading off the hall into an empty future awaited her at home. She hesitated on the pavement and then found herself walking, determined to put one foot in front of the other until she got home even if she was mugged, raped or killed in the attempt. She saw, some way ahead of her, a man clanking along on his aluminium sticks and set herself to race him to the end of the road. In the blackness of Olive's heart, special bitterness was reserved for this elderly person, the sight of whom, had Olive been an ant, would have triggered the flow of enough formic acid to sting him to death; had she been a skunk, the toddlers whose heads he patted would have fled screaming from the stench in which she drenched him. His crime? It seemed that whenever she was most in torment, most self-lacerating, he would materialise on the pavement, swinging along between two aluminium crutches, at a fast and virtuous lick, shopping bag slung round his neck like a nosebag to leave his hands free to grip his sticks. He covered miles; she had seen him on Beulah Hill and in Brixton, in Crystal Palace and Streatham, always alone, speeding stiffly on his silver supports in snow and rain, his thin hair streaming in the wind. She hated him most on Sundays, sighting him matins or evensong-bound, no discouragement making him once relent his first avowed intent to be a pilgrim; an inspiration to the congregation and a reproach to her. Sometimes she believed that he was a minor demon, conjured up out of her guilty unconscious, sometimes that he had been sent to torment her.

Olive overtook him as they came into the home strait, just pipping him to the post. With a new spring in her step, she passed the rubble of what had been until recently a ruined Georgian house which had stood empty, except for secret itinerants and birds, for years; and then gypsies had moved in and filled its overgrown garden with caravans and scrap metal, broken cars and rubbish. They had disappeared overnight, thrown out probably by the police, and the bulldozers had moved in. Olive thought of *Dunedin*, as she had known it as a small girl before her grandparents moved back to Scotland, and as it was now. It opened like a dolls' house, and she saw its dark little rooms peopled with broken dolls, and the grubby New Zealand boy doll sprawled on a miniature stained mattress among dinky little black garbage sacks.

The same morning, as soon as Olive had left for work,

William unlocked the garage, took out the gardening tools which he had managed to conceal from her, and set out for work himself. It felt strange, a back-to-school, first-day-of-term feeling. He had been unable to eat any breakfast. Ridiculous, he told himself as he washed Olive's breakfast dishes.

Mrs Handisyde's house was decked like a dowager in amethysts, dripping necklaces of wisteria. The front garden was a tangle of unpruned stems and litter from the street; the back garden had been taken over by borage which rampaged in bright blue flowers and empty seed heads, tiny fresh green seedlings starring the dry soil and great rotting dead bats of leaves flopping over any other foliage that attempted to survive it.

'If only there were just one or two ... ' Mrs Handisyde sighed '... I would think they were lovely, but it's completely out of control. I'm in despair. You'll need gloves – the stems are covered in tiny prickles which get into your skin, and days later you find little poisonous spots on your hands, and wonder what they are.'

There was the crack of a snail's shell as she stepped back.

'Oh God!'

They stared at the wrecked mollusc writhing, beginning to foam and ooze. William saw that it was his responsibility.

'No hope there, I think,' he said, flicking it under a draggle of borage leaves with his toe.

'You might have put it out of its misery first ... '

'I didn't tread on it,' he started to snap, and stopped, embarrassed to realise that he was in the snipey mode that had become his and Olive's currency.

'I'll make a start, then,' he added as she wiped her shoe on the ragged grass.

He took a folded copy of the *Streatham Guardian* from his pocket and laid it down as a kneeling pad; his own face would be ground into the earth. *Have-A-Go Bill Is Hold-Up Hero.* Despite his plea for anonymity, Jenella Abdela had sent round a photographer the day after her visit, and he had succumbed. He had not confessed to Olive; her derision when he failed to repel Jehovah's Witnesses and jobless youths selling dusters and ironing-board covers was hard enough to bear. And the thought that his and Olive's pictures stared from opposite pages of the same newspapers, locally famous and infamous, might have been amusing, were it not so frightening.

He had made page two while Olive was a page three girl. Mrs Da Souza next door had waved a copy of the paper at him that morning and he had scuttled into the house. There had been no other reaction, no reprisals from the boys' families or friends and, thank God, no connection had been made with the notorious ex-headmaster. He did not see Jenella as a future First Lady of Fleet Street.

Half an hour later he was at the back door.

'I don't know what to do.'

He opened his hand and there on a handful of black compost sat a toad. Its body pulsated gently and its long toes, sensitive as antennae, tensed.

'The place is hotching with them. There's a colony in that old gro-bag.'

'Hotching?'

Mrs Handisyde put out a tentative finger. The toad made a bravura leap onto the bristly doormat and then walked out over the step and onto the path.

'Show me.'

They were under leaves, half-buried in the worn-out compost of the gro-bag, sharing cobwebbed flower pots and a thick sack of ancient garden refuse with encrustations of snails; big brown and olive drab toads and babies the size of her fingernails on their mothers' backs.

'I'm afraid to dig . . . '

Her eyes glanced off the silver prongs of the new fork.

'Nothing to be done. We'd better have a drink.'

'But . . . the patio . . . '

He stamped earth from his feet and followed her into the kitchen.

'Bugger the patio – I'll just have to leave the garden as a toad sanctuary. Whisky? Vodka?'

Would it be too suburban to point out that it was only ten thirty?

'Seeing as the sun's over the yardarm . . . I'll have a large whisky – I don't know why I said that, I meant to say a very small one, please.'

'I don't know why they should have chosen this garden, it's not as if I've got a pond.'

As he sipped, a green-and-yellow memory surfaced, of carrying a toad in his hands to the river, long grass and buttercups brushing his bare knees; when he had described his feat at Cubs that evening, expecting a hearty pat on the back from Akela, she had told him that the toad had undoubtedly drowned. His socks, he remembered, had been the wrong green, with flashes cut from an old yellow taffeta dance frock, sewn onto garters of knicker elastic. The whisky made a sickly sunburst in his chest.

'They just like a bit of moisture,' he said.

'Well, anyway, that should get the neighbours off my

back – I'll just tell them it's a wildlife sanctuary and I'm doing my bit to save the planet, endangered species and what have you, and they'll just have to lump it. Personally, I don't give a monkey's about the wretched garden, just thought a patio would make me a bit more socially acceptable, tubs of busy lizzies and perilgoniums sort of thing, instead of standing accused of spreading weeds into their ghastly flowerbeds. Honestly, the whine of lawnmowers and hedge clippers here on a Sunday is enough to drive one mad, and the pollution from a dozen barbecues . . . 'Fraid it means you're out of a job though. Sorry.'

'Oh well, I – we could still get a few tubs, I noticed some of those half beer barrels going cheap at the garden centre, and perhaps a buddleia to attract butterflies and a few nettles.'

'Hmm. OK, then, I'll give you *carte blanche*, and perhaps a hanging basket in the porch might placate them. Did you notice by any chance that hedgehoggy thingy, bootscraper, by the back door? Very realistic, with its bristles and little snout, don't you think? My late husband did – gave it a saucer of bread and milk the day we moved in. A little while later he came in with such a long face: "Bad news, old girl. I think Mrs Tiggywinkle's popped her clogs."'

'No, I won't, thanks,' William protested as whisky was sloshed into his glass.

'God, I miss him. Cheers. This house is too much for me. I should move to a bungy on the coast somewhere and spend my days in a shelter on the prom, wearing a plastic rainhood and overshoes. At least I'd have some company. I could go to bingo.'

'There's bingo at Crystal Palace, and Streatham. Have you thought of . . .'

William had been going to suggest lodgers, students perhaps,

223

but, looking round the kitchen, he knew that Mrs Handisyde would never be able to cope. His eye fell on a photograph of two little boys in school uniform. A different Mrs Handisyde had washed and ironed those white shirts, straightened those ties, slicked down the glossy hair for the camera. The boys smiled out from another world, a world from which he had been banished too. Maybe it had been matron or an au pair who had buffed and polished the boys to an ideal shine, it didn't make any difference; their bright eyes were unbearable, watching the birdie, saying cheese.

William pictured their mother crouching in a damp bedroom, terrorised by lodgers, afraid to creep down to her own kitchen, and then standing in a wintry seaside amusement arcade in transparent plastic overshoes, with a clown's mouth of lipstick, feeding coins into a one-armed bandit.

'I think they're called perlagoniums,' he said.

Mrs Handisyde twisted her wedding ring, slumped in a kitchen chair.

'Geraniums might be a better bet,' he compromised.

'You're the gardener. What about some music?'

She reached for a once-white, nicotine-kippered radio and a pack of cigarettes.

'May I always listen to the Anniversary Waltz with you . . .' boomed out, sending a spider scuttling back up its web to the ceiling. Mrs Handisyde held out arms in shrunken cashmere.

'I won't dance, don't ask me, I won't dance, merci beaucoup', William was surprised to find himself accompanying the Anniversary Waltz . . . 'I won't dance, m'sieu, with you . . .' But he did, steering her suavely round the floor, until a chair with two left feet stepped on his toes.

Something splashed onto his hand; he thought it was a spider, then he realised it was wet.

'I'm afraid your ceiling's leaking. You haven't left a bath running, have you?'

She shook her head, dancing on; a tear rolled down his neck.

'So sorry. Not like me to blub. Just that it happens to be m'anniversary. Or near enough, can't recall the exact day, but I know it's sometime around now.'

She grabbed a handful of kitchen paper from the roll on top of the fridge and trumpeted into it as they shuffled round. The kitchen roll toppled and fell and bounced, unwinding round their shoes. It caught William's ankles, bandaging them together, and he stumbled, pulling Mrs Handisyde down on top of him as they sprawled on the floor. A wraith of sexual possibility wriggled between their bodies, fled as she struggled up on her elbows, and was exorcised.

William got to his feet and brushed fluff and crumbs from himself.

'I'd better be going.'

'Better for whom?'

'I'll see about those tubs and the hanging basket, get some prices for you. I'll come round tomorrow afternoon if you like and let you know. I could clear a bit of that blue prickly stuff, borage, or is it anchusa?'

'Fine. Oh Lord! I've just remembered, a very tiresome person is coming to lunch. Don't suppose you'd care to join us?'

William pretended not to hear the plea in her voice.

'Very kind of you, but I'd better be going. I don't want to intrude. I'll just pack up my things.'

She was opening the fridge and taking out little paper

packages. She opened one and sniffed at it. He glimpsed blue circles of meat; she put it on the table with a hunk of bread, and began wrenching a jagged lid from a tin of tomato soup with a black tin opener as he reached the back door. She dumped the soup in a pan and bunged in a dusty stream of dried basil and a slug of vodka.

Sunshine smacked a headachy sobriety into his head as, avoiding the hedgehog bootscraper, he turned and said 'Pelargoniums' and left her stirring and sipping her Bloody Mary, adding a dash of Worcester.

He gathered his tools and took the dank and ferny passage that ran alongside the house to the front, crumpling his newspaper into a dustbin, and passing Mrs Handisyde's guest, a surprisingly ordinary woman in a summer dress.

'The garden's just at that betwixt and between stage . . . ' Mrs Handisyde's sigh followed him. 'Late spring's such a difficult time, isn't it?'

'Yes,' her visitor might have agreed, 'the crisp bags almost over and the beer cans not fully out yet . . . '

'Of course, all Roderick's roses have gone to dog.'

'Gone to dog?'

'Gone back to dog roses or wild roses from neglect. Reverted to type. And the hyacinths are all bluebells now.'

'Oh well, up to them I suppose, if that's what they prefer . . . '

The guest washed her hands of Mrs Handisyde's feckless bulbs, like a social worker dismissing a problem family. She poked at a drift of polystyrene pieces which had blown in like blossom from the pavement and lodged among the fresh green leaves and last year's skeletal flowerheads of a hydrangea.

'You'll have to excuse me,' Mrs Handisyde said, 'I've got an awful woman coming to lunch and I've been fortifying myself somewhat. Not wisely but too well, I suspect,' she added in the silence offered by the other woman.

William stayed to hear no more, but caught the visitor's, 'I always sink jamjars filled with beer into the earth. At least they die happy.'

And Mrs Handisyde's reply. 'What makes you think that? How many slugs have *you* seen going down the pub?'

15

There were no signposts to the Victorian edifice of pinnacles with conical caps of grey-green purplish lead, crenellated turrets which flew no flags, glassed-over walkways in the air and fretted iron fire escapes, sealed at either end, curvetting dizzily round the brickwork. There was no name on the electronically operated gates, set between stone pillars topped by spread eagles with open beaks caught in mid-cry. This vast house was not on the current local Ordnance Survey map; it was not listed in the telephone book; it was as if it did not exist. There were pigeons who had colonised the broken cupolas and the loftiest windows and, with visiting gulls, clotted the sills, drainpipes and window bars with marbled guano and feathers, who knew about it; there was a great bell which hung exposed to the weather but it had lost its tongue; and there was a small army of people who had sworn to be as dumb as the bell and whose tales, if told, would have sounded as foreign, incomprehensible and deluded as the cries of the birds. They never left the building and its grounds and many of them did not speak English. These workers, men, women and those of indeterminate gender, wore heavy green dungarees which faded with time to a soft sage shade, specked with bright orange lichen where the metal fastenings had rusted.

Above the greens ranked the white-overalled contingent and the blue-uniformed. Minibuses picked them up early in the morning, and deposited them in the evening at their homes, where invariably they made for the bath or shower, sluicing and soaking away their day's work in hot water and scented or medicated shampoos and foams. Their midday meals were prepared in the modern kitchen and their uniforms dry-cleaned, and bleached and starched to dazzling whiteness in the subterranean laundry; and yet they, and their children, fell victim to more stomach bugs and sickness than their neighbours and schoolmates, ailments for which they were compensated by bonuses and holidays in the firm's time-share complex in the Algarve. Several among them lived on the same small private estate. Their social life was limited, and they kept aloof from other neighbours, who guessed them to be security guards and lab technicians and agency nurses, and some of the respect that adheres, with an indefinable institutional smell, to members of the caring professions clung to the last-named. Yet they slept uneasily under the padded and quilted headboards of their valanced beds, sniffed their skin surreptitiously, and picked up regular prescriptions of antidepressants and tranquillisers from the company pharmacy.

Then there was the admin team and, at the tip of the hierarchy, the director. His 1964 E-Type Jaguar glittered like a silver bullet in its reserved spot in the car park, whose tarmac, like all of the grounds, was immaculate; there was no shortage of gardeners to rake gravel and tend the rockeries and shrubberies of heathers, leathery-leaved hostas, sedum, berberis, spiraea, spotted laurels and dwarf conifers which gave a wintery and withered aspect even in the spring, when a subversive splash of snowdrops, then coltsfoot and celandines, rogue wood anemones and a brief blaze of bluebells staged a short-lived protest. Dandelions, buttercups and daisies were put down without mercy; balsam, cow parsley and all its cousins, nettles and willowherb buckled, blackened and melted before the flame-thrower brandished by the most senior trusty. Tall trees screened the perimeter fence topped with razor wire and rolls of barbed wire. Behind it was the original brick wall which was studded with jagged shards of broken glass. Set in the folds of the hills, the buildings were invisible except from the air. Had the locked windows not been shrouded by wire without and paint within, a view might have been had across the treetops, of the grey corrugated roof of the nearest neighbour, a mushroom farm, and the windowless galvanised gothic of a chicken farm. Consignments of misshapen mushrooms and cracked eggs arrived regularly at the back entrance, as did severed heads and trotters, strings of glistening offal gouted with blood, red, raw and faecal, grey sponges and honeycombs, lengths of diseased rubbery tubing, all to be boiled and boiled in aluminium vats and the brownish grey froth they exuded stirred in or skimmed off in the main kitchens.

Nothing of this was known yet to the men and women who were pushed or stumbled from a windowless van onto the pebbles where, some of them picking themselves up painfully, they stood blinking on the crunching gravel as if they had been cast up on a beach at sunrise. Or, city children on a treat, disgorged from the coach, they gazed around, puzzled to encounter trees, cheated of the sea. They were separated roughly into two groups according to gender, their garments, which hung wetly on them although it had been a dry night, providing a not infallible guide, for several had lost all distinctions of sex. A couple who clung together were wrenched apart.

Among the men, the youngest of them, was Jay. He had been one of a group of people and dogs making quiet shapes on the wide paved portico at the top of the flight of shallow steps which led up to a church. The heavy vehicle, marked Department of the Environment, had screeched up, men with truncheons had jumped out, a hose had been unreeled, a flat serpent suddenly swollen and jumping and ejaculating, sousing the brazier in a sizzle of black smoke, assaulting the sleepers. Cries, shouts, barking, curses, breaking glass; the people had been beaten with sticks and water, dragged, shoved and thrown in the van and driven away, with the barking and howling of the dogs fainter and more frantic behind them. From the windowless interior they had not been able to see a second van draw up, and men with guns jump out.

A man had beaten on the steel doors, leaving smears of blood, howling his dog's name. The four broad backs of their captors had been crammed along a bench seat in front of the grille which separated them from the prisoners. One of the uniformed men had cracked open a can of lager and opened a foil packet.

'Anyone fancy a sarnie?'

'What you got in 'em?'

'Cold turkey.'

They had laughed. A sudden dazzle of early sunshine had bathed them in a golden fuzz. The van had filled with the stench of unwashed flesh, wet clothes, exhalations of wine and cider and blue and the metallic smell of blood and cigarette smoke. The shaking, crying and coughing up of distressed jellyfish had increased as they hit a motorway.

'Welcome to Butlin's, boys and girls!' the officer who unlocked the doors of the van had said.

Through the bushes glittered the chlorine peacock-blue rectangle of a swimming pool. A girl was running slowly on poised toes along the dipping diving board; she poised in her petalled cap, somersaulted through the blue sky, and broke the surface into a fountain of diamonds and peacock feathers. The pink hydrangea of her cap floated on the blue water. Those last vivid man-made colours were the last Jay knew as they were herded inside, into the reek of misery and rot, those and the girl's white body, arched in a shiny turquoise swimsuit.

They were being addressed by a man in a quasi-uniform of navy blue: ' . . . and just in case there should be any barrack-room lawyers among you, with any fancy ideas about Human Rights, I should point out that you lot have renounced any claim you might once have had to humanity. You are no longer human beings. You are the scum of the earth. Your subscriptions to Amnesty International have been cancelled. If you have any friends, which I very much doubt, they won't find you here. Oh yes, one more thing, there is no way out, so don't even think about it.'

He turned to the two guards lounging against the wall like Sumo wrestlers gone to seed, in sagging sweatpants; tsk, tsk, tsk sizzed from their personal stereos.

'Right. Get them out of my sight, before I lose my breakfast.'

In the sunny ground-floor room at the front of the building, the director looked across his desk at the lipsticked mouth and the glossy hair, blow-dried and conditioned after her swim, of his secretary.

'What is it, Cheryl?'

'It's, er, a Father Jeremy, Dr Barrable.'

'Who? How the hell did he get in? What the fuck does he want? I gave strict orders ...'

'He was very insistent, he ...'

The doctor rose, extending a hand to the untidy impression of denim and wool, spectacles, teeth and hair.

'Father Jeremy! What can I do for you?'

The curate had to stretch across metres of rosewood and a marbled deskset to grasp the soft waving fingertips. He resisted the impulse to wipe his hand on his trouser leg, and sank uninvited into a low chair, looking like a toy which somebody had knitted with more enthusiasm than skill for the Christmas Fayre.

'Actually, I rather hope it's a question of what *I* can do for you. And your patients, of course ...'

He ran a finger under the slip of white collar which encircled his throat.

'I'm new here, as you may know, and I've been doing my homework like a good boy. Local history's rather a hobbyhorse of mine, the oral tradition and so on ... I managed to get hold of some old Ordnance Survey maps, and I discovered that there's a chapel attached to St Anne's, as it used to be called, and, as such, it falls under my jurisdiction, as it were, well, that of the vicar really, but in effect ...'

'The vicar ...'

'Oh, I realise that Mr Stebbings wasn't aware of the chapel's existence but I was wondering – you see, you look after their

233

physical welfare and do a grand job, I don't doubt, but as to their *souls*, well, that's *my* job . . . '

'Father Jeremy, we have one of the finest psychiatric teams in the country and, frankly, tragically, the majority of our patients are beyond . . . you'd be wasting your time.'

'Nobody is beyond God's love.'

'Oh, for Christ's sake!'

'Precisely.'

'Well, goodbye, Father. I appreciate your coming to see me but I'm an extremely busy man and I've got a hospital to run.'

'Anyway, the chapel's derelict,' put in Cheryl, shuddering as if a bat had flapped through the ivied dusk and tangled in her hair.

'They don't,' said Father Jeremy.

'Who don't? Don't what?'

'Bats don't get in your hair. It's a popular misconception. As a fully paid-up member of Batwatch, I could give you some literature, if you're interested.'

Cheryl's mouth dropped open.

'No doubt your experience of belfries proves invaluable, Father Jeremy. Now, if you'll excuse me,' said Dr Barrable.

He picked up one of the telephones on his desk.

'Cheryl, don't stand there gawping like a . . . ' He had almost said 'like a pig', for he often fancied that when she turned round he would see a little curly tail peeking from the perky curved butt. 'Show Father Jeremy to his bicycle. No, don't.'

He pressed a bell on his desk.

Father Jeremy rose.

'And the little crematorium, is that derelict too?'

A man dressed like a Securicor guard with, Jeremy thought, the eyes of a disgraced policeman, materialised.

'McPhee, show Father Jeremy out, and then I'd like a word.'

Cheryl stood at the window on her trotters, in her tight skirt, watching an orange Beetle with a BABY ON BOARD sticker on its rear window clacking down the drive, a plume of smoke attached to its exhaust, towards the electronic gates, followed by McPhee on his BSA Thunderbird.

'How on earth could he have known, about the bat, I mean? That I was thinking about bats? I never said nothing, anything, I mean, did I?'

'I could say that there are more things in heaven and earth than are dreamed of in your somewhat limited and banal philosophy, Cheryl, or I could say get on with your work, and call a full meeting of all security staff for after lunch. And make sure that snooping little God-botherer, Father frigging Jeremy, doesn't get within a five-mile radius of this place again, or I shall see to it personally that he never fathers anything.'

'He did have kind eyes, though,' said Cheryl, 'shame about the glasses. And the hair. It was uncanny, ooh, my arms have gone all goosey just thinking . . .'

'Cheryl, just get out, will you, before I make you into a pound of pork chipolatas . . .'

'Yes, sir!'

Cheryl wiggled delightedly.

The doctor banged his fist on his desk and his wife and children jumped in their silver frame. There could be no doubt that he had mishandled the interview. He had admitted far too much, and he could be in very serious trouble. Not since his days as an ambitious young abortionist in Earl's Court, when that slag had died of septicaemia, had he felt in such danger.

*

'I was right, Heather.'

Jeremy buried his face in the hair of the baby in the high chair, reviving himself on the healing smell of baby shampoo and apricot yoghurt.

'You mean it *is* a hospital, or a home? Mrs Matthews said it was some sort of government research station, to do with AIDS or animals or chemical warfare, something top secret ...'

'She may well be right about the government bit, but as for a hospital or a home, those have got to be euphemisms, I fear.'

'Well, did you see any, um, patients, then?'

'A couple of chaps in the grounds who looked as if they'd been lobotomised. I bluffed my way past the guard on the gates, whose head I imagine is rolling even as we speak, but I'm sure I won't be able to do that again. I met the director and his secretary, and a heavy who gave me a motorcycle escort off the premises.'

'Your hand's shaking.'

Jeremy gulped the coffee which Heather had handed to him.

'What's he like, the director?'

'Smooth. Sleek. A fat cat, no, slimy rather than furry. Probably owns the E-type in the car park. He kept his temper with difficulty. Just. Obviously had me down as yer typical wimpish curate as portrayed in a thousand amateur dramatic productions and TV sitcoms ... perhaps you could give me a trim later ... I don't want to sound dramatic, darling, but I really did feel that I was looking into the face of Evil.'

'Don't! You're making me go all funny ... look!'

She held out her arm, and pulled the baby from his chair and hugged him with arms blurred with a fuzz of fair upstanding hairs.

Jeremy stared at the pale skin in the rolled sleeves of her

236

washed-out mauve jumper. Heather, who had spotted the untidy doll and perceived it as the most desirable object on the stall.

'Heather, I . . .'

He stooped to pick a yoghurt carton from the thin acrylic carpet patterned with orange and brown and lime-green sycamore leaves.

'I am so . . . blessed. I love you, and Danny and our home, and the cats' – taking in the material flowing from the stilled needle of the sewing-machine, the plastic sack of disposable nappies, the two cats, smooth Jacob and fluffy Esau, moulting on the nylon chintz stretch covers of the sofa, all bobbled and snagged by their claws, the dried palm crosses stuck behind the pictures, the jar of nasturtiums with blackfly-clotted stalks. 'These look good,' he went on. 'They for the Malawi Steering Committee?'

He lifted from the paper-doilyed plate a white iced fairy cake tipped with a glacé cherry; some of the cakelets in their fluted paper cases had aureoles of hundreds and thousands too. He bit off the cherry. It swelled in his throat so that he had difficulty swallowing it. He could have wept at the innocent little breast which he was eating, at the rumpled bridal lace of the doily, at the ingenuous leaves of the carpet.

'It was such a beautiful morning,' he said through a mouthful of cake, making a fan of the paper case and handing it to Danny, who put it in his mouth, 'and yet I felt that if the wind had been in the wrong, or the right, direction, it would have blown a stench out of that place that would asphyxiate the whole of Surrey. I can't put my finger on it, but I know something's wrong there, and I know that God wants me to find out what it is.'

Heather extracted the soggy paper from the soft wet lips. Tiny teeth, all four of them, closed on her finger.

'Who's got the cleverest, sharpest, pearliest little toothy pegs in the whole world, then? Jem, you don't think there are any *children* there, do you?'

She handed him the baby, and scrubbed at the slop of yoghurt on the carpet with a damp cloth, scrubbing out of her mind a photograph of a monkey, on a poster, with tubes and electrodes coming out of his scalped head, and agonised eyes.

16

SERIOUS CRIME the poster at the top of the escalator at Brixton was headed: CAN YOU HELP? DO YOU KNOW THIS WOMAN? DID YOU SEE ANYTHING?

'That's Olive.' Terry stopped to stare at the assembled features. 'Could be.' He was tempted to take out his pen – a smidgen off the nose, bit of shading on the cheekbones, lower the hairline – the eyes were wrong, but it could be. What had Olive's double been up to? Murder? Armed robbery? Baby-snatching. Faintly disappointing. He could dob her in, for a laugh. 'Officer, the woman you're looking for is Olive Mackenzie, proprietor of *Ideas*, and I claim my community Service Award . . . ' He pictured Olive's rage and revenge, spitting at him, flailing with handcuffed wrists; perhaps it wouldn't be that much of a laugh. Tempting, though. There was no way Olive would take a kid, it just wasn't in her nature, he thought as he shoved past a couple of girls on the escalator, foreign lumps who hadn't mastered the first rule of escalator etiquette – stand on the right to let others pass. Feet were thudding behind him and there was almost a pile-up. It was rare to find even one escalator working; alongside, people were toiling up the fixed staircase, boys taking the broken upward escalator in one effortless go, several stairs at each bound. Of course, Olive had hinted more than once that she would like to have a child, but that was because of him; it had been his child that she wanted. Good job he hadn't listened.

There are two platforms at Brixton, the south end of the Victoria line; all trains terminate there. As one train disgorges its passengers, the other closes its doors and heads back north. Today there was no train on either platform and people jostled about between the two, their numbers swelling all the time to fill the gaps left by those who gave up and made for the buses. It was a not untypical state of affairs. God, they ought to ban pushchairs from public transport, Terry fumed, his way barred by a mother with several small children. Serve them right if their kids got snatched, getting in the way of bona fide travellers. He bit into the big yellow microwaved Jamaican patty he had bought in the booking hall. It was getting cold. It was impossible to enjoy your food in this crush. A message was coming over the loudspeaker; every fourth word or so was intelligible, something about an earlier incident at Pimlico ... subject to long delays ... advised to ... How to make yourself the most hated person in London in one easy step – chuck yourself under the tube. Terry was swept along in the wave towards the exit, trapped for a while in the whirlpool of people still descending. He could have grabbed any number of brats if he'd wanted to.

Fragments of a conversation with Olive were coming back to him. 'I know what it's like to be the only child of elderly parents,' he had told her.

'Who said anything about an only child? I'm not elderly. Lots of women my age . . . anyway, your mother's different from me.'

'You mean thick, working class?'

'She was a lot older than me, is all I meant, and times have changed.'

'Just because she lives in a mobile home. Anyway, *you're* almost old enough to be my mother.'

'Your mother's old enough to be my mother.'

'One major difference would be, you'd be bringing it up on your own.' Not handled with the greatest diplomacy. On either side, he conceded.

'Brixton?' Terry's mother interrupted his denunciation of London Transport, when he finally arrived, having been unable, of course, to telephone to say he'd been delayed. 'That's where that baby was snatched, wasn't it? We saw it on *Crimestoppers*, didn't we, Dad?'

'Reconstruction,' said Mr Turner.

'Yes, that's right. Shall I warm this through for you, Terry? We had ours. It's that poor mother I feel sorry for; of course we should never have let them in in the first place.'

'We?' asked Terry. He saw his parents in uniform at Immigration, at Passport Control.

'You know what I mean. I was talking to Mrs Jeffries, you know who I mean, used to clean the aeroplanes at Heathrow before she was married, and then she was at Gatwick, in the Ladies, till she retired.'

The remains of a Fray Bentos steak and kidney were heating in a pan of bubbling water on the Baby Belling, to be served with sprouts out of season and scalloped potatoes. Condensation ran down the windows.

'She said they used to come off the aeroplane in a crocodile, kiddies first, then the women, then the men, in their summer clothes, expecting sunshine. Well, they would, wouldn't they? The air hostesses used to give them blankets to wrap around theirselves. You had to feel sorry for them, she said. She was invalided out of the WAAFs, in the war. You know who I mean, Dad?'

'This is good, Mum. Any ketchup? Thanks.' Terry unscrewed the top of the salt and extracted a damp lump.

'How's your chest, Dad?' he asked with some trepidation.

'Not so bad, son. This weather seems to agree with it. Mind you, we could do with some rain, they had us all queuing at the standpipe last week, a right old carry-on we had with our buckets.'

'What a bore,' said Terry. 'I mean, it's a disgrace. People your age shouldn't have to go through that.'

'Oh, we managed, didn't we, Dad?'

Terry supposed it had given them something to think about, taken them out of themselves.

'The old Blitz spirit, eh?' he laughed.

'No, it was nothing like the Blitz,' his mother snapped.

'How's Literature?' Mr Turner smoothed things over.

'Oh, bearing up. Musn't grumble.'

'It must be nice for you to meet all those famous writers.'

'Mum, I'm a famous writer, you know. These people meet me on equal terms.'

'I'm sure they do. Hand me your plate, I'll fetch your afters.'

'Leave the washing-up, Mum, I'll do it in a minute. At least wait till I've finished eating, for God's sake.'

'Oi! Don't talk to your mother like that.'

'Sorry, Mum, but couldn't you just sit down for a minute? The dishes can wait.'

'I wouldn't like to see the state of your kitchen!' His mother squirted washing-up liquid briskly. She was unlikely to. The thought hung in the cloud of steam from the kettle, visible to all. His father made the tea and sponged down the windows and window frames.

'Yoo hoo. It's only me!' Fingers rapped and a face loomed through the wet glass. 'Mohammed comes to the mountain,' announced the neighbour known by the courtesy title of Auntie Edie, stepping inside. 'I thought I saw young Terry arrive and I thought, I'll give him time to have his dinner and then I'll pop round to say hello.'

'Hello, Auntie Edie.'

'Should have been put the other way round,' the mountain thought, pushing away his plate. Auntie Edie seemed to fill the room.

'You're looking well,' he said, hoping her condition had not been diagnosed as life-threatening.

'Terry was just saying, weren't you, Terry, he was just saying "I must pop round to say hello to Auntie Edie in a minute, as soon as I've drunk my tea."'

'Pull the other one,' wheezed Auntie Edie cheerfully, accepting a cup and easing herself on to a chair. 'I know our Terry's much too grand for the likes of us nowadays – too busy consorting with the hoi polloi at all those literary soirées.'

'It's not like that,' Terry protested. 'Well, of course I do have to attend a certain number of parties and . . .'

'Got a drop more sugar, duck? Ta. We'll be seeing you win the Booker Prize soon I dare say. Your dad was telling me your latest went down very well. Are you putting in for the Booker Prize this year? You should have a go. After all, when you see some of them that win it ... Oh, look at him, Dot, he's gone as red as a beetroot!'

'Actually, I think the Booker has a very corrupting influence on writers and publishers.'

'Wouldn't mind the money, though, eh, would you?' Auntie Edie laughed.

Terry tried to catch his father's eye. If only he would come out with something manly like a suggestion of a visit to the pub or the allotment.

'Take us all on a cruise.' Edie was waltzing on the deck under a midnight-blue sky, shooting stars and an orange tropical moon.

'"I've never sailed the Amazon, I've never reached Brazil ... "' she sang. 'Remember, Dot? When we were at school.'

They sang together:

> '"Yes, weekly from Southampton,
> Great steamers, white and gold,
> Go rolling down to Rio
> (Roll down – roll down to Rio!)
> And I'd like to roll to Rio
> Some day before I'm old!"'

'Remember Singing with old Mr Benson? Ooh, he was a tartar! Bandy Benson, we used to call him.'

'Was that "before I mould", or "before I'm old"?' Terry was wondering, noticing a small growth of what looked like gorgonzola under the window frame.

'Dad?'

'Just a minute, son. I'll just make a fresh pot,' the old fool said, evidently believing that they were all enjoying a cultural afternoon.

'Almost forgot,' said Edie. 'I've got some nice rhubarb for you, Dot. My grandson brought a load round, much too much for me. Your dad misses his allotment, Terry; shame it's got too much for him.'

Two at one blow, the grandson and the allotment. Nice one, Edie, Terry congratulated her silently. Auntie Edie smiled, grandmother of seven, great-grandmother, and still with a soft spot in her heart to spare for young Terry who she'd known since he was knee-high to a grasshopper.

'I suppose I'd better be getting back, Mum.'

'But you've only just got here!'

'It's been a good couple of hours ... '

The clock, his father's presentation on retirement, gave the lie to his statement, but Terry felt as if he'd been there at least four hours. He swallowed a yawn. As he departed he realised he had come empty-handed. He was leaving with a food parcel; well, a carrier bag of goodies that he was too depressed to investigate. He stopped off at a florist's in Redhill to remedy his omission.

'That's pretty, how much is it?' He pointed at a delicate arrangement.

'That's a floral tribute. Were you looking for something for a funeral?'

'No, I bloody wasn't. How soon can you deliver? Later today? Great. I'll have some gladdies and roses, lots of roses, delphiniums, irises – what are those big suede things, are they real?

Gerberas? I thought they were desert rats – never mind, I'll have some of those and some nice greenery and that white stuff.'

'Would you like to write a card to go with your flowers?'

Terry chose a little card and wrote on it 'To the Best Mum in the World, all my love, Terry.' The whole thing cost him twenty pounds. That should put Auntie flaming Edie in her place. Take them all on a cruise, I should cocoa!

'Now that you've won the Booker, Terry, how do you feel and what do you plan to do with the money?'

'I'm over the moon, Melvyn. It's always been my dream to take my mum and dad and Auntie Edie on a cruise.' Gordon bleeding Bennett.

When Terry climbed the escalator, his lungs expanding with relief as he drew in the healthy air of Brixton sizzling with onions and burgers, his heart quickening to the music pulsating from the little record shop in the booking hall, he noted that somebody had added a moustache and beard to the Olive look-alike, and somebody else had scrawled 'Liars' across the fading notice promising that the escalator would be repaired as soon as possible. The usual beggars were on the steps; two evangelical prophets of doom, one black, one white, had come to blows at the top of the steps that led to the street, imperilling the flower seller's display and the stall that sold socks and boxer shorts. The pavement outside Murray's Meat Market, the mirrored emporium reflecting glistening heaps of white and scarlet, was slippery with blood. Terry felt he had come home.

Later that evening as he and a friend arrived at the Ritzy to see *Wings of Desire* Terry caught sight of Olive with some women in the foyer drinking coffee and eating carrot cake.

'Let's go for a drink instead,' he said. There was no chance of avoiding them in that tiny plush auditorium.

Olive, watching the stylised machinations of angels with their hair tied back in ponytails like Terry's, had no idea that her face, or an approximation of it, now bearded and moustached, stared out at the indifferent crowd at Brixton tube. She felt safe in the darkness, happy to sit on with Betty and Hazel and let the late-night, women-only showing of *Desert Hearts* wash over her; she just wished she could spend the rest of her life in a cinema, like a fish fathoms deep on the ocean floor. Her greatest fear was of encountering that woman on the bus who had sympathised when Theo was sick; no doubt it was she who had gone running to the fuzz, sitting self-importantly at the station, flicking through transparencies of eyes and mouths and noses; the sort of woman who wouldn't hesitate to shop her own mother to *Crimestoppers*, the arch-vigilante of Neighbourhood Watch, snooping behind her net curtains, sneaking out at night to drop poison-pen letters into the pillar-box. Women like her shouldn't be allowed, they should be ... feeding off human weakness and misery ...

'Olive, are you all right? Do you want to leave?' Hazel whispered.

'No. Never. I'm fine.'

Miraculously, Charlene had either not seen them or not noticed any resemblance to Olive in the picture in the papers, and no customer had done a double-take. Hardly surprising; it was perfectly hideous. Artist's impression indeed. Some artist. Yes, the sooner somebody put a stop to that woman's nasty little games, the sooner she was behind bars, the better. Olive sucked an irritating shred of carrot from a tooth. There was nothing at all to connect her with Theo, nothing in the world; and for God's sake, she'd given him back after a few hours. The whole thing was a storm in a teacup; the police would be better employed catching criminals, like that woman of the poison pen, or those thugs who had gone up the road last night smashing the windows of every parked car. A few hours – he probably spent longer than that every day strapped in front of a television with a dozen other babies in the room of a sleazy babyminder, or crying alone in the dark while gas seeped through a faulty pipe and his parents rapped and hip-hopped the night away. She had seen those blackened, boarded-up windows which told their own tale.

Somewhere, not very far away, a woman going about her evening in her home or garden might suddenly have felt her ears on fire, or a stab in her heart like the pricking of a pin in a wax image, or an invisible cold tornado of ill-will lift her up and set her down again, shaken, as Olive's thoughts left her. Olive sat, not seeing the screen, an unconscious smile flickering her lips as she reflected that, after all, she and Theo had had fun. He would always have some brightly coloured elusive memory of the lovely time he had had, like a magical lost toy or a glimpse of fairyland.

There are writers who concern themselves with the good of their fellow artists, who make the time to sit on committees, to fight injustice, to make speeches and to write letters on behalf of those silenced victims of torture and oppression, sending flickers of hope into dark and bloody cells. Terry was not one of those. Today it was as much as he could do to order, on Joyce Jauncey's behalf, a pair of double jersey elasticated waist trousers in burgundy, a pink ribbed polo-neck, 85 per cent acrylic, 15 per cent wool, and a pair of French knickers with lace trim in champagne, and then, crumpling the catalogue, aim it at the wastepaper basket and miss. He threw up the sash window and leaned out over the montana into a waft of mock-orange blossom and a subliminal whiff of Whitsun weddings as two neighbours passed below with shopping bags. They certainly went in for pair-bonding in this street, he reflected, and called out, 'Phew, what a scorcher!' to the couple in their dove-grey summer plumage shot with pink and turquoise.

'Thought that chap was supposed to be a writer,' the male partner remarked as, nodding agreement, they bobbed shopwards, leaving Terry to ponder the wisdom of the deliberate cliché, and Clichy and Vichy France and Vichy water and vichysoisse, and watch a man in a parked car peel back the bread of his sandwich and sniff the filling and a silver cigarshaped plane dissolve in the blue. Had he only filled in the order form at the back of J.J.'s catalogue he might have been more dissatisfied with his morning's work, but he had spent some time adding spectacles, moustaches, beards, pipes and cigarettes to the smiling faces of the models, and bandages and elaborately laced and eyeleted high-heeled boots to their shapely calves. He decided to give *The Archers* a miss and set off for Brockwell Park Lido with suntan oil in his shorts pocket and a neat swiss roll of trunks and towel under his arm.

'All right for some,' one of a pair of neighbours remarked; the same couple, or a different one? Terry didn't know; to his writer's eye they were indistinguishable. He idled at the bus stop behind a gaggle of pensioners, waiting for one of them to say '2B or not 2B, that is the question' when the top of a bus

appeared above the clogged traffic. It was a 196, and a piece
of dialogue lodged in his head as one old woman, descending,
encountered another boarding the bus.

'Oh, ello, uh huh huh.'

'Ello uh huh huh.'

'All right, then?'

'Keepin' on the move, so I must be.'

'Right. Ta ta, then.'

'Ta ta, then, uh huh huh.'

Terry observed them like a zoologist recording the encounter of two animals, and registered the little uh huh huh laugh
indicating friendliness, and membership of the same group, or
herd; there would be no clash of lowered heads and spectacles,
and the ritual enquiry had established that neither had crawled
away yet to die in a dark place out of the sight of the pack which
might turn and rend it.

At the Lido, Terry swam, dried himself and anointed himself
with oil. Pillowing his head on his shirt and wallet, he stretched
out face downwards on his towel on the stone, feeling slightly
sore where a black bacchante in wisps of nylon leopardskin had
detached herself from the throng, pursuing a youth along the
poolside, and jumped in feet first onto Terry's basking stomach.
He felt the earth's faint heartbeat, or the pulsation of traffic on
the road, through the grit and tiny plants of the insects' world,
and heard the whooping of a police car and shrieks from the
pool, arcs of coloured sound exploding in bright stars against
the blue sky and fizzling out; the pyrotechnics of a summer
afternoon. Squinting up through prismatic sunshine into a
tree, he wondered drowsily if it were possible to get away with
candelabra imagery describing a chestnut tree, if the candles

were burned down and melted in post-modern sconces. Vivid geometric shapes and sounds, voices and patterns on shirts and shorts, neon fish and tropical birds darted through blackness as he rested his closed eyes on his arm; 'keepin' on the move so I must be', stylised laughter, shoals of black, pink, white, brown bodies tumbling through the water like dollops of ice cream, a fountain of diamonds, a head breaking the surface with brilliants, jewelled colours slicked to loin and breast flashed through his brain. He slept.

Terry woke to find that his shorts had been nicked and went home, slightly lobsterous where the oil had not lubricated him, in his trunks and a sarong made from his towel, picking up a *Standard* on his way. Waiting at the bus stop, he turned to the books pages: there was no reason to expect his name to jump out of the newsprint but it was always possible that some reviewer might cite him in favourable comparison. Not today, though. He flicked back to Londoner's Diary where he read that the Literary World was saddened by the death of Enid Masters, a writer whose star had dwindled and gone out. The implication was that it was not a natural death. There would be a memorial service. A sour acid, such as he had swallowed when he had found his shorts missing, filled his chest. He had not been told about her death; he was not saddened by it; ergo, he was not part of the Literary World. He could not be seen to be of it by attending the memorial service in a dark tie with his linen suit, because two weeks ago he had written a snide and dismissive notice of the reissue of one of her early books. He supposed it was too late to write to the *TLS*, complaining that a sub-editor had changed his distinguished into undistinguished and dateless into dated.

Tricky. He had corrected the proof himself and insisted on the reinstatement of a semicolon.

The phone was ringing when he got home. It was a poet named Mollie Mitchell.

'Well, I trust you're feeling proud of yourself?'

'How d'you mean?'

The words 'prize' and 'genius' floated in the room, dark after the sun, and were burst like balloons.

'I suppose you've heard about Enid?'

'Mmm. Topped herself, did she?'

'You bastard. And don't try to tell me that shitty piece you wrote, designed to show your own cleverness at her expense, had nothing to do with it.'

'Now look here! I will defend to the death my duty to protest about bad art!'

'I think you just did.'

The phone was slammed down. Stupid old bat. She must've been about two hundred years old anyway. Terry's anger was making his sunburn tingle. Even as he was pouring blissful cold aftersun lotion over his shoulders, a biographer in Hampstead, at a loose end, idling through the evening paper, suddenly sat up straight with shining eyes, stopped chewing one end of her pencil and sharpened the other.

'Probably done old Enid the biggest favour of her career,' Terry muttered as he cracked open a can of Red Stripe. 'She'll be a Virago Modern Classic before you can say "knife". Anyway there must have been more to it; nobody kills themself over a review. If you can't stand the heat stay out of the kitchen.' That cow who'd called *Wraith Rovers* gratuitously nasty and grubby, all he'd done was get her phone number and call her up a few times in the night and give her a bit of heavy breathing. There were ways of handling these things if you were a pro. His thoughts turned to Una and the beer gushed back up his throat in a bilious geyser.

17

The women were disposed about the small walled garden on cushions laid on the silvery herringbone brick paving studded with creeping thymes, in the blue-green, yellow-green bitter scent of rue crushed from leaves rubbed between Olive's fingers.

'I think this is my favourite smell,' she said. 'I love all those strange bittersweet sharp-sour scents like this and elderflowers and geranium leaves and flowering currant and snapdragons, that lots of people dislike.'

'But it is melancholy and has sad allusions.' Betty had rolled up her trousers and was dabbling a foot in the little pond to entice a silver carp or the frog who had fled under a waterlily leaf; a stone fish dribbled brightly onto the cresses she had cloven with her toes, and her arm was loosely round Hazel's somnolent shoulder. Beyond the perimeter the dozy sounds of Sunday afternoon traffic were shattered by postprandial ice-cream chimes and then drifted back. The back wall was a torrent of ivy, and half-glimpsed statues among fragrant bushes made the garden a secret and aromatic place; green and silvery plants trailed from the heads of stone goddesses and satyrs among the clematis and passion flowers and old Russian vine, and blossom from another garden spiralled slowly onto the friends, their used plates and into their glasses, floating on yellow wine and the green water of the pond. It was Hazel, an acupuncturist who had at times stuck needles in them all, who reintroduced the topic which had engaged them on more than one or two occasions: why are some people grown-ups and others not, whatever their ages? She was worried by a streak of silliness in herself which did not become narrower with the years, and a flippancy which might prove fatal. It was Hazel who, on being introduced to Olive, as Olive Schwarz, had replied: 'Look on the bright side – you might have married someone called Stuffed With Pimentoes, or even Anchovies.' Olive, who had suffered years of Olive Oyl, drew her dark brows together and narrowed her eyes. That had been some years ago and she had long since forgiven Hazel for remarking that her maiden name, Olive Mackenzie, sounded like a green waxed raincoat with a tartan lining. She had stuck to Schwarz for a long time after her divorce.

'It's an attitude of mind,' Betty said. 'How often have you heard an old person say she feels just the same inside as she ever did? It's how you perceive yourself. If you are a grown-up, you don't even think about it.'

'Well, why do we?'

'I'm a grown-up,' Olive said. Nobody answered and the aluminium aquamarine arch of climbing frame with slices of blue sky between its rungs curved in her mind, set in the scrubby grass of a post-war Utopia of sand and water trays and Marian Richardson handwriting. Despite the idealism, the new buildings, the teacher with her hair in a bun like a dried fig and her flowery smock had been brutal to her chosen victims;

the girl who was permeated with the smell of the chip shop where she lived, the runny-nosed, the boys with holes in their trousers and no underpants, the twins from the orphanage. She did not know why that school, one of many, its daisied playing field and little camp beds where the children rested after dinner-play, had swum into her mind, and did not like the implication that she had stuck at five years old. She looked at her friends, sprawling like schoolgirls on hot asphalt; the Radio Luxembourg generation, disaffected members of Jimmy Savile's T and T Disc Club, who would never be at a loss for the spelling of Keynsham, Bristol: Ashley, a few years younger, thin and fair, and looking even younger than her years; Rosemary, mother of two grown-up sons, whose voluptuous blondness suggested a sympathetic bosom leaning on a bar, and the skilful dispersing of solace to the tired and lonely; brown Betty, and Hazel in baggy floral shorts and green espadrilles which almost matched her T-shirt; Lizzie too hot in black Levis and vest, and around them the brightly coloured pieces of Betty's prized Depression china.

'Of course it was much easier for our mothers' generation.'

'Why?'

'Well, they had those lovely forties frocks cut on the bias, floral crêpe de Chine, and clumpy peeptoe shoes, and flowery wrap-around pinnies to do the housework and baking. You had to be grown-up in those clothes.'

'You can get all that stuff,' Olive said.

'But that's retro. It's dressing up, so it negates the whole thing.'

'They addressed one another as Mrs. I think that about sums it up.'

'And lovely kitchen cabinets in lemon and eau-de-nil and Goblin vacuum cleaners and the kind of gas you could kill yourself with. There was some point to their lives.'

'There was in the war. God, they were lucky, I mean, what could be sexier than wearing those stunning uniforms and dancing with officers while the bombs were falling? Or they could work in munitions factories with their hair in turbans and listen to *Music While You Work*. There was so much scope ...'

'Remember parachute knickers?' Hazel said. 'Transparent and freezing, with pilch edging! Ah me, takes you back ...'

'My mother never had a Goblin.' Olive was slightly smug. 'It was always a dustpan and brush.'

'Yes, but they were all in it together. That's the point ...'

'I expect I'd have gone to the bad and painted my legs with cocoa and drawn seams up the back and got nylons and chocolate from GIs while my man was fighting for his country.' Olive looked not at all put out when her friends agreed, 'Yes, you probably would have.'

'I always wanted to be a land girl. You used to see them in the fields for a few years after the war. I wanted the britches.'

'Well, you got them in a way, didn't you?' Olive touched Betty's khaki knee. 'Laurence Corner lives.'

'Hey, do you mind? These are designer dyke.'

'I'd like to be the Andrews Sisters.'

The danger that Hazel might break into a rendition of 'Boogie Woogie Bugle Boy' hovered, and passed.

Olive went through the French windows and rooted through the records and put on 'In the Mood'. She opened another bottle of wine.

'Stuff to give the troops!' said Hazel.

'Trains were so glamorous. Steam trains! The roar, the steam gushing out round the wheels, hissing, Stanley Holloway and whatsername, that actress, in the buffet. All lost and ruined. Where's the excitement for children today? *Network Southeast!* It makes you want to cry.'

'Don't,' warned Betty. 'You'll only regret it.'

'Sorry.'

'It can't have been very glamorous sending your children off as evacuees, not knowing if you'd see them again. Those awful newsreels of bewildered kids with teddies and gasmasks and labels round their necks. And then lining up in some village hall to be chosen, and there was always some unfortunate kid who nobody wanted, who'd get punished for head lice and bedwetting, and being stoned by the village children ... used as cheap labour on the farm ...'

'Oh shut up, Lizzie,' was the consensus.

'A nippie in Lyons Corner House, in a black dress and frilly cap and apron; the corner houses were the acme of glamour and sophistication to us ...'

'Murder on the feet. Varicose veins.'

'Lizzie!'

'Sorree. But, anyway, the fifties were so drab – so sort of post-war, if you know what I mean. The sixties had to happen.'

'Yes, it was inevitable after 1959.'

Olive thought of her own upbringing, so far from the *Good Housekeeping* fifties' ideal. She had wanted to be a bus conductress, a clippie, to get the pastel-coloured tickets and the clipper. She hadn't achieved her one ambition. Not too late, she supposed, but the uniform was nowhere near as nice now or the passengers so docile. Tacky and racketty, that had been her life. She'd better imbibe some bonhomie so she wouldn't scream at Rosemary droning on about hop-pickers and Butterick sewing patterns and Dewhurst's Silko-Perle.

'Olive? How about you?'

'What? Sorry ...'

'I was asking if anybody was interested in staying in the cottage this summer.'

'Oh, no, I don't think so, thanks, Liz. I hadn't really planned to go away. When I've got no one to bloody go with. Except William ...'

'How's William?' Ashley asked.

'Just William.'

She had seen photographs of Lizzie's cottage in Hampshire; it looked pretty but she had no intention of incarcerating herself there when she could be just as lonely at home. Besides, she didn't know how to work an Aga. She lay on her stomach, gazing into the water, watching pond-skaters like floating sunflower seeds zipping across the surface on hair-thin legs. She wondered if it would be possible for a woman to drown herself at a lunch party, by dipping her face in the water, without her friends noticing. Then she realised Rosemary was talking about her.

'I always envied Olive St Martin's ... she seemed to have such a dramatic life, and she was so thin and her friends all called her Oliver ...'

'What went wrong, Oliver?' Hazel interrupted. 'When did you start to suspect yourself of unnatural heterosexual leanings?'

'It wasn't like that – it was just to make myself more

259

interesting I suppose. I went through a phase of calling myself Olivia before that. I think I must have been rather a nasty child,' she mused.

'You're rather a nasty woman,' her best friend reassured her. Olive had to make a quick decision about sulking. It was too hot, the sky too blue, a butterfly too languid. She drank her wine.

'What's the score with Tina Turner?'

'*Terry* Turner. I wouldn't know. He may be performing live at Wembley Stadium even as we speak, for all I know, or care.'

If anybody said she'd never really liked him, or that he'd made a drunken pass at her, she'd push her in the pond. The wine and sunshine had got to Rosemary: 'I was a grown-up until the children left home.'

'The Kleenex is on the kitchen table. Coffee, anyone?'

Betty began clattering dishes briskly onto a tray. Olive squinted up through the leaves of next door's eucalyptus.

'I think the sun's over the yardarm.'

She'd better watch it, she thought as she drank, or she might be overcome by the urge to confide in someone about Theo. The smell of a barbecue drifted over the wall.

'Long pig,' said Olive, 'if I'm not mistaken.'

'What?'

'Long pig. It's what the Maori called human flesh.'

'Yuk.'

'Oh, I don't know ...' She let her glance linger on Rosemary's white leg, tinted pink by the afternoon. Rosemary was dabbing her eyes.

'My grandfather brought a shrunken head back from New Zealand.'

260

'How perfectly horrible. Where did he keep it, on the mantelpiece?'

'No, in an old shortbread tin. I sometimes wonder if it wasn't the cause of all the bad luck that's befallen our family over the years . . .'

'Like in all those films where haunted houses inevitably turn out to have been built on an old Indian burial ground?'

'Possibly. I shouldn't have mentioned it. I think it's better not to talk about it.'

'How shrunken?' asked Hazel. 'Grapefruit size? Orange? Kiwi fruit?'

'We can have any exotic fruit from any part of the world all the year round,' said Rosemary, 'and we want the first bananas after the war and a tangerine in our Christmas stocking.'

Olive reached for another of Betty's Camel Lights and lit it without answering Hazel. She was remembering that she had seen the New Zealand boy again, about ten days ago, on a bus. He hadn't spotted her; she'd glanced up from her paper as he passed and ducked her head as he headed for the front seat, where he leaned forward, no doubt pretending to be the driver.

'Palace, please,' the girl behind him said to the conductor.

'Palace, please.' The boy echoed her confidently.

'Palace?' repeated the conductor, scenting a victim. 'Which palace have you in mind? *Buckingham* Palace? *Kensington* Palace? *Blenheim* Palace? *Lambeth* Palace, the Czar's *Winter* Palace? Come on, mate, I'm a bus conductor not a mind reader. State your destination, or you'll have to get off. If you don't know where you're going, how am I supposed to?'

He winked at the girl seated behind the blushing lad. She responded with a feeble, cowardly grin.

'Crystal Palace,' the boy muttered, his happy look replaced by bewilderment.

He had gone downhill since their meeting. Olive had to feel sorry for him, the poor sap.

Now, in the garden, she was putting off thinking about getting herself home by public transport. Eventually, she found herself in a minicab driven by an evangelical lay preacher who sang hymns all the way. Everything about him, his broad rigid back, his black hat, his eyes in the mirror, declared that he condemned her as a harlot.

'One more river and that's the river of Jordan ...' he sang as they took Vauxhall Bridge.

'I always thought this was the Thames,' said Olive.

'You will not enter the Kingdom,' he told her.

As they approached Herne Hill she told him to go to Temperance Terrace, and then had enough sense left to change her mind again.

'Thanks for the in-flight entertainment,' she said as she got out at home. She did not tip him.

18

Returning from a solitary walk to Norwood Grove, William stopped halfway down Knight's Hill; on the amethyst horizon shimmered the little onion of St Paul's dome, flanked by hazy glassy green tower blocks as perspective and pollution and the late afternoon sunset conspired to create the Celestial City in a dazzle shifting through violet, gold and rose. As he walked downhill, the vision was lost behind the shop signs and bunched-up buildings of Norwood Road and the tree tops around St Luke's church This massive biscuit-coloured structure, one of the Waterloo churches built to commemorate Wellington's victory in 1815, with its cupola and columns and portico and dark red doors, had always fascinated William, but he had never entered it. Coral pink roses, like nail varnish or lipstick, bloomed in its garden, the sort of roses he had noticed in the khaki-coloured rock-hard clay outside the gents in Brockwell Park by the bench where drinkers gathered, municipal flowers with little charm, no scent and no trailing or abundant companions to offset their starkness. Children from a playgroup were trundling about on plastic vehicles while a young woman read a story to those who would listen. These little ones and the memory of St Paul's onion simmering in an amethyst broth touched his heart and straightened his shoulders and brightened his face so that, when he came through the black-and-gold gates of Norwood Cemetery, Rosetta Snyder, listlessly holding onto the hem of her daughter's dress while she scattered crisp crumbs to the indifferent goldfish in the pond, did not recognise him.

She was wearing a pink velour jogging suit which had lost its lustre and whitish trainers crazed with grey, with pink flashes at the ankles. She had lost weight and wore no makeup. William could hardly express his opinion that the recession suited her, and said, 'Hello, it's Mrs Snyder, isn't it? Rosetta. And, er, Chantal?'

'Who wants to know?'

She tightened her grip on Chantal's dress, glaring in a defiant and frightened way, as if at some bailiff or DSS snoop.

'William Mackenzie. Liam's former teacher.'

'Oh, yeah, sorry, didn't recognise you. Come on, Chantal, we've got to go home now.' The empty crisp bag lay glassily on the water; Chantal leaned over to try to reach a water lily and was jerked roughly back. She filled her lungs with the air necessary for an open-mouthed bellow of frustrated aestheticism and was dumped and strapped into a buggy with some force.

'Look,' William said over her howling. 'Why don't you and Liam and Chantal come to tea some time? There's a nice, well, biggish, garden for her to run around in. How about Sunday?'

'What for?'

'Well, it would be nice to see you all – catch up on old times with Liam ... Olive, my sister, would be delighted, I know. Come about three, or four.'

'I'll have to ask Liam. We might be going out.'

'OK, I'll give you the address anyway. Come if you feel like it.'

As she stumped towards the gate William could feel her wondering: what's his game? Does he fancy me, or is he into little kids, or has he got his eye on Liam? Bloody schoolteachers ...

He walked on past mausoleums and graves wondering what on earth had possessed him to invite her, and was brought up short by a photograph in a plastic frame, attached to a headstone, of a smiling girl in a blue-and-gold blazer and tie, hair washed to a gloss and tied up in ribbons for the school photographer. Old times with Liam. How could he have said that? How could he have forgotten?

'Have you gone *completely* mad? Are you *totally* out of your skull? What on *earth* possessed you to ask them here?' The Double Biological Ariel which Olive was decanting into an Ecover bottle dripped unheeded into the sink as she confronted him.

'I don't really know. It was a beautiful day, I felt sorry for them. I dunno ... I don't suppose they'll come anyway ...'

'Too bad if they do. I'm out to lunch.'

'And have been for some time.'

'Oh, ha ha. Better save your schoolboy wit for your little schoolfriend.'

'Does it ever occur to you that I was fond of my pupils? That I might miss them? Good God, woman, what do you think I was doing all those years? I have no life, no social life. All my friends were colleagues and ex-colleagues, now I don't see them any more ... Couldn't you make an effort just for once?'

'All right, all right, keep your wig on. Do you want to put anything in the machine? This is a whites wash.'

'No, I'm all right, thanks. In fact, I picked up a couple of new shirts in Brixton the other day, just BHS seconds,' he said stiffly.

'Well, there's no need to sound so guilty about it. You could have got them in Turnbull and Asser and it wouldn't have been a crime. You're entitled to a new shirt or two every few years.'

William saw himself purchasing, in some sort of punishment shop, two hair shirts lined with harsh grey bristles. Even prisoners, though, in this country at least, were entitled to a clean shirt every week, or fortnight. It came to his mind that he had read in Olive's morning paper that two more youths on remand had hanged themselves in prison, bringing the year's total so far to twelve. What are we doing to our children? He banged his fist into his palm. And who was he to feel anger about it? Grey concrete filled his chest and head as Olive ventured brightly, 'I don't suppose you bought a sweater, did you? Any chance of the grey cardi going to its last resting place? No? Oh well, the compost heap will have to wait ... You're cooking tonight, don't forget. What are we having?'

William, who had indulged earlier in two eggs, beans, a fried slice and two cups of strong tea in the ALL DAY BREAKFAST, felt little enthusiasm for the project, and mumbled something about it being too hot to eat much. When Olive had got out of the way he began to wash a lettuce but found it so colonised by greenfly that he had to throw it out in the garden. It seemed simplest to take Olive out for a meal.

Crystal Palace was a bottleneck every night of the week. They parked behind the Pizza Hut, walked round to Lorenzo's, found it packed and crossed the road to the Pizza Express, where they sat opposite each other on iron chairs at a round marble table in the bluish light, the oldest couple there.

'Well, this is cosy,' said Olive.

'Ea-g-les!' came the hollow, drawn-out cry of a lost drunk Crystal Palace supporter.

Early the next morning, at the time when dreams are often most vivid, William was running down corridors opening doors on empty classrooms, late for the assembly which he was to take, unable to find the hall, in a black gown which flapped round his knees and tripped up his feet, shod in cracked white trainers like Rosetta's. He was carrying a boxed pizza and a pile of books which he kept dropping and scrabbling to pick up. He heard children's voices singing, and burst through the swing doors into the hall. Hanging against the window swung the body of a boy, rotating slowly, strangled in a sheet. William rushed forward and dragged him down, weeping, and put him on the platform, kneeling and unwinding the sheet now enclosing him like cerements. It was Pragna Patel. She sat up smiling, with daubs of black grease on her face. William embraced her, stroking her hair, wiping the oil from her face.

'You're not dead, you're not dead,' he was sobbing and laughing. 'All this time I've been thinking you were dead. I must telephone your parents. Somebody, ring Pragna's parents and tell them she's here, at school. Where have you been?'

'I've been in hospital in France but I'm better now.'

A low humming from the children broke into song; he saw they had linked arms and were swaying in alternate rows, right to left, left to right, in a rippling Mexican wave, and they had garlands of red and blue flowers round their necks.

He woke with a jolt to his heart as if a doctor had resuscitated him with a blow to his chest, and lay sweating, his pyjama jacket open, the sheet binding his legs, trying to get back into the dream, grasping at images whirling as if on a black cylinder and disappearing. The singing, sweet and triumphant, hardened into black characters of a language, Gujerati, Hindi or Bengali, which he could not decipher, and dissolved.

Out of that rehashed mishmash of the previous day, had there come a message? He did not know. Was he comforted or distressed? He kicked the sheet from his legs, and knew he was not absolved. Yet Pragna's smile, the silky warmth of her skin, the touch of her hair falling through his hands, and her words 'I'm better now' remained, almost persuading him that she was alive somewhere, and happy and forgiving.

When Olive came into the kitchen in the morning, he dropped her car keys on their plastic tag from a local Indian restaurant on the table. He had noticed one or two foolish mothers leaving their babies outside shops again.

'I think it's probably safe for you to use the car again now. There's never been any mention of it.'

Olive snatched the keys and dropped them into the pale canvas sack she was using that day. She was humiliated by any suggestion that she might have done wrong.

'Look at the state of that window.' She indicated the glass mottled in the sunshine, with a branch of the elder tree which had sprung up beside the drain draggling across it, its leaves drooping under the weight of black insects.

'Sometimes this house really gets me down. How I long for something neat and pebbledash with one small pyracanthus and a forsythia – have a nice day.'

She left William to organise secateurs and window-cleaning

things. The sound of her car failing to start set his heart jud-
dering with anxiety. When she stormed back into the house to
ring AA Home Start, he had fled to the drawing room with the
paper and a mug of tea. The pages were in disarray, a tomato
seed adhering to a photograph of neighbours and police fanned
out across a field, searching for a missing child. It seemed that
Olive had glanced at it earlier and disregarded it, making no
connection with herself, feeling no guilt. The ring left by a
coffee cup corroborated the evidence. He scraped the tomato
seed from the picture, and almost unthinkingly popped it into
his mouth.

'Ugh.'

What did they hope to find, those people combing – they
always combed – the fields and woodland with their long
sticks? Did each one believe that he or she might be the one
to find little Marie whimpering unharmed in a badger's sett or
discarded fridge, or did some of them secretly or unconsciously
hope for a grisly discovery?

He could hear Olive bashing about in the cupboard under
the sink, hauling out cleaning implements to attack the
window, as a reproach to him while she waited for the AA.
He felt trapped. Black insects and their sticky exudations were
scrubbed away.

One of our children is missing. Each time a child is taken,
habitual lurkers in playgrounds and alleyways, parked cars and
woods, must hear the parents' anguished pleadings breaking
into tears on television and radio, must witness the blanketed
rush through spittle and abuse from police van to courtroom.
They must know what horrors awaited the debased bodies of
the convicted at the mercy of fellow inmates and screws in a

system which condones and tacitly approves. Yet the urge to violate and seek the hideous thrill which culminates in murderous panic is stronger. William prayed silently for the safe return of little Marie, as he had prayed for the restoration of Jermaine before he knew the truth, and for his safety after he had dumped him at the Maudsley, and with as little conviction that his prayer would be answered or even heard.

'What's up? Are you all right?'

Olive came in and sat down, raising a swarm of dust motes from old velvet, which swirled around, trapped in a shaft of sunshine which gilded the leaves of the weeping fig and threw watery reflections from the glass parrot onto the floor.

'William?'

'It's nothing, just something in my eye.'

'A beam, I expect.' Olive smiled at her own wit.

'"Why beholdest thou the mote that is in thy brother's eye, but considerest not the beam that is in thine own eye?"'

'I said it first,' she countered as William shuffled out, weighed down by the millstone round his neck, the comfort of his dream fading. He reminded himself that Jesus had said that it would be better for whoso should offend one of those little ones which believed in Him that he should have a millstone hanged round his neck and be drowned in the depth of the sea, and that Pragna had not believed in Him. Even so, his neck was bowed by the feathery bulk of an albatross, and he realised the horror of such a burden, for the size of the bird meant that the great dead pinions would have scraped along the deck.

When the telephone rang early that evening, Olive took the call.

'That was Ashley. She's coming round for supper.'

'Fine. Do you want me to make myself scarce?'

'Why should you? After all, you've done the cooking, such as it is. It hardly seems fair.'

'OK, I'll make some more salad. There's plenty left.'

Despite what she had said, she had expected William to have the grace to disappear, surrendering the garden and his food to Ashley so that they could get pleasantly tipsy in the summer evening and talk at ease about things to which he wasn't party. He heard her dragging the garden furniture about in a bad-tempered way as he boiled potatoes for more potato salad and chopped chives and made a dressing.

'Why don't you just bung it all in a screw-top jar and shake it?' she said, infuriated by the sight of him pounding away with pestle and mortar when she came into the kitchen. If only he had some friends or a committee meeting or something to go to.

'I like doing it this way.'

'Thought you were going to join the Norwood Society? It would do you good to have an interest, get out of the house. I mean, it's your sort of thing, local history. You'd have a ball grubbing about in overgrown cemeteries, hacking down brambles and rooting up old graves ... sorry, I mean, you told me yourself about all those eminent Victorians in Norwood cemetery – Mrs Beeton and "Mr Bovril" and Sir Henry Tate and Lyle – are they all foodies buried there?' She popped a cherry tomato into her cruel mouth.

'No,' said William with restraint although the Sabatier knife was to hand. Local history was Anne's thing. 'There are navigators and architects, soldiers, sailors, the inventor of the flying boat, philanthropists, musicians, Edgar of Swan and Edgar, Reuter, Cubitt, a champion prize-fighter. There's the whole Greek cemetery. Charles Bravo, the victim in the celebrated Victorian poisoning case is there . . . ' The menace with which he left that hanging in the air made Olive pay attention to his preparations.

'Those potatoes will be mash if you don't watch out,' she said in a minute. William rescued them.

'*Juste à point.*' He tasted one, finding it just this side of being soggy. He felt her hovering and, hearing the crunch of celery, remembered the torture of lying in bed with the agonisingly slow and juicy sound of Olive chomping an apple in the other bed ruining what he was reading. She had eaten her way through the deaths of Aslan and Aloysha, Ayesha, Beth, the little crossing sweeper, Little Nell, Sydney Carton, Brother Hilarius; and then she had bounced on his bed, mocking his tears, a fiend in faded winceyette. Nowadays a brother and sister over a certain age were not supposed to share a bedroom, but their circumstances had often made this necessary. In his case, the incest taboo had been reinforced by Olive's nocturnal eating habits, her predilection for crisps, rubbing salt into his wounds, and a peculiarly painful way she had of pinching.

Once, at the age of thirteen, feeling bored and curiously rest-less on a rainy afternoon and believing himself to be alone in the house, he had succumbed to a vague desire to investigate Olive's underwear. He had been standing with a circle of suspenders dangling down his legs, wrestling to hook a bra round his skinny chest when his mother popped her head round the door.

'Oh Olive, when you're dressed, would you nip down to the shop for ten Woodbine and a tin of Chappie? Put it on the bill.'

Clad in grey school trousers, his father's cut-downs nipped in at the waist with a boyish snake-belt, his flirtation with cross-dressing over, William braved the fierce Mr Snell at the corner shop. His heart stopped when he saw a notice stuck to the door: 'I Habakkuk G. Snell of Snell's Stores, hereby publicly blacklist the following *former* customers for the nonpayment of overdue debts ...' Sandy Mackenzie's name led all the rest. William sensed that the family would be on the move again soon.

Now, dressed in faded Levis and a faded Black Watch cotton shirt, he was concocting a red salad from radicchio, finely grated red cabbage, radishes, beetroot, red pepper and the cherry tomatoes.

'You're going to a lot of trouble. It's only Ashley.'

'This is beautiful.' Ashley held up the red salad in its glass bowl in the garden. 'It's too pretty to eat.'

William thought she looked pretty edible, albeit frail and tired in her old chinos and T-shirt, like a soldier who had changed into clean fatigues after combat.

'Let me be the first to violate it, then,' said Olive tearing a segment of garlic bread from the loaf. 'I'm starving. How are all the lame ducks, then?'

'I wish you wouldn't call them that, Olive, they're my family.' Ashley flushed.

'Sorry,' said Olive without contrition. Ashley's father was linked up to an oxygen cylinder for his emphysema, her mother was diabetic, she had an aunt in a hospice, and a depressive cousin. There were also brothers and sisters and nephews and nieces in ordinary and sometimes exuberant health. She had telephoned that evening from the callbox in the foyer of the hospice. Olive did not know it but Ashley would never quite forgive her for laughing when Hazel had suggested substituting a cylinder of calor-gas for her father's oxygen. That was the sort of flippancy expected of Hazel and although Ashley had sent her to Coventry for weeks, Hazel had not noticed. The wound had healed leaving only a small scar.

'Cheers,' said Ashley, raising a glass of the wine she had brought. 'Your off-licence really is the pits, isn't it?'

'Booze is just a subsidiary line there, really, although desperate drinkers too ill to go further afield hang out there. They do a flourishing trade in video nasties but we wouldn't know about that, unless William spends his idle afternoons watching snuff movies, of course, while I'm at work.'

'Really, Olive!'

'Everything round here's the pits,' Olive continued. 'I'm seriously thinking of moving north of the river when the lease on the shop runs out. Islington's a paradise compared with this – they've got everything there. Or W11.'

'What would you do?'

'God knows, get a stall in Camden market or Portobello ... I'm heartily sick of it all. How I wish I'd done something proper with my life, like the rest of you. Anyway, I've had enough experience selling tat ... Charlene thinks we're running a charity shop – only today she took delivery of hideous and unsaleable silk flowers made by some battery hens' co-op.'

'Surely you mean battered wives?'

'Battered wives, battered cod – who cares? I made her take them back.'

'You're going to lose Charlene if you're not careful, Olive.' Ashley had the licence of long friendship to warn her.

'Nonsense, she's devoted to me. And I can see a real recession coming. She's lucky to have a job.'

'How are the cats?' William asked Ashley. Harlequin and Columbine were white, splashed black and orange, with long expressive brindled tails, and black masks which turned their most mundane activities into a masquerade. They seemed poised always for a performance. Ashley smiled, knowing that her friends laughed at her close relationship with the cats: recently she had been stung into telling Rosemary that her children were substitute cats.

'They're becoming more environmentally aware – they've switched to a new brand of litter which is made of naturally replaceable wood.'

'Anyone consulted the trees on that?' Olive said. 'They happy to do their bit?'

Ashley sighed.

'Haven't you got a cat flap?' asked William. He was on the point of offering to install one but Ashley shook her head.

'No garden. They've got their balcony – I never intended to have cats, but they were sort of wished on me. I'd love to get a place with a little garden, but the flat downstairs has been on the market for over a year. Nobody's even coming to view it.'

'William's got a chum who's an estate agent, haven't you, duckie? Perhaps the mysterious Mr Snyder might help. If he ever graces us with his presence ...'

She rose and went into the kitchen to make coffee.

Ashley and William heard the grinding of beans. The sky was sapphire blue deepening into darkness, with smears of knickerbocker glory melting in the west.

'I'm sorry. Olive's really in one tonight. I should have left you two alone. I feel very *de trop*.'

'You mustn't.' Ashley touched his hand quickly. 'I'm glad you didn't.'

'I don't suppose you'd – no, sorry, silly idea . . .'

'No, it isn't. Yes, I would.'

'Are the stars out tonight? I don't know if it's cloudy or bright . . .' Olive came out singing with a tray of cups and saucers and the coffee.

'They are,' said William.

Olive remembered how she had said once, '"Oh Terry, don't let's ask for the moon, we have the stars,"' and he had replied: 'What are you on about?'

'I was a fool to think I could be happy with someone who had never seen *Now, Voyager*,' she said, savagely pressing down the plunger in the coffee pot.

Neither Ashley nor William could think of anything to say, then,

'It does get better, you know . . .' Ashley told her. 'Honestly, love.'

'Hmm.'

William wished Olive would go away. He knew that she, not he, would walk Ashley to her car.

'This is quite ridiculous,' Ashley was thinking. 'Why can't he just ask me out properly? Why do we have a tacit understanding that Olive won't approve?'

An owl hooted from the line of poplars two gardens away.

'"Come indoors – come indoors! I cannot bear the whip-poor-will!"' Olive cried, striking an attitude.

That was the trouble with William and Olive: they were

always quoting from some film she hadn't seen or book which had informed their bizarre childhood, and then they would laugh their exclusive laughter. Watching television with them was no fun, as they were always in competition to shout out 'Keenan Wynn' or 'Naunton Wayne', 'Chips Rafferty', 'Donald Meek', 'Spring Byington'; or 'It's 'im – Orry, from *United*' or Gussie from *Compact* or David Rome or Mother from *The Brothers*, characters from long-extinct soaps, or Rank starlets who had glittered for a day. There had been that tedious evening recently when William had claimed to have scored the definitive triumph by having spotted the Smout family from Streatham, failed finalists in *Telly Addicts*, shopping in Sainsbury's.

'They had two trollies, absolutely loaded with junk food: crisps, cokes, beer, frozen burgers, pizzas, cakes, snacks.'

He had tracked the four couch potatoes in their leisure suits to the DIY superstore, he said, and was in no doubt that they were the genuine article.

'That proves it couldn't have been the Smouts of Streatham,' Olive objected. 'They'd never have time for DIY.'

'They were checking out plastic clip-on trays for TV dinners. I rest my case.'

'What's the time?' Olive said. 'When a sudden silence falls, it's always twenty past or twenty to.'

William could not say 'Time you went to bed, Olive, and left us alone' or 'Time for Ashley and me to go to bed'. He could not say 'early yet' or Olive might sit on, or 'late' because then Ashley would leave. He remained silent.

'That's only true if there's a crowd,' said Ashley, as if three wasn't. 'Anyway, I suppose I'd better make a move.'

'You are a fool,' Olive told William, finding him still in the garden, 'sitting there to the bitter end. Couldn't you see Ashley wanted to talk?'

Later, as she settled on the sofa with the remains of the potato salad and cold garlic bread, to watch *Prisoner: Cell Block H*, she felt a frisson of fear as the steel gate clanged. She had felt it earlier when Charlene, bringing through their pot of afternoon tea, had said 'Will you be mother?' 'No, you go ahead,' she had said. For all she knew patient police procedure was even now tightening the net around her.

19

Terry had been relieved that his companion had not telephoned to cancel lunch; he had feared that backs would turn
on him, after the Enid Masters incident.

'I'm going for the lambs' tongues and arugula with raspberry
vinegar,' Derek Mothersole announced. Once a misogynistic
womaniser who had made his reputation with a novel con-
cerning an angler who netted schoolgirls and kept them in
a subterranean tank, trussed with barbed and hooked fishing
line, he now drove a Metro with beaded seat covers and a KIDS
ON BOARD sticker. Terry watched his face as he outlined
his travel piece, an account of a trip to Romania, which Terry
had missed in *Granta*. Terry thought he might turn his own
hand to some travel writing, obviously money for jam, while
his novel failed to materialise. A 68 bus lumbered through his
mind – *Joyce Jauncey's Jaunts*. No.

Derek had a fringed circular mouth, of which the upper lip
was curiously flat, in a cylindrical face. There was something
self-congratulatory about his choice of clothes, always in colours that echoed tones of his own hair and beard. He had a
tumty-tum delivery that savoured and munched his words as if

reluctant to let them leave his mouth. Terry pictured some mid-land or northern county of stony dales populated by Mothersole look-alikes, all tumty-tumming away at each other. He ordered a Bloody Mary. Derek chuckled into his mineral water. The raw smell of his sandals, hacked from the hide of an animal recently dead, added to Terry's discomfiture. He had sneaked a glance under the table to check that he hadn't trodden in anything, and glimpsed bare tufted toes.

'Shame about Enid.'

Terry looked to see if Derek's words held any more than their apparent weight but his napkin was being applied to his beard.

'Did you go to the funeral?' he ventured.

'No. I would have but I was stuck with an *In Conversation* at the ICA. Just as well, who wants to schlep to Potter's Bar in this heat?'

'Quite.'

Potter's field, where the poor and strangers are buried; a rough sour patch of grass and thistles outside the graveyard wall. He helped himself to the house white, Derek having become one of those bores who don't drink at lunchtime. His heap of artichoke leaves was removed and he lit a cigarette while waiting for his spinach salad and fries.

'That's all one wants really, this weather, a couple of starters,' he said, feeling that he had come a long way from the Baby Belling cuisine of Sub Rosa, although he had been pretty sure that Derek had paid over the odds for a dish of the weeds which he could have retrieved from his father's little compost heap. Derek was exuding silent implications that Terry's cigarette would somehow be responsible for a Mothersole child's asthma attack that very night.

'My mother's definition of a wild mushroom would be a Chesswood Creamed Button which slipped off the toast,' he remarked, seeing Mothersole frown. Derek was keen on roots, and loquacious on the pain he felt at his parents' touchingly clumsy attempts to accommodate their gifted son: he had had a poem about it published in *Stand*.

Terry continued: 'Did she leave a note or anything, do you know, old Enid?' and mimed a gesture of grinding a large pepper mill at the cheerful antipodean waitress. The wheels of a small industry were clicking into motion even as Derek replied.

'Not that I know of, but I gather there's a journal. Some of it fascinating, she knew everybody in her time. Real documentary stuff but a bit of a downer towards the end, self-pitying rambling about people not paying her for work and the Inland Revenue and suchlike. Real dark night of the soul territory – can't afford to have hair done. Moisturiser dried up, no more mascara, washing powder . . .'

'Oh, laundry list stuff,' Terry interrupted contemptuously. 'Watch out for the Life next year: *No More Mascara – a Critical Biography*.' He laughed.

'Still, they say she was quite a beauty in her day. I suppose that sort of thing mattered to the poor old thing.' Derek relished and digested his own tolerance. It came to Terry that in Derek's books people were always munching food and washing it down with whatever beverage was to hand.

'How come you know so much about it? Have you seen the diary?'

'Uh uh. But my editor's her literary executor . . .'

Terry felt defeated, as though standing outside wheels within wheels.

'Oh well, she had a good innings,' he concluded. He recognised a Radio 1 DJ at the next table but decided it would not improve his standing to mention it.

'They say she only weighed five stone when they found her. Lucky the bailiffs broke in when they did, or she'd still be lying there. In this heat – the mind boggles ... Hadn't been eating properly – total squalor. It's terrible when people let themselves go, lose their self-respect. Are you having a pudding?' he asked, as though his mouth was full of his own already.

Terry shook his head, seeing the old lizard curled on the unmade bed, desiccating in the sun. Shades of Una Ogilvie.

'Let's have one brownie with two forks, and coffee,' Derek suggested to the waitress, who thought it a good idea. 'How's Olive? Are you two still an item?'

'Not really. I don't know.'

Derek chuckled again, a noise like pebbles in a grinder being polished to make pendants of local stones. 'Time you settled down, lad. Did I show you the polaroids of Arthur's birth? I was determined to deliver him myself after that set-to we had with the Whittington over Milly. No idea, these people. Bloody medics.'

'I thought Meg had it in hospital? I meant to send flowers ...'

'Oh, that was afterwards, she had to go in. Just bad luck really. I'm working on a different design of birthing pool for the next one.'

'Yes, thanks, I've seen them,' Terry said quickly to forestall the hand reaching for the folkweave bag hanging from Derek's chair.

'Oh. Right. You can see the video when you come round; I just took these to have something portable.'

Terry looked at Derek's breasts nestling snugly in his brown polo shirt. 'Are you breastfeeding?' he asked.

A shabby man was working his way round the tables with a black velvet tray of gilt earrings. Terry was tempted to buy a pair to divert Derek from his question and babies in general but the vendor assessed them, and did not approach, so he said, 'I had that Mollie Mitchell on the phone the other day,' signalling for another glass of wine. 'Abusing me. Drunk of course,' he added with inspiration.

'How come? What did you do to her?'

'Oh, she took exception to my rather less than ecstatic review of Enid Masters. Seemed to think I was somehow to blame ...'

'Daft bitch. Where was it? You know I never read reviews, unless I've written them myself, and not always then.'

'What? Oh, it doesn't matter – God, what a dog!'

He directed Derek's attention to a girl on her way to the Ladies. Her ears seemed to spring scarlet from the sides of her head as his words hit her. When she returned some time later, head at a defiant angle, ears still red, he tried to put it right by saying loudly: 'Yes, we're thinking of showing him at Crufts' this year. Should get best of breed, if not Supreme Champion.'

'What the blue blazes are you on about? I've rather lost the plot, old son.'

'You and me both, old son,' said Terry recalling the blank pages of his novel and jotting down in his mind: girl in restaurant overhears man call her a dog. Kills herself in Ladies. How?

'Well, see you post-Prague, then, Tel old son.'

'Post-Prague?'

'Yes, British Council gangbang – thought you might be coming along ...'

'Shame you have to be away so much, when the kids are so young; they change so quickly at that age, don't they, Del, me old mate? You must miss out on such a lot if you're not there all the time.'

Such a shame, Terry thought, when Derek might have been at home in his study at the top of the house while Meg kept the kids quiet until Daddy descended to give them Quality Time and she did the dishes.

There comes a time in a man's life when he can no longer spend afternoons watching Australian soaps, when the neighing theme song of *Neighbours* twice daily grates on his ear, and one of the episodes is, besides, a repeat of the previous day's; when baddies from *Prisoner*, turning up in the guise of goodies in *Home and Away*, forfeit credibility; when old movies lose their charm and quiz shows their magnetism. What does it profit him to answer all the questions in *Going For Gold* when he will never carry off the trophy or win the star prize trip to Kenya where he can observe the Masai and lions and hippopotami in their natural habitat? The moment of truth came to William when his remote control gave up the ghost in an episode of *Take the High Road*. How he envied those Scots not only their landscape but their problems; how pleasant to agonise between commercial breaks in the knowledge that there was a scriptwriter, like God sitting at a celestial word processor, to set them all right. He realised that there was no scriptwriter for his own life and that he must get himself out of this appalling fix, this futile self-laceration and lassitude, sitting like a man of dust boring himself to death with fictional lives and spectator sports and useless general knowledge. 'It has always been my conviction that one must work one's passage through this world,' he thought. The memory of the Mrs Handisyde debacle, and his promise to return, struck him. He had not been back, and never would, he knew.

He rose decisively, crumpled that morning's *Sun* into the bin and set off for the shops to buy a new battery for the remote control. He walked, his mind channel-hopping from the ongoing non-drama of himself to events in Eastern Europe, to the story in the local paper of pizza delivery boys knocked from their bikes and robbed, to an ice-lolly melting like a Tequila Sunrise on the pavement. Outside Doolally's he stopped suddenly, staring into a box of red and yellow plum tomatoes blazing in blue paper like the Mediterranean. That programme he had watched, for the deaf. Surely that was something he could learn, teaching the deaf something useful, where his skills could be put to use. The hot colours excited him. The idea excited him. He wanted to tell somebody, enlist in classes immediately; he saw a child's blank face break into a smile of recognition. Mandy Miller in pigtails.

'Oi! Cloth-Ears! I'm talking to you!' Doolally shouted at his wife who, oblivious, was stacking cat food, with headphones embedded in the yellow spikes of her hair.

'How much the plum tomatoes? Talking to a brick wall,' he grumbled, dumping them into the silver scale and lobbing a bruised peach at his wife to attract her attention.

'Got any broken biscuits?' a defeated voice said from the doorway.

'Nah. Sold out.'

The customer turned to go.

'Hang on.' Doolally reached for a packet of Happy Shopper

Country Crunch and smashed it on the counter. 'Ee-ah. Thirty-five p.'

'But.'

'That's what it says on the packet. Take it or leave it,' he said indifferently. After some dithering, she took it, but did not escape Doolally's scorn.

'We get 'em all in 'ere!' he told William. 'She asks for broken biscuits, I give 'er broken biscuits. Some people don't know *what* they want.'

'Have you heard anything more about those boys who tried to rob you?'

'Only that they've been remanded. Case hasn't come up yet. I dare say they'll be wanting you as a witness.'

'That is the fear that haunts me,' said William. He regretted profoundly his involvement in the affair.

'I'd put them up against a wall and shoot them,' Mrs Doolally opined. 'Teach them a lesson they wouldn't forget in a hurry.'

'Bleeding holiday camps, prisons, these days,' Doolally added. 'Don't know they're born.'

There had been a time when William would have refuted this with statistics but, having forfeited the right to moral judgement, he paid for his purchases and left, with the dull spark of his idea faltering in his returning depression. When he got home he was almost forced to confront his own weak nature as he unpacked the two punnets of mildewed raspberries Doolally had offloaded onto him, but sidestepped the issue by putting them straight into the bin.

The burning wheel of red and orange-yellow circles on a blue plate, the yellow-green drizzle of olive oil and sharp fresh green scent of basil charged his senses and he was suffused with longing to share the summer evening. Ashley's number was in the book; he dialled, not knowing quite what he was going to say, and found he had been handed a script when she answered in tears.

'Ashley, what is it?'

'Oh – I don't know. You caught me at a bad moment. I've really got the blues. Everything's all right really, except that it isn't. Everything's terrible. It isn't really of course. Sorry. I just saw on the news that they found that little girl, Marie, safe and well. That's good news, isn't it? Despite the fact that at least five hundred people have been drowned in Bangladesh. Sorry. I know I'm being boring. How are *you*?'

'I'm fine. Um – shall I, would it be all right if I came over?'

'I've got the car. It would be quicker if I came to you.'

Quicker. Let joy be unconfined. He punched the air like the scorer of the winning goal. They decided on a restaurant in Clapham, of which Ashley had read good reports, and which was able to provide at short notice a table for two. Was that Terry Turner sloping off with some woman, leaving an ashtray full of butts and a stained tablecloth? They thought it was and didn't care. Ashley, it turned out, was knowledgeable on Italian regional cooking: William, who thought pasta was pasta, despite Olive's tutelage, and secretly didn't mind if it came from a tin, was enchanted. He was a willing convert to the subtleties and nuances of food, to acupuncture, homeopathy, psychother-apy and tarot cards. He was touched by her faith in astrology which made her seem so brave and lonely, looking up at the stars. She chose a wine tasting of blackberries, blackcurrants and Ribena, with the scent of flowering currant leaves, wet with rain, crushed between the fingers. He was in love with her fork smeared with the unfinished tiramisu, with the cheque book and credit card stamped with her name, which he persuaded her to put away.

'My mother had a crush on Leslie Howard,' she explained. 'That's why I'm called Ashley. I suppose it's marginally preferable to Rhett.'

'It's a beautiful name. Blue-grey, like your eyes.'

'Or Confederates and Yankees.'

She did not add that on a bad day she saw a grate filled with last night's ashes or an overflowing ashtray.

Ashley was successful in her job. She had her family and friends but she knew Sunday afternoons when the chimes of an ice-cream van cranking out the first few bars of Lili Marlene like a broken mechanical glockenspiel struck desolation into her heart; solitary walks when the plywood backs of dressing tables in bedroom windows exuded melancholy and a curtain blowing at an open window was as sinister as a noose; hungover mornings when the cats turned into wolverines. There were times when it seemed as if all her friends were frightened, huddling together on a ledge above the abyss of old age and loneliness; there was talk of all sharing a house and forming a co-operative of skills, walking sticks and zimmer frames. Most of the time, though, she was contented enough and never sufficiently desperate to contemplate an affair or marriage merely as a buffer against the horrors of Saturday shopping for one in a scrum of families. She had always liked William, even when he had been a draggled old outcast bird in his grey cardigan, but until the day when she had come round to look for her diary, and the evening when they had had supper in the garden, she had thought he had no time for her. Now, sitting opposite her in the restaurant, his plumage looked glossier. In fact, it had been trimmed that morning in *Haircut Sir?* of Tulse Hill.

Had they been written by Mothersole or Turner, they would have found themselves completing their meal in bed tearing at one another's clothes and gobbling each other up with relish and sound effects. As it was, they went for a walk in Norwood Grove. Ashley, who had drunk only one glass of wine, parked the car in the rutted lane that led to the little park, and as they walked hand in hand to the gate, a fox appeared on the path in front of them, paused, poised, black and silvery, then flattened itself into the black of the brambles and was gone. The gate was open because the house, built on the site of an eighteenth-century shooting box which, with the park, had been presented to the local people, was now the meeting place of several societies. Tonight it glittered magically white in the moonlight, as if floating on the brow of the grassy slope. Ashley and William stopped at an ancient mulberry tree, with branches both as scaly and contorted as dragons and as smooth as pale silk, hidden by cascades of leaves; a smattering of unripe fruit lay on the grass under the almost horizontal trunk. Then they walked under flat cedar branches studded with young pale green soapy cones towards the house where figures moved behind the windows of the glassed-in terrace like ghosts playing ping-pong. On the benches with memorial brass plaques inscribed with the names of people who had been happy there, sat the ghosts who loved the park, taking the night air. Marigold petals glinted like goldfish in the basin of the fountain supported by the four seasons, blue-green metallic children offering fruit and flowers and elaborate autumnal and wintry grapes and leaves, and the moonlight picked out the mosaic names of the months running round the rim. William and Ashley kissed in an iron pergola hung with roses and honeysuckle. Then Ashley dropped him off at his house, and went home to give the cats their supper.

Under the roses and honeysuckle William had put aside a pang of guilt towards Anne, who had shown him that hidden park, and the memory of weeping there for Pragna while a pair of bullfinches flew in and out of the iron tracery pecking the scarlet honeysuckle berries, taking little sips at the seeds among the thorny tangles.

20

'Refuse to be incinerated', said the notice above the row of steel bins on wheels lined up in the corridor. Each time Jay read it a tiny spark flashed for an instant in the blackness of his mind. 'I will refuse,' he vowed. 'I am still myself. I won't let them destroy me. I will get out of here.'

He pushed his broom along, disturbing the old greasy grey deposits of dust which clung to the walls and which no sweeping could dislodge.

'What's needed,' he informed one of the guards who was friendlier than most, 'is one of those heavy-duty industrial cleaners, like they use in factories and hospitals, to really get to grips with this ground-in dirt.'

'You've got a point there, son. I'll put it to the guv'nor at the next staff meeting. He's always more than happy to bend an ear to suggestions as to the more efficienter running of the place. Or you could make a note of it yourself and pop it into the Suggestion Box. Do yourself a bit of good at the same time, too; there's plenty of opportunities here for an intelligent lad, taking an interest in his work.'

'Beauty!' Jay was beaming as, like a conjurer's bouquet,

remission, release, unfounded fear, rationality, exploded into bloom. 'Thanks, mate. I didn't know there *was* a Suggestion Box.'

'Yes indeed, laddie. So if you've got any more bright ideas . . .'

'Well, I have. Lots of them. For instance, to do with the more democratic running of the place, there are some glaring injustices. You must be aware, must have observed . . .'

'Trouble, Eric?'

Fulcher, huge, shaven-headed, with a Union Jack tattoo fading in the rolls of fat at the back of his neck, had come up on silent feet while they were talking.

'Not at all, Mr Fulcher,' Eric said affably. 'Our young friend here has just been giving me some very useful tips as to how we might improve our working environment.'

Jay hazarded a smile at Fulcher, who was reputed to be ex-SAS, standing there, relaxed in his sweatpants, his gun at ease like a toy in its leather holster.

'Thinks a hoover might be in order . . .'

'Heavy industrial vacuum cleaner, one that washes as well as sucks up the dirt,' Jay explained.

'Vacuum cleaner eh?'

Fulcher seized the broom and danced in a grotesque parody of the housewife in the television ad singing 'Do the Shake 'n' Vac, put the freshness back!' Jay was laughing with them when Fulcher snapped the broom handle across his knee and jabbed him in the stomach with the splintery end. He doubled up in astounded agony.

'Let's see you do the bloody Shake 'n' Vac with that!'

Then he caught Jay behind the legs with the broken bit of handle, making him fall and bang his head against the wall as he went down.

'Get to grips with that ground-in dirt,' he heard as Eric's foot smashed into his ribs and then he was in a crumpled heap on the floor trying to protect his face and head and groin with his hands as they kicked him into blackness lit by flashes of pain.

'They give you the black aspirin,' the old man whispered.

'What?'

'That's what we call it, the cosh over the head, the black aspirin. They give you the headache, then they give you the cure.'

Jay saw two blurred bearded faces hanging over him. The pipes running along the ceiling seemed to wobble and sag; two bare bulbs dangled from each flex. He was back in L-Block under the lights which burned all night. He had been dragged from the barred room where he had lain for some days, and thrown back onto his mattress, one of thirty that covered the floor.

'You don't half pong,' the old man told him without rancour. 'Not that you'd notice with this lot.'

The mattress in the strip cell had been sodden when Jay was dumped there; now its next occupant groaned on Jay's blood and urine stains.

'I keep seeing things double. What am I doing here? I don't know where this place is. What have I done?'

'Nurse! Nurse!' It was the voice of Mad Taffy who was under the delusion that he was in hospital.

'You fell foul of Eric,' came another voice. 'Under that smiling exterior, he's possibly the most dangerous of them all.'

'Screw!'

The sibilant warning told Jay he was in prison but his head

hurt too much for him to remember why. A stick was banged on the grille that looked onto the corridor and a face leered through.

'Pleasant dreams, wankers. Sleep tight, mind the bugs don't bite.'

They did, the real ones and the crawling bloodsuckers of the DTs.

'Goodnight, John-Boy.'

'Goodnight, Mary-Ellen.'

'Nurse! Nurse! Nurse! Nurse!'

'Somebody put his mattress over his face.'

'How the fuck are we going to get out of here?'

'Oi, Mick, remember that offie we done over in the Walworth Road that time?'

'"I remember, I remember, the house where I was born".'

'What we need to do is form an Escape Committee. Now, I propose that . . .'

'Nurse, nurse, nurse, nurse!'

'Pack it in.'

'"It was a childish ignorance but now 'tis little joy to know I'm further off from heaven than when I was a boy."'

'You can say that again. You're in L now, sunshine. We've all died and gone to L.'

'Shut the fuck up.'

'Nurse, nurse, nurse, nurse . . .'

'Go on, Andy, for gawd's sake, then we all might get some sleep, and never wake up, if we're lucky.'

'Why is it always me who has to be bleedin' nurse?' Andy complained as he climbed over bodies, some as if lifeless, new-comers in the throes of the horrors at being dragged off the drink, many ill, without medication, coughing their lungs up, in pain.

'Because you're a bleedin' poofter, that's why.'

'Sorry, sorry,' he apologised as he trod on bits of bodies. Toothless gums snapped at his ankles; a hand grasped his foot. He kicked it off.

'All right, Taffy. Nurse is here. Let's make you comfy, then. Lift up your head, so Nurse can plump up those pillows. Here's your milky drink, get it down you and swallow your tablets like a good boy. There you go, those'll make you sleep like a baby. Night night, and not a peep out of you till morning. Let go of my hand, Taffy, I've got my other patients to think of too. Spoiled rotten, you are, now off to sleep with you or I'll have to report you to doctor. Night night, lovey.'

Some of the others started calling out mockingly or with longing 'Nurse, Nurse'.

'Will you all be quiet! I'm reporting the lot of you to doctor.'

Jay was thinking about a book he had loved as a child. It was called *Visiting Mr Bee*. Mr Bee had taken a little boy into the hive and shown him over it, all the hexagonal rooms where the bees made their honey. He wished he could be there, with wise, kindly fuzzy Mr Bee holding his hand.

A few miles away the night was young. Dr Barrable's E-type was among the cars parked on the forecourt of the Firefly Motel with the reflection of a fizzling neon pink cocktail glass, swizzle stick and green cherry flashing on and off in its silver skin. Inside the doctor swirled bourbon round his glass, watching Cheryl siphon up her third Margarita. The advantages of this place, which had once been the hang-out of louche local youth, with a refulgent throbbing juke-box, were its location, hidden in the hills, and the row of unseasoned pine cabins at its rear. The doctor reckoned Cheryl would be ready for action after one more. He looked at his watch. One too many, and she could become sentimental and lachrymose, then sullen and malicious. The mattress in the cabin was thin, the doors and windows didn't fit, but the director liked to slap her around a bit and she enjoyed being treated like a naughty little pink piglet, so both were happy.

'I wish we could be together always,' said Cheryl.

'My dear, so do I.' He put his hand over hers. 'You don't know how much I wish it. But you know my situation . . . '

'Redvers, I do understand about your poor wife. It must be awful for you living with somebody so – unstable. I really respect you for the way you handle it.' She squeezed his knee while sucking up her straw with a sound like bathwater gurgling down the plughole. She had no desire for him to leave his wife but felt that it behoved her to pretend that she had, and assumed, wrongly, that it kept him on his toes.

'Did I tell you my friend had her baby?' she asked. 'A lovely little girl called Kayleigh?'

'Yes, you did.'

Cheryl breathed a sigh of sacrificed motherhood into her empty glass. Kayleigh was a little doll, she had to admit, but really she found the whole business of pregnancy and child-birth distasteful: messy, animal and really old-fashioned, you'd think they could've come up with something better by now. If only you could just order one, toilet-trained, from the Next catalogue. She was wondering what to wear to the christening. Shame Lisa hadn't got her figure back; some women never did really. She pictured Father Jeremy conducting the ceremony, herself in something summery and sophisticated.

Great vulgar cocktails of laughter were being shaken over a long table nearby, spattering Dr Barrable in sticky droplets. Cheryl's coevals, the *jeunesse dorée* of Surrey, stubbing out their Marlboros and Mores in saucers of tepid tapas. He went up to the bar and caught Cheryl looking at them as he came back.

'You should be over there, with them. Not stuck with an old fogy like me,' he said sleekly.

'Redvers! No, funnily enough, I've always related more to more mature people than my own age group.'

'I'll bet you have, my little gold-digger,' he thought. 'Bottoms up.'

Cheryl squealed; his little loin of pork, well-basted and succulent, ready to serve. And then:

'Redvers?'

'Darling?'

'You know some of those people at the – at work, I mean?'

His eyes froze to ice cubes.

'Now, Cheryl, you know the rules. No office gossip out of hours.'

'No, I know, but what I mean is, some of those people, I mean what's the point? Wouldn't it be better just to ... well, I mean, for their own good, more humane. Like with animals. I mean, when our little dog started going to the toilet on the carpet my mum was down the vet's so fast – it was the kindest thing ... basically, they ...'

'Cheryl, have you been snooping beyond your parameters? If I thought you had ...'

'No, I haven't, honestly! Only, you can't help but notice things.'

'You're not paid to notice things. You are paid an extremely generous salary to do your work and mind your own business. I hope I don't have to remind you of the legally binding declaration which you signed at the commencement of your employment. I *have* to be able to trust my staff implicitly, Cheryl.'

'I only meant, well, they're no use to anybody, are they? It really turns me up, the state of them, I've been literally sick in the toilets more than once. I mean, it's like all down to the quality of life, isn't it?' she amended lamely. 'Let's face it . . . '

'You haven't been mixing with the caring staff, have you? Tell me the truth.'

'No, no, I haven't, honestly, I swear.'

'Methinks the lady doth protest too much.'

'No, I don't, honestly. I've got no complaints. I love my job.'

'That's all right, then. Subject closed. We won't refer to this conversation again.'

He popped a peanut into her snout, tipped with its pretty little greasy cupid's bow.

'Just remember that what you were hinting at would be quite, quite morally indefensible, and practically non-viable. Genoci— euthanasia is an emotive word, Cheryl. My work, in which you share as an important member of the team, is to do with rehabilitation and the care of those who cannot care for themselves.'

'Yes, sir.'

Cheryl faced him with the subdued yet sulky look she wore when rebuked in the office. What a waste of precious time, when he was entirely of her opinion, and the operation could be carried out cost-effectively, but he dared go no further than he had been authorised to do when the DoE had intimated to him that he need not strive officiously to keep alive. Time was ticking away.

'I've been thinking about your birthday, sweetheart.'

'So?'

The child who had been told off was not to be won round too easily.

'How d'you fancy popping over to Paris for lunch and then a bit of shopping for you to choose your present? Romantic dinner *à deux*, a small hotel . . .'

Cheryl's eyes sparkled.

'And what makes you think I'm to be bought for the price of a ticket on Concorde, Dr Barrable?' she countered archly.

She smirked to herself as they walked to their chalet; it was pathetic how she could twist him round her little finger. Dr Barrable was thinking hard about her previous remarks; he would be sorry to lose her, and was not sure if it would be safe to let her go. Still, she was hardly the type to write a letter to the *Guardian*. He would just have to keep an eye on her. If the worst came to the worst she should be fairly easy to neutralise with a handsome pay-off, or the fear of God put into her, or to discredit. But any breath of scandal would finish him . . . He buried his face in her hair as he fitted the key into the lock, humming.

'Your perfume fills the air and oh, the night's so blue. And then *you* have to spoil it all by saying something stupid . . .'

21

There could be no doubt that it was Mrs Handisyde sitting on the wall outside the Maudsley. William's arm jerked up in guilty salute, and he almost stopped to excuse his defection. She was staring straight at him. It was clear that she did not know him at all.

His instinct was to turn left towards the Phoenix and Firkin at Denmark Hill to deal there with the emotions the sight of Mrs Handisyde had provoked, but the thought of that converted railway station full of noise and real ales and young people and mental patients scrounging drinks propelled him on towards the Fox on the Hill. There he sat, a Dr Jekyll waiting for the potion to restore him to a Mr Hyde, who would stay at this bar in an invisible circle of darkness over whose edge no one would dare step until he lurched out into his unreal reality in a mad dark afternoon. As if in atonement, tribute or self-punishment he had chosen a large whisky, such as he had drunk in that macabre kitchen when he had been a gardener for a morning. Of course, the whisky told him, it is perfectly possible that Mrs H was merely waiting there outside the bin, for a bus; several buses stopped there. Her glazed aspect contradicted that comforting theory; the eccentricity had developed into full-blown derangement. Well, even so, it had nothing to do with him, she was not his responsibility.

He had enough difficulty keeping his own head above water without taking on a deluded stranger's unhappiness. Was he not entitled, even obliged, to clutch at the straw he had been offered that might pull him back to life after floundering in the cold dark water for so long? Yet the thought that a hanging basket or tub of busy lizzies might have saved her would not be drowned like a slug in beer. He sipped slowly. Knock it back. Have another. No, don't. That way lies madness. He would go home and do something about his own garden.

When he came in from the garden to wash his stinging hands at the kitchen tap, he remembered Mrs Handisyde's warning about the prickly plants: ' ... days later you find little poisonous spots on your hands'. It had come true. He scrubbed at earth and dandelion stains. The free newspaper had been delivered while he worked. There it was, on page two. The youths who tried to rob Doolally's had been sentenced. The black boy got youth custody; the white boy had been put on probation. William had not been called as a witness. He felt angry despair at the injustice of the sentencing, mixed with guilty relief that he had not been forced to appear.

'Herne Hill is populated entirely by grotesques,' Olive came in saying. 'My God, the adipose tissue alone ... the fat would keep McDonald's going for years. Might that not be an answer when the oil runs out – recycle the populace of south-east London?'

'Olive ... '

'Yes, that's the solution. To think of the toxic waste from

those burger-fed bodies oozing into the soil, poisoning the crops. Let them drive their cars and heat their homes and fry their chips in their own oil. Fat fuel. Fast food.'

'Olive.'

'Fresh pasta, from Lina's. Look, isn't it beautiful.' She unwrapped the big white squares for his inspection.

'Well, hooray!'

'What? And garlic olives. Smell.'

'I meant, hooray, you actually said something nice about something. Do you have to despise *everybody* you see?'

'No. Not at all. There were two stunningly attractive and superior people waiting outside that ghastly supermarket by the bus stop.'

'There you are, then . . .'

'Both of mixed race. One was a cross between an Alsatian and a Collie with a wonderful long nose with a white blaze and the most elegant white legs, and the other was chunkier, a gingery colour with a white chest and a Mastiff sort of face, but smiley.'

'You're impossible. Will the pasta keep?'

'Why should it?'

'I shan't be in for supper.'

'Well, thanks a bunch. You might have given me some advance warning, and I wouldn't have bought all this stuff. Where are you going? Staff meeting? PTA? Graffiti in Toilets and Textbooks subcommittee? You're always sloping off somewhere lately.'

William opened his mouth and snapped it shut without speaking.

'How am I supposed to eat all this stuff on my own?'

'Put it in the fridge. We can have it tomorrow.'

'That's not the point,' she shouted as he retreated. 'What am I supposed to do? Put myself in the fridge, put my life on ice until somebody condescends to buy it?'

She thought she heard William mutter something about sell-by dates as his cowardly and treacherous feet took the stairs. What should she do; read, watch the box? A bit of ironing? William had done it all. Knit, sew, paint? The only hobby she had had since her schooldays had been a small stuffed bird of prey, given to her by her grandfather, which had collapsed in a mound of dusty feathers years ago. After a while she decided that she could indeed eat all that stuff on her own, and she did.

Much later, rising to pull the curtains against the moon, she saw that man clanking past, and clashed the curtains together, almost wrenching them off their rings, obliterating him. She realised what his aluminium crutches reminded her of: a pair of stilts she had received one Christmas. She remembered the feeling of power she had had, towering over William, a capricious dictator, deciding who should or should not have a go. William hadn't got the conjuring outfit his heart was set on, for some reason. Just as well, he'd only have muffed all the tricks. He had saved up for some indoor fireworks once, for Mother's birthday; damp squibs all.

Days passed, and still the weather did not break. Gardens had a jaded July look about them as summer flowers bloomed too soon and scorched. Charlene had broken up with her boyfriend and moped apathetically in the scented oven of the shop; dust and litter blew in off the street if they left the door open for air. Plastic and paper fans sold out; an electric fan whirred on a shelf, out of the reach of little fingers.

'I wish we had one of those big wooden ceiling fans,' Charlene grumbled, 'or a punkah wallah.'

'If wishes were horses, Charlene ...' Olive felt obliged to point out.

There was one dramatic thunderstorm and deluge, on the day of the Reggae Festival in Brockwell Park.

'Such a shame,' Olive said, 'perhaps Jah doesn't like reggae after all.'

Charlene didn't answer. Later, though, she suggested that Olive engage a Saturday girl for, although she had time off during the week to compensate, she was finding Saturdays a real drag. Olive said she'd think about it, but the thought of thinking about anything in this heat was too much.

Sunday found Olive on the bus – William had borrowed the car – with nothing better to do than visit the Horniman. True, Hazel and Betty had suggested she join them at an Older Lesbians' Tea Dance; Olive had exploded with outrage: 'Older indeed! Thanks but no thanks.'

She hadn't bothered to ask why he wanted the car. Now she was mildly curious, but forgot about him as a small bee bounced off her nose.

Olive opened the window and forgot about it; then she heard the flapping and thwacking of a newspaper behind her.

'There is a bee,' said the old man in the back seat, in what Olive took to be a *mittel*-European accent, leaning forward to flap.

'I know.'

At that moment a young black man who had been sitting at the front came down the aisle and stopped at the top of the stairs.

'Don't kill it,' he said.

'I wasn't going to,' Olive retorted indignantly.

'Won't sting you if you don't touch it.'

The old man snorted.

'I wasn't going to kill it! I opened the window for it.'

'It's gotta live, right, just the same as us.'

'Right.'

Olive managed to scoop it off the window with her own paper and out into the air. The young man descended the stairs.

'He was trying to chat you up,' came venomously from the back seat.

'Oh, I hardly think so.'

'They got their own rules, those people, make them up as they go along.'

Olive tried to see through the window if the young man with the nice smile, who had seemed pleased with himself and life, had actually got off the bus.

'Mmmm,' she tried to agree and disagree simultaneously.

'He was smoking at the front of the bus and when the conductor asked him to move back, he told him to "piss off".'

'Really? And when did this great empire of ours grant you refugee status, may I ask?'

When she next turned round, the back seat was empty.

The painted colours of the totem pole outside the museum fading into the wood and the odd humpy castle of the Horniman building, like something out of Heath Robinson, reassured her as she approached and went up the familiar steps in a scent of philadelphus.

The walrus had been shot in Hudson Bay. In about 1870

the taxidermist J. H. Hubbard had bulked out its vast grey skin with stuffing and preservatives and it was displayed in melancholy splendour at the Great Colonial Exhibition of 1886. Unfortunately, Hubbard had never seen a live walrus, and so he had filled its folds and rolls of fat, giving it a smooth, anomalous hide. The walrus had arrived at the Horniman in 1893, and had been re-stuffed in 1986. It wasn't so bad from the back, looking as manufactured as its iceberg, but when Olive had walked round it, she was confronted by the glass eyes, the tusks, the bristles of the pepperpot muzzle of a creature which seemed to know that it had been murdered, robbed of the ice and seas, and sentenced to hulk there as an undead condemnation of all empirical follies.

She moved away, past the eagles and the condor, to the parrots. Behind her, she heard a mother cry to her children, 'Oh look at the little darling fledglings!', calling them to admire two tiny miracles of the taxidermist's art, fluffy and nestling against the parent bird's breast.

The kakapo, and the kea, with its bronzed green feathers and orange-lined wings, represented New Zealand in the gaudy display of scarlet, emerald, sapphire, gold and amethyst. A flock of those mountain parrots, the keas, had once revenged themselves on Jack Mackenzie by ripping his tent to shreds. There had been a Maori chief's kiwi feather cloak in the dressing-up box, a hamper big enough to hide a child, when they were little. Once a source of family pride, it had lost its glory with the years until, mothy and dusty, no longer worthy of loan to school plays and amateur dramatics, it had become a children's plaything, and had ended its days as a pile of ragged feather dusters. On her first visit here Olive had come to the small Maori exhibit in the Horniman with a shock; there was the twin of the long, lidded, carved box which stood on her mother's dressing table holding a tangle of beads and pearls, labelled Chief's Feather Box. There was another, intricately swirled and sworled like Father's pencil box, which she had borrowed from his desk and taken to school with a rubber band binding on its lid, until the scorn of her best friend, with her two-tone, green and white, double-decker Rolinx, with special compartments and retractable lid, had forced Olive to abandon it and demand a Rolinx of her own. There were these funny, dusty bits of her childhood in a glass case, lost family clutter which here retained its magic and ceremony; and there stood a Maori chief in the selfsame cloak that had decorated their games, served as dolls' bedspread, and the bed of dogs and kittens. The cloak was woven from flax, open work entwined with kiwi feathers, and edged with red and yellow; above it, the chief's face was tattooed, grooved like his feather box and the ornamental prow of a canoe. Round his neck was hung a jade tiki, a writhing green gargoyle, which looked both foetal and ancient; he clasped a staff topped with a stylised human face whose large protruding tongue expressed contempt and defiance.

If the dead animals and birds, the pillaged gods and artifacts, the jewellery and weapons and cooking utensils were a monument to colonial impudence and greed, they spoke too of courage, exploration of an unknown too terrifying to contemplate, where you might sail over the edge of the world into a fathomless and eternal abyss, of impenetrable darkness split by shrieks and painted faces and flames, magic beyond comprehension and powers against which there was no appeal or redress, unthinkable agonies engulfed in a vast blackness, after which there was no memorial.

Olive felt the floor rock under her feet, as if she were balancing on a fragile globe. She thought of her grandparents in a boat that seemed as small as a painted tin clockwork steamer in a bathtub, borne across the Pacific by faith, conviction and the will to do good. Where was her faith? Evaporated like weak communion wine. Her conviction? Nonexistent, like her scientific curiosity and her sense of adventure. Her will to do good? She went to have a cup of tea.

The warm, English smell of the tea, drawing one to the refreshment room, redolent of urns and church halls, rained-out subdued festivities, usually cheered her with its sense of small expectations. Today it failed to touch her *mittelschmerz*.

The ruins of a piece of fruitcake lay on her plate and a stubbed-out cigarette in the tinfoil ashtray. She didn't know why she had bought the cake. At another table a man was twirling a match in his ear while crunching a chocolate biscuit, reminding her of a recent journey home on the tube. She had sat, fearful and yet longing for Theo and his mother to board, in straw hat and shades. The carriage was invaded by headbangers bound for a heavy metal concert at Brixton Academy, in stinking clothes thick with grease, swigging lager, terrorising the people sitting down quietly, minding their own business and eating bits of dead animals in buns, or bits of themselves, and picking and flicking scraps of skin and nail onto their library books and fellow passengers.

Olive went to get another cup of tea, and sat down where she could not see the man. No mad Kiwi to plague her today; she would almost have welcomed his company, until she remembered how he had degenerated when she had seen him on the bus. Perhaps Ashley should adopt him as one of her lame ducks. Reluctant to go home, she made another circuit of the museum, carefully avoiding the display of dogs' heads. She could take everything else, the Egyptian skeleton with bracelets circling bones, a necklace of stones falling from crumbled vertebrae into the sand, a fragment of leather sandal on an ivory foot; she was almost fond of it, and would stand gazing for a long time through the glass tomb smeared with the breath of the curious. But those mounted, decapitated dogs' heads seemed an affront to nature. Dogs ought to lie in little cemeteries in the corners of gardens or churchyards, with names like Laddie or Bess or Jock incised on the mossy headstones.

22

London had a drainy smell. It hung over the streets and collected round the overflowing rubbish bins and black sacks of garbage, the drunks in doorways and the crowds of young people drinking on the pavements outside every Soho pub, in the evenings that sweated menace. Faces were glazed like the flattened lacquered ducks hanging in the windows of Chinatown restaurants; raw provincial adolescent laughter, threatening smashed glass and vomit, sprayed in thick volleys over passers-by through the police sirens and burglar alarms frazzled into dementia by the heat. People at the best tables in restaurants shifted their chairs and sniffed the air, as if they had been placed too close to the loos.

'What do you think?'

Olive waved the empty blue glass bottle at a passing androgyne in a white apron to give herself time to think of a plausible reason for refusing Lizzie's offer of her cottage. She was being very persistent.

'I'm sorry, we've run out of mineral water,' the waiter said without apology. 'Iced water?'

'Fine,' said Lizzie, over Olive's disgusted protest. 'Really,

Olive, you could do with a break, for all sorts of reasons. The cottage is there, you'd be doing me a favour in keeping an eye on it.'

'What all sorts of reasons?'

Olive's heart had jumped, as if Lizzie had brought her here to confront her with the theft of Theo.

'You're looking tired, for one thing.'

'You mean old.'

The water arrived, cloudy with chlorine. Lizzie fished out a tiny shrimp on her finger tip.

'Well, you're hardly looking your best, you must admit.'

Lizzie could be relied on to dish out brutal truths, so Olive did not pursue this line of conversation. An emaciated girl, trying to sell wilted red roses, which would never open, passed their table by.

'You've had a rough time with Terry – though what you see in that little creep beats me. OK, I know anything I say will only make you jump to his defence. Go on, you old bag, say yes. Charlene can look after the shop, or you could close for a week. Think of waking to birdsong, taking your coffee into the garden, no need to get dressed. It's quite secluded, nothing to do all day but read and sunbathe . . . '

'Skin cancer,' said Olive. 'And I bet it's haunted.'

Her dress, unbuttoned as far as she dared, was sticking to her, thin and tissuey like the paper round a tangerine. She felt that if she were to rise and walk towards the Ladies, or the telephone, the chair would accompany her. All around mouths were shouting, closing on forks and glasses, exhaling smoke in a haze of grilled meat.

'Somebody else's ghosts would be a change,' she conceded,

as she pictured herself slim, brown, looking ten years younger, insouciant in bright cotton, waving casually to a pale and sweaty Terry, his hair broken into a frizzy mass of split ends by the rubber band that dragged back his ponytail.

'There aren't any ghosts. If there were, they would be benign. It's a happy house.'

The disruption that preceded Olive's departure tempted William to have the locks changed the moment she was safely out of the house. Should she drive or take the train; would Charlene manage or should she close the shop? What did her friends think she should do? At least half a dozen people might have heaved a sigh of relief when her minicab arrived, but it did not arrive.

'I knew I should have driven down. Or got a bus to Waterloo. Even crawling along the Walworth Road in a 68 would be preferable to this. I blame you, William. "Leave the car at home. Take a complete break,"' she bleated in imitation. 'I won't even get there – and if I do I'll be stranded without a car!'

'You're right on the edge of the village – there are local shops, and walks, and if you want to explore further afield you can use local transport.'

'Everybody knows there's no such thing as local transport any more. All the trains and buses were axed long ago. I should never have agreed to this stupid plan. I don't even want to go. Why are minicab drivers such inveterate liars?' she screamed, dancing on the carpet in rage, with flailing arms, flashing eyes and teeth. 'I told the bastard ten o'clock. At ten fifteen I rang to ask if it was coming and he said "One minute, young lady. It's on its way." If he's not here in one more minute I'll have to cancel and try someone else, and then the same thing will probably happen all over again. I'm going to kill that driver if he shows!'

'It's not really the driver's fault, you know, the controller just ...'

'Don't you dare to try to see both sides,' Olive shrieked. 'There's only one side. Mine. That's your worst fault, you know. Can't you just be on my side for once without having to be the Secretary General of the bloody United Nations? All I want you to do is agree with me occasionally and then I'd feel better and get on with it. As a psychologist you're on a par with Pollyanna. No wonder your staffroom was a hotbed of intrigue and jealousy ...'

As she ranted, William was dialling.

'Should be outside now. A dark blue saloon ...' he informed her.

Olive seized her bags and rushed into the street, dropped them in the road and hammered with her fists on the wind-screen of the car pulling up.

'What the hell do you think you're doing?'

The driver jumped out and grabbed her wrists, trapping her fists in front of her like a bouquet of snakes. As she realised that she was in the grip of their neighbour and had banged furiously on his Porsche, a car screeched to a halt behind them, pulsating with music which shook the windows of the houses and sent birds squawking into the sky.

'My brother will explain.'

She struggled free, wrenched open the passenger door of the blue saloon and sprawled into the blast of music with her luggage.

'Waterloo, and step on it. You've ruined my life.'

Through the black nylon hair of the miniature shrunken heads which hung in the rear window she saw Roger Da Souza shouldering past the mallow and marching down the peacock path in a way that meant business; the successful receiver of stolen property, of whom she had remarked more than once, 'Good fences make good neighbours'.

'Would you mind turning down that . . .' she stopped herself from saying jungle music ' . . . thing, and put your foot down.'

The massive nest of locks was impassive. Typical. Normally you could rely on these drivers to let you out on the pavement a trembling wreck. This jerk was not only sticking to the letter of the highway code but displaying quite uncalled-for courtesy. She was getting the headache all right, though, colours thudding through her skull, and that hideous plastic replica of the head that had grinned through her childhood nightmares bobbing about behind her didn't help. Emboldened by rage, Olive tapped the driver on the T-shirt.

'Excuse me, I've got a train to catch, which I've probably missed thanks to your incompetence.'

'There *is* some other traffic on the road, in case you haven't noticed.'

Self-righteous prig, like all of them. Taking over our God, sitting on the tube with their Bibles feeling superior and drinking little bottles of Lucozade . . . As if he was aware of her thoughts he launched into kamikaze mode, zooming through changing lights, missing buses by inches, scattering pedestrians on zebra crossings and almost depriving a minibus load of senior citizens of their lunches at the day centre on that or any day. Olive was delighted with him. Flung from side to side, she clung onto the handle, and tapping the beat with the fingers of her other hand, she sang along: 'I need your body tonight'.

'Get him!' she commanded, as one of her bags slammed into her shins once again and a cyclist teetered into the kerb. 'Missed. Damn! Still, that'll teach him to wear those disgraceful shorts that make his thighs look like a pair of black puddings. The arrogance of displaying oneself like that!'

The glossy haunches and obscene gesture of the cyclist appeared briefly in the window. Olive had a sudden memory of herself, aged fourteen, mounted on an old black Rudge, freewheeling past a cornfield with all her eggs in one basket and her cotton skirt catching in the mudguard and a black oily diamond imprinted by the chain on one white ankle sock. It was a pleasing picture.

They arrived in time for Olive to buy her ticket.

'Spare some change, please.'

'Got any spare change, please?'

Olive stopped to buy a crusty baguette filled with salad and brie and a fresh orange juice, almost tripping over some great hulk slumped on the concourse with a piece of cardboard hung from his neck saying 'Homeless and Hungry'. Encumbered, she found her way blocked by a pushchair in the hands of a girl so drunk that she could hardly stand, and two companions, one opening a can of lager which exploded in a yellow fountain and fouled the transparent hood under which a tiny baby slept. The buggy whirled on its hind wheels as the young girl, in a shrunken pink jumper, her flushed face bleared with tears, turned in some altercation with one of the others. Olive had an impression of staggering figures, unkempt hair, loud thick obscenities, swollen childish faces. She hurried to her train carrying the image of those three drunken children in charge of that baby. A courtroom, a crying girl in a police cell, a baby confiscated and never returned flashed through her mind as two uniformed policemen passed her. She didn't want to know what happened next. Besides, she was hardly in a position to offer her services in any capacity. She addressed herself to the problem of eating a long baguette filled with salad and brie discreetly.

William's wrists felt light, as if manacles had been struck from them. There was Roger Da Souza hulking on the step.

'Fancy a drink, old boy?' William deflected him.

They sat in the back garden, Da Souza's jacket draped over the rusty iron chair, his telephone on the curlicued table.

'Absent friends.'

The men raised their cans of beer. Da Souza's phone shrilled like a cicada in the heat haze. He shrugged his feet out of his Gucci loafers and let it ring, loosening his tie.

'So what's with your sister? Good-looking woman like that, you'd think ...'

William examined an empty snail shell, faded and light.

'She's never had much luck, I suppose.'

'Unlucky in love, eh?'

William felt that he had been about to say 'Lucky in cards, unlucky in love', but he had stopped, remembering an unfortunate evening of bridge at the Da Souzas' from which he and Olive had retired, if not quite in disgrace, in a coldness which had nothing to do with the frosty air in which they had padded down the path, with an unspoken accusation of Olive's cheating hanging like the aureoled moon above them.

'Yes, she's got a lot of style.'

Now William feared that he was about to be made an offer for his sister, like those men who return from holidays in Morocco and boast about the numbers of camels they had been tempted to accept in exchange for their wives. Of course, they'd never get them through Immigration.

'How's her business? Doing well?'

'Oh, ticking over quite nicely, I think. Of course, the lease comes up for renewal in three years, and you know what that means, and she's worried in case they implement this poll tax.'

He remembered standing in a stifling classroom, the windows closed against the shrieks and thwacks from the tennis courts, boring a group of disaffected pupils with the poll tax riots and the Peasants' Revolt.

'Same again, Roger?'

He had heard himself droning on like an untidy insect, a drone in fact, as he hovered over the dapper Da Souza flapping wings of shirt, or a dull grasshopper emitting a dreary song. What had been the cruel words of the sleek ant to the starving shivering grasshopper in the winter? 'You sang through the summer, now you can dance'? Something of the sort. He shuffled towards the fridge as the telephone burst into song, marking the end of a little idyll. Roger Da Souza, seen through the kitchen window, leaning back expansively in his chair among the weeds, talking into his portable telephone, brought to mind Sandy, his father, at his most affluent. He noticed that Roger had managed to get some orange pollen on his shirt sleeve now; William knew it of old; it was tenacious, like curry powder, and would never come out. Despite his recent efforts, the garden was still a disgrace. He would get to grips with it now Olive had gone.

23

Olive stood in the bedroom feeling the quietness of the house drift down upon her like disturbed dust, in the faded pink arcadia of the wallpaper among shepherdesses and little shepherd boys and sheep and sheaves and hayricks, willow trees and rustics dancing by flowery streams, and swains kneeling to proffer primroses, and distant castles on gently wooded hills. It was evening and the sound of rooks was in the air and in the branches of the great copper beech. There could be no doubt that they were having a meeting. Rook after rook flew in with information which was delivered in a distinctive voice to the committee in the tree and discussed excitedly before being relayed to a group in a poplar on the edge of a field. Each messenger circled the copper beech several times and landed with a crackling of twigs and leaves; others were dispatched, cawing. The conversation died down to an occasional remark and the tree fell into silence, but all around, from other trees, came the voices of rooks overlaying the softer twitters and flutters of small birds.

'What were they saying about me?' Olive wondered. She was slightly afraid of the black harsh-voiced residents, lest they be stern and punitive elders of a narrow church; then she was enchanted to notice house martins flying in and out of baked cups of mud under the eaves. She felt they did not judge her.

In the morning, curled up in the no-man's-land between sleep and waking, Olive was aware of light and birdsong behind the faded birds on her curtains but chose darkness, keeping her eyes shut. Twin babies hatched in her brain, bright against the blackness; ceramic black babies in scarlet and emerald knitted suits and booties. She saw herself, six years old, lifting the naked dolls from a nest of excelsior in a parcel. A birthday present from her grandmother. What should she call these African babies? Seretse and Kama. The names had been her mother's suggestion. It must have been around the time of that brave and scandalous marriage. No doubt now the names would be seen as a racialist slur but how she had loved them, about six inches high with painted hair and eyes and red lips, and limbs and head hooked to the torso on an elastic band inside the body, as was the way with dolls then. Elastic bands broke and had to be replaced, with a mother's skilful fingers hooking them out with a pencil or knitting needle and reassembling the body. The suits had been knitted by a neighbour, Miss Souness, in the spirit of missionary zeal with which she rattled the velvet bag at Sunday School: 'Hurry, penny, quickly, though you are so small, run to tell the heathen, Jesus loves them all.' Seretse and Kama had excited the envy of Olive's latest best friend Gwenda Jones, who wore patent leather shoes with ankle straps.

'I know you're trying to take Gwenda away from me,' Gwenda's erstwhile best friend Janice had accused in tears. Olive had shrugged, grinned enigmatically, wobbling a loose tooth with her tongue and jumped into an infuriatingly prolonged display of double-bumps with her skipping rope, the ballbearings in the handles clashing and the whippy white new rope skinning Janice's shins. Janice had trailed Olive and Gwenda home from school, dragging her dirty length of clothes-lines behind her. A few days later Olive disappeared leaving them to mend their lives, until somebody new came along for Gwenda to appropriate. Olive could still hear the sibilant wheedling tones of certain schoolgirls: 'I'll be your best friend ... I won't be your friend if you don't ... I'll like your drawing if you like mine ... be my partner ... I won't be your partner unless you ... you can't come to my party ... I'm getting a gang onto you ... ' Even as a child she had suspected that such bargained-for, conditional friendship and praise was not worth the having, but a best friend had been a social necessity. The only best friend she had actually liked had been Rosemary; she smiled now in recollection of what had been falling in love for the first time. Seretse and Kama had been lost long ago in one of the many moves, like so many pretty things they had had once. Olive felt a hot spear of guilt in her heart – dolls, dolls' clothes – was that how she had seen Theo, a doll to be played with and dressed up? Someone else's doll snatched in the play-ground? A replacement for lost toys? She writhed in white-hot colonial shame.

'Charlene?'

'Oh hullo! I wasn't expecting to hear from you.'

'Just thought I'd give you a quick ring to see how it's going.'

'I've only been open five minutes!'

'Yes, well ... '

'Look, don't worry, everything's under control. You're

supposed to be on holiday, remember, so just go on and enjoy yourself!'

'Yes, thanks, Charlene, I will.'

Olive put down the receiver wondering just how to do that, and realised, in the archaic shower, that Charlene would be muttering 'Old bag, checking up on me!' or, worse, had detected loneliness.

She wandered down the enclosed garden with a cup of coffee, barefoot on the springy lawn of tiny flowers which, when she had stood at the window earlier, had looked like embroidery under tulle burned by invisible flames as the sun consumed the last of the dew. She stood under the copper beech. Seen from below, as she gazed up into the greenish, serpentine, monumental branches, repositories of time formed by time, the leaves were not copper at all but a bronzine alloy of copper and green. She felt pleasant dizziness, an immobility, as if she would stand until roots grew deep and long, snaking under the grass to twist through the foundations of the house. Birdsong and the conversation of sheep, pleated bleats of off-white cotton wool or little bits of knitting, mesmerised her as the coffee cooled.

On her way to the shop, Olive noticed that the church door was open and two cars were parked outside the lych gate. She surmised that they belonged to two ladies – they were always ladies rather than women – on the Church Cleaning or Altar Flowers Rota. As she walked on alongside the stream, passing an iridescent dragonfly hovering above the yellow flags growing out of the water, she decided to have a look inside the church on her way back.

With her light bag holding nectarines, tomatoes, a newspaper and several postcards showing a garish aerial view of the village which gave it all the charm of an industrial estate plonked down in a viridian field, Olive entered the graveyard by its back gate, feeling slightly unnerved by the friendliness of the woman in the shop and the 'Good morning' of a man on a bicycle; she had forgotten that strangers could be nice to one another. She walked between old sunken tombstones which swooned in the heat and would have fallen were they not held tight in the rough arms of the long bleached grass. '*In Affectionate Remembrance*.' Was that the best anybody could do for somebody who had died aged fourteen years? She put away from her the inevitable thought of the girl whose death would not go away, but lay in wait everywhere, even here. She was glad that William was not with her and that she did not have to divert his attention from the inscription, which he would surely have sniffed out. Inside the church she felt the coolness of stone, smelled wet flowers and encountered buckets of water, a litter of damp paper and cut stems.

'I'm just looking at the church,' she told a kneeling woman who looked up at her from a pail of blooms.

'Oh yes, do. I expect you can see we've got a wedding tomorrow,' she said over white irises and white peonies. Faith, Hope and Charity, three stained-glass sisters, threw muted confetti of coloured light onto the pews and the floor. Beneath Olive's feet a brass plate commemorated a former vicar of the parish; a Bible lay open between the spread wings of a golden eagle on the lectern. She thought of her grandfather perched like an eagle in the pulpit with black wings folded. The altar, dressed in white, was attended on either side by a tall vase of white flowers. Olive studied glass and wood and embroidery, silk and stone, and stopped at a tablet set in the wall in memory of a young wife who had died in childbed. Had the baby perished too or had it been delivered safely, to be a living reproach to its grieving father? Had he loved it the more or had it crept about with a black burden of guilt on its puny shoulders? It was unbearable. She must get out.

'Oh, I'm sorry.'

She had blundered into another woman with a cathedral of white delphiniums and canterbury bells filling her arms. The woman smiled.

'We've got a wedding tomorrow.'

'Yes. What time is it, the wedding?'

'Two o'clock.'

'It's going to look lovely.'

'Well, I hope so . . .'

A bee rolled out of a flower, a drunk old bell-ringer making his unsteady way down the aisle to the door. Olive followed him out. The women, the flowers and the bee had brushed a peaceful pollen onto her. She walked into the sun, and felt no sorrow for those who lay under the hillocky grass; nor, for the moment, did she fear her own death.

'Upon Paul's steeple stands a tree, As full of apples as can be . . .' the bells seemed to sing, pealing her back to an infants' singing lesson. From her vantage point at her bedroom window she saw confetti-coloured dresses, skirts like shop carnations, yellow, pink, clove, pale green and blue, the lacy white legs of little girls skipping up and down the path, risking smears of moss and lichen from the gravestones; little boys with haircuts and bow-ties; prenuptial cigarettes smoked among the

323

buttercups and daisies. She watched cars arrive and debouch, onlookers gather to sit on the churchyard wall among the white valerian, the bridal limousine crossed with long white ribbons. The bride on her father's arm, matching pairs of bridesmaids, two taller, two tiny, in pale yellow with chaplets of flowers on their hair, processed inside, and the church door was closed with a clang of its iron latch. Olive rushed round doing the few chores the place required, an ear cocked for the muted triumph of the organ and the rejoicing bells.

The bride and groom emerged wife and husband and, as they stood among the people, the bride in white with flowers in her hair and a bouquet of rosebuds and baby's breath, the groom with his dark suit and white carnation scattered with confetti, were part of an ancient pastoral; the corn in the fields around them, the dead below their feet, the buttercups and daisies, fresh flowers on graves and plastic blooms bleached colourless in broken globes, the buttonholes in silver paper, the nosegays and little trailing baskets and wreathed hats were all part of it; the dead were at one with the living and the instamatics and camcorders might have been pipes and viols. To Olive, alone in the bedroom, the sentimental arcadia on the wallpaper around her illustrated the truth: love can be king, happiness is possible. Celebration and flowers and music demonstrate the best in people, illumine for a moment or two their souls, honour the past and affirm the future; nymphs and shepherds still sport and play.

'I am not part of it,' she thought, turning away. The ceremonies of the world went on without her, festivals that mark the year passed her by almost without touching. She was the stranger who hurries past the war memorial where others have laid their wreaths, with a poppy in her lapel only if it enhanced her lipstick or coat; death as an accessory. The observer of firework stars falling against distant blackness. Red, gold, green and purple Harvest Festival, spicy, orangey, nutty magic Hallowe'en, candle-lit tender Christmas Eve, they were all ordinary days on her calendar. The cycle of the seasons the rituals that give life comfort, hope and purpose, the fires lit against the darkness: because she was not part of them, she lived in unhappy exile from the tribe.

'Well, I'll leave them to their bucolic revels and bawdy jokes in the village hall,' she thought. 'Lambrusco in a plastic glass has never been my idea of a good time.'

Nevertheless as she lay in the garden with her book and a cold beer, Olive drank a silent toast to the bride and groom. She fell to thinking of the other England, that she had left behind; it might have been centuries rather than miles away. A sense of incredulous shame tinged her skin like that of a pale sausage under the grill, that she could have expected people to be nice living in conditions such as theirs; she had been guilty of an unforgivably Victorian prejudice of dividing people into the deserving and undeserving poor, doling out barbaric punishments; the workhouse, the poorhouse, the hulks, the gallows for that one and that one, awarding the nourishing soup and cast-off clothes of her approbation for those who touched their forelocks and kept their cottages clean. Not that anybody in the city rat-runs had noticed of course. If she had no real experience of the hardships and deprivations, the squalor and discrimination suffered by those she had condemned, how much less did the people of this village? There could be no doubt that the real power in England still lay in the land, behind high walls in the shires, at the true heart of England, among horses and dogs and ruddy men with guns. Easier to be patriotic here, with the sun and shadow moving across the hill, than in Railton Road, Brixton, or the North Peckham Estate. The misery of rural poverty and the galvanised animal concentration camps set in stinking yards were remote from the wedding and from this garden.

She was browning nicely, watching a bee back out, powdered gold, from the crimson heart of a peony, hearing little dropped stitches of the sheep's voices, and their sound prompted thoughts of their fate, the arcadian lambs, and she remembered lunching with Terry in a Smithfield wine bar and crossing part of the market, deserted in the afternoon but smelling of all the butchers' shops of London, skirting vast parked container lorries stuck with wisps of straw.

'I hate those things,' she had said. 'They remind me of those things the Nazis used to pack people in to send them to concentration camps; what were they called?'

'Cattle trucks,' said Terry.

'Yes, well.'

Terry Turner, the hermit of West Norwood. Where was he now? Working out at the Y, lying beside the pool at Brockwell Lido, lunching somewhere? No, it was Saturday. Probably poking round Brixton market for the ingredients for dinner for two and a couple of T-shirts. Anywhere but chained to his desk. Frankly, my dear, I don't give a damn. A children's choir was singing. 'Nymphs and Shepherds, come away, come away . . .' at the back of her brain, ' . . . this is Flora's holiday.' She slept, and woke among wisps of dream like rosy clouds on a painted ceiling, dissolving into blue, fading memories of something more Boucher or Titianesque than Terry Turner's Rottweiler amorousness.

It was a summer when a contagious madness had struck the nation's dogs, if the papers were to be believed. Scarcely a day went by without a distressing account of some family pet turning savage and killing or disfiguring its owner or a child, or some scarred urban beast kept for fighting taking its revenge. It was as though the order 'Kill!' was passed from dog to dog in the parks and bloodlust charged their veins. If canine revolution had been planned, it failed. The leaders, Pit Bulls and Rottweilers, were captured and put to death, and life went on as before; all that had changed, as far as Olive could see, was that the Alsatian, once feared for its sudden regression into wolf, took on the mien of a safe and cuddly family friend, guardian of pushchairs and prams. She had toyed with the idea of a Peke, a Pomeranian or a Chihuahua, something small that she could have in the shop, but was deterred by the picture of it vanishing into a pair of slathering jaws. Besides, she really preferred bigger dogs. Ashley's cats were very decorative, but too demanding; she remembered the croaky phonecall two years ago, when Ashley had had the flu: 'Please come. The cats have made me their slave.' She decided to give Ashley a ring, but only got her voice on the machine. She hung up without leaving a message, as she realised she hadn't really anything to say. She thought of William then, but did not ring and was pleased she hadn't got Ashley, because it would be like breaking a spell to speak to anybody in the other world. Charlene had her number, and William's, should an emergency arise. Truth to tell she had hardly given the shop a thought; it was as if the lease had run out already and the estate agent's board was up.

She had a sudden flashback, of running out on Charlene in Casualty that day. She would make it up to her, and with more than a box of bashed lavender soaps; Charlene would find her a model employer. She might even consider a small rise, or a Saturday girl.

The morning after Ashley had warned her that she risked losing Charlene, Olive had taken the girl by her shoulders and whirled her round.

'Really, Charlene, must I take you to task once again? You know I have a total, absolutely total, phobia of labels sticking up at the necks of clothes.'

'Sorry, Mrs Schwarz.'

'Do try to be less slapdash. If I want to know the size, composition and washing instructions for your garments, I have only to ask you, I'm sure. And by the way, I wish you would remember not to call me Mrs Schwarz, I'm Olive . . .'

'OK, Olive. Customer.'

' . . . Mackenzie, now. I reverted to my own name some time ago, as you should be aware, so it's Ms Mackenzie. Attend to the customer, please, Charlene.'

'Yessum!' Charlene had dropped a subversive curtsey.

In the cottage kitchen Olive felt a wave of affection for her assistant. She was not perfect by any means but perhaps it was not entirely her fault that she was younger and more attractive than Olive.

She woke early the following morning and took her coffee into the garden. The house martins were flying out of the eaves, taking insects on the wing and carrying them back to their nests. She put down her coffee, was dragging a chair into the sun, and stopped, shocked. A baby house martin on the grass, black, blue, white, out of its element; she might have trodden on it; could almost feel the sickening squash under her foot. Olive stared at it helplessly.

'You!' she shouted at a passing bird. 'Do something!'

It ignored her. Was the fallen bird a fledgling? Could it fly? Did it fall, or was it pushed?

'Get up. Look. Sky. Lovely sky. Go on, fly! Do you want to be a sitting target for any cat that comes along? Well, do you?' She clapped her hands. 'Shoo! Shoo!'

Its sides were heaving like a tiny pair of bellows, its beak was open, it seemed to be gasping. She thought the sun would shrivel it up, it would die of heatstroke. There was no help for it, she would have to pick it up. Perhaps it was trapped by its feet in the grass. She didn't even know if house martins had feet. She knew there were legless birds of paradise, and there was that song about a little bird who lived on the wind. The last line was something about 'the little bird dies'.

Olive positioned herself behind the bird and steeled herself to pick it up, dreading that the feet, if it had any, were tangled in stalks. She got it, holding its wings to its sides. She set it on the palm of her left hand. It sat. She could see each miniature feather, perfect, iridescent in the sun, its tail feathers not yet grown, its bright eyes. She stroked its head with her finger, hardly daring to touch, it was so fragile, wanting it to sit there for ever. She looked up at the window and saw that there was no way she could place it under the roof or in the gutter. She knew there was no ladder. Olive raised her arm and batted the bird, a weightless shuttlecock, towards the sky. It took to the air, it was flapping, flying, it fell. A low bush broke its fall, it was on a perilously bouncing broad leaf. Olive picked it up again and this time, eyes shut tightly, threw it upwards with all her strength.

It must have caught a current of air, for it soared with spread wings, then flew directly towards the roof and disappeared under the eaves. Olive breathed out deeply. She was jubilant, but there were only the birds to share her joy. She felt tears on her face, salt, burning and stinging; the first tears she had cried for years that were not for herself. Saving the bird seemed the only worthwhile thing she had ever done. She let the tears dry on her skin, mineral signs, a sort of stigmata, which proved that she had changed utterly, and she felt a hard crystal in her heart dissolving and charging her arteries with benevolence.

She was different; everybody, William, Charlene, her friends, would see that she was different.

In the garden, Olive faced for the first time the pain she had caused Theo's, no, Jermaine's, family. She saw that there was no point in giving herself up, for she knew she would never steal a child again. She thought of her failure to comfort William in his distress. She forced herself to listen to her last conversation with her mother, when she had been too full of her own troubles to hear the alarm in her mother's voice or the crackle of flames behind her. It had not been her fault that her mother had chosen to answer the phone to her while leaving a low gas under a pan which boiled dry, or that a plastic colander had rested on top of the pan and had melted in an explosion of green fire, or that her mother had thrown water on the burning cooker, sending a sheet of flames to the ceiling tiles so that the whole kitchen became an inferno and choking black smoke engulfed her lungs, but she had been so angry with her mother for years, for this final, fatal, act of foolishness.

330

The baby bird was her Dostoevskian onion, that would pull her up to heaven like the old woman in the folk tale he described; she would not let future sins pull her back down to hell; she was the Ancient Mariner who, when he blessed the water creatures unaware, felt the albatross fall from his neck; she was restored to life. All shall be well and all shall be well, and all manner of things *would* be well: if she used other people's imagery to describe her altered state, that was all right, she thought, because she was part of them as they were part of her and of the garden, the fields around her, part of the universe and of the human race and of eternity.

24

"'The kiss of the sun for pardon, The song of the birds for mirth, One is nearer God's heart in a garden centre, Than anywhere else on earth,'" William said and Ashley joined in on 'centre'. He felt a wild happiness in being with her, excitement at the exquisite ordinariness, the Englishness of pottering round a garden centre on a Sunday afternoon, joy in her selection of the plants in little black plastic pots for the balcony, the snake's head fritillaries of reptilian velvet, black snake's beard or dragonbeard like flowers from the underworld, the scarlet geranium, the eau-de-cologne mint.

One thing only cast a shadow over the afternoon: Wandsworth Prison. It hulked over the garden centre with its walls and castellations, barred windows and tower topped with a geometric glass skylight or observation post. It was impossible not to wonder if there were faces behind the bars watching the Free coming and going with their trolleys of peat and compost, plants for borders and rockeries; a captive audience in the gallery watching players on the far-off stage in a symbolic enactment of all that they had lost or never had. The moist black smell of earth and greenness could not penetrate those walls or drift into the room where the prisoners received their visitors. Meanwhile, stone angels and cherubs smiled on Ashley and William, who felt like a released prisoner himself, seeing everything for the first time for years, on probation, fearful of violating his parole, aware that the face of a flower, the scent of thyme or a rose might break his heart.

'My father used to say, "You're nearer God's heart in a chemical garden,"' Ashley told him. 'He gave me one one Christmas. It was beautiful.' She saw the crystals growing into magic pinnacles and stalactites in the old aquarium, pink, purple, blue and green spikes like a coral reef or fairytale castle. 'Perhaps I could get him one, he might like it. If one can still get such things.'

'Every Christmas I wanted a conjuring set from the Gamages catalogue,' said William. 'But I never got it.'

They walked on past tiny irises and lilies in bubbling water tanks, coloured with intentions towards conjuring sets and chemical gardens, redemptive gifts to each other.

William bought her a small stone tortoise, putting aside thoughts of Mrs Handisyde and the hedgehog bootscraper. Aphids and wireworms of guilt must be kept at bay. Then they were drawn like bees by the perfume of white camellias; with faces nearly touching the petals, they discovered the scent was almost unpleasant. 'That symbolises nothing,' William decided, withdrawing his head into sweetness once more. It was getting late; the staff were becoming impatient to be gone. The gates were locked; the plants were banged up for the night.

Yesterday, Saturday, they had taken Ashley's small great-nephews, a slightly daunting pair at the dinosaur stage, who wore T-shirts emblazoned with endangered species, to

Crystal Palace to see the lifesize models of prehistoric animals which reared out of the landscape of the park. William had dreaded that the boys, who had sunk into a condemnatory silence in the back of the car after he had stopped to fill up with leaded petrol, would spot some Mesozoic error or denounce the arrangement of spike or scale or tail, but they had been enchanted. Ashley and William had shuffled through old cereal packets and tea-bag cards in their minds for plastic models and information to answer their questions and had acquitted themselves well enough. It was when they were leaving the park and William was explaining, with some mischievous satisfaction, that the car belonged to his sister who was, alas, not as environmentally aware as she might be, but he was trying to persuade her to have a catatonic converter fitted, that they came upon their own example of an endangered species in the grass. The Snyders huddled together in their bright clothes as if the slopes of grass were too vast for them.

'They didn't look very happy,' said Ashley.

'No. I'm a bit worried about them. Ashley, I've got to get a job.'

'Yes, I know.'

'Not just for something to do. Financial reasons, too, make it essential. Urgent, even.'

'Will you go back to teaching?' she asked hesitantly.

'I don't know. Something – useful, at any rate.'

'I could do your c.v. If you like, of course.'

For a moment then it seemed as if the getting of the job would be a mere formality. Everything seemed possible, and in the morning, waking with Ashley's warm body entwined round his, reading the papers in bed, breakfasting on red orange juice and bagels with cream cheese and scallions, going back to bed, everything seemed possible still. They had lost their fear that the other might find some fatal flaw, that it would not work; Ashley knew herself to have become beautiful because she was loved and so was less shy with him. William was suffused with tender gratitude; a hoover hummed in the flat above them, sweetpeas fluttered in a glass on the sill.

'I thought that part of life was over for me. And I didn't care, until I met you.'

He was at pains to say nothing which might cast her as simply the restorer of tired loins, some patent aphrodisiac such as those that used to be sold alongside trusses and surgical corsets in the Charing Cross Road: Damaroids, the Great Rejuvenator, or Phyllosan which Fortifies the Over-Forties.

Now, walking to the car from the garden centre, he felt desire, and honoured too. Anne had been as voluptuous as a peony; Ashley reminded him of the sea with her eyes like agates changing with the light from heavy salt-grey to moonlit calm, moonstones to flint; he thought of salty succulents, sea pinks, shells.

'Is something wrong?' he asked in sudden alarm on the way home.

'Oh, just Sundayitis.'

'We'll have to do something to get rid of it,' he said. 'I know it only too well myself. It can strike any time on a Sunday afternoon, something to do with Monday and school and homework not done.'

As he described the symptoms he felt the familiar palpitations and buzzing in his chest.

'I get it really badly, I don't know why, after all these years.

It's worse when I'm alone. Talk to me, about anything. Tell me about your mother; Olive always clams up if one asks too much.'

'She died in a fire.'

'What?'

'She died in a fire.'

'Oh darling, I'm so so sorry. I didn't know.'

'No, it's all right. It was worse for Olive, because she was on the phone to her at the time.'

'But, how? How could she have been?'

The green verges of Wandsworth Common shimmered in a heat haze as the car crossed false puddles of vapour on the potholed road.

'Is this some kind of sick joke?'

'No, really. You have to understand that my mother was rather strange in some ways. For example, if ever she went out leaving things less than immaculate, she'd leave a note saying something like "Back in ten minutes to scrub the floor", just in case some burglar should find the place not up to scratch. She used to sing a song that went "Don't take my prayerbook, Mr Burg-u-lar ..."'

'But ... ?'

'Well, she was always very – diffident, never wanted to upset anybody, self-effacing almost to the point of disappearance. That night Olive had rung her and she noticed something a bit strained in her manner, more distracted than usual. Olive was in a bit of a state about her marriage and going on a bit, when my mother said, "I'm sorry, pet, would you mind if I rang you back, I think the kitchen's on fire", and those were the last words anybody heard her speak.'

'But that's terrible! How absolutely – ghastly. I'm so, so sorry.'

'Thank you.'

'But poor Olive! Did she – does she . . . ?'

'Blame herself? No, not now anyway. She called the fire brigade but it was too late.'

Back at the flat they flapped in a desultory way through the remains of the papers.

'There's a piece by the dreaded Terry Turner here. Want to read it?'

'No, thanks. It can be of no interest to anybody. What's the little creep on about now?'

'"My Herne Hill" by Terry Turner.'

'Gordon Bennett.'

'Poor Olive,' said Ashley again. 'I wish she could find somebody.'

She poured William a drink, treating him gently, seeing him as an orphan now, who had lost his mother tragically.

'Down with Sundayitis,' he said.

Harlequin and Columbine were wreathing themselves round them. Ashley took 'My Herne Hill' by Terry Turner with her when she went to feed them, placing it with the papers she would use to line their tray, although the glossy surface was not of the right absorbency. It seemed to her now that one of her fears, as exemplified by a headline in the local paper – 'Woman's Body Eaten By Cats' – would not come true; the flat with two coffee cups in the sink and divided newspapers felt like a home.

25

In most penal institutions hierarchy develops naturally, cream on the top of the milk or scum rising to the surface; there is a pecking order, a system of commerce, a protection racket; there is collusion between some prisoners and screws and there is a grapevine so that the prisoners know what is going on almost before it happens. In the institution where Jay Pascal had found himself the normal rules did not apply: the prisoners had nothing to bargain with or barter, no visitors to bring anything in, no meagre wages and no rations of tobacco or sweets to buy; there was no fraternisation by any of the staff, and the men in Jay's block had no knowledge of what was taking place outside their limited parameters. Those with superior strength or more brain cells in working order were free to tyrannise the weak, incontinent and stupid under cover of darkness, and although fights did break out, there was nothing to tyrannise them for. Two of those who had been taken at the same time as Jay had disappeared and it was rumoured that they were dead: one old man had died in the night and the screws had removed him the next day in a heavy-duty plastic sack.

Jay had plenty of time for thought as he lay awake in the

babel of snores and groans and wrecked stomachs. Until coming to London he had spent most of his nights in dormitories: from the ages of five to sixteen, when he had been launched into the world, he had lived in the St Kilda Homes, an institution founded by the philanthropist Dr Murdo Aitchison at the beginning of the century and still run with his Calvinistic precepts not much modified. Jay had brought with him no garment embroidered with a coronet, no crested signet ring which hinted that he was of noble birth, a prince or duke in disguise, no letter to be opened when he came of age. All he knew of his ancestry, and it was memory which told him rather than information given to him by the authorities, was that his great-grandmother had been part Maori and his great-grandfather had been a Scottish minister. It was not until he was in his teens that he had realised, with the shock of a betrayal, that they had not been married, and that the respectable and ordered life in a big manse with a garden, which he had imagined for them, was a wishful fantasy.

A young teacher from England on an exchange visit, dismayed by the lack of music and drama in the St Kilda children's lives, had, against some opposition, mounted a production of *Annie*, with more enthusiasm than tact. Jay was cast as one of the orphans, dressed in an orphan costume of cut-off trousers and urchin cap, while the little Maori Annie sang of her lost parents: 'Betcha they're young, betcha they're smart, bet they collect things like ashtrays and art . . . ' Jay had not made a success of his part; he lacked the chirpiness of a credible orphan. There were no ashtrays and not much art at St Kilda's. As the years of his residence passed, discipline became slowly less draconian; for example, bedwetters were no longer publicly humiliated, but they did spend a lot of their free time in the laundry and they seldom got a slice of Sunday cake.

The children, many of whom, like Jay, were of mixed race of one sort or another, lived in what were termed family groups, each family in the care of an 'auntie'. Not surprisingly some of the aunties were as dispossessed as the flotsam and jetsam of children washed up and marooned at the St Kilda Homes, that remote island with its own culture and laws, set in a suburb of Dunedin.

For a long time Jay Pascal had been classed as educationally subnormal. 'He lives in his own little world,' Auntie Kilbride would say, and add 'autistic', tapping the side of her head. She was wrong; sounds and colour flooded into Jay, he saw too much, heard too much; his brain was bombarded by scents, details of leaf or flower or the pattern of Auntie Kilbride's tartan skirt or the flecks of colour in her tweed jacket; his breakfast puffed wheat was pebbles on a beach or people engulfed by a tidal wave of milk, his mashed potato formed grey cumulous clouds, his peas were a green hill far away topped with a crucifix of carrot: 'Come *on*, slowcoach,' Auntie Kilbride would cry, 'Hurry up!' and Jay would sit picturing the bus which took them to the beach on treats labouring up a tortuous hill, until she was forced to give him a clip round the ear to bring him to his senses above his congealing plate. She predicted confidently that Jay would end up in Seacliff, the loony bin immortalised by Janet Frame, whose books Auntie Kilbride had not read. Jay loved too much; he could fall in love with a painted rubber ball, which he saw as a little boy in a rainbow suit, with a shell from the beach, a pair of new shoes, a fragment of china found in the earth of the garden, whose crazed surface and speck of blue rim whispered half-heard memories of his life before St Kilda's. He had a series of doomed love-affairs with insects. When he had found a boiled caterpillar in his cabbage and protested to Auntie Kilbride she had said, 'Well, you've got more than your meat ration,' and, exasperated by his tears, had eaten it herself. She had called him 'a big wet lettuce' so often that his self-image was of a bright green dripping plant with drooping mud-streaked leaves. He even loved Auntie Kilbride on Sports Day, when she tossed the caber further than any of the boys or men, her strong arm drawn back, the small tree-trunk hurtling to the blue sky; Jay was in no doubt as to what Scotsmen wore under their kilts: interlock bloomers to the knee, the colour of elastoplast.

One day when he was seven years old Jay found that he could read. It was as if a colony of ants scurrying in different directions had suddenly drawn up in military formations; the letters on the page swarmed into solid shapes and held their positions and Jay saw in a flash the meanings of their shapes. The wet lettuce was changed into a bookworm chomping its way through the limited school library and beyond. 'Get your nose out of that book,' became Auntie Kilbride's constant admonishment as she snapped the volume closed on his offending feature. By the time St Kilda's closed its gates on him, his nose should have been honed to a fine point. He was still, as Auntie Kilbride took pride in remarking, a duffer at games, and his academic record was undistinguished to say the least.

A place had been found in a hostel for him where he put to use the simple culinary skills that leavers were taught and found his experiences in St Kilda's laundry had not been wasted.

They found him a job in a shoe shop but his dreaminess,

alternating with over-attention to detail, did not endear him to the customers.

'Don't get me wrong, son,' the manager had said with real regret, dismissing him. 'You're a nice lad and I like you, but you'd put me out of business if I kept you on.' He had discovered Jay's practice of selling shoes of different sizes to people with different-sized feet. 'How can you guarantee another bloke with a size nine left and a size ten right's going to come along, eh?'

Jay regretted the bright new shoes in their neat white boxes piled up in the storeroom like blocks of flats. He had enjoyed fitting the kiddies, watching them walk over to the mirror to admire themselves, and remembering his own pleasure in new shoes, so intense that he had smuggled them under the bed-clothes inhaling the intoxication of their smell. He backed the children's pleas for pretty and fashionable shoes, so that more than one mother stalked out, dragging a wailing child, to buy sensible school shoes elsewhere.

'Come back and see us!' everybody had said when he left St Kilda's, and Jay had taken them at their word. After the first visit nobody had much time for him and when he turned up on the fourth consecutive Sunday Auntie Kilbride had said: 'Now, Jay, I don't wish to be unkind but you really must stop hanging about here. St Kilda's gave you a home and an education and equipped you for the outside world. If you demonstrate that you are not making your own way in the world, then you're suggesting that St Kilda's did not do its job. That smacks of ingratitude, don't you think? I am sure that you, who have so much to be grateful for, are not intentionally letting down the school but that in effect is what you are doing, Jay. You do understand, don't you?'

342

Jay had found himself outside the gates with his bunch of wild sweetpeas and bag of lollies for the younger kiddies.

After the shoe shop, he had worked in restaurant kitchens and selling ice creams at the racecourse; he had tried working on a sheep station but had not liked the bullying dogs, the sight of struggling sheep, the snipping and cauterising in the burning iron sheds, the team of shearers with their mechanical clippers reducing the animals to skinny statistics. As Jay worked at a succession of low-paid and short-term jobs, spending his leisure in libraries, parks, graveyards, travelling around a bit, he slowly accumulated a little hoard of savings, and all the time he was aware of the Pacific rolling green, a vast bolt of shot-blue silk, whale-grey, dolphin-backed between him and part of his ancestral past. He had looked for his mother among the graves at Anderson's Bay but there was nothing, not even the cheapest municipal marker, to indicate that she had ever existed. All that he had of her were the garbled memories of things she had told him; the fragment of story about a great-grandmother named Myrtille and a great-grandfather who was a minister. A shadowy figure named Madge had written to his great-grandmother from London, from a house called *Dunedin*, but Madge must have been dead for many years now. Jay knew nothing of his own father; Auntie Kilbride had told him that his father was dead but he had no means of finding out if this was true. Another young person in Jay's situation might have discovered channels or agencies for information and pursued the matter but Jay was not equipped for that sort of detective work, and had never felt an inclination strong enough to attempt it. What was the use anyway, if all it would yield was a dead father or a dad who didn't want to know; but he still dreamed of meeting his mother again. He remembered very little of her now, but from time to time something, a string of pastel beads across a pram, a faded gnome fishing from a rustic bridge on a garden pond, the smell of cooking drifting through a fuchsia hedge or the scent of a woman's hair as she bent to fasten a child's sandal, or coloured embroidery on a white blouse, pierced him and left him with a sense of loss as vivid as the blue edge of the bit of china he had loved as a little boy and a feeling of something broken, with missing pieces, which could never be restored.

There were days when he ate and drank loneliness, when he mopped it from his plate with his bread, when it lay down beside him at night and got up with him the next morning but, for all that the blokes he worked with never saw him as one of them, that the girls who teased him and joked with him at work would never come out with him in the evening, he was for the most part content. He could look at things, staring, other people said; he had his library books, and the freedom to put his hands under the covers at night without Auntie Kilbride ripping back the sheet, just in case. One day he answered an advertisement and found himself, to his own surprise, one of a group of six heading for the UK in a white dormobile plastered with pictures of Kiwis. They took the well-worn route to Earl's Court.

It was there that disaster struck. Jay, out alone, was mugged and badly beaten and robbed. He lay bleeding in the street for some time before somebody rang an ambulance and he was taken to hospital, where he spent the night. On his discharge he wandered the streets trying to find his friends; he was sure that the van had been parked somewhere called Philbeach Gardens but when he found the street at last the van and his companions were gone and he never saw them again. It took days of waiting and searching before he accepted that they were not looking for him and that they were not coming back.

By the time that a man he met on a bench in Holland Park suggested that he go to the New Zealand Embassy for help, Jay was so filthy and dishevelled from sleeping rough that he was turned away from New Zealand House without a chance to tell his story. He sat in Trafalgar Square for a while watching the pigeons and the starlings in their suits of lights; the fountains had been turned off and the square was dusty with litter bowling about in a hot wind. He watched the tourists go up and down the steps of the National Gallery and marvelled that such a short time ago he had been one of them.

His first attempts at begging had been fruitless: 'Excuse me, I'm a New Zealander who's down on his luck and I wonder if you . . .' proved to be a hopeless opening gambit. He was getting the hang of it now a bit better.

It was when he walked into the park and was trying to make friends with a pelican that he saw the black swans on the lake. Then he wept, for he was weak and hungry and bewildered and they reminded him of the only home he remembered. He stood on the bridge snuffling into his sleeve, unaware of passers-by who found him a distasteful blot on the beauties of the park. Suddenly one of the black swans stretched its neck and spread and flapped its wings, rose in the water so that it seemed to stand on the surface and launched itself into the air, flying low, and skittered across the lake, braking just in front of him and folding its sooty wings on its back. Jay looked into the bright eyes set on either side of the neat head and at the red beak and the feathers bouffant in the little breeze.

'Sorry, mate, I've got nothing for you.'

Then he lowered his voice, but not enough, for a girl's snigger burst like a vicious firecracker behind him as he said: 'I'm from New Zealand too.'

The swan nodded.

'I got mugged. Look, I'll show you.' Jay leaned forward, parting his hair with his fingers to show the dried blood matted in the dark curls. 'The rotten mongrel took everything I had, except what's in this bag, my washing gear; at least I've got that.'

The swan looked sad, as if he knew that such terrible things happened in this city.

'What do you reckon I should do?'

The swan shook its head slowly and turned in a circle and began to glide away, cleaving a glassy wake, as a duck rose from the rushes shouting, 'Dunedin Dunedin Dunedin'.

Jay slept in a doorway in the Strand that night, huddled up against a girl who took pity on him and gave him a sandwich as well as a corner of her sleeping bag. He told her about his unsuccessful attempt at busking, how he had stood there at the bottom of the escalator, forgetting every song he had ever known except Auntie Kilbride's party piece, 'A Scottish Soldier' (the break in her voice on 'and fair as these green foreign hills may be, they are not the hills of home'), and a couple of numbers from *Annie*. People travelling upwards ignored him, people travelling down averted their eyes. Then he was joined by an expatriate Scot; it was as if Auntie Kilbride in her gardening mac, tied at the waist with twine, and having fallen into the compost, was at his side, singing her heart out. Then a black guy with a load of electronics and a saxophone had told them to clear off because it was his pitch, and the Scotsman

346

had vanished with the Spud-U-Like carton which had been Jay's collecting box and the coin which an American tourist had thrown in it out of pity.

'It seems there are rules and regulations everywhere,' Jay told his companion.

'You said it.'

She explained some of the intricacies of the network of streetlife to him but Jay was finding it hard to take it in.

'I should have tried something a bit more trendy, one of The Clean's numbers maybe.'

'Who?'

'The Clean. They're very big in New Zealand. Don't you get their records over here?'

'Where have you *been* all your life?' she asked him later, exasperated by the exposure of some fresh naivety.

'I'm not sure really,' he had to admit.

'All that Vegemite must've done something to your brain,' she told him, gnawing on a chicken leg from the kitchen of the Savoy.

'We could team up. Be mates, friends. Look out for each other,' Jay said. His voice was too hungry, his eyes were too pleading.

He hadn't seen her again; she had decided to swallow her pride and go back to Birmingham whence she had fled from the attentions of her mother's latest boyfriend, and her mother's rages. Thereafter he had slept in Lincoln's Inn Fields, once or twice in a hostel, and anywhere he found himself at the end of the day, slowly drifting south of the river.

Children are born with a concept of fairness. Protests of 'It's not fair!' ring out in classroom and playground, and the fact

347

that the child usually means 'It's not fair to *me*' does not detract from their statement of an ideal. By the time most people reach the age that Jay was at the time of his incarceration they have acknowledged that the adults who retorted 'Life isn't fair' and 'Who said it should be?' were right all along. Jay, lying awake on his smelly mattress, still believed that there would be some sort of hearing or tribunal, when somebody in authority would see that it was not fair that he and his companions were held here, in these conditions. There would be a trial, at which he would explain that the only thing he had done wrong was to take that library book of Russian stories, and that he had meant to put it back; that was what libraries were for, lending books. He was sorry he had lost it and he would pay for it when he got a job, if he could remember where he had borrowed it. Some of the people here had committed crimes, stealing, smashing windows, attacking one another with bottles, fists and feet and sticks, but surely they were entitled to a fair trial? This was not a proper prison, even for people on remand; a man should be presumed innocent until he was found guilty; and they were subject to arbitrary and savage punishments by Fulcher and his heavies. On television people arrested by the police always demanded to see a solicitor, and they were not punched in the mouth for asking.

If only he could get into the garden, he might be able to see some means of escape. He pondered the wisdom of telling one of the guards that he had had experience as a gardener, that he had been put in charge of the vegetable garden at St Kilda's; the smell of earth, the sharp, warm scent of watered tomato plants brought tears to his eyes as he lay in the almost tangible, solid atmosphere of confined sick bodies, blocking his ears against the muffled groans of somebody's bleak and unsatisfied attempt to gain relief. One night he dreamed that he had a job, picking up litter on Streatham Common with a silver spike in the sunshine. When he woke, he cried.

He thought about *Dunedin*, its overgrown garden where he had found the secret Solomon's seal, the big gnarled rosemary bush whose blue flowers and dark green feathery branches looked so pretty in the fading evening light; the photographs of the maids Madge and Lil. He thought about Kirsty, who had been kind to him in her way. He would have given anything for a lick from Gnasher's friendly tongue. He remembered the woman who had given him a lift in her car, and the rabbits and birds and wallabies in the garden of the Horniman, and the black swan, far from home like him, on the lake in St James's Park.

Now he employed the trick he had devised for getting off to sleep; he imagined himself lying on the swan's back on a bed of downy feathers, soft, soft against his face and aching body, sinking in to dark softness, with the black wings folding over him, the tips of the feathers like lace against the night sky. As he fell into sleep he was jolted by the image of a room he had passed in this place where he had glimpsed before the door was slammed naked men huddled on a bare floor awash with urine and excrement, and one rocking backwards and forwards, beating against the chains that bound him to the wall. He buried his face deeper into the swan's feathers to blot it out, and thought of the diving girl he had seen on his arrival, the swimming cap like a flower, her body arched over the chlorine-blue water.

26

Olive knew something was wrong the moment she entered the house. Odd sounds were coming from the bathroom. She raced up the stairs.

'My oh my, what a beautiful day ... '

She steadied herself on the landing, hand on her thudding heart. William was sitting in suds with a bluebird on his shoulder, singing 'Zip A Dee Dooh Dah' with the lack of inhibition of somebody who believes himself to be alone in the house. Everything is satisfactual? What the hell was going on? She banged on the door. A startled whale dived, creating a tidal wave.

'Come in, darling. I wasn't expecting you so soon ... '

'Evidently,' said Olive, although no sound came out.

'Ashley?'

Olive was sitting on the top stair raising a face greenish beneath its tan towards William when he appeared beaded with bubbles and girt in a towel splashed with starfish shells and crustacea.

'It's me,' said Olive. 'So you can get Mr Bluebird off your shoulder.'

'Olive . . . '

'That's *my* beachtowel. What the hell's been going on?'

'I've got some wonderful news!'

'You've got a job?'

'Ashley thinks she may be pregnant. In fact, we're pretty sure . . . '

'It's not fair! You cheat! You horrible little liar! She can't be! I'm . . . ' Olive looked as if she was about to say, 'I'm telling Mummy'. 'How could you? When you knew how much I wanted a child! Ashley's *my* friend. How long has this been going on?'

Olive sank into a chair with her face in her hands and ugly sobs bursting through her fingers.

'I thought you'd be pleased. Olive, please, look at me.'

She shook his hand from her shoulders.

'Oh did you? Did you really? Well, you should know me better than that. And now you can get on the phone to Ashley and tell her how vile I am and how I greeted her good news. My God, no wonder you wanted to get rid of me to the country!'

Olive rushed out of the room, upstairs, and flung herself on her bed, on to a rocky shelf above a chasm of loneliness. The swine. The pair of them. A couple with a pram. A family. And herself a dark figure trailing behind. 'I suppose we'll have to ask Olive to be godmother.' 'Must we?' A wicked fairy, evil with hurt, cackling into a white frilly bassinet. She could tell them a thing or two about each other. And would, with pleasure, standing up at their wedding to denounce their shabby secrets to the world. Wedding – of course Ashley had brothers and sisters, who would give the brat cousins – she might not even get to be godmother – Jesus, she might not even be favourite auntie.

351

Her heart started pounding with shame as she began to acknowledge she had behaved disgracefully. As for their guilty secrets – she saw, sick with jealousy, the two of them lying between clean sheets, telling the worst things about themselves, each charmed by the other's disasters, forgiving the past.

'In fact, we're pretty sure . . .' He had entered an exclusive intimacy of pregnancy testing kits and antenatal appointments, the goat. She had lost brother, friend, status at one blow. Well, she would fight back. She would be the glamorous one who took the kid on treats and outings the others could not afford. Its first pantomime, ballet, opera, sip of champagne, trip to Venice, if the bloody place hadn't sunk by then, if the rotten planet hadn't frazzled, been drowned by the melting polar ice cap, engulfed by waste and the corpses of extinct species or blown into kingdom come. Perhaps there wasn't all that much time. Her first move was to wash her face, comb her hair and put on some mascara and lipstick.

'William, darling, I'm so sorry – I was just overcome. I'm so happy for you – it's the most wonderful news ever! Have you spoken to Ashley? Well, give her *all* my love if you do, but I want to ring her myself.' She flung her arms round him and hugged him. 'I'm over the moon, I really am. You clever old thing! Well, not so old, obviously. And you want to lay off that stuff, now you're going to be a dad!' She indicated the glass of whisky to which he had resorted after her onslaught.

'A daddy. I can't believe it!'

It was true, she couldn't. They must have been sneaking off for ages, under her nose, behind her back.

'Neither can I, quite . . .'

He kissed the top of her head, so that for a moment she felt as though she had not been left off the team, was not the only girl without a partner for the sixth-form dance.

'Oll, thank you for being so generous.'

'Generous? I'm over the moon! Sorry I can't stay to celebrate, I've got to go out for a while. Shampoo later, OK? Oh William,' she called over her shoulder as she went through the door. 'Just one stipulation – I insist on being favourite auntie.'

Amazingly, a black cab was coming down the road with its light on. Just like when she had taken Charlene home.

'Hamleys, please.'

As William finished his drink in the aftermath, he realised that, in her excitement, she had not asked when the baby was due, or how Ashley was feeling, or if they were getting married; any of the normal questions, such as did he want a girl or a boy. He pondered her uncharacteristic use of the expression 'over the moon'.

Those words came to him again when he found his arms full of objects disgorged from Hamleys carrier bags and wrappings, among them a giant teddy the size of a six-year-old child and a nursery light shaped like a smiling crescent moon. The smile on his face froze to a rictus, and embarrassed excuses to Ashley, frantic thoughts of hiding the toys, raced through his mind as a cab driver appeared on the doorstep carrying a plush Shetland pony on rockers.

Olive arrived at the shop early the following morning, looking forward to seeing Charlene again, to making amends in subtle ways which would erase her old bad-tempered image, and to sorting things out after her period of idleness. Still shaken from

William's bombshell, pale from lack of sleep, but resolute, she unlocked and switched off the alarm.

'No, Charlene, I'm afraid that won't do,' she said aloud, removing from the door a card which advertised 'Mature Nurse Gives Enemas'. Definitely a dubious one; she was amused by Charlene's naivety, bless her. Then she noticed a layer of dust on a shelf, on the counter, on the till. The till drawer was open, as they always left it at night, to show prospective burglars that it was empty; but this morning a white envelope lay in the drawer.

Olive felt the blood drain from her heart in a red sluice, leaving her cold, and then it flooded back painfully. 'Mrs Schwarz' it said, crossed out; 'Ms Mackenzie' was written below that. She couldn't pick it up. It lay there, white and malevolent. Shakily, Olive went to make herself a cup of coffee; the water hit the side of the kettle and sprayed her. At last she sat down under the motionless parrot mobile and slit open the letter.

Dear Ms Mackenzie,

I hope you enjoyed your holiday, and find everything in order here. Sorry it's short notice but I have decided to get myself some qualifications and do something with my life. I'm starting college in the autumn and meanwhile I am taking a holiday myself, as you know I haven't had one this year. Hope this doesn't inconvenience you too much. Things have been pretty quiet on the whole.

Best wishes, Charlene.

There was a scrawl which might have been an uncertain kiss, or a slip of the pen. Olive sat there, feeling sick, a sip of bitter coffee in her mouth. She traced the seeds of Charlene's defection to that day in Casualty, with litter and balls of fluffy dust bowling about like tumbleweed. She blamed the hospital, those Third World conditions; she blamed the government for its cynical destruction of the health service. She blamed the youth who had punched Charlene so cruelly and casually; she blamed Charlene. After all she had done for the girl; that beautiful dress, all those chipped soaps, honeys past their sell-by date, enough joss sticks to make a fragrant funeral pyre. If Charlene had waited a few weeks, Olive would have been able to give her her marching orders. Well, she needn't come snivelling to her for a reference. The Beatles' song 'She's Leaving Home' played in her head: 'Daddy, our baby's gone . . . ' Stupid, stupid selfish girl.

She got home that evening with the desire to lay her throbbing head, which felt as heavy as one of the stone balls which topped the pillars of the Da Souzas' gate, onto a cool pillow in a darkened room, and the certainty that tomorrow was to be one of her Tuesdays; indeed the rest of her life might be one long Tuesday.

A child's pushchair stood in the porch. Olive stopped dead on the path. Theo's parents were inside, waiting to accuse her. The police were in there, waiting for Theo's mother to identify her. Theo! Would he put out his arms to her, his face light up with recognition and betrayal? There was no help for it, she would have to go in. Shaking, she managed to fit her key to the lock and step into the hall. Jermaine.

A small girl was rocking wildly with screams of delight on the Shetland pony she had bought for the baby; shreds of its polythene wrapper still clung to the pony's flanks and there was something sticky on its teeth.

'Ah, Olive, thought I heard you come in. This is Chantal. I knew you wouldn't mind.' There was a pleading note in his heartiness.

'That's the baby's rocking horse! How could you? She's putting dirty finger marks all over it!'

Chantal rocked on, no longer laughing, as if she would have galloped away, but the pony's hooves were firmly fixed to its frame.

'Come into the front room a minute.'

Chantal had wrapped her arms round the pony's neck tightly and lain her head on its neck, staring defiantly.

'She thinks it's hers. There'll be trouble when she goes home. You are a fool, William.'

'That's just it – she won't be going home. I've asked the Snyders to stay for a while. Their flat's been repossessed. They're homeless.'

'You've what? How dare you!'

'Just till they get back on their feet. Please, Olive. Don't make it difficult.'

Olive felt she could not breathe; she felt trapped by the furniture, the weeping fig, the portraits of her grandparents, the glass parrot with the pane which she had broken in a childish rage. She clenched her hands to stop them from hurling and smashing something now.

'How could you? How could you? The Snyders! You're as feckless as Father and as mad as Mother!'

'Mother wasn't mad.'

'Of course she was. She must have been, to give birth to you.'

'Please, Olive, they'll hear you.'

356

'Oh, hear me! So I've got to speak in hushed tones in my own home to protect the sensibilities of the Snyders?'

'They've had a tough time. Listen ...' His face broke into a proud proprietorial smile.

'Hossy hossy don' you stop
Dus lat your feet go
Clipperty clop!
Hossy hossy don' you stop ...'

'Stop her, I can't stand it. Get her off that horse before my head splits in two, and before she ruins it completely.'

'Come on, Olive. Be nice. You know how much you wanted a child about the place.'

His parting shot. So that was it. Blackmail.

William: 'Your tail goes ...'

Chantal: 'SWISH!'

William: 'And the wheels go ...'

Chantal: 'Wound!'

Both: 'Giddy up! We're homeward BOUND!' and squeals of laughter as he cantered her into the kitchen and her mother.

Some of the pounding in Olive's head declared itself as the spinning of the washing machine, chuckling and gurgling away the dirty water from Rosetta's second wash. The garden was a-flutter with their garments in the warm wind which would bring no rain. Olive went up to the bathroom, fearful of the paraphernalia of Snyder toilet requisites, potties and plastic ducks which she would find. The door was locked, and behind it a boyish voice was singing as its owner splashed. She heard the slide of his bottom on the bath's enamel base; she was outraged;

and the slap of a tidal wave and a clicking which sounded like some mechanical toy, a wind-up frog or duck or dolphin; and the scent of Floris Special 127 bath essence seeped under the door.

She ran downstairs and dialled Terry's number.

'Terry? Something outrageous has . . .'

'Hang on, do you want Terry? I'll just get him for you.' It was a girl's voice.

'No, wait, it doesn't matter. Just tell him – tell him Joyce Jauncey called.'

She rang Ashley.

'Ashley, have you heard? About the Snyders?'

'Yes, great, isn't it? You know, the more I get to know your brother, the more I love him. Olive?'

Olive had put down the phone. She went bleakly to her room to write stick-on labels for all her bottles and jars. As she worked grimly, she reflected that at least she would have given Terry Turner a nasty turn.

Terry spent an uneasy night. While the girl beside him lay as immobile as a doll, he sweated in a fitful half-sleep, hearing a woman's voice in his ear: 'You will wake one morning, Terry Turner, to see that you have worshipped false gods, that polenta is no more glamorous than semolina pudding without the blob of jam.'

Terry whimpered, 'No . . .'

'Go back to your roots, Terry Turner, to Redhill and Merstham, known locally as Merstram, to the small light-industrial estate at Salfords where you belong.'

'Terry, wake up! You're shouting in your sleep. Are you having a bad dream?'

'What? What's the matter – oh! It was that Joyce Jauncey again. She's haunting me.'

'What? Go back to sleep, or get up and read a book or something, only let *me* get some sleep, please. Stop it. Don't – I can't, I've got a breakfast meeting.'

27

After that aborted phone call, when she had slammed down the phone without mentioning the baby, Olive had put off ringing Ashley, whose own silence pressurised her, begged her to make that call. She gave in, and dialled Ashley's number, determined to strike the right note of congratulation and excitement this time.

'Well, hello, my little elderly primagravida ... '

Afterwards when she put the phone down she remembered an old joke of her father's: Dai Jones is killed in an accident down the pit and two colleagues are sent to tell his wife. On the way they discuss the gentlest way of breaking the news. They knock on the door. Mrs Jones opens it. 'Good evening, Widow Jones.'

She tackled William later.

'But, William, have you really thought about what it entails? You'll be taking on Ashley's whole flock of lame ducks – limping and quacking all over the place ... '

'I want them.'

'I only want what's best for you. Oh, you're impossible!'

'And you're poisonous.'

After Olive's furious and tearful departure, William contemplated his guest list for the wedding. He saw a church, Liam acting as usher. 'Bride or Groom?' 'Groom.' The Patels were in the front pew of course, moving closer together to fill an empty space; Anne and her husband and children; Mrs Handisyde in a straitjacket, with an attendant from the Maudsley; Olive in poisonous green with a wreath of deadly nightshade on her black hat, carrying a bouquet of hemlock, laburnum, digitalis, rhubarb leaves and deathcaps.

'I'm not poisonous.' Olive denied the charge in the front room. A handful of dry leaves fell from the weeping fig. 'I'm just ...' She could not think what she was. 'I'm just an ordinary woman doing my best.'

> 'Good, better best.
> Never let it rest
> Till your good is better
> And your better best.'

It was her mother's voice.

'Huh, that's rich, coming from you.'

She saw herself, small, with dark hair cut in a heavy fringe; loved. The little Olive wanted to climb on her mother's knee and feel arms around her.

> 'If I were hanged on the highest hill,
> Mother o' mine, O mother o' mine!
> I know whose love would follow me still,
> Mother o' mine, O mother o' mine!'

The brittle leaves crumbled in her fingers as she gathered them up. She felt somebody watching her and turned. Chantal was standing in the doorway with round eyes and a dinky feeder in her mouth. Olive blew her nose and blinked away tears.

'Hello, Chantal. Do you want to come in the garden with me? Shall we pick some flowers?'

Chantal stared silently.

'Chantal! Chantal! Where've you got to?' Rosetta's voice was panicky.

'It's all right, she's here,' Olive called. Rosetta rushed in and scooped up the child.

'Did you come down those stairs by yourself? Daddy's going to have to fix up a gate.' Her tone seemed to accuse Olive of all the inadequacies of the house.

'That's great,' Olive thought. 'I'll have to climb over a bloody gate every time I want to get to my own room.'

It was a pity Chantal was such a plain little thing, with those big eyes set too close to that beaky little nose. Funny how William and the besotted parents couldn't see it.

'Won't that damage her teeth?' she asked. 'That coke, or whatever, constantly dribbling over them?'

'It's Baby Ribena. Sugar-free,' retorted Rosetta.

'Only trying to help.'

The house was filled with talk of the future: Ashley and William and the baby, and Liam and Rosetta and Chantal. Olive felt like a blasted tree with snowdrops blooming above her shrivelled roots. Well, for a long time she had known that snowdrops were little white lies. There were five for dinner that night; there would have been six had not Olive retired to her room with a headache, only to be confounded when a sharp ring at the bell brought William to the front door. Olive cursed; she had hoped the merry laughter in the kitchen would drown the sound, and she'd get there first.

'There must be some mistake,' William was saying to the boy in striped livery and cap who stood on the step holding a steaming box containing a large deep-crust pizza. Olive elbowed past her brother.

'That's for me.'

Chantal had run out of the kitchen and was jumping up and down shouting, 'Pizza! Pizza! Pizza!'

'You can have a slice if you fetch me the black pepper. Go and get the pepper for Auntie Olive, Chantal, run along now.'

'Pizza! Pizza!'

This was intolerable. Olive went upstairs, minus the pepper. And nothing to drink. At this rate she'd be keeping bottles in her room next. William was carrying the screaming Chantal back to her dinner. He was right; the pizza had been a mistake. Olive thought of a dipsomaniac friend, now dead, who had been such a secret drinker that she even hid the bottles from herself. Probably a bottle in her room would be the beginning of the end. She ran a speculative eye over the bottles on her dressing table as she ate without pleasure, using her hands. She would have felt ridiculous if she had not fuelled her sense of exclusion with cardboard dough and greasy olives.

Later she heard the click of the latch on Chantal's gate and a tap on her door.

'Can I come in?' Ashley hesitated in the doorway.

'Feel free. After all, privacy's the last thing I've come to expect in my own home.'

363

She waved at the detritus of pizza in its box on the dressing table. 'Want some? You are supposed to be eating for two . . .'

'No, thanks. Olive – I just wanted to say – why don't you come down for a drink? We've got lots to talk about.'

'Have we? Everything's changed. It's all different now.' Olive punched the bed savagely.

'Of course it's different. Better. Look on the bright side; you're not losing a brother, you're gaining a sister. Come on, Olive,' she wheedled. 'How can we be happy when you're like this?'

'Oh, please!'

'Really, Olive, it's true. You're my best friend.'

'What are we, in the playground?'

Ashley withdrew.

It was so obvious she'd done it on purpose. Nobody had to get pregnant nowadays unless they wanted to. There was a screech of brakes. Olive thought of the pizza delivery boy: if he should be knocked off his scooter or mugged for his takings, would that be the fault of her sulks? She decided to go down and face the music, which turned out to be the theme tune of *Sportsnight*. Ashley had gone, Rosetta was gathering up a sleeping Chantal and William and Liam were settled in front of the television. It became clear to her, and at once urgent, that she must find somewhere of her own to live; but with Liam sitting there like the ghost of the property market and things being as they were in the shop, she felt defeated by the prospect of getting a mortgage. Surely there was some form of legal redress, some sort of sisterly palimony?

Ashley's pregnancy became obvious almost at once, manifest by a penchant for mineral water and the company of Rosetta

Snyder. Olive observed this softening of the brain, this demonstration of hormonal imbalance, with incredulity and distaste. She came home one evening to find them clucking away like two old hens over decaffeinated coffee.

'Funnily enough, I went right off coffee,' Rosetta was saying. 'Even the smell turned me right up. I didn't have to give up smoking, though, I was lucky; I never smoked then.' She puffed away on her Berkeley.

Ashley looked a little wistful. 'Of course, I hardly smoke anyway – it's just knowing that you *can't* have one ... I'll just have to sublimate it with these tomato sandwiches. Want one?' Rosetta shook her head. 'They have to have really soggy white bread, that's essential, like we used to have on picnics when we were kids.'

'It was sandwich spread in my case. I used to eat it by the jar.'

'Oh, for fuck's sake,' said Olive. As she shut the door behind her she heard Rosetta say: 'I've always hated that expression. I mean, it doesn't really mean anything, does it? Really common.'

'Well, thank *you*, Miss Manners,' she said to the empty hall.

It was on Wednesday morning that Olive, having decided not to bother to open her shop, was setting off for the local shops. It seemed hardly worth going further afield for delicacies which would be appropriated and wasted on the house guests' dull palates.

'Are you going to the shops?' The shopping bag answered Rosetta. Olive did not deign to.

'Only I was wondering, if you wouldn't mind, if you could pick up a couple of Toddler Dinners for Chantal – she won't eat what we're having. I'll give you the money. I would go myself only she's having a nap, she was up half the night, and Liam's gone down the Housing. I'll give you the money.'

'Never mind,' said Olive, not asking why Chantal had been up half the night. 'You can give it to me later.'

Rosetta's thin old battered purse, the careful counting out of loose change, would be more than she could bear.

'Anything except . . .'

Olive was gone. Presumably all Toddler Dinners were much of a muchness; no child of hers would be fed on manufactured food. She had been going to purée Theo's in the blender. She saw his face clearly, the perfect skin, soft dark lips slightly open, the curling lashes closing over eyes of purest opaque white under brows like two fine feathers stroked on by a delicate finger. And besides, some loony had been going round putting poison and broken glass in jars of babyfood in an attempt to blackmail the manufacturer. Had the panic that it caused passed over Rosetta's thick and careless head? Olive stood behind another woman at Doolally's checkout, unaware of the old-fashioned flypaper, the sword of Nemesis twirling slowly above her head. She had noticed that much of the shelf space had been given over to videos. Mr and Mrs Doolally stood side by side at the till.

'Did young Kim's pals come round to give you a hand with the car boot, Sister, like they promised?' Mrs Doolally was asking.

'Yes, indeed, thank you. Diesel dykes both, bless 'em, but hearts of gold.'

Olive realised that the woman was a nun in the sort of quasi-mufti they affected nowadays. Most unsuitable.

'That's all right, then. Ta-ra, Sister Swastika, God bless,' said Doolally.

'Scholastica, Tom. See you tomorrow, I expect.'

'Did you have to show us up like that?' grumbled Mrs Doolally. Then they both turned their attention to Olive. It was almost as if they were confronting her. She was pretty sure she hadn't slipped anything into her bag absentmindedly but one never knew; perhaps she had reached that age without realising. Why were they staring?

'Yes,' said Mrs Doolally.

'You was right, then?'

'No question of it.'

Olive's mouth was dry. Her throat painful. They weren't the Doolallys, small-time comedy duo, but Mr and Mrs Dooley, witch-finders, inquisitors, executioners.

'Something's been niggling me,' Mrs Dooley said. 'Ever since that poor little black baby was snatched, only I couldn't put my finger on it.'

Olive's own finger was being nipped painfully between the handles of her wire basket. Part of her mind, ice cold, sneered, 'Poor little black baby! You won't like it so much when it is a bit older, will you?'

She licked her lips. 'Would you mind? I'm in rather a hurry.'

'I should think you are,' said Mr Dooley.

'I shouldn't be in too much of a hurry, if I was you,' said Mrs Dooley. 'You see, I never forget a face. You develop a sort of sixth sight in this business. It pays you to. They never caught that woman who took the kiddy, did they?'

'Didn't they? I've no idea.'

'The thing is, when I saw that photofit picture in the paper, it really niggled at me. "I've seen her somewhere," I said to my husband, didn't I?'

'You did, my love.'

'Only, I couldn't place it. Then one night I sat up bolt upright in the bed. "It's her," I said. "That woman in the shop. She was buying nappies and a little pair of dungarees. She had a little T-shirt too and a tin of tapioca pudding, if I recall."'

'Ambrosia Creamed Rice – you're not infallible after all,' Olive almost betrayed herself by retorting, too clever by half.

'Tapioca pudding? You must be joking,' she said.

'I spotted you for a wrong 'un right off. Call it a woman's intuition if you like ...'

Olive saw then, beside the till, an incongruous, unseasonal box, covered in Christmas wrapping paper, with a wide slot, labelled 'Staff Christmas Box'. So that was their game. Blackmail. Evidently the police were not to be involved. If she paid up now, she would go on paying for ever, her own shop's slender profits feeding the Doolallys' rapacious business.

'I don't like. I'm afraid your intuition has let you down this time. Now, are you going to take for these items, or shall I take my custom elsewhere?'

'Not so fast. I told you I never forget a face and I'd swear on my own mother's life that that day the baby was snatched, you was in here buying baby clothes and baby food. Deny it if you can. And your face fits.'

'I have no intention of denying it.'

'Now you're talking,' said Mr Dooley, picking up the Staff Christmas Box.

'I have no intention of denying it,' Olive repeated, 'because no doubt I *was* in your disreputable shop that day, and no doubt I *was* buying baby things. As I am today.' She produced her ace. Two tins of Toddler Dinners. 'They're for my friends' little girl.

They're staying with us, as they do from time to time. Chantal, she's called. I expect you know her? Pretty little thing – she's on to the toddler food now, bless her. Grow up so fast, don't they? Into everything at that stage ... still, this won't buy the baby a new frock, as they say. How much do I owe you, for my shopping, that is? And I'll take a packet of those revolting-looking dolly mixtures.'

Doolally started hitting the keys of the till so hard it jammed. He did indeed know Chantal, into everything as that snooty bitch had said. He had roared at her for helping herself to a grape and then failed to placate her with a black banana.

'Thank you so much,' said Olive. 'Oh, by the way, Mrs Doolally, I do understand your concern, in view of your own black roots. Have you thought of trying Empathy Shampoo? Works wonders on older hair, I've heard.'

'Well, you really blew that one, didn't you? Swear on your own mother's life! The old boot's been dead thirteen years,' Doolally was grumbling, and Mrs Doolally snapping dispiritedly 'can't win 'em all', as Olive stuck her head back into the shop.

'I should be very careful in the future if I were you before making slanderous allegations like that. You could find yourselves in very serious trouble.'

After her triumphant exit she had realised that she had not protested enough, and had returned to finish them off with a display of outrage and unspecified threat. Outside again, she felt post-battle fatigue suddenly draining her. A man was entering the shop with a sheaf of papers and brown envelopes, and Olive saw clearly the photocopier at the back as the recipient of confidential, and useful, information, an insatiable mouth gobbling secrets and regurgitating them.

'Oh, there you are, I was beginning to think ...'

'No, Rosetta, I hadn't forgotten. Here you are, and I got her these little sweets. Don't suppose they'll do her much harm. God, what a rip-off, that shop, and filthy! They'll be having the health inspector in again soon if they're not careful, and it's not that long since they were closed down before. Honestly, it really is worth it to make that little extra journey to the supermarket, makes economic sense and, well – a child's health's just too important – don't bother now, give it me any time. I've decided to go in after all.'

Satisfied that she had nobbled Rosetta, Olive left for the shop, where the sale of a pair of expensive earrings and a bracelet which she had despaired of shifting confirmed that this was a lucky day.

'The house is overrun by Snyders,' Olive complained to Rosemary on the telephone, from the shop.

'So what else is new?'

'No, Snyders! It's intolerable. And what with William and Ashley billing and cooing all over the place ...'

She had begun to suspect that Lizzie had been party to their plot, conspiring to send her off to the country to get her out of the way.

They arranged to see a film and then have something to eat. As they walked from the cinema they became aware of music.

'Sounds like *Turandot*,' said Rosemary. 'Do you think they're beaming it out of the Opera House?'

'Must be, I suppose.'

They were pulled along by the music, which became louder as they neared the centre of Covent Garden.

'Look!'

'Oh, it's BSB.'

British Satellite Broadcasting had set up an enormous screen in the Piazza and was projecting images on to it.

'Sure it's not *Butterfly*?' said Olive, registering two Japanese women and a sliding-walled paper house and blossom, just before her friend did the same.

'I think you're right.'

Olive smirked imperceptibly.

Beyond the screen the sky was turquoise printed with swirling wheels of starlings. Olive and Rosemary stood on the edge of the crowd, some sitting, some standing rapt, others caught for a few minutes by the music. On screen, a dot matrix of tiny coloured squares created jasmine and almond blossom; the gigantic Butterfly and Suzuki, and the doomed child in his white sailor suit; bland Sharpless holding a panama; Pinkerton in uniform and a stout Mrs Pinkerton in grey with a hat tied on with a veil. Olive said, 'I've got to sit down. These shoes are killing me.'

She spread the thin jacket, which she had regretted carrying, on the dirty cobbles and arranged herself on it. Rosemary moved slightly to the left to get a better view. Olive jumped at the tap of a hand on her shoulder. A matted face breathed foulness into her face and tangled hair brushed her cheek as an old man asked: 'Would you mind keeping an eye on my things for a few moments while I'm away?'

He indicated a clutch of bulging and splitting plastic bags. Olive nodded brusquely and he set down the bags and several empty beer cans a few inches from her and went. Olive shifted a little bit away from them and dismissed their owner from her mind.

371

Waiting in the wings, and fortifying himself for his performance, was a man who Jay Pascal would have recognised as Unlucky Oswald. His timing as hopeless as ever, Unlucky took what he perceived as his cue, and capered and gesticulated in front of the immense screen, pirouetted in lurching balletic mimicry and lay down on the cobbles waving his feet in the air. Then, as if he had pulled off the most daring stunt in the history of the circus, he staggered to his feet and gave a little leap and a theatrical bow and swayed sideways in slow motion to the ground again. He crawled to his knees and righted himself, and mopped and mowed ingratiatingly along the front row of the audience watching Butterfly's farewell to her child, thrusting a filthy hat under their noses. Embarrassment and hatred rained into his hat, and from the back of the crowd tribute whizzed towards him in the form of an empty Carlsberg can which struck him on the head and felled him. Madame Butterfly plunged the knife between her breasts. People turned to go in tears, stepping over the fallen Pagliacco as the credits rolled.

Two days later Terry stumbled out of the French pub in Soho into the microwaved afternoon and encountered Derek Mothersole emerging from the Groucho looking very pleased with himself.

'You're looking very pleased with yourself. As always.'

Mothersole tapped the side of his nose and wagged his beard, exhaling garlic. 'I'm sayin' nowt, young Tel.'

As the last thing Terry wished to hear was the account of some Mothersole coup, he grinned and fumbled in his addled brain for a bit of body language to imply that he had pulled off a more spectacular deal, and failed to find one.

'Yours was a liquid lunch, if I'm not mistaken, it does you no good you know, our Terence.'

Derek wagged his finger now in mock mock-admonishment. 'What have you been up to?'

'Oh – owt and nowt . . . '

'I was going to give you a bell later on anyhow,' Derek went on. 'Care to join me in a dish of tea and a bit of a chinwag? I might even stand you a pastry if you twist me arm.'

Terry found himself sitting opposite Derek and his glass of lemon tea, scalding his mouth with a small espresso. Mothersole was obviously bursting to divulge something. Terry hoped it would not be the account of his latest success, or something paediatric, but could not imagine what else it might be.

'I don't know if I should be telling you this . . . ' with the air of somebody who had every intention of doing so.

'Telling me what?'

'It concerns your friend Olive.' He bit into a pastry which oozed.

'What about her?' Terry was preparing to deny any friendship if necessary, but felt his heart thudding nevertheless.

'You're not going to like this, old son.'

'For God's sake, get on with it.'

'Well, you did ask. And I did warn you. Happened to be passing through Covent Garden t'other night, just back from Prague, as it happens, on my way to – well, never mind that. I stopped for a few minutes because BSB were doing *Butterfly* on a big screen, with whatsername, you know, the Jap one as Butterfly. Well, then I saw Olive . . . '

'So?'

'There she was, sat in the middle of the Piazza surrounded

by carrier bags with empty Carlsberg Specials stacked around her.'

'I don't believe you! Never!'

'God's truth, I swear it. I thought it was just another derelict at first, then I recognised her.'

'I still don't believe you. It's just not possible.'

'Face it, Tel.' Mothersole sucked tea through his lemon. 'Olive has become a bag lady.'

'What did you say to her? Did she say anything?'

'What could I say? I mean, put yourself in my shoes. She didn't see me: too far gone, I guess. I just fled. I was really gutted.'

'It couldn't have been Olive. What was she doing?'

'Just sitting there, surrounded by all those old bags and cans.'

Terry felt a small electric shock to his brain, his heart raced, a rusty gear shifted in his head.

'Poor Butterfly,' he said softly.

The rusty gear creaked. A ratchet caught. Something shifted. His block.

'Carlsberg Special? What sort of carriers?'

'Plastic. All sorts. One was from Harrods, one Kwik-Save, I think, maybe a Europa.'

'And she didn't speak? Not to ask for the price of a cup of tea or anything, not recognising you?'

'I told you. Look, Tel, I'm sorry, really I am – don't torture yourself – there's nothing you can do. She was really out of the race. You mustn't blame yourself, Terry.'

Povera Butterfly, Terry thought. Carlsberg, Harrods, Kwik-Save, Europa. Asks for change, perhaps, not recognising . . .

'I've got to go. You understand . . . ' He stood up.

'Sure, Tel. I'll get these.'

It was all he could do in decency, to pay for the lemon tea and small espresso and pastries, Derek thought, as he finished Terry's.

'Cheers. And Del . . . thanks! You're a pal.'

Mothersole answered with a manly nod. 'Po-ver-a Boo-ter-fly,' Terry sang under his breath in Old Compton Street.

'Spare some change, please. Spare some change, please.' A sibilant voice pursued him down the steps of the tube as he hurried home as fast as public transport would carry him, to begin work.

28

Jeremy's inquiries had led him nowhere. He was certain now that he was confronting a conspiracy of silence, but it was impossible to know which of those he questioned were genuinely ignorant, and who was involved in the cover-up. He had become suspicious of the residents of one private estate in particular as door after door was closed in his face.

'We're Jehovah's Witnesses,' he had been told at the last house. 'You'll find most people on this estate are. You're wasting your time, Reverend.'

He knew the woman was lying.

The vicar, Mr Stebbings, called him into his study.

'Ah, Jeremy. Good of you to spare the time – I was just working on my report to the Bish. I've been hearing splendid things of you from all quarters ...'

'Oh, really? Thank you.' Jeremy blushed. 'I'm just trying to do my job.'

'Yes, yes. About the job, Jeremy. I wonder if perhaps you haven't, in your enthusiasm, which is most encouraging of course, rather overstepped the mark. Trodden on a few toes. One or two brickbats among the bouquets, I fear. There are plenty of people in the parish in genuine need of your counsel and support and I shouldn't like to think that they are receiving less than your best because you have embarked on some cock-eyed quixotic quest which can lead nowhere. You must stop harassing people, Jeremy; it gives us a bad name. New brooms sweep clean, but they can raise a lot of dust in the process. I suggest you think about that, and concentrate on your real responsibilities. I've got great hopes of you, you know.'

Jeremy, in one of the disconcerting flashes of intuition which he had sometimes, as when he had known that girl was imagining a bat tangled in her hair, sinking fangs into her scalp, saw the vicar speaking on the telephone and the sleek director of the institution on the other end of the line with his hand up Cheryl's skirt.

'It was a warning-off, Heather,' he reported later at home. 'The implication was clear; either back off, or I'll put in a bad report to the Bishop. He was putting my career on the line.'

'What will you do?' Heather asked. Jeremy shrugged.

'I felt like a schoolboy who had been caught doing something naughty in the bicycle shed. It was humiliating.'

'Did he tell you to pull your socks up?'

Jeremy looked down at the old football socks wrinkling over his trainers.

'Virtually. Listen, Heather, I don't think I've been neglecting my duties, do you?'

'Absolutely not. No question. Speaking of which: Mrs Anderson and Miss Johnson rang, they'll call you back. Will you take communion to Mrs Widdoes, as she's too frail to come to church any more? Deaconess Lesley says the photocopier in the parish office is on the blink and she'll need volunteers to do some typing; Chris Martin wants to talk to you about theological colleges, and I want us to take a holiday.'

'We will, darling, I promise.'

'Oh yes, and Tim and Karen want to discuss their wedding.'

'Well, that's a pleasant duty at any rate.'

'Karen wants her dog to be one of the bridesmaids.'

'What kind of dog is it?'

'A Jack Russell.'

'Shouldn't be a problem. I don't think there's anything in canon, or should I say canine, law, which expressly forbids it. After all they have ecclesiastical connections – the Parson Jack Russell Working Terrier, they were known as originally.'

'She's quite a pretty little dog, and she can walk quite a distance on her hind legs they say. But I don't want you to get into more trouble. What are you going to do?'

'I can't just let it rest.'

'No. After all, you'd be going against God if you did, wouldn't you?'

'Yes, I would. I'll just have to wait for Him to show me my next move.'

Heather slept badly, getting up twice in the night to check Daniel who was sleeping peacefully under a mobile of butterflies turning gently like moths in the moonlight. Jeremy was sleeping too, for which she was glad because he had been looking so washed-out of late, and because he could not guess how she was fighting against wishing he had never discovered That Place. She half-dozed at last, imagining a little dog in a bridesmaid's dress with a circlet of flowers on its head and a posy in its paws, then the director of the institution reared menacingly over her. She concentrated on flowers, daisies, her own wedding, and thought of a fox in *Gone To Earth*, and had to pray hard when she saw Jeremy hunted across the fields by the director and his heavies, crashing through hedges armed with guns. A report in the local paper had told of a cat killed by hounds, pet rabbits torn to pieces; if that had happened to Esau and Jacob, with Danny screaming ... She had to get up and go downstairs and sit with the light on.

The next morning she went to deliver some papers to the vicarage.

'Is anything wrong, Heather?' Mrs Stebbings asked in the kitchen over coffee. 'You're looking a bit washed-out.'

'Well,' said Heather. 'There is something I'd like to talk to you about ...'

All at once, the dogs' tripe boiled over on the stove, Danny pulled down the vegetable rack in a cascade of potatoes and spinach, the telephone rang and somebody knocked on the back door. The dogs leaped up barking. The moment was lost. By the time the caller had been admitted, Danny comforted, the potatoes and spinach leaves retrieved, and Mrs Stebbings returned from the telephone, Heather was ready to leave.

'Jeremy's looking a bit under the weather too. You must come and have a word if things are getting a bit – the secret is to set aside a little bit of each day for yourself. I should know, being an old hand at the game.'

'Something smells good!'

The caller was lifting the lid and peering into the battered enamel saucepan whose sides were scummed with the brown spume of boiled-over tripe.

'Jeremy's got some holiday owing, hasn't he? Have you booked up anywhere?'

'We were thinking about a cottage in Wales, but I don't know if – we're definitely planning a few day trips, anyway.'

'That's the ticket! Get right away from it all. You know, my dear.' Mrs Stebbings, who had taken Heather's arm as they walked down the path, stopped and drew her attention to the green wooded slopes in the distance. 'I take great comfort from the hills. "I to the hills will lift mine eyes . . . "'

Heather strapped Danny into his seat and headed for the hills. She drove for miles, uncomforted by their undoubted beauty, but could not find a secret set of electronic gates and would not have known what to do, except be strengthened in her resolve to support Jeremy, if she had confronted them.

Later that day McPhee reported to Dr Barrable: 'I saw that orange Beetle nosing around again. Looks like the Reverend didn't get the message,' and Cheryl pricked up her ears. The director was in a foul mood; it seemed that his wife had had one of her nut-dos and gone for him; he had a scratch on his face and a plaster on the knuckles of his right hand. Cheryl would have felt sorrier for him if he hadn't said her birthday outing might have to be postponed. She wouldn't have minded so much, only she'd told her friend who'd been really impressed, although Lisa's husband Peter had passed some sarcastic comment; now she couldn't face telling them it was off. She felt sorry for Lisa, really; she and Peter had got unofficially engaged when they were eleven and all at middle school together, and Lisa had never been out with anybody else. And then Peter had had the nerve to accuse her, Cheryl, of trying to get off with him while Lisa was in hospital with complications after having Kayleigh, which was the thanks you got for trying to be a good mate to your friend and making sure her husband got a decent meal when he was on his own. She had stalked out of the Pizza Hut leaving him to stew in his own juice, pick up the tab, and make his own way to the hospital. She had worked on her version of events, until she would be word-perfect if ever it should be necessary to deliver it to Lisa.

'Beetles are pests, McPhee. They must be dealt with. Eradicated. Pesticides are called for.'

'You said it, Doc.'

'Cheryl, get your butt off my desk and do some work.'

Much of Cheryl's work was to do with Dr Barrable's partnership in a clinic associated with the Harley Street practice, which he attended twice weekly, and with his other business interests. That afternoon she made the rash mistake of answering sulkily: 'I haven't got any work to do.'

She was counting the minutes to her date that night with one of the blokes from Research, with a pleasure sharpened by the knowledge that she was cheating on Dr Barrable, and serve him right. To kill the time she took out a fat paperback tale of bestiality in Hollywood. Her eyes grew round as marbles as she read; she didn't care much for animals really, and had urged her mother to have Topsy the geriatric Cairn put down for months before she had seen sense, but this was something else. Those horrible, fluffy and slimy wriggling things. Uuugh. How *could* they?

'Get me the file on Pascall, J.'

'Sorry?'

'I said, get me the file on Pascall, J.!'

'Which one's he? Sounds like a fruit drop.'

Cheryl handed him the thin file which contained a single piece of paper.

'What does it matter which one he is? They're all the same. Fulcher had some trouble with him, that's all. He's a troublemaker.'

'There's hardly anything in his file. Seems a bit pointless really,' said Cheryl as she filed away Pascall, J.

'Everything must be done by the book, Cheryl.'

She went back to hers.

There was her birthday celebration with some of her colleagues to look forward to; some of the girls had wanted it to be a hen do with a male stripper, but Kelvin McPhee had muscled in on the arrangements; couldn't stand the competition, she supposed. Needless to say, Redvers wouldn't be joining them: it wouldn't be politic, he'd said. Cheryl was secretly relieved, as she pouted in feigned disappointment.

The proprietor of the Blossom Garden Chinese restaurant would have requested the party at the long central table to leave, had not one of his staff still been recovering from the fractured skull sustained at a similar celebration the previous week. They had demanded knives and forks, all but that one who had downed two margaritas on arrival and had now switched to beer; she had determined to show her sophistication and superiority by using chopsticks.

'You're making a real pig's ear of that, Cheryl,' the bloke on her left had told her.

'It probably *is* a pig's ear,' retorted Cheryl and one of the gales of laughter which were making the diners at the other tables wince rocked the restaurant.

'D'you mind, this is a new shirt,' grumbled the man opposite Cheryl, scrubbing at the spray of black bean sauce on his chest. Cheryl called for more sizzling prawns. The remains of several spatchcocked ducks littered the table. Any minute now she would go lurching into the Ladies gagging herself with her napkin, to be retrieved by a friend in time for the birthday cake stuck with sparklers, if she were lucky. Beside her Kelvin McPhee watched with some disgust; at this rate the evening would not end as he had planned it.

'Take it easy, Cheryl.'

'What do you mean, take it easy? Whose birthday is it anyway? Waiter! Twelve more beers.'

The waiter responded without enthusiasm. When this lot had got out their calculators and, after much dispute, slapped their plastic onto the plate there would be no tip, he could guarantee that.

'You can never tell what they're thinking, can you?' Cheryl complained.

'Inscrutable,' said McPhee.

'Mind you, I quite fancy that little one.'

'All look the same to me. Yellow.'

Cheryl was constructing a pancake filling of splinters of duck and fried seaweed topped with a prawn.

'Then we had the bang-bang chicken with buffalo fries, or was it buffalo wings?'

Two girls were discussing a meal they had eaten last week. Next week they would sit in another restaurant trying to recapture the details of this one.

'How 'bout me, Cheryl? D'you fancy me? Pardon me,' McPhee leered with a fringe of foam on his lip.

'You? I couldn't fancy you in a hundred years, Kelvin, belching like that in public.'

'S' only nature's way, innit, pardon me. Better out than in. Anyway, what's a certain lab technician got that I haven't got, eh?'

'Meaning?'

'Leave it out, Kelv,' warned a friend.

'No, I want to know what he's insinuating.'

'Let it go, Cheryl. He didn't mean anything, did you, Kelvin?' One of the other girls attempted to distract Cheryl with a bowl of cold noodles, but Cheryl's eyes were dangerously bloodshot and she had the fixed glassy stare of a boar about to charge, and would not be deflected.

'Well, Kelvin? I'm waiting for an explanation.'

'Leave it, Cheryl. He's drunk.'

'Oh yeah? On five pints, do me a favour! You asked for it, Cheryl, so here it is for all to hear. Daniel Robinson, lab technician; Paul Mitchell, care assistant; Mark Flynn, kitchen supervisor ...'

'Liar! You liar!' Cheryl was screaming, standing up, throwing a glass of beer in his face. A phalanx of waiters was forming.

The people either side succeeded in pulling Cheryl down on her chair. Kelvin wiped his face.

'Liar, am I? Well, what about a certain director, then? What about our revered Dr Barrable? What about ...'

'Shut up, Kelvin! You know the rules.'

'No talking shop out of hours.'

'Sssh.'

'Cool it, Kelv.'

'Leave her alone, it's her birthday.'

His colleagues' consternation, their fearful glances lest he had said too much, could not silence McPhee.

'What about the Firefly Motel, then, Cheryl? You think you're so clever, don't you? So discreet. Well, let me tell you that lover-boy Barrable and myself have had many a good laugh about it. Oh yes, great sense of humour has our Redvers.'

At that Cheryl flung off the restraining hands that held her down, and grappled her way clumsily out of the Blossom Garden screaming that she was not staying there to be insulted, leaving a heap of wrapping paper and presents under the table.

McPhee was lying about Barrable confiding in him, had in fact followed them once on his bike, but Cheryl knew nothing of that as she galloped down the pavement, outrage and humiliation steering her on a fairly straight course, ignoring the faint cry of 'Cher, wait!' from one of the other girls. She took the corner too fast and skidded off the kerb, wedging her foot in a drain.

There he found her, trapped like a ram in a thicket.

'Alleluia!' breathed Father Jeremy. 'You appear to be somewhat stuck. Can I help?'

He could smell the alcohol gusting from her open mouth; in fact she reeked like a Chinese restaurant too. 'It might be an idea if you stepped out of your shoe. Lean on me, that's right, and I'll just – a little twist, there you are! It's Cheryl, isn't it?' he continued, holding the shoe.

'Gimme my shoe.' Cheryl was swaying against him, grabbing at the air; she nearly had them both in the gutter.

'Here, let me put it on for you. What's the matter, had a row with the boyfriend?'

'That bastard! He's not my boyfriend. I wouldn't go out with him if he was the last man on earth. Showing me up in front of everybody on my birthday!'

'Is it your birthday? Not a very happy one from the sound of it.'

The sympathy in his voice broke Cheryl; she sobbed in his arms.

'There, there.' He patted her shoulder, fishing out a man-sized Kleenex. 'Let's go and get ourselves a cup of coffee and you can tell me all about it and then I'll run you home.'

'There's nowhere to go for coffee,' said Cheryl in a moment of lucidity.

'Pub, then.' Jeremy's cheerful tone disguised his anxiety about feeding Cheryl more liquor and being spotted in her company.

'I'm going to be ill.'

She was. Jeremy turned away tactfully but stood his ground, removing his collar.

He sat under a coleus in a brass pot in the quietest corner of the noisy pub while Cheryl cleaned herself up in the Ladies.

'Haven't you got them in yet?'

She had returned looking waxy.

'Oh, sorry. Do you think they serve coffee here? Or would you like a fruit juice or a mineral water?'

'I'm on margaritas. Never mix, never worry,' she added.

'Oh, right.'

Jeremy fought his way to the bar, thinking it unlikely that any of these kids would recognise him, deafened by music.

'A – er – margarita and a St Clement's, please. Thank you. I say, is that really what they cost? Good Lord!'

The barman held out his hand with a pitying look while Jeremy fumbled with his wallet. As he carried the drinks back he reassured himself that it would be a small price to pay for the information he wanted.

'Did you get any crisps? I'm starving. It's true what they say about Chinese food, isn't it?'

Two packets of prawn cocktail crisps – never mix, never worry – and three margaritas later, Jeremy felt he had more information than he could handle. He felt quite sick, rather than triumphant. It was clear that Cheryl had been kept in ignorance of much that went on, and of who sanctioned it ultimately, but what she told him had him writhing in pain on the banquette, and he slumped with his head in his hands.

'Oi! Sit up straight, you're making a spectacle of us!'

'Sorry.'

As Cheryl spoke of vans disgorging broken people into the courtyard, of black-windowed private ambulances, the stench of offal from the kitchens, the armed guards, the secret laboratories, locked rooms where naked men and women roared and rocked silently in filth, the faint far-off cries of children, it was as though a troop of demons streamed from those rosebud lips. They swarmed everywhere, settling on the leaves of the plant, the fixtures and fittings, the fake Tiffany lightshade. The air was black with them, the glasses encrusted. Jeremy dashed them like insects from his eyes and stood up, making a sucking sound as his trousers clung to damp vinyl where he had sweated, leaving burn marks on his legs. The demons were clustered on Cheryl's lips. He had to support her to the car. The air was stale and warm with cooking smells, but above it were the stars.

'Have you got kids, then?' she asked, seeing the child's safety seat.

'A little boy – Danny.' His voice broke on the words.

'I love children.'

Jeremy drove carefully, aware that he must contain himself, and worried that a pothole might cause Cheryl to be ill in the car. She was seriously drunk, his wallet was empty, but the end surely justified the means.

'Cheryl, would you like to say a prayer with me?'

'No, I'm all right, thanks.'

The telephone was ringing in Redvers Barrable's bedroom. As he answered it he registered that his wife had slunk away to the spare room.

'Dr Barrable. Who is that?'

'It's me, Kelvin. Kelvin McPhee. There's something I think you ought to know, doctor. Cheryl ran out on us and I've just seen her coming out of the pub with that Father Jeremy. Out of their trees both of them and they both got into his car.'

Later McPhee would curse himself for a lost opportunity for blackmail or for exacting money from Barrable for information received, but he put down the receiver with satisfaction that Cheryl had sealed her fate in a bowl of sizzling prawns. He lifted the telephone again and dialled.

'Police?' he said when he was put through.

'I want to report a drink-driving offence. Bloke in an orange Beetle, pissed as a fart. Heading north up the High Street.'

McPhee was on his bike roaring into the hills by the time the squad car reached the phone box, which they had traced almost immediately. When Jeremy was stopped and breathalysed he was found to have no trace of alcohol, and there was no way the girl snoring in the passenger seat could have driven anywhere.

'Enjoy your evening, vicar?' the constable asked, handing back Jeremy's licence.

'Oh, I – I hardly know her. I'm just giving her a lift home. It's her birthday and she's been celebrating, not wisely but too well I'm afraid and got separated from her friends.'

The policeman winked.

'If you say so. Don't worry, we see it all in this job.'

Jeremy sighed and drove on to deposit Cheryl on her door-step and let her in with the key he found in her bag. As he closed the door on her she said woozily: 'You know that time when you knew I was thinking about how bats get in your hair; well, how did you know I was thinking about it?'

'I sometimes get a feeling about something, a kind of intui-tion,' he replied through the letterbox.

Jeremy drove home and took a very long, hot shower, and then spent a long time praying for guidance as to what his next move should be. He rose from his knees, opened his desk diary and began to write.

Cheryl was absent from work the following morning. The driver of the minivan which usually picked her up reported that her mother had said she wasn't well. Kelvin McPhee, who was himself nursing a savage hangover, smirked. Barrable was in an evil mood, not made better by the report that somebody had been caught tying a message to a pigeon's leg.

'They'll all have to be shot. Do it. I mean the pigeons, you fool, so you can wipe that grin off your face.'

'Some of the inmates have been making pets out of rats as well.'

'Deal with it. For God's sake, man, get out and stop bother-ing me with these footling matters. Rats and pigeons! What do you think you're employed here for? I don't buy a dog and bark myself. Get out and get on with your job while you still have one!'

'Yes, sir.'

Out there, beyond the walls and perimeter fence and razor wire, rolled an emerald sward, studded with bright flags and scoops of golden sand and gorse and neat holes like eggcups waiting for snowy white eggs; it was gently, greedily, insistently drinking the rainbow spray from the sprinklers which defied the hosepipe ban; and here was he, stuck with vermin, human, feathered and furred, scuttling filthy things which spread disease. There was a clubhouse where a man could enjoy a civilised drink under a striped umbrella on the terrace; the nineteenth hole. Barrable went out into the grounds. Guards lolled around smoking, keeping an eye on the trusties who worked in the dull beds; an imbecile carrying a sack stumbled and almost scattered grass cuttings over the director, and cowered, wrapping its arms round its head, as if expecting blows from those smooth hands, a crack from the signet ring. Barrable strolled on, his mind in a turmoil of what to do about Cheryl, and what she had said to that pathetic but dangerous curate.

He heard raised voices and then someone was racing across the lawn towards him pursued by a guard, was on him, gibbering and clutching at his jacket.

'Get your filthy hands off me.'

The guard got the man in an armlock.

'Sorry, sir.'

'Just let me speak, just let me speak,' the creature was gasping, its bearded face suffusing with blood as the guard got an arm across its throat. 'Please . . .'

'What's the meaning of this?'

'It's Pascall, sir. Broke away from the work party. A troublemaker.'

The guard's muscles, huge from pumping iron, tightened on Jay's throat as he twisted his right arm tighter up his back. Jay's eyes were bulging; he was gurgling something about demanding to be heard.

'All right, Dennis, let him speak. I've been getting disturbing reports about you, Pascall.'

The arm was relaxed a fraction. Jay gulped painfully.

'I thought you must be the governor, the director; there's been a mistake, I shouldn't be here, I haven't done anything. I'm a New Zealander. Why am I being kept prisoner here? And it's not just me, all of us, we haven't committed any crimes and if we had we're entitled to a hearing, not just to be locked up and beaten and the conditions here are terrible, terrible, the things that go on, the food it's worse than pigswill, they beat you up for nothing, there's a man in a coma, they say he's diabetic, he should be in hospital but he's covered in bruises like I am, look – here and here – I'm sure if you knew what was going on, you'd ... '

'If you've got any complaints about the food, take them to the appropriate department. Get him inside, Dennis. This is a serious breach of discipline.'

'You don't understand! I shouldn't be here! People are dying!'

'You are being held under the Vagrancy Act. And you'll be held here until further notice. Now, get back to whatever it is you're supposed to be doing.'

Barrable turned to walk away, hearing the sound of knuckles on skull and Pascall shouting, 'At least let me work in the garden. I'm a gardener by profession, I can grow vegetables, let me be in the fresh air – I want to see my solicitor!' until he was silenced. Grow vegetables! Pascall must think they were stupid – obviously he'd head straight for the wall although cut to pieces or electrified might be the best thing. Dennis would deal with him for now. Barrable went back to his office where he had to make his own coffee, thanks to Cheryl.

What a bed of nails this job had turned out to be; he cursed the DoE and Jeremy and Cheryl. His diary told him that he had promised to go to some school play tonight, which was just the icing on the cake. He rang Cheryl's number but there was no reply.

In fact as the telephone trilled in the empty house, Cheryl, feeling very fragile and wearing dark glasses, was leaving the building society where her account had swelled nicely during her time at the institute, and making her way to the travel agent's. Sun, sand, surf and male company was what she had in mind, somewhere as far from Surrey as possible, although now she felt seasick, and the glare of the brochures made her dizzy even through her shades. She must book the first available flight, for she was very frightened, even if it meant buying all her holiday requisites at Gatwick or Heathrow or Luton.

Back at the institute, Jay Pascal was lying in darkness where he had been kicked, at the bottom of a flight of steps. Pascall. They had taken even his name away from him. He was clammy, ice-cold, sweating; waiting for them to come.

It was while dozing through *Murder in the Cathedral* at his daughter's school, watching her lacklustre performance as a novice in brown acrylic habit and Nike trainers, that the idea which had been floating formlessly in Barrable's mind hardened into resolution. It would necessitate the cooperation or coercion of McPhee, and would involve nothing so crude as painted swords or knitted string sprayed silver.

'Get on with it,' he muttered, shifting meaty buttocks in silk and linen on his uncomfortable chair, so that his wife gave him a look, which was all that she dared. 'Well, I can't stand this medieval claptrap. T. S. Bloody Eliot. Why can't they put on a musical, something by that chap who wrote *Cats*, something with a bit of life in it?'

'Sssh,' hissed someone from behind. His wife bit her tongue; as a mother of four she had sat, without him, through three productions of *Joseph and the Amazing Technicolor Dreamcoat* and two of *Jesus Christ Superstar*, as well as that ill-starred performance of *Cats* where there had been some backstage disaster involving superglue, whiskers and tails. Her name had been Edna until she had changed it to Hedda at secretarial college. It was hard to believe now that she had ever been that student who queued for the ballet, the Royal Court and the last night of the Proms, one of a laughing group. 'Suits you, seeing as you're forever gabbling,' her father had teased, revealing hitherto hidden theatrical depths, when she started to sign herself Hedda; but over the years she had become almost silent, as though four children at private schools, the two Great Danes as tall as ponies, the swimming pool and tennis court, the skis and golf clubs and dinner parties, the quilted leather bag whose gilt chain she was twisting round her finger now, were no compensation for something. When Redvers addressed her as Edna, their friends, more business acquaintances really, took it to be a jokey term of endearment, but Hedda's smile was sickly with fear. More than once she had done the school run in dark glasses, with a scarf printed with stirrups and bridles wound tightly round her face and neck. Hers was the familiar tale of the secretary who married her boss but she had not known then how his title would stick throughout their marriage. The only holidays she enjoyed were the times when he was away at a conference, lecture or on business; she would like to have taken the children somewhere simple like Wells-next-the-Sea or Budleigh Salterton or Lyme Regis, some bleached Edwardian haven of sunhats and shrimping nets. She wished she had stayed Edna. Beside her, Redvers – that was his real name – was looking at his watch. He would have called McPhee if he had had a portable phone. As it was, he waited until the morning. He called McPhee into his office as soon as he arrived.

'Kelvin, I'm putting you on special assignment. Surveillance. Think you can handle it?'

'I can handle anything if the price is right.'

'It's a delicate matter, Kelvin. I've got to be able to trust you implicitly.'

'Delicate? You mean there's a lady involved?'

Barrable looked at Kelvin's swaggering stance, legs apart, lewd and macho.

'Not delicate in that sense, although you never know . . . that might be a consideration . . . use the wife to get at him . . . no, at the moment anyway, Father Jeremy is your prime concern. I want him off my back. How you do it is your affair. I don't want to know anything about it, but here's something on account. You'll get the rest when the job's completed.'

'It'll be a pleasure,' said McPhee, rolling the wad into his pocket. 'Cheryl still sick?' he asked as he went out.

'Apparently, poor kid. I might pop in on her later – just to let her know we're all missing her.'

Barrable sat at his green leather desk at the heart of the day that was getting under way all around him. The sun was warm on the face of the institute, striking the incised name of a forgotten Victorian philanthropist, whose vision yet lived on; for his building still provided shelter for the feeble-minded and criminally insane, was a repository for moral defectives, and it had kept pace with the times, evolving into a vast sports and leisure complex which provided them with punch bags and footballs, a shooting gallery and snooker cues which, pointed along green baize or elsewhere, were a challenge to their precision and ingenuity.

29

On summer Saturdays and Sundays, South-east England is one gigantic car-boot sale. William, passing the forecourt of a Methodist church where traders were setting out their wares, was tempted by a box of 78s in friable brown sleeves. 'The Golliwogg's Cakewalk', 'Pixilated Penguin', 'La Mer, J'Attendrai', 'Among My Souvenirs' – 'I count them all apart, And as the teardrops start, I find a broken heart, Among my souvenirs . . . ' Among his souvenirs were memories of similar sales on the school tennis courts; pieces of his former life, discos and forms in triplicate, wine and cheeses, tombolas, timetables, rosters, sponsored sports, steering committees, Christmas Fayres, all jumbled in his mind, like the drab and gaudy clothes and artifacts spilling on to the asphalt here. He thought wistfully of Anne, the architect and artist of the timetable, as one might remember the scent of a rose in a summer long ago. He had wanted to ask her blessing on his wife and child, but knew that he had no right to do that. He suppressed the recurring thought that if he had ordered his life better, he would have had many more years with his child. That seemed justice; just towards him, in the circumstances, if not perhaps to the child.

Past days came back to him, when he had drifted like a ghost through car-boot sales, taunted by the parable of the talents, going to waste, unable to exact any grim pleasure or licence from being beyond the pale, seeking the apathetic company of strangers with dull eyes and painful bodies who did not question their right to consume the worst food served with the illest grace. Seated among them, he would sift in his mind through the hate mail that Pragna's tragedy had inspired; the red and green, bloody and venomous marks on lined paper, the purple felt-tip approximations of his address on brown envelopes; the inverted commas and exclamation marks which, scoring the paper, must be impressed for ever on their writers' tables. Worst were the congratulations from racists, with crude biro or, more sinister, professionally printed depictions of the Union Jack. None of them bore an address. They might have been sent by that couple at the café table, or anybody smiling in the sunshine over a display of assorted crockery. At that time he had had no doubt that his heart was broken; he felt its jagged edges grating, like the halves of a broken plate.

William put the records back in the box. He must always honour Pragna's memory, even if his pain could do nothing to lessen her parents' or bring her back. If watching his own child grow up brought him tortured awareness of all that had been stolen from her, that was only right. There was Mrs Handisyde: he might have saved her, but he hadn't. Olive. Who was guilty there? Ashley, who had cancelled lunch that day? Had she kept the date, Olive would not have been in the wrong place at the wrong time, would not have snatched the baby. Or the person who had called that last-minute meeting which made Ashley cancel? And Olive? Olive. Well, she maun dree her wierd, as his grandmother would say. The bus which doesn't run; the train which glides away early leaving a weeping passenger pleading at the closed barrier; the man who makes a dash across the road as the lights change, knowing in the split second of his momentum that an old lady will follow his lead: each of us has the power, almost every minute, to alter, unknowingly, other lives for ever. The heavy links of the causal chain ran backwards out of sight, disappearing into the past. He had been given a gift and he was not going to break it.

Drifts of yellow lime flowers were banked round the trunks of thin urban trees whose leaves, glazed with sticky sugar, shone in the heat, and lay in heaps in gutters and across the grids of dry drains, waiting for rain to infuse them into a tisane. Forensics could have had a field day with the pavements under the lime trees, stained, spattered with fluids and detritus; but no scientist, analysing the grey slabs, could have detected the pleasure that they gave William that morning. It rose with the warmth of the sun from the paving stones; the glint of minerals and fool's gold, the papery glittery blossoms, were as beautiful to him as specks of true gold sluiced from the gravel cliffs of Otago. The world was precious, full of treasures; a bird's wings lit from below, like mussel shells or the wings of a Flemish angel; the creaking of a pigeon's wings in flight; the lilt of a cat's legs disappearing through a cat flap.

He had left Ashley sleeping and come out to her shops to buy breakfast. The eggs were scrambling in their shells in eagerness to get to her, the juice swooshing in its carton, the croissants clawing the paper bag. He smiled to himself as he realised that he didn't know if she ate eggs; a lifetime of breakfast discoveries. A high chair. He felt like a thief, making his way like a reckless robber with his stolen happiness to the flat which Ashley had described as 'quite ugly, purpose-built, in a sixties block. You'll know mine by the hydrangea on the balcony, the best in the street. Very Fantin-Latour, or do I mean Rennie Mackintosh?'

He walked towards a quite ugly purpose-built flat on the second floor of a sixties block, partly tile clad and faced with panels of peeling white-painted wood, which was redeemed by massive, delicate blooms of pinks and mauves and blues; carrying the breakfast, walking on eggshells.

The Sunday papers were missing from the mat when Olive came down in her dressing gown, wrapping it round her, without William's protection.

'That's pretty,' said Rosetta, in the kitchen. 'Is it Marks?'

'No,' said Olive. She had cut out the label, as was her custom, except when the label was sufficiently distinguished; so Rosetta would never know.

'There's some tea in the pot,' Liam told her, looking up from a newspaper.

'I prefer coffee in the morning, thanks. Where's my kettle?' She looked around, treading on an eggy bit of toast dropped by Chantal. 'Stainless steel. Have you seen it?'

'Oh, the Alessi,' said Liam. 'It's in the sink. We had one, didn't we, Rosie, but it went with everything else.'

'Had enough? Do you want to go on your horsey, then?' Rosetta lifted Chantal down from her chair. Olive was rigid with rage; she didn't know what to do with herself while she waited for her coffee and toast. The silence grew so strained that everybody was grateful when Chantal started her little song. Olive, thwarted of a leisurely and civilised breakfast, put her mug of instant and toast on a tray. She could not bring herself to sit down with the Snyders.

'Mind if I take a piece of one of the papers?' Her voice was expressionless.

'Help yourself. Take them all if you like, they're yours after all.'

'It's all right, just give me a couple of sections and a magazine, and a property section. Thanks.'

Rosetta and Liam exchanged a glance. Olive caught it, and did not explain that she wanted it on her own behalf, and it had not been meant as a hint to them. Olive departed, in her oyster satin, with her tray. The Snyders heard a faint thud from upstairs; it was Olive hurling a magazine across her room: 'Sacred Cows no. 29. Terry Turner Trashes Tolstoy.' Olive noted the number. After the Oxbridge and UEA boys and girls, the suburban iconoclast is allowed his say. 'Next week: Una Ogilvie Susses Sylvia Plath.' Olive sipped her coffee and read the papers. Lying on her bed, she scanned the property columns. Nothing. She skimmed the pages: 'Hell on Earth: Greek Island of the Insane Exposed. Why it couldn't happen here: our investigative team of writers . . .'

Bloody foreigners, thought Olive. What could you expect?

She read about a curate and his family, wife and child, who had been killed in a freak accident, when their Volkswagen Beetle had run off a seemingly empty country road in broad daylight and somersaulted down a chalky bank. 'They'll be all right,' she thought dully, turning the page. Leaving behind the car lying on its roof on the green-gold turf with chalk flowers and rabbit droppings, wheels spinning unconcernedly, the robin's pincushions, and wayfaring trees, a tangled wreath of green bryony berries: then the fatal spray of red fire, the deadly tendrils rushing to grasp the car, the explosion of glass and metal and squawking crows against the cliff face; three souls slipping from blackened seatbelts upwards into a blue sky and clouds whiter than the chalk.

From her window she could see Liam bowling a car tyre down the path, intent on fixing up a swing in the garden. She felt like a prisoner in her own room. It was ridiculous; she would just have to co-exist peacefully with the Snyders while they were here, or while she was. God knows, she'd have to get out before Ashley and her cats and baby turned the place into a bloody commune. Worse, she had overheard a snippet of a hideous conversation about opening a nursery school. Rosetta had been complaining that Chantal's nursery had been closed down and William had made a joke that had dangerous possibilities of turning serious. She had to admit that Liam had looked quite sweet with that tyre. She would shower and dress and go down to fraternise.

Rosetta was at the sink peeling potatoes.

'Are you in for dinner? Only I thought . . . ' Her voice trailed off, and Olive perceived that this sullen-looking woman in unbecoming shorts was afraid of her, was unhappy at living in someone else's house and terrified of the future.

'Well – yes, I am. What shall we have?' She opened a bottle of wine and gave a glass to Rosetta. 'There you are. Cook's perks.'

After her own first glass, peaceful co-existence seemed a pleasant prospect. It was soothing to watch Rosetta preparing vegetables. Liam came in, ducking through the door with Chantal on his shoulders. Olive poured him some wine.

'Cheers.'

With a smudge of earth on his cheek, his tousled hair and rosy skin, Liam looked much as he must have after an afternoon on the cricket field, when he had been William's Head Boy.

'Guess who I saw at the garage?' he said to Rosetta. 'Old Clive who you used to work with. He's on the buses now.'

Chantal was banging a doll on Olive's knee. It was the first time she had come to Olive. Olive picked her up and set her on her lap. She really was quite a charming child. Bright as a button. And Olive owed her one – for the first time she acknowledged her enormous, overwhelming debt to Chantal, but for whom she would even now be behind bars contemplating a plate of something unspeakable, which someone had undoubtedly spat on, in Solitary for her own protection.

'Lucky sod. Wish it was me,' Liam was saying.

'What's dolly's name?' asked Olive.

'Ayesha.'

'That was her friend at nursery,' Rosetta explained. 'I wouldn't mind being on the buses myself.'

'Listen,' said Olive. 'Why don't you? I mean it. You could be a team, Liam driving, you the conductress . . .'

'I want to be the driver,' said Rosetta.

'And I want to be the driver,' said Chantal. Enchanting little feminist. Olive's face grew pink.

'Whatever. I wouldn't mind helping to look after Chantal . . .' Now she trailed off between the slow shakes of Rosetta's head.

'I couldn't leave her with anybody. It wouldn't work out.'

'You don't mean you couldn't leave her with anybody, do you? You mean you couldn't leave her with me!' She slammed down her glass, thrusting Chantal from her knee, and rushed into the front room. Her grandparents' portraits stared at her from the walls. Granny, sad in faded silk, Grandfather, smug, ecclesiastical and disappointed in her.

'It's all your fault! All of it! You are to blame for everything!' she shouted at the Reverend Jack Mackenzie, and turned on her heel and stalked out of the house, slamming the front door, striding down the peacock path.

Her feet consumed the pavements as she walked, blind to the gardens and trees, frightening families on Sunday walks with her fixed stare. The steeper the hills the better as far as she was concerned. She found herself at the big crossroads at Crown Point, going down Crown Lane towards Streatham, and stopped at the flourishing shrubbery of the Home and Hospital for Incurables, her rage somewhat abated. Which were more tactless, she wondered, deciduous trees which lose their leaves, reminding people of their own mortality, whose bare branches hint at springs which they might not see, or evergreens flaunting their glossy immunity to time? Intolerable, both. She had given a donation to the home once, she remembered; Charlene had a relative, mother perhaps, or father, who worked there. A sign was fixed to one wall of the building, with a gigantic thermometer painted on it, red mercury representing the level of money raised for refurbishment; they were aiming for £1.1 million. £50,000 so far. Not bad. Olive wondered where her own two-pence piece lay.

On to Streatham Common where she sat on a bench at the edge of the grass and watched some hopeful halfwits trying to fly a kite in the humid air. As the coloured thing fluttered and fell from the damp blue, Olive remembered her bird, the house martin sitting on her hand. Tears came to her eyes at the joy she had felt and she gave a bitter snort for having thought it would change her life. It was nothing, the incident had been nothing.

The long length of Streatham High Road; Streatham Hill. She could feel every piece of grit through the soles of her shoes now and her heels were rubbed red, threatening blisters, but she walked on, doing the large circuit which would eventually bring her back to where she had started, past castellated villas, terraces, council blocks, thirties seaside extravaganzas in ice-cream colours, art-deco zigzags, concrete, brick, Tudoresque beams and sunbursts; music from an open window followed her down the street for a while; sometimes she was blasted briefly by passing cars. On she walked, alongside shops shuttered in steel or boarded up, clotted with fly-posters, letterboxes disgorging junk mail on to the pavement, down Brixton Hill; here and there a vivid blur of plastic grass, reds, oranges, yellows, purples heaped on viridian outside a small Asian supermarket; a crescent of houses set back behind trees and gardens; at the foot of the hill, The Fridge, venue for music and dance, with its six white refrigerators suspended in chains above the black fascia; and the great ship Lambeth Town Hall riding at anchor.

There were more people around here; there were always people on the streets in Brixton. Cutting through, Olive came eventually to the corner where the George Canning pub bulked out of Effra Road, and her eye was caught by a poster in one of the windows: 'TONITE. KIM DOOLEY AND THE DOOLETTES'. So those guitar lessons hadn't been wasted after all.

Then, if such things are possible, a kindly thought would

have brushed Jay where he lay, like the tip of a black swan's wing and shielded him for a moment; if goodwill had any power against evil, a spark flared for a second in the darkness. Olive, passing a boy squatting outside the pub with his head wrapped in his arms, remembered Jay, wished him well, and forgot him.

The sun was low over Brockwell Park and the railings jumped in optical confusion past her tired eyes. A blackbird's song was fluid among the heavy, limp leaves of the chestnut trees. Then she saw him bearing down on her, her *bête noire* on crutches; an ordinary brave man overcoming handicap to pursue his life, sweating painfully with effort in the heat. As they approached each other Olive felt shame for her monstrous feelings towards him, and also shame for resenting William's happiness, as though it were a betrayal of her own misery, for having wanted him to be punished for ever, to keep her company. They were getting closer; they met. Olive took a deep breath.

'Good afternoon,' she said.

He turned on her a look of such hatred, such utter contempt, that Olive shrank against the railings. It was as though he had known her and despised and hated her all along. She crept on, quite exposed, the last vestiges of protection torn from her. Totally alone on the surface of the earth. William, Ashley, Terry, Charlene, Rosetta, Liam, Chantal had all fled from her, left her as a bare tree shivering in a desolate landscape. A group of Evangelicals dressed to kill in dark suits and hats heavy with white camellias and roses flattened her against the railings again, and passed.

'Have you got the right time, please?' a man stopped to ask.

'No, I haven't. My watch is ten minutes fast.'

Olive strode on, sick, sick of herself.

'Well,' she thought. 'Seeing as no one else bloody well wants me, I'd better see if God will take me back.'

PART THREE

New Zealand 1910

30

Jack Mackenzie's Bible class flourished, although Myrtille remained its only pupil. Madge joked to the mistress that it would not be long before they saw yon Myrtle enrolled at Knox College and then up in the pulpit herself, but nobody was willing to make any remark in the minister's hearing which might disturb the new golden atmosphere, like the summer itself coming in through the open windows. Voices were heard singing and the laughter of children was unchecked. The baby, discovering the world, found it to be a place of kisses and smiles. Myrtille, who had begun to walk to church with Lil and Madge, wearing shoes and the outlandish rig that was her Sunday best, sometimes seemed to be laughing at them with her great dark eyes under the brim of her hat. There were those among the congregation who thought that trimmings of flowers and an array of cheap glass and stone and ivory beads were quite unsuitable but they kept their mutterings out of earshot of the minister. Miss Kettle and other ladies voiced their disquiet to Louisa over needles and teacups, but she told them with a new authority which brooked no disagreement that they must all rejoice over a lost sheep brought to the fold.

While the manse basked in sunshine, the great big world kept turning of course. Sparks flew in the shipyards of the Clyde, icebergs broke away at the start of massive inexorable journeys, painters, musicians and writers went about their work, ants toiled, grasshoppers danced, gilded blowflies feasted; boys, Maori and Pakeha, played cricket in Dunedin and lolled in the grass thinking that meadows would always be green and golden, unaware that far-off fields could turn to murderous khaki-coloured mud. Meanwhile, as the resourceful Scots planned new railways, cable trams and electric illuminations, Louisa began to enjoy the city, a mirror image in a slightly distorted antipodean glass of Edinburgh, Dun-Edin, Edin on the Hill, half a world away. She took the children to the art gallery where, standing in front of a river petrified in dull varnished swirls and curls peaked with meringue between yellow hills, Sandy exclaimed indignantly: 'Madge can do much better than that!'

'And who might Madge be, my little man?' an old gentleman nearby enquired indulgently.

'She's one of our maids, and she's an artist.'

The old gentleman bowed stiffly to Louisa and moved on to a miniature of Franz Josef Glacier, white snow and crimson rata against a cerulean sky. It was true that Madge had recently taken up watercolours and had proved a dab hand with the paintbrush. She spoke with admiration of the young Dunedin lady artist Frances Hodgkins who was travelling in Europe, and she cast wistful glances at the Art School when they walked past.

'There are many fine paintings here,' Louisa told Sandy, but it did seem as though many of the artists were defeated by the landscape. The Mackenzies visited the Botanical Gardens and museum too, although their own house was becoming more of a museum all the time; perhaps, thought Louisa, the Maori, with their convoluted and stylised carving, restricting their palettes to natural pigments, red, black and white when painting patterns of their great tribal meeting houses, had made a wise choice in not attempting to engage with nature. 'I have come to appreciate this beautiful island,' Louisa wrote to her mother, 'although Scotland will always be home of course. Even though I miss you all as much as ever and I do so wish you could see the baby, I am very happy and determined to enjoy my good fortune in being here. The children and I plan to take the steamer to Port Chalmers tomorrow. Unfortunately Jack will not be able to accompany us, as he has a great deal of work to do . . . '

Lilian had succumbed to a summer cold with an annoying cough, and Louisa had instructed her to take to her bed if she felt the need, worried that it might develop into an attack of the quinsy which had laid her low in the winter. Jack came into the kitchen to find her spluttering with streaming eyes over a cup of red sage tea.

'That's a sair hoast ye have there,' he said genially, broadening his accent to match his ingratiating smile. 'Ye should be in your bed, you're awfu'nae weel.'

Lilian nodded, a sorry sight with her red nose.

'I won't be needing anything today, Madge. I've urgent business in town, and then I'll be occupied with my work until the family gets back. Why don't you take advantage of their absence and get out with your sketchbook and paintbox in the garden or further afield?'

'What about luncheon, Mr Mackenzie?'

'Dinna fash yersel', lassie, I'll have something in town. Away and enjoy yoursel'!'

Satisfied that he had disposed of the maids, he took his hat and stick and set out. How wise he had been to turn a blind eye to their true relationship, the hussies; he smiled indulgently. He was safe today, and if ever they should discover his secret, they would be in no position to divulge it to anybody. He walked on until he had given Madge time to settle Lil and set off with her things, and even if she should return soon to stay with her friend, she would not be looking for him. As he turned back, towards Myrtille's dwelling, he saw Madge disappearing obediently through the orchard, carrying a light easel, with the dog Hamish running in front of her, taking advantage of the day; a waste of a fine woman.

A lizard flickered in the corner of his eye, too quickly for him to identify it. Myrtille would have said it meant bad luck; Jack wondered if it had been named. He had yet to discover a new species or variety, or to catalogue any albino or sport.

Myrtille was treading sheets in an old zinc bath with her skirts girded above her knees, stomping sullenly up and down. Jack thought that she should have been treading grapes, with purple juice rather than soap suds squelching between her toes, with a jug of rich red wine to hand.

'Myrtille.'

At his low call she stood in the sodden sheets, pushing back her hair with a damp wrist. A bubble flew from the tub, floated upwards, an airy globe of faint swirling colours, and shattered against the delphinium-blue sky.

'*Bonjour*, Myrtille, *ma chérie*,' said Jack in an arch tone which would have astonished his wife, taking off his light straw hat with a flourish.

'I am sick of washing dirty sheets.'

Jack smiled, 'Come away, then, lassie.' He held out a hand and she took it, stepping onto the grass, and he led her into her house. It was dark inside for a moment or two, out of the bright afternoon; then the seagrass chair, the stove, the disembodied head came into focus, and the colours of the patchwork cover on the bed in the alcove shaped themselves into harlequin diamonds, triangles, hexagons and squares. Jack took her in his arms, crushing her to him, bruising her lips, breathing into her mouth the scent of a violet cachou which he had dissolved in his mouth to sweeten his kisses. He manoeuvred her into the alcove where, lying beside her, raised on one elbow, he licked a row of tiny seed pearls from her upper lip. He could see her diving into a turquoise sea, breaking the calm surface with pearly shells in her hands and teeth, her head sleek as a seal's.

As he was leaving, Myrtille caught hold of his sleeve.

'Jack . . .'

He had slaked his thirst on exotic fruit and now he was impatient to be gone.

'Stay and talk to me.'

'We can talk at the house tomorrow, at the Bible class.'

'I don't want to come to the house any more. I hate the Bible class!'

Myrtille was looking down, watching her bare foot drawing circles on the floor. Jack saw that she was wearing fine stockings of dried soapy water, the tidemarks of her equivocal life.

'Finish your work, and then go and find Madge,' he suggested. 'Or Robert – I've seen you talking to him often enough!'

If there was any indication, in her stance, of loneliness or a troubled conscience, Jack chose to see only a mutinous aborigine to be placated with gewgaws, fripperies and beads.

'You are very wicked, Jack, to use God as an excuse ...'

'Here,' he said, taking something from his pocket. 'A wee present. Buy yourself something pretty.'

Myrtille took the money, which she would place in the tin box under her bed which held her savings, her travelling fund. Jack reached for his hat. He must be at his desk when Louisa, who had been much more pleasant a companion of late, and the children returned.

As he went out, he said, "*Dieu me pardonnera. C'est son métier.*"

Jack was chuckling as he emerged into the bright afternoon. His smile died.

'Good afternoon, minister.'

The black shape of a cart loomed; holding the reins was the old rogue Michael Flannery who made deliveries and did odd jobs, a tinker sort of fellow.

'I've just taken a package up to the house, from Forsyth's, the taxidermist. There was nobody about, so I've left it in the kitchen.'

He sat there, leering, as if expecting a tip, in rusty black with blackened teeth, a slow wink and rasping of the dirty hand across a stubbled chin indicating that his lewd mind had taken in at once the minister's flushed face and flustered air, the abandoned washing and their implications.

'Thank you, Flannery. It'll be some specimens I've been expecting.'

'I'll be on my way, then. Come on, old lady.' Flannery spat a quid of tobacco, flicked the reins and the cart went shambling off behind the grey mare, with its wheels buckling in all directions. The spat tobacco glittered loathsomely in the grass. How long had Flannery been there? If only he had not given Myrtille all the money in his pocket. A coin or two might have bought Flannery's disreputable goodwill.

When Madge, having seen the minister's hat and stick in their places, knocked on the study door to see if he wanted any tea, she found him with his head in his hands, too abstracted to remove them at her entrance, not at all the jocose fellow of the morning. She hoped that he would have regained his good humour by the time the family returned from Port Chalmers.

'There's a big box from Forsyth's in the kitchen, sir. Dead things, by the look of it,' she added to cheer him up.

'Michael! Michael Flannery! Come here, I want you to sharpen some knives and a pair of scissors!'

Nellie the old mare ambled to a stop at Miss Kettle's shrill voice, twitching her ears as if at troublesome flies.

'It's a terrible hot day, missus. A day to give a man a terrible thirst,' said Michael at the kitchen door.

'You'll get no beer in this house, Michael Flannery.'

'On my mother's grave, I have not touched a drop since I signed the pledge on my sixteenth birthday.'

He stood there with the grog blossoms on his face until Miss Kettle was forced to offer him tea in the tin mug she kept for such emergencies.

'Ah, you're an angel straight from heaven, so you are.'

Michael put an edge like a razor on the worn knife blades and twirled the shining scissors on a black finger.

'Speaking of angels,' he reflected, 'as we were, puts me in mind of certain other feathered individuals ... I was witness to a very strange sight only yesterday. ... ' He drummed broken nails suggestively on his empty mug.

'I've no time now to listen to your stories, Michael.'

Miss Kettle opened her purse, which had sloughed many of its scales. No doubt the man had fancied he had been visited by an angel while lying drunk in the gutter. He had spoken to fairies with hair of finest thistledown, she remembered him telling her, and had once met a leprechaun who had led him to a crock of gold, and he had woken clutching an old milk churn in the light of day beating through the barred window of the lock-up. 'It's not for us to fathom the ways of the Little People,' he had explained.

'Mrs Forsyth had asked me to deliver a package to the manse, stuffed birds and creatures for himself at St Enoch's. So I hitched up Nellie and when we arrived there was nobody there, so I ...'

'The family was away at Port Chalmers. Mrs Mackenzie happens to be a dear friend of mine, so I know. They asked me to go with them as a matter of fact,' Mrs Kettle cut him off, half-mendaciously.

'That's just it, missus, the minister was not at Port Chalmers, wherever the rest of them might have been. He was not in the house, nor yet in the garden, in fact he was somewhere else entirely, where he had no right to be. And I've no right to be telling you this, so I'll bid you good day and be on my way.'

'Sit down a minute, Michael, I'll just put on the kettle again. Will you have a scone with your tea?'

*

Mistress Cameron, the wife of the most venerable of the elders, was so astonished to see, through her window, Grizelda Kettle rattling up to her door side by side with Michael Flannery on that terrible old cart that she dropped the precious cup which she was dusting, an heirloom too valuable to trust to her maid. Flannery was handing Miss Kettle down as she stepped over broken china to open the door herself.

'Come away, Miss Kettle. Whatever can be the matter?'

The poor old thing was in a state of extreme agitation. May Cameron pitied her, fending for herself since her maid Jeannie had left on account of her stinginess, and alone in the world, repelling not only moths with the odour of respectable poverty. Michael Flannery fed Nellie the sugar lumps he had taken from the bowl under Miss Kettle's very nose, patted Nellie's whiskery old velvet nose, and went on his way.

'Mistress Cameron, I must speak to you at once. It is a matter of the utmost gravity!'

Jack was in his study pecking away at a piece of rock with his little geological hammer. Kitty was on the rug with a book of Edward Lear's bird paintings. Jack glanced out of the window and crashed down his hammer with such force that the stone shattered and Kitty screamed. They were moving across the grass towards him, grave and black as vultures against the green, a convocation of elders.

There was no rainbow the day the Mackenzies set sail from Dunedin, nobody on the quay to wave them off. They were a party of seven, for Madge was with them, with Jessie in her arms howling bitterly enough for all of them. Jack Mackenzie, who had wanted a botanical specimen to be named after him,

Mackenzia officinalis, had after all left behind something that might bear his name, but he did not know it, and neither, yet, did Myrtille. She could not have failed to notice, however, that the preserved head was missing from her shelf.

BIBLIOGRAPHY

The New Zealand Index 1915

The Geography of New Zealand, P. Marshall (c. 1910)

The Fatal Impact, Alan Moorehead

Joyful Melodies for Young People's Missions etc. compiled by
Newton Jones (1903)

DANCING ON THE OUTSKIRTS

SHENA MACKAY

A wonderful collection of short stories by the writer known for 'the Mackay vision, suburban – as kitsch, as unexceptional, and yet as rich in history and wonder as a plain Victorian terrace house, its threshold radiant with tiling and stained-glass birds of paradise encased in leaded lights'
Guardian

Shena Mackay, who first came to fame before the age of twenty with two novellas, is the doyenne of the short form. In this volume of previously uncollected stories – including those read on radio – she constantly surprises with a view of the ordinary world that is not at all ordinary.

'Mackay will introduce us to the apparently trifling thoughts of a host of solitary characters and show us, with wonderful imaginative power, interior lives that are expansive, wondrous and tender. And even when her subjects are sad, the great power of her noticing, and her frequently piercing prose, transforms them into something vibrant and tender'
Daily Telegraph

THE ORCHARD ON FIRE

SHENA MACKAY

Shortlisted for the 1996 Booker Prize

'An extremely beautiful and funny novel ... *The Orchard on Fire* is probably Mackay's most perfect book, produced with a technical adroitness and shapeliness which one can only envy'
Philip Hensher, *Guardian*

When Percy and Betty Harlency abandon their seedy Streatham pub for the Copper Kettle Tearoom in Kent, life for their daughter April changes dramatically. She is befriended by the wonderfully dangerous Ruby, whose red hair and brutal home life emphasise her love of fire, and by the immaculately dressed Mr Greenridge who likes to follow her around the village. Mingling the innocent with the sinister and laced with the tragic and the bizarre, this is a rare evocation of a 1950s childhood.

'A celebration of childhood as well as a mourning for the loss of innocence ... a bitter-sweet, gentle novel, not given to grandstanding or preaching, but shot through with humour and compassion. Her writing brilliantly captures the spirit of the place, where every present sensation has ghostly overtones that make the experience all the more sad and lovely'
Times Literary Supplement

virago

To buy any of our books and to find out more
about Virago Press and Virago Modern Classics,
our authors and titles, as well as events and
book club forum, visit our websites

www.virago.co.uk
www.littlebrown.co.uk

and follow us on Twitter

@ViragoBooks

To order any Virago titles p & p free in the UK,
please contact our mail order supplier on:

+ 44 (0)1832 737525

Customers not based in the UK should contact
the same number for appropriate postage
and packing costs.